WITHDRAWN

FEROCITY

Nicola Lagioia

FEROCITY

Translated from the Italian
by Antony Shugaar

Mount Laurel Library
100 Walt Whitman Avenue
Mount Laurel, NJ 08054-9539
856-234-7319
www.mountlaurellibrary.org

Europa
editions

Europa Editions
214 West 29th Street
New York, N.Y. 10001
www.europaeditions.com
info@europaeditions.com

This book is a work of fiction. Any references to historical events,
real people, or real locales are used fictitiously.

Copyright © 2014 by Giulio Einaudi editore s.p.a., Torino
First Publication 2017 by Europa Editions

Translation by Antony Shugaar
Original title: *La ferocia*
Translation copyright © 2017 by Europa Editions

All rights reserved, including the right of reproduction
in whole or in part in any form.

Library of Congress Cataloging in Publication Data is available
ISBN 978-1-60945-381-7

Lagioia, Nicola
Ferocity

Book design by Emanuele Ragnisco
www.mekkanografici.com

Cover photo © Dieter Spears/iStock

Prepress by Grafica Punto Print – Rome

Printed in the USA

CONTENTS

Prediction is very difficult, especially if it's about the future.
—NIELS BOHR

FEROCITY

PART ONE

Those who know say nothing;
those who speak do not know

A pale three-quarter moon lit up the state highway at two in the morning. The road connected the province of Taranto to Bari, and at that time of night it was usually deserted. As it ran north, the roadway oscillated, aligning with and diverging from an imaginary axis, leaving behind it olive groves and vineyards and short rows of industrial sheds that resembled airplane hangars. At kilometer marker 38, a gas station appeared. It was the last one for a while, and aside from the self-serve pumps, vending machines that served coffee and cold food had recently been installed. To promote the new attractions, the owner had installed a sky dancer on the roof of the auto repair shop. One of those puppets that stand fifteen feet tall, pumped up by powerful motorized fans.

The inflatable barker fluttered in the empty air and would continue to do so until the morning light. More than anything else, it made one think of a restless ghost.

After passing that strange apparition the countryside ran on, flat and unvarying for miles. It was almost like moving through the desert. Then, in the distance, a sizzling tiara marked the city. Beyond the guardrail, in contrast, lay untilled fields, fruit trees, and a few country houses nicely concealed by hedges. Through those expanses moved nocturnal animals.

Tawny owls traced long slanting lines through the air. Gliding, they waited to flap their wings until they were just inches from the ground so that insects, terrified by the sudden tempest of shrubs and dead leaves, would rush out into the open, sealing their own fates. A cricket, perched on a jasmine leaf, extended its antennae unevenly. And, all around, impalpably, like a vast tide suspended in the air, a fleet of moths moved in the polarized light of the celestial vault.

Unchanged over millions of years, the tiny, fuzzy-winged creatures were one with the equation that ensured their stability in flight. Tied to the moon's invisible thread, they were scouring the territory by the thousands, swaying from side to side to dodge the attacks of birds of prey. Then, as had been happening every night for the past twenty years or so, a few hundred units broke their link with the sky. Believing they were still dealing with the moon, they homed in on the floodlights of a small group of detached houses. As they approached the artificial lights, the golden angle of their flight was shattered. Their movements became an obsessive circular dance that only death could interrupt.

A nasty black heap of insects lay on the veranda of the first of these residences.

It was a small villa with a pool, a blocky, two-story construction. Every night, before going to bed, the owners turned on all the outdoor lights. They were convinced that an illuminated yard discouraged burglars. Wall-mounted floodlights on the veranda. Large oval polyurethane lights at the foot of the rose bushes. A series of faint vertical light fixtures lined the path to the swimming pool.

This kept the cycle of moths in a state of immanence: carcasses on the veranda, tortured bodies on the scalding hot plastic, in flight among the rose bushes. Just a few yards away, as it had the night before and the night before that, a young stray cat was moving cautiously across the lawn. It was hoping for another bag of garbage left out by mistake. Beneath the branches of the rhododendrons, a snake was splaying its jaws as it struggled to devour a still-live mouse.

The heavy barrier of leaves that separated the villa from its twin next door started to shake. The cat cocked its ears, raised a paw in the air. Only the moths continued their dance, undisturbed in the spring air.

It was against the background of the impalpable grey-green bank of haze that the young woman made her entrance into the garden. She was naked, and ashen, and covered in blood. She had red polish on her toenails, nice ankles, and a pair of legs that were long but not skinny. Soft hips. A full, taut pair of breasts. She put one foot in front of the other—slowly, tottering, cutting straight across the lawn.

She wasn't much over thirty, but she couldn't have been younger than twenty-five because of the intangible relaxing of tissues that turns the slenderness of certain adolescent girls into something perfect. Her fair complexion highlighted the scratches running down her legs, while the bruises on her ribs and arms and lower back, like so many Rorschach inkblots, seemed to tell the story of her inner life through the surface. Her face was swollen, her lips slashed vertically by a deep cut.

That the animals were alarmed was to be expected. The fact that they hadn't remained so was far stranger. The snake returned to its prey. The crickets resumed their chirping. The young woman was no longer of any concern to them. More than her harmlessness, they seemed to sense that she was dragging herself once and for all toward the place that eliminates all differences between species. The young woman stepped on the grass, surrounded by this sort of ancient indifference. She was bathed in the glittering mantle that the swimming pool was reflected onto the walls of the villa. She passed the bicycle abandoned in the drive. Then, just as she had appeared in that small corner of the world, she left it. She went through the hedges on the far side of the yard. She began to vanish into the underbrush.

Now she was moving through the fields in the moonlight.

Her blank gaze was still locked onto the spool that was draw-ing her along a route that ran identical and opposite to that of the moths: one step after another, drawing blood as she crushed sharp stones and branches underfoot. This went on for some minutes.

The underbrush turned into a floury expanse. After not even a hundred yards the path narrowed. A dark surface, far more compact. If she'd been in full contact with her nervous system, at this point the young woman would have sensed the strain on her calves as she climbed uphill, the wind freely whipping her skin. She reached the top and didn't even feel the chilly metallic 500-watt power that once again revealed the curve of her waist.

Five minutes later she was walking on the asphalt, straight down the center of the state highway. The streetlamps were behind her. If she'd lifted her eyes she'd have seen, beyond the curves of the gas station sign, the pathetic profile of the sky dancer lunging skyward. She followed the roadway as it bent to the right. The road straightened out again. It was in this way—a pale figure equidistant from the lines of the guardrails—that she must have been reflected in the animal's pupils.

A gigantic sewer rat had made it that far and now it was looking at her.

Its hair was bristly, its head square. Its enormous yellowish incisors forced it to hold its mouth half-open. It weighed almost ten pounds and it did not come from the surrounding countryside. It came from the foul-smelling collection of sew-ers that fed into the tunnels that reached the outlying urban areas. The rat wasn't frightened by the young woman coming toward it. In fact, it watched her curiously, stretching the whiskers on its spiraliform muzzle. You'd almost have thought that it had its sights fixed on her.

Then the animal detected a vibration in the asphalt and froze. The silence filled with the roar of an engine coming ever closer. A pair of white headlights illuminated the woman's silhouette, and finally the girl's eyes were reflected in the horrified expression of another human being.

In the muggy, suffocating night, he went on telling the story of the crash.

"Completely fucked up. You're just doing your job but that day Christ on the Cross decides to turn a blind eye to you. When He abandons you, He abandons you. I'm just saying that already that morning, things had started off badly."

He'd told the story in the spring, and even before that, when the old single-pipe steam heating system was still struggling to ward off the chill in the recreation center, so that he, Orazio Basile, fifty-six years old, a former truck driver and now disabled, was forced to sniffle constantly. He sat there hunched over in his seat, his crutches crossed against the poker machine, with a grim, disgusted look on his face. And his audience—men on unemployment, steelworkers with ravaged lungs—listened closely every time, though not a comma of the story ever changed.

The rec center was in the old section of Taranto—the *borgo antico*—a small bean-shaped island connected to the rest of the city by the spans of a swing bridge. Charming, unless you lived there. Buildings with fronts eroded by time and by neglect, empty courtyards overgrown with weeds. Outside the rec center's front door was a parking area where semitrailers were left overnight. Between one truck and the next you could see fishing boats bobbing in the water alongside the deserted wharf. Then huge red forked tongues of flame. The sea crisscrossed by reflections from the oil refinery.

"That fucking city."

As Orazio said it, he widened his eyes. He spoke in dialect and he wasn't referring to Taranto. The others pricked up their ears even before he opened his mouth. Watching him over time, they'd learned that the metronome preceded the opening notes of the music—the trouser leg stitched shut at knee length was coming to life. The stump bounced up and down, increasingly rapid and edgy.

That morning a faint blue haze covered the fields between Incisa and Montevarchi. He'd been at the wheel for hours, driving his delivery van down the A1. His passenger just wouldn't stop talking. Orazio regretted having picked him up.

He'd left Taranto the previous afternoon and spent the night at a service area in Mugello, lulled to sleep by the reefer units on semitrailers packed with perishable food products. By 8:30 that morning he was on the outskirts of Genoa. He picked his way through the industrial park, down roads marked by implausible points of the compass. Electronics. Toys. Household Goods. One after another, he passed wholesale warehouses. Apparel. That's where he slowed down. He rummaged through his pockets for the crumpled sheet of paper. He'd been there once months ago, but still he was afraid he might get mixed up. When the letters of the sign matched what was written on the paper, he stopped.

He let the warehousemen unload the merchandise. Five hundred pairs of jeans made in Puglia and destined for retail outlets across Northwest Italy. While the men were unloading the clothing, the owner emerged through a glass door from a small office.

"Nice to see you again," said the wholesaler with a smile.

The man was about sixty, and wore a pinstriped three-piece suit that had seen better days, his choice of attire suggesting superstition more than stinginess. Business must have been thriving for years, as many years as it had taken to fray the jacket cuffs this badly.

"Let's go get a cup of coffee."

The wholesaler acted like someone who was sure he'd neither stepped across the watershed that marks the midpoint of a lifespan, nor was running the risk of doing so in the future. It would take more than twelve hours of driving to get back to Taranto; every minute was precious. Orazio was trying to come up with an excuse when the man laid a hand on his shoulder. Orazio let himself be jollied along. That had been his first mistake.

When they got back from the café, he'd followed the owner into his office to get his signature on the bills of lading. Only then did he see the cell phone salesman. The young man was sitting at the desk, reading the paper.

"The son of a longtime friend," said the owner.

The kid stood up and came over to introduce himself. Slim-fit suit, black shoes. Just as relaxed as the wholesaler was, that was how hard it was for the thirty-year-old to keep both feet flat on the floor for more than three seconds at a time. Without moving his head, Orazio looked out the window at the leaden sky outside. He was eager to get going. The same kind of impatience that, Saturday nights in Taranto at the rec center, drove him to get into an argument with someone after a glass or two.

"It's practically a miracle that he's alive," said the wholesaler.

The previous afternoon the salesman had crashed his Alfa 159 outside of Savona. A curve taken too fast. He was looking for a ride home.

"He's Pugliese, too," added the wholesaler.

Orazio snapped to. "Where from?" he asked.

The kid told him. The wholesaler nodded with satisfaction. One crash leads to another, thought Orazio. He considered the fact that giving him a ride wouldn't take him out of his way. He

could drop him off right after the toll barrier and then continue on to Taranto. Easier to say yes than to say no. And yet
he could say no. The problem was the wholesaler: the bubble
of bliss he was floating along in was a way of presuming—to
the point of imposing—total understanding between Orazio
and the salesman. Joviality capable of showing itself for what it
really was—suspicion and arrogance—only if and when the
bubble popped. But that hadn't happened, ensuring that the
wholesaler chose, like the last time, not to have the items of
clothing counted before having them stacked in the warehouse
along with other identical garments. All jeans of the same
brand. An attitude the truck driver had counted on for this
second trip. And so he'd had to give the youngster a ride.

The second mistake had been to let him spew all that nonsense.

His passenger had behaved perfectly until they stopped for
coffee at the Sestri autogrill. Which is to say that for the
remaining 560 miles, he'd never once shut up.

"First there's the panorama of the Riviera di Ponente. You
know what I'm talking about, I'm sure. Pine trees and citrus
groves just steps from the sea. At that point, *wham!* and I'm
sitting on the asphalt without even a scratch on me. Jesus
Christ, you can't begin to imagine. I didn't really get what had
happened myself. It was a brand new 159. Before that, I drove
a VW Golf Variant."

He burst out laughing for no reason. "A Variant," he said
again.

The accelerated precision of someone who'll go on being
thirty well past the age of fifty. After all, he came from the
regional capital. He spoke lightly of the danger he'd escaped
. . . When His talon sweeps past, just grazing you and inflicting nothing worse than a scare, the thing to do is shut up and
keep going.

Orazio continued to drive and pretended to ignore him. He was forced to acknowledge his undeniable existence, though, when, at Caianello, he wasn't able to pull into the gas station. That's where, if he hadn't had the salesman along, he'd have met the fence and handed over the forty pairs of jeans he'd pilfered from his freight.

He would have set aside part of that money and whatever else was left after rent. The cash would come in handy the next time he had an argument with someone at the rec center. Like other times before, he'd choose to leave the center rather than get into a fistfight. He'd drive through the outskirts of Taranto until the lights of the refinery illuminated the city limits ever more faintly. A swarm of sparks would carve out the darkness at the end of a dirt lane. Whores. He'd head straight for them, thanking his lucky stars for leaving out on the streets the women he didn't have at home.

Instead he'd had to keep going, which left the salesman free to take the initiative a little further down the road: "What do you say we stop here for a piss? Let me buy you an espresso."

They set out again after a brief break. Orazio was on edge. He kept brooding over the income he'd so recently missed out on. He totted up numbers in his head as he drove, as twilight erased Irpinia and a clear, metal-black evening in late April descended over the plains of Puglia.

As they approached Candela they saw the enormous pylons of wind turbines in rows across the fields in the moonlight. They suggested a landscape imprisoned for too long in the realm of the imagination. Cars instead of horses. Mechanical towers instead of windmills. After ten minutes, the wind turbines vanished, and the horizon flattened.

The kid should have gotten off at the South Bari toll plaza. But just before they got there he said: "Now, please, let me repay you."

He spoke of a restaurant in the center of town. From how he described it, a very fancy place. He reeled off dishes and brands of wine, and when he stopped he still hadn't finished— Orazio had nodded in agreement. His third mistake. It wasn't greed but exhaustion that had convinced him that, when the kid offered to treat him to dinner, the damage was going to be made whole, at least in part.

They pulled through the South Bari toll barrier and headed toward the coast.

Quídde paíse de mmerd'!

At this point in the story—when he referred in dialect to "that fucking city"—Orazio was usually already standing up. He'd hoisted himself erect with one hand gripping the armrest of his chair while, with the other, he harpooned his crutches. The effort charged him with an angry energy that swept over the counter and the bottles behind the bar, as well as over his audience as they nodded, in the throes of indignation, well aware that their own city might be an endless list of disasters and infamies of every kind. But Bari was even worse.

Any mentally sane individual would feel dismay upon entering Taranto from the Ionian state highway. The tranquil promise of the seacoast shattered against the crusher towers of the cement plant, against the fractionating columns of the refinery, against the mills, against the mineral dumps of the gigantic industrial complex that clawed the city. Every so often a foreman would be carted off in an ambulance after a grinding machine spun out of control. A plant worker would find his forearm stripped bare to the bone by the explosion of a machine tool. The machinery was organized so that it hurt men according to a cost-benefit equation calibrated by other men in offices where they optimized the most unbridled perversions. The regional assemblies ratified them, and the courts acquitted them at the end of battles the local press fed on. Thus, Taranto was a city of blast furnaces. But Bari was a city of offices, court-houses, journalists, and sports clubs. In Taranto it was possible to link a urothelial cell carcinoma classified as "highly improbable in an adolescent" to the presence of dioxin, used in ninety percent of Italy's entire national production. But in Bari, on Sunday afternoons, an elderly appeals court judge might sit comfortably on the living room sofa watching his granddaughter pretend to swing a hula hoop around her hips, dressed in a filthy pair of sneakers and nothing else. That episode had been recounted by a worker at the cement plant whose own daughter was working as a maid in the regional capital.

That's why he shouldn't have accepted the salesman's invitation. What did it matter if he'd gotten a home of his own out of the story? Four sparkly clean rooms in a building in the better part of Taranto.

In Bari, after dinner, he abandoned the salesman to his fate.

He had no time to enjoy the solitude because he immediately got lost. He made a left turn, then a right and then another right, and found himself right back under the blinking neon owl outside the eyeglasses store. He cursed as he swung the van around. An advertising panel scrolled vertically from a sunny ad for toothpaste to a velvety one for a clothing store. That was when Orazio thought about the jeans still hidden in the van.

After driving around aimlessly for half an hour, he pulled onto the bridge that connected the center of town to the residential area. Ten minutes later he saw the Ikea tower and felt relief. He realized that he was on the state highway facing the cement barrier that separated the traffic going in opposite directions.

The person he was all this time later made a tremendous effort to lift a crutch to shoulder height. Wild-eyed, he pointed to the dark space beyond the breakwater, as if to say that not even a Man who'd come walking over the waters could have warded off his accident. The mistakes had piled up in the empty primordial space where life stories are written before the events make them indelible and comprehensible.

He barreled down the deserted state highway, jamming on the accelerator. The roadway rose so that the vineyards stretched out as far as the eye could see. The moon was just a few days short of full and right now it gave the illusion that it could wax ad infinitum. He accelerated into the curve, altering the relationship between the passing seconds and the reflectors on the pavement. In the distance, beyond a second curve, he saw the inflatable man flailing wildly atop the roof of an auto repair shop. There was something ridiculous about the dance. Orazio furrowed his eyebrows without losing sight of the angle of the road: the absence of lights in the visible stretch corresponded to the lack of dangers in the blind spot. He would have been able to see a car with its parking lights out of order. But what happened was impossible to avoid.

A woman, or maybe she was a girl. She was walking in the exact center of the roadway, completely naked, and covered with blood.

He violently jerked the wheel to the right. That was a mistake, since the van immediately shot in the opposite direction. It went whizzing past the girl. It hit the guardrail. The van slid across the road until it smashed into the barrier on the opposite side. It tipped, flipped, and landed on its side, so that he could very clearly see the wall of metal coming back toward him.

He woke up again at Bari General Hospital, in a room with bare walls where an old man with a fractured femur kept moaning.

The first signs of a sunny morning entered through the

window. Dazed by the pain medicine, Orazio reached his arm out toward the nightstand. He felt his other arm. He grabbed the bottle. The long drink of water refreshed him—his thoughts lined up in a bridge of light, but then collapsed, jumping back into line in a different order.

He'd had a crash, but he was alive. A nasty crash. He remembered the highway, even the salesman. The van must be a wreck. Then something. An opalescent marble glittered amidst the rough gears he was using to reconstruct what had happened. That was strange, because the gears were interlocking, while the marble floated in thin air. It gleamed again and disappeared. The girl. That had to be a ghost, an imaginary shape risen from the depths of consciousness. He felt an itch. The patient in the adjoining bed wouldn't stop whining. He scratched his face. He scratched his left hand with his right. Still, an itch. He jerked himself upright, into a sitting position. He felt a tug, reached his arm down toward his right leg.

Two nurses came running at the sound of his screaming.

The next morning, as he lay in bed with the stump of his leg draining, the head physician came to see him, accompanied by a nurse. From that point on, Orazio began to believe that the girl was real.

The doctor was an old man, tall and deathly pale, with wispy white hair. He leaned over him. He observed him longer than was necessary. He smiled. He re-assumed the chilly persona that must have fit him comfortably and spoke to the nurse. The stump needed to be washed with delicate soap, he told her. An antiperspirant would reduce excessive sweating, while the inflammations should be treated with lotions.

"A corticosteroid cream," he specified in a voice that was a caress to the patient's ears, and an order to the nurse.

Public hospitals. Orazio knew those places. Once a cousin of his had had her appendix removed, and after the operation they'd left her in the hallway for five hours. The head physician was a nameplate on a door with no one ever behind it. However much the old man might look at him, from behind the protection of his summa cum laude degrees, Orazio recognized in his eyes a strange eagerness to please.

And so he lay motionless in the bed. He stared at the head physician so that the old man's eyes followed his as he shifted them toward the other bed.

"Isn't there a fucking thing you can do to make him shut up?"

Two hours later, he'd been moved. A single room with a private bathroom. Really, an oversized room overlooking the eucalyptus trees in the courtyard. Maybe an oversized records room, emptied out at the last second, to which had been added a bed, a bedside table, and a television stand. Each of which now emanated the dreary aura of objects out of place.

They got him settled in the bed, vanished for a few hours. In the afternoon, a nurse came in carrying a tray with coffee and grapefruit juice. He furrowed his brow and glared at her. He pushed aside the tray, freeing up his line of sight. "What a pathetic excuse for a screen." He asked them to replace the television set. The next day two attendants were carrying in a 32-inch set fresh from the mall.

When the head physician came by to see him again, Orazio asked to have the nurse stationed outside the door. His request was granted.

The next day, the head physician returned, escorted by two men in dark suits. Under the jacket of the first man he glimpsed a dangling hem that looked very much as if it, too, might belong to a labcoat. The second man was in his early fifties, and his hair was brylcreemed. Notable polka-dot tie, chunky-toothed smile. He introduced himself: "I'm Engineer Ranieri." They started talking. The first man felt called upon to lower the shades, thinning the light.

*

At this point, no one was bringing up blood alcohol levels. At the rec center, no one was making any more wisecracks about the possibility that the crash had been fatal mostly for his memory. Those jokes had been made at first. He'd tell the story and the others would shake their heads. One of them had gotten hold of a copy of the paper from the day when the news report should have been published. "Well?" He slapped the counter with the rolled-up paper. There they are, the things that happened that day. An out-of-work man had set fire to himself outside the Apple Store on Corso Vittorio Emanuele. The daughter of a well-known builder and developer had killed herself by jumping off the top tier of a parking structure. There was also a car crash on a highway, but on the Autostrada Adriatica. No reports of a girl on State Highway 100 at two in the morning—neither naked, nor dressed, nor blood-smeared, nothing at all.

"So, Ora', do you want to tell us what really happened?"

But a few weeks later, Orazio had moved house. From the one-bedroom apartment in the old part of the city he'd moved into an airy apartment overlooking Via d'Aquino. The only problem was that there was no elevator. Absurd as it seems, he only realized it the second time he tried to climb the stairs, hobbling up them on his crutches. He didn't like it one bit. Three months later, a team of construction workers was hard at work on the scaffolding that rose up the side of the apartment building.

To anyone not convinced by the stump of his leg, this was more than adequate.

But Orazio hadn't stopped thinking about the girl.

It was early May, his hospital stay was coming to an end. One after the other, they'd unhooked his tubes and lightened his dose of pharmaceuticals. They'd given him a pair of crutches.

After his conversation with the head physician, it had become clear to him that it had been no dream. From a simple ghost, he had transformed the girl into the cause of the accident. Only that meant he'd now placed her in a service role that likewise stripped her of significance. She became the cause of the crash just as a tree or an oil patch might have been, as if tree and oil patch were logical transitions capable of leading to the word "amputation."

Every now and then, curses echoed through the hall. That's when they called for the orthopedic surgeon.

It wasn't just the fact that he mentally perceived the presence of his leg. He caught himself actually *moving* the toes of his right foot, he felt an *itch* on his right ankle, and *pain*— piercing stabs between his kneecap and shinbone, or on the knee that was no longer there. He clenched his teeth and broke out in a cold sweat.

Then, one night, he tracked the girl down once and for all.

The hospital was shrouded in silence. The laments of the other patients didn't reach his room. Neither, for that matter, did the sounds of the voices of the staff on duty. He had fallen asleep watching TV. He'd awakened with a start to a commercial for a jeweler offering to buy gold at twenty-five euros a gram. Two young men were rummaging around in a corpse's mouth, and in the next scene they were handing over the gold teeth to the jeweler. He switched off the television set, and rolled over onto his side. He must have fallen asleep at the precise moment he felt the urge to go to the bathroom. He dragged himself out of bed with his mind elsewhere, convinced he'd be able to support himself on both legs. He collapsed face-first onto the floor.

Angry, discomfited, he felt the chill on his forehead.

He tried to get himself into a sitting position by lifting with both hands. His breathing was labored. The room was immersed in quiet. The shadow of the eucalyptus trees stretched across the ceiling so that the leafy branches turned into seaweed, coral branches tossing in the shifting currents. His eyes grew accustomed to the darkness. It seemed to him that the floor was swept by a faint luminescence—the catalysis of fireflies and sea anemones—the radiance of the early May nights that the absence of artificial light gradually revealed. But the light that was capable of leaving him open-mouthed was right in front of him.

Further on, beyond the wide-open bathroom door, the magnifying mirror fastened to the wall was flooded with the moon. Reduced by half up in the sky, it still appeared full in the concavity of the reflective surface—a silvery puddle that emerged from the past, at the bottom of which he seemed to find her again. The small opaque patch took form, drawing closer. Orazio realized once and for all that she was beautiful. He realized that she was in her death throes. He realized, with a shiver, that sheer will couldn't have kept anyone on their feet like that, which meant there had been something else making her place one foot in front of the other. Movement itself, more than that from which the movement physically derived. A quicksand, a dead swelling beneath the summer rain.

He understood, above all, that he'd swerved not to avoid her but to save himself, because everything about her was a magnet and an absence of will, the hypnotic call that, once followed, makes everything identical and perfect, so that we cease to exist.

S eated on the sofa, his legs crossed, he crooked his arm
along the armrest so that he held the handsome gold
watch dial up before his eyes. It was a quarter to three in
the morning, and Vittorio was waiting for the phone call that
would tell him whether or not his daughter was still alive.

He was breathing slowly in the den of the villa that he'd
purchased after the birth of his eldest child. The first person
to live there had been a large landowner under the Bourbon
dynasty. It had become the property of the local *podestà*, and
then passed into the hands of an elderly senator who wisely
stopped thinking of it as his home when, sensing as he dozed
the pull of the thread tying him to Rome, he attributed, night
after night, a syllable to every jerk of the string, so that he
was able to read in advance the judicial sentences of the
coming year. At that point, Vittorio Salvemini made the first
bad bargain of his life, purchasing the building at market
price.

It was 1971, and the employees of the neighboring South
Bari Tennis Club saw him arrive one morning, escorted by a
small team of men, the bare minimum necessary. Tall and tan,
dressed in a tailor-made linen suit, he clenched between his
lips a self-satisfied smirk that no tailor would have attributed
to a tradition older than ten years. The others were too rough
even for the furthest outlying areas—five men, short and muscular, to whom even dialect was an achievement. They walked

up the drive, one after another taking the lead with sharp shouts, sniffing the air like the vanguard of a barbarian king who had just crossed the sheltering Alps.

Here comes another one who doesn't know his place, thought the custodian of the tennis club, lowering his gaze to the chalk lines he hadn't stopped tracing.

The senator had come close to transforming the villa into a modern residence behind the art nouveau façade. Vittorio was of another mind. He had the furniture heaped up in the garden. He ordered his men to uproot the marble statues, and beneath them reappeared the slabs of stone aggregate. Every time he heard a hollow sound when he rapped his knuckles against the wall, his face lit up. Away with the partition walls, away with the false ceilings. The workers knocked down one wall after another.

The men, it later emerged, came from the same town where he was born. They would have been normal farmhands if the times they lived in hadn't left them unemployed before they could learn the trade from their fathers. More than out-of-work laborers, they were his slaves, creatures without a past, faithful and willing to do anything. They hauled sacks bursting with rubble and garbage without ever taking a break, and they'd have tried to rotate a house barehanded if he'd asked them, because he, not they—at least so they believed—knew precisely the point beyond which they would collapse, never to rise again.

Vittorio wanted them to finish the work in just a few weeks. To save time, he one morning authorized them to burn all the furniture he had no intention of reusing down at the far end of the garden. After half an hour, one of the workers came running up to him, out of breath. He was gesticulating. On his face was an expression of disbelief. Vittorio followed him. Just on the other side of the boundary line between properties, a number of men were gesturing in indignation. Two of them wore shorts and polo shirts. They were pointing at the black column rising into the sky.

The smoke, after drifting across the tennis courts, was brushing against the gazebo, where loungers had been hastily abandoned by ladies in swimsuits who were now chattering indignantly, their hands on their hips.

"I'm so sorry. I hope you'll forgive me."

He made a show of bowing in an exaggerated fashion. He was smiling. A part of him was flattered by the idea that he'd bought a house in a neighborhood where, albeit for a complaint, he could attract the attention of these kinds of people, men who, even in their underwear, could evoke the image of a gold nameplate screwed into the door of an office that they had never needed to take by storm. Their faces luxuriated in a special form of relaxation, the apparent state of idiocy particular to the privileged, in which Vittorio identified a further form of intelligence. No trace of the metal foil that darkens beneath the skin thanks to friction with the world. Their grandfathers might perhaps have felt fear in their lives, and their fathers only the volatile apprehension that filled the monarchs of bygone times with wisdom.

Still, a part of that part of him would instead have led him to kneel at their feet, to kiss the marks of the tennis balls that they'd been driving for decades over the red clay.

"My workers must have thought that the wind would blow all day long toward the road," he lied, because it would have been worse to admit that it had never occurred to him that at that time of the day men might be doing something other than work, or that women would be out of the house for reasons other than adultery.

"I see that there's a bar," he went on, pointing to the gazebo, "and I realize that I've inconvenienced them as well. And so . . . "

"You have *first-rate* powers of observation."

No one laughed. The man who had spoken was in his early fifties, not especially tall, all gussied up at ten in the morning. Jacket and trousers draped in a facsimile of elegance, an intentional step behind genuine elegance, but only so as to show it the way. Vittorio decided that this must be the club director. He remained confident: "And so, in the hope you'll forgive me . . . " he went on, and as he spoke, he felt a twinge of hope quiver in his chest, "I'd like to treat you all to a nice round of champagne."

Two men turned on their heels then and there. They headed off toward the tennis courts as if the offer had settled any remaining doubts about the stranger.

"Signor . . . ?" the director smiled with venomous charm.

Vittorio uttered first and last name, hoping that the man was capable of glimpsing them from the future, the letters, from that perspective, written in an ever larger typeface, the way he saw them himself on the days when inspiration (nothing but the anguish of the talented) allowed him to perch at the far end of the decade.

"Signor Salvemini," the man went on, "to enter this club all you need is a membership pass. It's small and rectangular, and to procure one you need to submit a request supported by five members who've renewed their own memberships for the past ten years. Which of our old friends have the pleasure of being yours as well?"

A few more men moved away. Vittorio did not retreat. As more and more men went to join their wives, he sensed that, for the director, questions of principle were once again mingling with practical considerations.

"May I speak with you for a moment?"

"Why of course."

"Earlier, you said that I had good powers of observation. I'm afraid for myself that you've put your finger on the heart of the matter."

The director's face continued to register curiosity.

A propensity for detail, Vittorio went on, had led him to notice the deposits of rust on the lampposts on the second tennis court, the pitted pavement at a certain point along the front drive—where the eye strained to reach, though not *his* eye, and not at sunset, since at that time of day the rainbows produced by the sprinklers faded away. He'd noticed the signs of wear on the façade of the administrative building and the necessity of replacing the modular dance floor from which at night (on those occasions he and his workers had stayed late working on the renovations) the notes of instruments playing mazurkas, polkas, and sambas floated across the lawn, along with the laughter of women and men hidden behind the hedges.

He kept to himself the fact that those voices constituted, for him, the sweetest of possible calls. In them he sensed the movement of surnames that appeared on zoning plans, flinty tablets of laws that he could only work around. He promised to take care of the small amounts of work required. It wouldn't cost the club a cent. In fact, he had no idea whether he could even afford to bring skilled workers over from the other construction sites. In all likelihood, the debts the banks held would require him to further speed up his schedule. And yet, hadn't he just undertaken the reconstruction of the entire dance floor, free of charge?

"Have you ever seen anything like it?"

He pointed to his workers. Without a word from him, they were doing their best to put out that small bonfire. Strong as bulls, intuitive as horses capable of sensing the coming spring from the scent of blossoming oats. He'd summon more men, he told the director. They'd be done applying new coats of paint to the lampposts before the members of the tennis club even realized they were there. These were men accustomed to far more demanding endeavors. Last year they'd introduced the idea of row houses to the province of Taranto; and now, in Santa Cesarea, they were completing in record time a vacation resort that would yank the district out of the past.

"Where were you born?" Vittorio asked, as he adjusted his jacket. The director smiled. Because Puglia was certainly not Bari, he went on. It wasn't Lecce and it was hardly Foggia. For that matter, it was a land that you had to have the guts to kneel down and kiss with the rat-tat-tat of a jackhammer. Vast expanses of wheat and fields of tobacco, dirt roads that fetched up in the piazzas of towns and villages whose inhabitants elbowed each other aside to hurl wads of cash into the faces of the statues of their patron saints. They prayed to God through the eyes of their parish priests for a building permit that would allow them to sell farmland that was ever less productive.

The proposal in question is approved by a majority. In Santa Cesarea they'd been forced to blow up a deconsecrated church. In the province of Taranto, they'd had to wait for a fire to devour 225 acres of pine grove before crossing the threshold of the city council.

Crossing that boundary had been nothing but a first step. Over the years he'd shared meals with mayors and struggled to follow conversations so tangled an interpreter should have been present. Men with shirts dotted with spaghetti sauce who practically forced you to take their cleaning women to bed as revenge for the favors *you* were doing *them*. Lunch after lunch after lunch. And now he was in the regional capital, at the age of thirty-five, the sole owner of a company that no one had ever heard of. But just ask the Bantus of Pulsano. Gather information from the aboriginals of Campi Salentina. Take a Southeastern Railroad train and admire, I beg you, in these northernmost reaches of the Horn of Africa, the first hotel in Puglia to boast a golf course, a hotel on whose cornices, if they hadn't already been covered over by blooming geraniums, you'd be able to notice the name of Salvemini Construction carved in bas-relief.

"Hurry up and get that little fire put out, or we'll have to call the police on you."

It was too bad that Vittorio took that phrase the wrong way. If pride hadn't blinded him, he'd have glimpsed in the eyes of the club director a very different signal. From a gentleman in pinstripes to a gentleman in a linen three-piece suit, the invitation was merely to raise the stakes. But Vittorio turned his back on the director without a word of farewell. He headed straight for his workers. He yelled at them to work faster until his scolding calmed them.

In the days that followed he extended the working hours. He was convinced that they could get it done in less than the short time he'd already allotted. He thought back to the members of the country club. Did they drive gleaming sports cars? He knew how much work went into paying for one. Were they napping in the shade of the city's finest lawyers? Vittorio knew that behind the zoning plans there was legislation, and behind that (which they considered the solid earth that had forever been beneath their feet) there was nothing but an initial act of arbitrary personal will.

He ordered his men to dismantle the old wall-mounted armoires. He had them hammer the granite flowerpots at the foot of the interior staircase to rubble and dust.

The morning he decided to knock down the large expanse of wall separating the front hall from the living room, though, the foreman finally balked. There was a good chance that the wall was load-bearing. Vittorio smiled. The foreman's fear confirmed the presence of a seal that remained unbroken.

Once the wall had been demolished, the bright light that poured in on the rubble gave him the impression that he'd finally burned through the faint patina of time, allowing him to see, and perhaps even to *touch*—as if the villa could rejoin something that reached back earlier than its own foundations: the Austrians before the Bourbons, and the Aragonese before the Austrians—an uncertain presence that he recognized from having perhaps glimpsed it in some recurring dream. Namely, glory. Impossible to give it a more specific name, because its power—provided a man was sufficiently daring to reach out his hand to it—consisted in the fact that any name would do.

The following year, Vittorio had won his first major contract, in Bari, for a small university cafeteria next to the building that housed the economics department. Ten years later, he was constantly shuttling between Sardinia and the Costa Brava, and so it fell to his wife to toss his invitations to evenings at the Rotary Club into the trash.

He looked at the hands on his watch dial once again. Upstairs, his wife and Gioia were asleep, blissfully unaware.

He left the sofa and went over to the window overlooking the garden. He watched the shadows of the trees around the fountain. Something moved in the leaves without discomfiting the shadows. The last time he'd seen Clara had been the week before. She'd come by to pick up an old trench coat that had lain forgotten for years in what she alone still considered Michele's bedroom.

The coat hung in the back of an armoire that by now was packed with all manner of things, wrapped in a plastic cocoon ever since the days when Gioia was still just a girl and Ruggero was shining at the medical school where he was specializing in oncology and on his way to graduating first in his class. They all still lived under the same roof, back then. And even if, with the passing of the years, that bedroom had been transformed into a sort of storage closet, every time Clara came by to visit, she lingered in front of that door as if behind it she would still find her younger brother.

It's not as if he's dead.

Then she'd continue down the hall, a glint of contrariness swallowed in her gaze.

Vittorio thought he knew what was bothering her. She blamed him and his wife for having, over the years, allowed dust to cover the star globe, for having let the ashwood furniture fall out of their shared tastes so that they had an excuse to discard every last stick of it.

If, however, the last traces of his son had almost evaporated, that was, according to Vittorio, not the reason. Quite the opposite. Since he'd left Bari, Michele hadn't come to see his family more than five times. Five visits in ten years.

Michele never spent the night. He'd arrive from Rome and leave the same day. Without wasting so much as a syllable, he'd made it clear what the odds were on the likelihood of his spending so much as a single night in the house where he'd grown up. Vittorio would have liked to know what urgent responsibilities summoned him back to the capital. He wasn't a successful professional the way Ruggero was. Saying "he works in Rome" was just a way of fending off the curiosity of his acquaintances. At thirty-three, Michele scraped by in Rome. He wrote for newspapers that went out of business after a month or else forgot about him, evidence that leaving Bari hadn't solved all his problems, as the psychiatrists had hoped. The train schedules even kept him from staying for dinner. In the implausibility of those obstacles, Vittorio glimpsed the pretense of a duty to safeguard. To safeguard *them*. As if sitting down for a meal with Michele exposed them, not so much to embarrassment as to danger. Were they still ready to leap out of bed at the sound of a beam collapsing, devoured by the flames of a fire set in the living room?

Clara would have run that risk. She and Michele were separated by hundreds of miles, their only contact reduced to cordial chats over the phone during the holidays. There was no longer the same asphyxiating intimacy that had so worried

Vittorio years ago. And yet, Michele's older sister would still have unhesitatingly rushed into the flames for him.

For that reason, the fact that the last time he'd ever laid eyes on her was as she emerged from that room struck Vittorio as the bitterest of coincidences.

Vittorio was climbing the last steps of the interior staircase. This was a complicated period. Business was creaking under the weight of uncertainty, and the whole Porto Allegro affair was robbing him of sleep. He'd heard the door click shut and then he'd seen his daughter suddenly emerge from the far end of the hallway: an elongated *s* in the darkness, miniskirt and white blouse, the trench coat she'd just taken from the armoire clutched firmly in her bejeweled fingers. She'd brushed past him saying "Ciao, Papà" with a faint smile on her lips. Vittorio hadn't been able to bring himself to ask her if she wanted to stay for lunch. Clara was already walking out into the garden, ready to head back to her own apartment or to take a stroll in the center of town, leaving, beyond the door, the idea of a flock of birds rising into the air from a beach without witnesses.

The equivalent of a filial benediction, Vittorio had thought vaguely, as if all his problems were on the verge of being solved.

He threw open the sashes of the casement window. He received the cool caress of the springtime night. The moonlit sky gave him the feeling that he could, paradoxically, read earthly distances, as if in place of the nothingness of space he could see Brazil, the United States, and China . . . The constellation of Los Angeles. The sleepless nebula of Tokyo. As he waited to learn Clara's fate, the sun had already been shining on Phuket for four hours. That meant that a small army of bulldozers was busying itself around the small hotel complex that he was building with his partners over there. By the time they stopped working in Thailand, it would be three in the afternoon in Turkey, where he was completing work on a spa. In Italy he'd call the supervisors of the various construction sites with the moon already high over the Bosphorus, leaving only the hours between ten and eleven at night empty of activity.

That was the only moment during which the machinery everywhere in his little empire would fall still. Vittorio ultimately came to consider that hour a dangerous vulnerability. Wasn't that the time of day he'd first received news of the problems with his vacation resort in Porto Allegro? And the heart attacks? Both of them right after dinnertime. "Not actually heart attacks, just particularly violent angina attacks, from which for that matter you've recovered completely," Ruggero repeated, barely concealing his annoyance.

Still, at seventy-five, Vittorio could no longer smoke. At tennis he wouldn't last past the first set, and his memory was no longer that prodigious thing men his age had envied him for so many years. To say nothing of how the world had changed. He'd have bet against Argentina in soccer a hundred times, but he would never have dreamed how the thoughts, frustrations, and shared confidences of millions of adolescents slumped in front of a computer screen could fatten the wallet of the most cunning of their ranks. There had been a time when all he needed was a little confidential information from a union organizer—a tip about Fiat management being ready to take to the streets in defiance of the striking metalworkers—and he'd buy some shares. Now there were algorithms sailing around the internet, issuing huge buy orders, canceling them a split second before they took effect, and instantly issuing new orders to profit from the price variations they themselves had generated.

There were nights when he looked up at the starry sky— the world was once again revolving upon its own axis, and he feared that the show was happening outside his line of sight.

Clara.

A ladybug came in through the open window. A nondescript black speck transformed itself into a handsome vermilion shell as it emerged from the darkness of the night. Its flight, slow and tremulous, could have been extinguished by a simple clap of the hands. Its pleasing appearance for humans made that eventuality fairly rare. Birds on the other hand were deceived for the opposite reason—they associated that spotted red with the poisonous nature of mushrooms and berries. In this way, the little ladybugs could better play the role with which nature had entrusted them: they managed to devour as many as a hundred aphids a day, and they did it with a voracity, a rapidity, a cold convulsive mandibular movement that on a large scale would have been intolerable to human sensibilities.

Like a Japanese umbrella, the insect resheathed its wings and paused on one of the doors of the bookshelf.

The feeling he had about Clara was that he never understood her quite well enough. Snapshots of his eldest daughter emerged, each detached from the others. The only objectifiable theme was the fact that she was attractive, and that was a puff of air no net could capture for long. Quiet and taciturn until the age of thirteen. Logical without being pedantic at fourteen. Magnetic at sixteen—jeans and long-sleeved cotton shirts, hair worn loose and long, straight-backed and composed on an armchair in the living room. A Mayan idol whose touch unleashed visions from the future: the caravels of Christopher Columbus, the mass rapes of the conquistadors.

At eighteen, she sometimes resembled certain movie stars after the va-va-voom period. Her curves soft, though not excessively so, a Natalie Wood without the final gloss.

Vittorio couldn't grasp what linked one transformation to the other. He'd had to wait for Clara to get married before he understood her place in the world. Until that moment, however, he'd struggled. The young woman passed lightly through the rooms of the villa. It was rare to hear her raise her voice or even try to start an argument. Calm incarnate. But she seemed to be the portion, as it were, favored by the light, and he was afraid to receive confirmation of the fact by those who, over time, really did enjoy the benefits of the presence of his daughter. Young men.

The specimens that appeared for many years at the end of the drive couldn't be described as anything but embarrassing. The important thing seemed that they be obviously marked by want and poverty. Lowlifes, practically. Individuals who were explicitly or implictly hostile to the paternal authority he represented. They would come pick her up in the afternoon and he wouldn't hear a thing from her until the middle of the night. As he lay in bed with his wife, Vittorio would hear the door click shut downstairs. He thought he could sense Clara's hair releasing the scornful nocturnal power with which a motorcycle ride had charged it.

When he tried to scold her, his daughter's lovely mouth lightened in an expression that had a hint of melancholy. Though she was still standing in front of him, she eluded him as surely as she did when she wasn't home. In those moments, Vittorio not only failed to understand *where* but *what* this daughter—whose essence dissolved, leaving in her place only the naked heartbeat of a regret, perhaps even of a sorrow, in the presence of which all were forced to take a step back—was.

Clara's voice materialized elsewhere, cool now and chiming, in a form her father did not have the privilege of hearing up close. Vittorio would walk along the upstairs hallway—a sudden silence after Michele's room. A few more steps and two peals of laughter that ended in an embrace, the excuse being they wanted to smother each other.

At that point, Vittorio would begin to worry. Young people are easily infected, and Michele was a hotbed of malaises. That was more than an impression. That had been certified by an envelope embossed with the seal of the board of education.

The letter, which was signed by the vice principal, had come several months into the new school year. Vittorio sent his wife to talk to the boy's teachers. That evening, Annamaria came home with the expression of someone who's just had her suspicions confirmed.

"Now I'll tell you, but you promise me you won't lose your temper," she said, pouring herself a glass of chilled wine.

The problem wasn't that Michele's academic progress was poor, but rather that his progress was impossible to verify. When quizzed in history, he hadn't uttered a word. Summoned to the blackboard by his math teacher, his greatest act of will had consisted of crumbling the stick of chalk in his fingers. For his Italian essay, he'd sidestepped the problem with an absurd burst of stream of consciousness. "This," said Annamaria, "will give you some sense of what we're dealing with." The prompt asked the students to analyze a statement by Marc Bloch that had been the subject of classroom discussion. "Misunderstanding of the present is the inevitable consequence of ignorance of the past." At the end of the second hour Michele had handed in a sheet of paper whose margins were illuminated with drawings of strange little creatures, while the main part consisted of a long sentence of which it was impossible to make either head or tail ("the room's window overlooks the garden," the incomprehensible opening phrase in the middle of the page), whose only connection to the writing prompt was to be found in a shrewd axiom copied who knows where: "But a man may wear himself out just as fruitlessly in seeking to understand the past, if he is totally ignorant of the present."

And as if that weren't enough, the English teacher had told her that during her class, Michele simply wouldn't stop asking to go to the bathroom.

"You see, Ma'am, I don't know if your . . . er, that is . . . "

"If my son," said Annamaria, presuming to divert and confirm the teacher's idea.

"*The boy*," the English teacher dodged her effort, "I can't tell if he's suffering from some kind of nervous disorder, or if he's just found a way to avoid being quizzed."

These weren't the first of Michele's odd behaviors. And obviously Michele was anything but stupid, Annamaria concluded, balancing her weight on the sofa. But the act of protest might perhaps have degenerated.

"Neurotically overwhelmed by narcissism. It happens to adolescents."

"What do you think we should do?"

That phrase gave Annamaria the license she never would have been so rash as to take for herself. Relying on the dedication that she had shown for Ruggero—and later for Clara and Gioia—she was willing to take on the burden of a problem that in theory was none of her concern, *the* problem that any other woman in her place would have brandished with all the power of extortion. Stunning, admirable. And those were the adjectives that in contrast echoed in Vittorio's head at the end of every discussion concerning Michele, because Michele was the ordeal, daily overcome, that gave proof of the solidity of their marriage.

Annamaria said that this was a delicate matter: "Don't think you can solve this one with the back of your hand."

Vittorio would never have raised a hand against one of his children. But having obtained the permission she didn't commit the error of claiming, Annamaria made use of a rhetorical trick to take the rest. She was the first human being with a college degree with whom Vittorio was on more intimate terms than those that bound him to the civil engineers working on his construction sites. While, deep down, that didn't impress him, what did feel exalted was the part—more superficial and concealed—we all look to in ourselves, every day, for confirmation of the progress of our lives. That degree put Annamaria in a position to complete thought processes that he chose to believe he was incapable of undertaking.

Vittorio had no objections when she told him that a psychiatrist would be the best thing for the boy.

It was a spectacular and unseasonable afternoon in the early nineties, one of those holdovers that summer stashes in a supernatural space to keep the temperature from spiking excessively, and that in cities like Bari ignites certain days of a beauty inconceivable even in the middle of August. Vittorio had come home early. He wanted a shower, and then to kick back on the sofa to think in peace about work until dinnertime. He'd forgotten what day it was, but the occupants of the house seemed to have been born to sabotage his every last little bit of amnesia.

He dropped his briefcase in the front hall. He rid himself of his jacket. He went upstairs. He saw her emerge—lightfooted and sleepy, wearing a blocky checked shirt and a pair of black Wranglers—through the door outside which she'd reappear eighteen years later with the old trench coat clutched in her hands. His daughter stood in his way. She asked him if it was true that her mother had made an appointment with the psychiatrist for that afternoon.

It was enough to hear him heave that long introductory sigh.

"I wouldn't recommend it."

She said it with a smile and downcast eyes, and didn't give him a chance to reply. It was unclear whether it was a reproof or a warning. *I wouldn't recommend it.* Then Clara headed off, barefoot, downstairs.

At eight o'clock Annamaria came home. Along the way, she'd picked up Gioia at the pool. Vittorio watched as they paraded by: a thwarted woman, a young boy who seemed as if the world had collapsed on his head, and a little girl floating two feet off the ground, excited at the thought that she didn't understand what was happening. Michele headed upstairs. Gioia went running past him. Annamaria steered straight ahead, into the kitchen. When Vittorio caught up with her, he found her slicing potatoes on the cutting board.

"Listen, I have a splitting headache. Let's talk it over, calmly, tomorrow."

It annoyed him to be shut out of family matters right when things were at their most interesting. It put him in a foul mood that only got worse the instant he went back into the living room and was dazzled by a flash of light through the window. The source of light wheeled around outside the gate. Without waiting for the intercom to buzz, Clara strode briskly toward the front door. She had a helmet in her arms. Through the living room window, Vittorio saw the cloud of insects intercepted by the beam from the headlight of a high-performance motorcycle.

She wasn't fast, she skipped frames—Vittorio didn't have a chance to start in on a discussion of when she should be home before he saw her, too through the glass, split in two by the reflection and reassembled on the back seat of the bike.

At dinner, Michele poked idly at his vegetables, head lowered. Annamaria read a magazine as she ate, and Gioia managed to imitate her without reading a single thing. Ruggero was upstairs in his room with the door shut, studying. Luckily the phone rang. Vittorio talked for half an hour with one of his engineers.

He went to bed, taking a copy of the newspaper with him. He fell asleep without even realizing it. When he reawakened, his wife was lying beside him, asleep. Silence filled the house. Vittorio wondered whether Clara had returned home. The LED on the VCR was blinking on and off without him under-

standing what time it was. He shut his eyes. A road on the outskirts of the city, a long straightaway. The shafts of light from
the streetlamps streamed past, reflecting off the speedometer.
The sky echoed with his snores. At the end of the road stood a
hundred-floor building. He saw the open space where the
motorbike was parked. He turned over between the sheets.
The bathroom faucet was dripping. Someone laughed. The
concentric circles dissolved, filling the sound with the power
of the image. His daughter was laughing between the pillows
in her bedroom. The girl's shadow bent forward, slithering
over the male shape, and then rose again.

"Vittorio!"

His eyes opened wide. Something moved between his fingers, and he clutched tighter. Annamaria's leg gave a second
jerk and pulled out of his grip entirely. Vittorio came to. The
videocassette recorder was blinking. There was something odd
about the light. He coughed. His wife coughed, too. From the
hallway a purplish glow swelled and contracted. He heard a
cough from the next room. There was a deafening crash downstairs. His wife screamed. Vittorio woke up for good. He leapt
out of bed.

He ran out into the hallway. He saw the dance of the shadows against the wall. He looked down the stairs and saw the
roaring bulb surrounded by billowing clouds of smoke.

"It's a fire! Wake up everybody!"

He rushed downstairs. When the rise in temperature
became unmistakable (his hair pushed back by the waves of
heat) he realized that it was the wrong tactic. He ran back up
the stairs. A shadow passed in front of him, running in the
opposite direction. Ruggero. Vittorio went back into his bedroom. He threw open the armoire and pulled out a wool blanket. He headed back downstairs. He thought he saw his wife
vanish beyond the billowing smoke. She had Gioia by the
hand. So he lunged forward with the blanket onto the fire. Just

as he was right on top of it, he realized that the wooden beam had collapsed. He heard roaring everywhere, he waved the blanket, kicking up swarms of sparks. As he was fighting, he thought he understood the intelligence of the flames, the obstinate will to devour everything that belonged to him. Which just made him push harder, ignoring the pain to his forearms.

He emerged into the garden, coughing. His face was blackened, the weave of his pajamas was fringed with burn marks, but he'd won. He ran the back of his hand over his forehead. At the foot of the stairs he found his wife and Gioia. The girl was sobbing in terror. "It's all okay, it's all okay," he muttered. In the meantime, he looked around. The tops of the pine trees were swaying in the wind. Whilever you were on the losing end of the battle, lucidity was lacking. Then your senses sharpened. The shadow crossing a face hours earlier. Vittorio walked down the driveway, moving confidently toward the fountain. He turned into the hedges, continuing to walk as the lights of the house receded behind him.

He found him sitting at the foot of a palm tree. He hadn't even bothered to get rid of the can of gas. He was holding it in his arms like a lifesaver.

Michele looked up. The guilty expression tightened a knot inside Vittorio that had already been reduced to the size of a pinhead. He would have had to kick the boy black and blue to make the feeling stop. "What have you done?" he asked, to give himself a moment's breathing room. Taking him to the psychiatrist had been a mistake, he thought. It amounted to attempting a superficial solution to the problem. Blood and its slow exchange. The sensations kept moving inside Vittorio, like plants in a single vase responding to the rising sun—he felt the pain of the two overlapping plans and only then did the betrayal fill him with its significance.

"Come on, let's go, get up!" he said sternly.

He let his anger flow in an incomplete form. If he'd had to trace it back to its origin—the woman who had engendered this son—he would have felt his strength grow fragile.

They walked, exhausted, side by side, taking slow steps back to the villa's front door. Michele still had the tank with him, absurdly, recklessly, clear proof of an impulse to self-harm in defiance of his father's vehemence.

Annamaria stiffened. Then Ruggero. Long-limbed and furious, his first-born took in the scene from the top of the stairs, dressed in a T-shirt and a pair of green underwear. He was ready to attack them. Not the absurd stunt his half-brother had pulled. Not Vittorio who was refraining from slapping him silly, and not his mother, either, so obstinate in pretending she could measure the same weight on a scale whose plates were of different alloys. Not the eight-year-old girl immune to the idea that there might exist girls of her same age untouched by the anguish of having lost a choker with a diamond, nor the eighteen-year-old girl that no one could force back by so much as an inch. But the family as a whole. That was Ruggero's problem: the concretion of lunatics with which fate had chosen to distract him from the only pursuit that would set him free, the nail he would continue to hammer until the particle of madness that fed, in a straight line, also into him, had been turned into a nude ring that transmits nothing; study, the fanatical study of medicine to which he devoted himself without wasting a second.

Vittorio saw Ruggero fold forward at the waist. He was ready to face even his eldest son. But before charging into the dispute, he heard a noise behind him. He saw the motorcycle's rear lights illuminating the bars of the gate less and less brightly, like water drying.

Clara appeared at the end of the driveway.

Vittorio descended the steps. As she emerged from the shadows, she appeared with her rumpled shirt and jeans-clad legs that showed no alteration of pace (if anything, her gait seemed to slow), which made her father even angrier. Putting on that display of unflustered calm was just a further lack of respect, as if there were nothing strange about finding them all on the front steps of their house at four in the morning, with smoke still pouring out the door.

"Where have you been until now."

He tried to say it as if he were spitting.

"We had problems with the motorcycle, didn't we?" She lifted her head and unsheathed a scandalized smile.

It sounded to Vittorio like she was stating the opposite (*I didn't have any problems with a motorcycle, I went to get myself fucked while the house went up in flames*) with a force he had not counted on and could not match, because then he would have had no choice but to admit that Clara's appearance was the perfect incarnation of the one he'd encountered in his dream such a short time before. Then Vittorio understood. She went on observing him with a sort of indignant astonishment mixed with composure, in such a way that Vittorio saw—dark brown in the clear green—her half-brother's eyes in hers. Michele had known. He'd known that Clara wasn't home. Otherwise he'd never have set that fire in the living room.

Vittorio moved away from the window. The curtains swung gently. The ladybug was still there, closed in on itself on the door of the bookshelf. He sat down at the desk. The black of the sky resisted the arrival of dawn. He put one hand over his eyes and imagined the worst.

He ought to have overcome the disparity between despair and the simulation of despair that he was now confronted with. He ought to have gone upstairs to give the news to his wife and to Gioia. Get on the phone to Ruggero. To say nothing of Alberto. He'd be willing to bet that Clara's husband was completely in the dark about everything.

But at that point, even if he wasn't carried off by a heart attack, they still wouldn't be safe.

Two hundred and fifty detached houses on the Gargano coast. Construction only recently finished, a few houses already sold. The Porto Allegro residential complex could prove to be the black hole capable of swallowing them all. The Foggia district attorney's office had already submitted to the court a seizure request because certain restrictions that even Vittorio was struggling to figure out had been violated. A terrible tangle in which experts, technicians, environmentalists, rival developers, and lawyers of every type had become involved.

He ought to have battled with all his might. That way, even if the worst had happened to Clara—he thought, staring at the screen of his cell phone—he wouldn't have had sufficient strength. In a last spasm, perhaps he'd have been able to bring home a mayor or deputy mayor for dinner. Then he would have begun retreating, overwhelmed by the force of events.

If he stopped to think, it was astounding. His whole life, luck and danger had risen in equal measure. He couldn't figure out whether it was something connected to the nature of individuals or that of business in general, the soul of which, if so, would really prove to resemble the little demon that you can spot from time to time on the façades of banks on days of blazing sunlight.

For that matter, everything that promised to return to its proper place went out at night in search of just the opposite. For all Vittorio could have said until last night, Clara had returned to the ranks. One day she had slipped into the finest hairdresser's in Bari, putting an end to the wild hair that hung down to her ass. Another day (a *magnificent* day) she'd cut ties with all those jeans and checked shirts. The dingy canvas shoes lay in a corner of the bathroom like proof of some crime committed the night before. At a certain point, they, too, vanished.

She had come shooting out of the revolving door of epochal changes showing off an outfit worthy of Jacqueline Kennedy. That happened during the period in which Michele had come home from his military service and yet another psychiatrist had told them that the only way to get him back to normal would be to change his surroundings. Michele had moved to Rome. Clara had started going to parties held by up-and-coming young lawyers. Parties held by engineers, doctors. Occasionally Vittorio ran into her at events where he was a guest himself. Evening gown. Skirt suit and high heels. Of course, not long after that she got married. Half an idiot, was what Vittorio had thought when he got his first look at Alberto. A forty-two-year-old engineer, intelligent, responsible, and pretty experienced. Over time, he'd been forced to admit that. Never a single problem with any of the construction sites he'd entrusted to him after the wedding.

Out of the corner of his eye he caught a gleam of something at the edge of his desk.

Vittorio reached out his hand, grabbed his cell phone. "Hello," he said. Then he nodded. He felt his throat tighten. He instinctively raised his right hand to his chest. On the other end of the line, the voice seemed incapable of getting to the point. He was the one who said it. *Suicide.* He said it before the voice could go on courting such dead-end words as "body" and "discovery." The hand clenched and relaxed on the shirt.

Five minutes later, Vittorio was looking around the room in bewilderment. He weighed the silence of the room, without finding any substantial differences between the before and the after. The world was still there. *He* was still there. Soon the sky would clear and he'd feel on his flesh the uptick in temperature. However possible it was that the news was plummeting down into him like a ball of cement tossed down a stairwell, he was still unequivocally alive. If there had been a change, it had to do with the perception of time. A mass of detritus had been steadily accumulating at a blind collection point. Now the hatches were open and he needed to act quickly.

From then to nine-thirty was still a long time. At that hour, a twittering would emerge from Gioia's bedroom (on the phone with a girlfriend from the university, with her boyfriend) capable of testifying to the little one's state of wakefulness.

At the break of dawn, though, his wife would appear in the kitchen. She'd ready the water for the tea and she'd stand there waiting, back turned to the solitary flame, erect and pensive in her translucent nightgown, observing as the garden slowly emerged from the shadows. There was no time to waste. He was awake while that little corner of the world still remained closed in the darkness.

Vittorio shifted his gaze to the bookshelves. The ladybug had vanished. He picked up his cell phone and started making calls.

Gioia tossed and turned in the sheets, warded off the faint glow that filtered in through the shutters. She curled up in the bed. The teddy bear on the chair lingered like a negative behind her eyelids, and vanished. Her neck muscles relaxed. Philosophy of language. It was necessary to imagine the exam as divided into interconnecting categories. If the first question were to be too complicated, she'd need to sort it into safer territories. But what were the odds that they'd actually ask her that one? She toyed again with the idea of not getting up at all.

Convincing herself that luck was on her side concealed the desire that during the exam itself, she'd be aided by a happy combination of physical appearance and veiled seductive appeal. Gioia persuaded herself of that further idiocy, feeling it rest on top of the only unconfessed presupposition actually capable of favoring her: her surname.

She embraced her pillow, peering over the edge of the bed.

The large rooms of the villa. The hand-wrought angels on the fireplace screen. And then the outside: the garden with the stone fountain, the palm trees and the oleanders. That was what gave her peace and, at the same time, ensured every morning that she could forget what rare good fortune was hers, and how she hadn't had to lift a finger to deserve it. She rubbed her heel up and down the calf of her other leg.

Like so many other young women brought up in accordance with the rhetoric of merit, she never made the mistake of using her status to stand out. Her strategy was subtler. Gioia immersed herself in the pretense that her condition was no different from anybody else's. Debunking that claim was hard for her friends to do without creating tensions—as if they were guilty of some reverse racism. And so the difficulties of her exam must be analogous to those faced by someone who lived off campus and had to work weekends. And since on Monday mornings Gioia was usually fresher, more understanding, and better tempered than most of her fellow humans, this attitude elevated her, in her own estimation.

The young woman transferred the concept to her family. What would have become of her father, always so tense and irascible, if she hadn't been there to temper his bad moods? And her mother? Signora Salvemini's discretion could be mistaken for aridity if it hadn't been possible with patience (and who if not the youngest of her children was endowed with the same?) to distill from her, every now and then, drops of genuine sweetness.

In her moments of optimism, Gioia convinced herself that it was she who held the family together. For the past few months, she'd been seeing a boy. She'd introduced him to her mom and dad. She'd even arranged for him to get to know Clara. Beautiful and inscrutable in a red Diane von Furstenberg dress, her older sister had come to the villa accompanied by her husband to celebrate her thirty-sixth birthday. Gioia's boyfriend had been daunted by the magnificence of the candelabras and the old, repainted pieces of furniture, without fully realizing that the objects revealed their true preciousness when they served as Clara's backdrop. After dinner, Gioia and the boy had gone into town to get a drink. There they'd had a fight over an old movie, suited to their rancorous dispositions in search of pretexts.

When they quarreled over trifling matters, Gioia could get him to fall back in line with just a few moves. Had he seen the house they lived in? The boy shrugged. "Do you seriously not see the kind of risks a family like mine runs?" The higher you fly, the more thunderous the fall. Every year they heard about similar cases. Very well-to-do families found themselves, out of the blue, shamefully sweeping up the shards. A catastrophe. Their villa, in contrast, reflected an unchanging bond. "Which, if you don't mind my saying so, is at least in part thanks to me." The bringer of harmony: that was her task, and she'd performed it well. If she was capable of managing the mood swings of a great man like her father, then how dare a student behind on his credits in business and economics contradict her? At these words, Gioia's boyfriend swallowed his pride—intimidated more by the mountain around which they were fluttering than by the fumes of her reasoning. She had him in her grip, and she was traversed by a quiver of pleasure.

Something similar to the sensation that, right this second, made her stretch a third time in the bed.

Gioia thought about her father and then again about her boyfriend, now more electric with allure. She thought about the exam that a little more sleep would do nothing to undermine. She felt her legs relax languidly. Her mouth stretched in a yawn. She plunged under the hot line that separates the illusions of our walking hours from the depths inside which flows the rest.

In her dream she was riding a train with her boyfriend. It was an old local train, its seats upholstered in fake leather, and the two of them were making their way from one car to the next, hand in hand. They were looking for the bar car. He must have said something funny, because Gioia couldn't stop laughing. The cars were packed with passengers. Her folks must have been sitting somewhere, too. A conductor went past them. The young man stopped to look at something in one of the compartments. Gioia went back to him. (It was only then that she realized they were no longer holding hands). She, too, peered through the glass door. She didn't like what she saw. A young woman was sitting between two old men. She was wearing a seductive red dress. She had an expression on her face that was intense and, at the same time, remote. Gioia felt uneasy. But what she saw when she looked down was even more unsettling. On one of the woman's bare knees there was a small dark seed, which started to wobble and then split in two. Two flies started moving, one atop the other. The old men seemed pleased. Gioia's boyfriend couldn't seem to take his eyes off the woman's legs. He was hypnotized. She gave him a tug, reminded him about the bar. The young man turned around in annoyance. He replied that there had never been bar cars on these local trains. But then where are we going? asked Gioia in alarm. To the bathroom, he replied.

She took a deep breath and clenched her fist. She unclenched it. On her palm the tension was released like a bodiless flower. She opened her eyes. The veil of morning let the stereo speakers sink into the eighteenth-century dresser. She pulled one of her two pillows out from under her head and wedged it between her knees. Her breathing grew jerky. She slid back into sleep. The restroom on the train was so small that now she couldn't move without constantly ending up pressed against her boyfriend. The train accelerated with a hiccupping motion. Gioia lost her balance and fell, her knees now on the filthy floor. Two flies sketched invisible helixes over the yawning mouth of the toilet. She asked, confused: what on earth is happening? He crouched down in front of her. He'd just seen something about her that she herself had no idea of. Something lovely, something irresistible. He laid a hand on her cheek. Then Gioia stretched out on her side and gently pressed her cheek against the filthy floor. She parted her lips, enjoying the wait. She felt him slipping his hand under the coral-pink silk dress. She squeezed the pillow harder between her legs. Her temples were overheated. Her eyes were closed, but she had almost entirely emerged from her half-sleep. First smooth, then soft—she felt the fingers sliding under the elastic of her panties. Gioia turned over on her side, and intensified the movement between her legs to ensure that the young man's profile remained alive in her memory.

Through the thin shutter of her eyelids, the screen suddenly lit up. The scene shattered. Gioia froze. Her knuckles in retreat beneath the cotton fabric, three small humps that vanished as they withdrew. She opened her eyes. The blinds were still closed, but now the window could be made out in its every slightest detail. And so she turned over onto her other side.

In the open bedroom door, the morning light was framing a black figure. Still stunned with sleep, Gioia struggled to comprehend. The silhouette took half a step forward. The profile devoured the light in a way that made it take longer than usual to reveal itself. Oh, Papà. How many times had she told him not to come in without first knocking?

She leapt out of bed, brow furrowed, blond and slender at five foot six and an eighth, offering up for an instant, possibly not entirely by chance, the tenderest part of her pelvis. "Listen," said Vittorio, moving toward her. She angrily tugged up her pajama bottoms. Her father's long and white and deflated face. The smell of old man. She found herself with his fingers blocking her arms.

Gioia found it necessary to think back on how she'd read his lips to get confirmation of what her ears were hearing. She managed to wriggle out of his grasp, fled from the room. My sister, my sister. She screamed and shouted. In the hallway she ran into a second body. Her mother almost fell to the ground from the impact. In the strong blinding spring sunlight, Gioia staggered senselessly to the door of her parents' bedroom, though they were right behind her.

"Who's going to take care of notifying him?"

Her mother had said it. She understood that she was talking about Michele.

The woman was dressed in a peach-colored silk nightgown
and slippers. Ravaged but freshly composed—a sorrow that
had dived into a ditch dug long ago. Her father seemed to have
returned from outside. Gioia couldn't manage to stop crying.
The mucus oozed out of her nose, her lips produced a series of
popping noises as if she were blowing raspberries, the way
children do, because childhood is the dimension in which sorrow and envy, sense of guilt and rancor, coexist with impunity.
Gioia ran toward her mother. She threw her arms around her
with violence. Annamaria put up enough resistance to stay on
her feet. Then she returned the embrace. She felt the warm
twenty-six-year-old body sink into hers, skinny and angular. In
the throes of her sobbing, one of her daughter's hands wound
up right in her face. Annamaria stiffened. She sniffed again.
She tore the hand off her, lifting her head in disgust.

The real estate lots stretched out dark and silent all the way
up to the state highway. Separated by surveyor's stakes,
pounded by earth tampers, or already covered with cement. At
six in the morning the light still hadn't stabilized between earth
and sky, so the construction site seemed to burn over an underground flame.

There were no practical reasons why Alberto would already
be there. The construction workers would arrive in two hours.
But the empty space surrounded by scaffolding was the ideal
place to reflect.

The night before he'd eaten dinner alone at home, lavishing
lemon juice on his carpaccio. He hadn't taken off his jacket or
his loafers, sitting at the table straight-backed and composed
to avoid giving satisfaction to the empty chair at the other end.
He'd loaded the dishes into the dishwasher. On the wall clock,
he'd found cause for optimism. The minute hand was running

slow with respect to his predictions. Then he'd moved into the living room. He'd taken a seat on the sofa, wandering through the channels until his thumb had remained raised at the sight of a film in black and white.

"Life would be very tolerable, but for its pleasures," the lead character was saying to his wife as he smoked a cigarette in a nightclub.

When, half an hour later, the same character asked "Do you often lose at this game?" while watching a young woman sliding her compact case across the floor of a half-darkened room, Alberto came to on the sofa. Now he sensed the passage of time, as if that scene were causing a drama, whose premise had been there from the outset, to resonate. The fifteen minutes gained on his watch contained the current delay, because even then no shop in Bari would have been open, no gym, no shopping center, and Clara, quite simply, would not be back until tomorrow morning.

At that point, Alberto had turned off the TV. He'd gone over to the stereo. In less than a minute, jazz from Minton's Playhouse was filling the living room, dismantling the rage and infamy that was in his heart. Competition contains friendship, envy contains admiration. The cross-accents on the piano keys, the tone clusters and sudden silences, remixed the concepts of before and after, making the world resonate in a single whole, each fragment already redeemed. Didn't adultery in some sense contain abnegation? The murder of mankind and the curse of a suffered faith? He'd turned off the stereo and gone to bed.

But two hours later, he was still lying sleepless. His wife's absence continued to make him uneasy. Just as he had earlier with the music, he did his best to reverse the point of view. Not letting him know, not phoning, not bothering to come up with an excuse. The more Clara failed to show him respect, the more the side that made her cleave to him could be reinforced.

A mine that produces a diamond's brilliance: down there, where true love sparkles; love that is not the balancing of a budget, not the caring for oneself or for others. Giving the beloved what one lacks and finding in the nothing one receives the excess that can never be repaid. That's what. Exactly the kind of experience that he—brought up in accordance with the rules of the provincial petty bourgeoisie—could never have otherwise had access to.

The idea of the sublime (but what evidence could be found to show that these weren't merely the ravings of an idiot?) went hand in hand with the computational obsession. If Clara was in the company of some other man, there must have been over the course of the evening a specific moment when the two of them had said hello, another when their arms had brushed with no specific intention. His footsteps just slightly ahead of hers. Then all the rest. It might have happened while Alberto was watching the movie on TV. Or else it was happening now—the ungraspable segment in which they weren't and therefore *were* a single flesh. Not knowing forced him to think about it continuously, so that it became his own, an instant made eternal until he saw her again, isolating the exact point in Clara's mind where his name had been uttered even as she betrayed him; or, even worse, isolating the instant of the leap that allowed a woman to keep from thinking about that name.

Or possibly none of that at all, he went on brooding even after four in the morning had come and gone. Clara might have been seized by one of her fits of melancholy. She wanted to be left alone. Like that Sunday so many years ago, at the start of their marriage. He'd woken up and gone straight into the kitchen, and she wasn't there. She'd vanished without leaving a word, written or spoken. If it had happened six months later, he would have panicked. He would have seen himself again at the steering wheel, with her sprawled in the passenger seat, messed up on Flunox, saying over and over with her eyes closed: "Forget about it, what the fuck, let's go back home . . ." But that time, he'd waited until early afternoon. Then he'd hopped in the car and gone looking for her. Through the windows, on both sides of the car, he saw a stream of low buildings and narrow courtyards surrounded by metal fences. Cocktail bars, theaters, fashionable restaurants: that was what he was taking care to avoid, as if he'd suddenly understood that the places his wife frequented were exactly those he'd need to pass through in order not to know her. He'd driven past the old hotel, the Albergo delle Nazioni. He'd continued down the road that ran along the waterfront and among the enormous boulevards on the outskirts of town.

At nightfall he'd finally found her. The immense parking lot around the San Nicola stadium, deserted at that time of day. She was sitting in her Audi, without so much as the company of a cigarette. Head down, she was staring at her right hand, where a scar dating from a couple of years back ran down her palm. When he'd pulled up, Clara had displayed no surprise. A small start. Then she'd lowered her window. Her face illuminated by the first streetlamps. "If you want to help, then please, don't ask me anything and just go home." At that point, Alberto had chosen once and for all, had realized that the only way (the only way available to him) to share in his wife's most distant side was to let her hand it over to him like a treasure chest we do our best not to pry open. That night, in the parking lot outside the large sports complex, what had been an irresistible source of attraction when he'd first met her (and a worrisome cause for embarrassment on their wedding day) had taken on the semblance of a love story.

Tonight, too, something of the sort might have happened. He imagined her alone in a room in a rundown hotel on the waterfront, sitting on the bed and looking out the window. Or not, or not . . .

After the first distant clatters of rolling shutters being

raised, he'd gotten out of bed. His insomnia had exhausted him, it was tearing into the barrier that separated the contemplative side from the garbage.

He'd grabbed his car keys. Without realizing it, he was driving toward the construction site even before day had dawned.

So now he was there, in the open air and silence of the morning. For the past few minutes, a tiny swallow had been wheeling through the scaffoldings. That meant that the number of live insects within its range of activity had already declined.

He inserted his key into the padlock. The chain fell away and he was inside the prefabricated shed. He pulled the can of coffee off the shelf. He twisted the coffeemaker tight and set it on the camp stove. He picked up the newspaper that had been forgotten there by the construction workers. With the paper under one arm, he turned off the flame, poured the espresso into a plastic cup, and sat down. As he was reading the news from the day before, he heard a bolt vibrate in its joint. He looked up, folding the pages of the newspaper. The oil tankers in flames got mixed up with the husbands clubbing their wives with shovels. The noise stopped. Alberto took another sip of coffee. He got to his feet and stepped back out into the open air.

The dawn was lighting the area all around. The sun was tinging the cranes and earthmovers pink, turning glassworks and printing plants in the distance red hot. Something had broken away from the background noise of the state highway. The cloud of dust, white and disintegrating, curved toward the right, tightening around a postage stamp of glittering metal.

The silhouette took on the features of a high-performance automobile.

The vehicle slowed down as it came even with the first bulldozers, stopping a few yards short of the columns wrapped in their scaffolding of tubular struts and joints. Alberto had the sun in his face, and all he could see was the black figure of a man carefully smoothing his suit as he walked in his direction.

It wasn't uncommon for his father-in-law to come and check on how work was progressing, but at this time of the morning it struck him as an intrusion. Alberto raised one hand, uncertain whether he was waving hello or miming the rejection of a nuisance. Nothing, in any case, compared with what the old man did once he was standing in front of him.

"So this is where you bring them, is it!" he snarled, slamming into him with his shoulder.

His father-in-law strode past him. Alberto was forced to turn around. With the sun behind him, he was able to focus on the man more clearly. He was wearing a lead-gray tweed jacket, and in his face there was a phosphorescent pallor. From his height of six foot one, he looked like a utility tower about to discharge its voltage into the earth.

"Here, on my construction site," he smiled horribly. He pointed to the pillars and the cars and the shed behind him.

"Signor Salvemini, sir, what are you talking about?"

Alberto immediately detected in that "sir"—which hadn't changed after years—a second source of weakness. The first was having opposed madness with common sense. Because it was obvious, something must have gone wrong with the man's arterial pressure.

"I pay my construction workers enough that they can afford a hotel room for their nights out," Vittorio hissed, "or do you think they don't cheat on their wives?"

Absurd though it was, thought Alberto, there was something theatrical about the situation—the aura of farce that sugarcoated the savage lunge with which Vittorio concluded a deal when he was dining with the lords of the steelplants, old satraps of the industrial aristocracy that he'd corner by telling a joke and then snapping right back to the importance of driving down prices.

"Signor Salvemini, sir, this is crazy. I don't bring anyone here."

"They don't tell *you* about it," Vittorio didn't even bother pretending he had to listen to him, "they catch a whiff of official documents and they steer clear. All they do is take your orders. But they tell me things. I'm the one of them who's made the most money. They tell me where they take the girls. How do you think all those shitty little hotels between Palese and Santo Spirito manage to stay in business?"

"What you're saying doesn't make sense. Would you please explain to me where—"

"You could actually buy yourself a small hotel," Vittorio started walking toward the prefabricated shed, the dust kicked up the wind caressing his shoes, "but you're such an idiot that you disrespect your wife in the last place you ought to—" he knocked twice on the aluminum wall—"I'm going in to say hello to your girlfriend."

He grabbed the door handle and two seconds later had vanished into the prefabricated structure. Alberto lifted a hand to his forehead. It seemed absurd to him that Vittorio should be lecturing someone for not handling his illicit affairs with sufficient prudence. Him, of all people, Michele's father. Alberto looked straight ahead again. Vittorio reappeared in the doorway. In one hand he held a small coffee cup. He was looking at him with a grin of relieved disappointment, the grimace the old use to scold the young for not having had time to make enough mistakes.

"Are you satisfied now, sir? Or would you like to go search on the scaffolding? Signor Salvemini—" Alberto clenched his fists—"I never disrespect your daughter. What's more"—he laughed bitterly—"you'll be surprised to learn that I also don't beat her on Friday nights and I even let her out to spend time with her girlfriends."

"But don't you see that *this very fact* is the point, you

miserable idiot?" Vittorio walked past the small mountain of cement bags and placed himself in front of his son-in-law, close enough to be able to take a swing at him, "the problem is that you do nothing. That *you've never* been able to do anything."

Alberto furrowed his brow.

"You might be good at calculating the sum total of static forces at work in a building," he went on, his face twisted by something grim, sorrowful, "but what you didn't know how to do with my daughter . . . "

"Signor Salvemini, excuse me, but has something happened?"

"That time with the barbiturates."

Alberto stiffened.

"That time she took all those sleeping pills, damn it!"

"That was a long time ago." Now Alberto found himself on territory where the burden of proof rested incomprehensibly on him.

"A long time or a short time, you were unable to do anything," said Vittorio angrily, "and in fact, this is where I found you today. Where were you when Clara took all those sleeping pills?"

"It was *me* who took her to the hospital, for fuck's sake."

"To which hospital?

"What do you mean, to which hospital?"

"You heard me loud and clear. I'm asking you which fucking hospital you took her to when she took those sleeping pills!"

He was red in the face, his pupils were dilated.

"To the Santa Rita." The words shot out of his mouth like bees from a burning hive.

"The Santa Rita clinic," the old man echoed.

Alberto added nothing, it seemed to him that his father-in-law was satisfied now, for some reason that he was struggling to comprehend.

Vittorio heaved a long, pained sigh. He took two steps back, stumbled, almost tripped over his own shoes. He set his sights on him again, enraged: "Do you or don't you know where she is right now?"

Alberto felt a wave of heat surge upward from his stomach. They'd never talked about it before, of course, but his father-in-law could guess the way things were between him and Clara. He'd come here to humiliate him. One of his arteries was blocked and now his true nature could be unleashed. A savage beast, eager to tear him apart. But, once again, Alberto was wrong. The insult was more serious. Did he have any idea what had happened to Clara? Because Vittorio, he did know.

After telling him, the old man went on looking at him. Before his eyes filled with tears, Alberto had the strength to ask him how she'd done it. Vittorio waved his open hand back and forth.

"Down," he said, "sixty-five feet."

Vittorio staggered backwards. He slumped against the bags of cement. Alberto followed his father-in-law's forefinger, which was pointed at him for the umpteenth time. Everything smacked of hallucination. The movement came to a halt before its time. Vittorio picked his cell phone from his inside jacket pocket, answered the call.

Ruggero slammed the refrigerator shut after drinking the milk straight out of the carton.

"Shit!" he shouted angrily. He hurled the carton against the kitchen cabinet on the wall, so that a spray of white droplets stuck to the smooth surface.

His father gazed at him, resignedly.

Ruggero displayed a sneer between his still-wet lips. He seemed to be blaming Vittorio, and a second later, himself, for the fact that they were there, like that, face to face, as if there were some unforgivable disproportion between the physical bodies of father and son and the silhouettes in which they should have been wrapped. The weave of his tracksuit was drenched with sweat. He'd gone for a run before heading to the clinic, where the deputy director of the Cancer Institute of the Mediterranean came in every morning at 8:50 sharp. The ritual of that run was important. Always three more laps around the track than he could take. The strain helped to lessen his tension, which in turn helped him face patients before whom he'd stage complicated charades that would carry them to the day of their deaths. The effort to resolve those charades confused them. An hour's run every morning to become a philosopher. Upon his return, he'd found his father waiting for him outside his apartment building, ready to give him the news.

The drops had dripped down the cabinet door. Vittorio explained the situation to him. He'd already told his mother, but Gioia was still sleeping.

"What do you mean, *sleeping?*"

They'd wake her up later, said Vittorio. He'd called Michele, too, but nobody picked up. The first thing he did, in any case, was go see Alberto.

"That asshole."

"Please," and Vittorio shook his head. He asked Ruggero if he could take care of his younger brother. Then he said something about the Santa Rita hospital.

But Ruggero was't listening to him. Now he was violently pulling the drawers open and shut. One loud bang after the other. *Slam! Slam!* When the sequence began to border on foolishness, he did the strangest thing of all. He picked up a bottle opener and held it in front of his eyes as if it were the first he'd ever seen. He threw open the fridge again. He grabbed a cold Schweppes, opened it, and drank it down. He started to hurl the little empty bottle against the wall. The gesture was so contrived that it failed to fool even him.

"What the fuck!" He set the bottle down on the table. He went back to looking at Vittorio.

They should have started showing her the back of their hands when she was small. Made her sit in a corner until she learned to say she was sorry. It wasn't Clara's fault. This is what happens to a troubled girl when she never feels the bite of discipline. Hadn't Ruggero been warning them for years? The absence of rules, the nauseating lack of authority that spilled out of even the family photos . . . *Freedom!* Nothing more disgusting under the sun than that word. Freedom was an empty proclamation, a dead animal in whose intestines an army of larvae was swelling its ranks.

"Let the damned fools think they're right!" he was shouting now, still standing in front of the refrigerator.

He phoned the undertakers himself. He phoned the diocesan administrator to arrange to have the Mass moved outside of Bari. He phoned Michele, but the line was busy. He phoned the assistant district attorney Piscitelli. He would arrange to send him the certificate they'd discussed. He phoned Michele and the line was free. The fact made him feel strangely uncomfortable. Vittorio hung up before his son could answer. He phoned Engineer De Palo, whom he considered his right-hand man. He asked if he had talked with Bari General Hospital. The engineer said yes, that the man from the crash was still in a coma. Vittorio went into the bathroom and splashed water on his face. He wanted a cigarette. With fingers still dripping water, he phoned Engineer Ranieri. He, too, would have been a worthy right-hand man, if his excessively servile nature hadn't compromised his reliability every now and then. Vittorio told him to get in touch with Engineer De Palo and to follow his instructions. Then he phoned his accountant. He asked if there was any news about the Porto Allegro affair. The man reiterated what he had told him two days ago. He spoke of the attachment order as nothing more than a regrettable juridical development. Vittorio interrupted him, annoyed. He asked him where he'd spent his summer vacation. Positano, with the family, said the accountant (his tone now perplexed). Vittorio asked him if he could guess where he'd be spending next summer if the investigating magistrate were to accept the request for protective seizure of assets. The man had the nerve to ask him if he felt well: his tone of voice was a little odd, he ventured. Vittorio told him that he didn't feel well. Not in your dreams. He hung up without giving the other man a chance to reply. He phoned the tax lawyer, an elderly practitioner who tended to wax dramatic over small mistakes on invoices. The lawyer confirmed that the situation at Porto Allegro was stationary. He said it as if he were announcing the end of the world. Vittorio tried to contain his pessimism. This gave him the push to do what he had intended to do from the start. He called the chief justice of the Bari Court of Appeals. The switchboard operator put him on hold. Vittorio used the melody of *Imagine* to destroy the minor causal nexus that trembled between him and the person who was about to answer the phone. The chief justice of the court of appeals said: "Hello." His voice strained to remain neutral. Vittorio informed him that Clara was dead. He said it immediately, without preliminaries. On the other end of the line, silence fell. Then the chief justice of the court of appeals spoke. He asked how it had happened. Vittorio was impressed by the man's ability to keep his cool. He answered the question. Only then did the judge say, in a faint voice: "I'm sorry." Now he gave the impression he needed to protect himself from something, and that in order to do so he'd need to take the condolences back in time a few minutes, so that the conversation could start over again from the routine formalities. They spoke about the funeral mass. They said goodbye. Vittorio's yearning for a cigarette had vanished. He phoned the director of the Banca di

Credito Pugliese. He told him that Clara was dead. He phoned the deputy mayor. He phoned the chancellor of the university, who was at the center of a conglomerate of local newspapers. He gave everyone the news. It wasn't he who was doing it. His fingers, on the keypad, were searching for the numerical equivalent of a hologram, the persistence of the nexus that he had tried to destroy a few minutes earlier. Between one phone call and the next, his cell phone rang. It was the accountant again. He apologized. He said that he'd only just heard. Word was beginning to spread, thought Vittorio. He set the cell phone down on the desk while the accountant went on apologizing. He shut his eyes. He heaved a deep sigh. The time had come to pay a call on his eldest son.

He phoned the clinic and told his secretary to cancel all his appointments. The young woman objected that his first patients were scheduled to be there soon. There were people who'd come all the way from Campobasso, from Reggio Calabria. She said it with an emphasis on how sorry she was, just enough to show it was false. Having to face them in person wasn't the same thing as dismissing them over the phone. Ruggero felt contempt for her. His secretary asked if he was still on the line. Ruggero replied that there had been a death in his family and hung up. He phoned his brother. After it rang twice, he hung up. He phoned Heidi. He told her that he was sorry, but their date for that evening was off. The girl told him that she had the afternoon free. If he wanted, they could even get together in the morning. Whatever the problem was, the girl's voice seemed to be saying, she wouldn't solve it. She'd have put it in perspective. She'd have softened it, caressed it. Ruggero said that he'd pay her anyway and hung up. He tried to call Michele again. He didn't even finish dialing the number. He phoned his mother. He asked her if she could do him a favor and call his brother in Rome. "I've been trying since this morning but the line is always busy." That's what Ruggero said. His mother replied coldly that she'd take care of it. They were about to hang up, but he took a deep breath and asked her. He could guess the answer. In fact, his mother told him that Gioia was still sleeping. All right, he thought. Clara had been dead for hours, and they still hadn't gotten Gioia out of bed. He had to get a hold of himself to keep from pitching a fit. He phoned Fatima. He told her that their date for that afternoon was off. Unfortunately, as he had expected, the girl started losing her temper. Ruggero assured her that he would pay her anyway. That's when something very strange happened: Fatima got even angrier. She started mixing her Italian up with her Portuguese. He told her to calm down. If he really cared for her, she replied, whimpering, then he would pay what he owed her right then and there via PayPal. She seemed convinced that she could claim a debt on the grounds of an emotional bond that they had never even considered as an object of negotiation.

The assistant district attorney Corrado Piscitelli laid a hand on Vittorio's shoulder and said: "I'm sorry."

The lights of morning had not yet penetrated the weft of the sky, and so the space around the parking structure was just a bare patch of asphalt discolored by the streetlamps. At the corners of an intersection, four traffic lights were blinking in solitude. The assistant district attorney was a man in his early fifties from Martina Franca. He was dressed in a casual style that courted fashion while denying the fact with excessive timidity. He used an Italian that had been cleansed of dialect with a skill that most public officials lacked. A trained ear would have recognized it as a nonexistent language.

Vittorio said nothing. The asphalt had been cleared. The carabinieri had left. By now she was already on her way to the morgue in the company of the medical examiner. The neon bar flickered between one floor and another of the cylindrically shaped parking structure. They were the only two left.

"I wouldn't want to make this any harder than it has to be," Piscitelli went on. "Well, you see . . . "

He tried to better modulate his tone. In the past he'd had his problems with them. The scope of the Salveminis' business was such that occasionally they overstepped the bounds of the law. That, unfortunately, was a normal thing. Put an elephant in a room full of glasses and then scold it if it breaks one. More than once they'd taken their respective documents before a judge. Skirmishes.

"Go ahead," said old Salvemini without moving an inch.

Already, putting his hand on the man's shoulder hadn't come naturally to him. There was a whole school of gestures of that kind, of which Piscitelli was no master. To find the right tone he tried drawing from colleagues of bygone generations, the ones who uttered their vowels so ineptly that they undermined the unity of the nation with the very tool that should have tightened its collar.

"It's something that might save time," the assistant district attorney said awkwardly, "so I wanted to ask you . . . Well. Was this the first time your daughter tried to take her own life?"

Vittorio's eyes opened a little wider.

There had always been gossip about the Salveminis, certain rumors had been circulating for years.

"I understand I'm just piling sorrow on top of sorrow."

The words that had come out of his mouth were faker than ever. And yet, the lack of naturalness made him feel in tune with the old man. Two elevators traveling in opposite directions in two shafts of clear glass, destined to intersect for a few brief seconds. A magnetic tension threw open and then reshut a door inside the assistant district attorney. He saw something incomprehensibly unsettling. The sensation passed.

"Oh," said Vittorio, "it was a long time ago."

The assistant district attorney felt relieved. He told Vittorio that if someone would let him have the medical certificate attesting to that attempt, the case could be filed away in a few days.

"Do you know what hospital she was taken to that time?"

Old Salvemini involuntarily raised an eyebrow. The assistant district attorney did the same.

In the distance, the rustle of the city rose just before its reawakening, the sound of cars without cars, the small electrical storm of the many who, on the verge of reopening their eyes, re-experienced in a few split seconds the film of the day that was about to begin.

The fluorescent light in the parking structure flickered.

"I have no idea where she was taken the other time," Vittorio's lips curled, "but I'll arrange to have you informed."

She phoned her boyfriend and he was unable to say a single word. (Every time he tried, Gioia just cried louder and told the whole story over again from the beginning). She phoned her best friend. She phoned a university friend with whom she had a fraught relationship. All it took were a few words for all the mistrust to collapse. She phoned the teaching assistant who was helping her with her thesis. She called Rosa, the daughter of the woman who had been coming to the villa for years to do their ironing. As little girls, they had played together, and it was only later that Rosa had developed a tendency toward submissiveness around Gioia; it was hard to say to what extent that tendency might grow after the news Rosa was about to receive. She phoned an ex with whom she'd had a nasty breakup. He said, "I'm coming straight over," as if he had never ordered her to ignore him if they ever chanced to run into each other on the street. With every phone call, she felt stronger and more desperate. She felt, growing within her, her power and her grace.

The spirit of her dead sister was filling every empty space.

C *hild of the pure unclouded brow.* He hid the little book in the drawer and picked up the missal.

Clara's funeral was held at six in the evening in a rural church thirty miles away from Bari, a small building dating back to the year 1000 that stood white and solitary on a hill in the Alta Murgia.

It had been such a beautiful day that a cascade of light still kindled the oaks and the asphodels, made the clouds of pollen blaze, and conferred on large, smooth, pale boulders the consistency of an optical illusion. Beyond the roof of a farmhouse, a small paved road ran downhill. There the trees grew thicker, giving anyone who looked a sudden sensation of melancholy, perhaps because the darkness—of which those shadows were a faint bellwether—would soon creep all the way up there.

Standing erect at the altar, the priest threw his arms open wide. He said that, having brought into the world nothing but his own soul, there was nothing else a human being could drag away with him. He had hoped that this formulation would express his regret for the poor girl. But the words came out of his mouth like an admonishment hurled against the congregation, by and large older people dressed in black, in whose midst anyone who kept up with the local press could recognize a few well-known faces.

Despicable old geezers, he thought.

The priest was thirty-two, four years younger than the woman who'd committed suicide. He was skinny and short, with small eyes and the complexion of someone suffering from stress. He saw the young woman, from his vantage point, upside-down. She lay in repose in her dark-wood coffin, dressed in an outfit of viscose and virgin wool with a V-neck collar and a white fur appliqué along the sides. A trumpet will sound and the face, nicely treated with cosmetics, will conceal the lesions brought on by stagnating blood. She had broken bones everywhere, he thought. But in spite of the violent impact, and the work of the undertaker's technicians, she had preserved a personality. There were bodies that death dispossessed instantly and bodies so lovely that they would admire their reflection for days in the survival of an idea. This young woman glowed in the offense. Her lips, stitched tight with thread, seemed to twist in a grimace of satisfaction. And then there was the residue of youth, the distant budding of childhood that the priest could still manage to glimpse.

He turned his eyes back to the attendees.

The morning had begun with a phone call from the diocesan administrator. He'd talked to the monsignor in the past few days, as well. They needed to make an appointment with the technicians to connect the parish website to the Episcopal Conference's server. The yeast of the Sadducees. Only now his superior wanted to talk about something else. The calendar of meetings with the families. The redesign of the parish newspaper. The priest was walking from the galley kitchen to the living room with the moka pot and a demitasse, the phone clamped between neck and shoulder, when the monsignor's voice grew thin. A funeral mass. To be celebrated that very day. People from Bari.

"A woman, very young."

This is what his superior had told him in response to his

request. But then he'd stayed silent, long enough for the priest to find, in the silence, wrath. He'd asked him the cause of death.

The monsignor's voice reemerged from the silence as if it had fallen into a crevasse and now showed the marks of a depth that overrode personal opinion. It asked him to reflect on the state into which anyone who uses narcotics sinks: "It seems that they found traces of cocaine." Moreover, the monsignor added, there wasn't any regulation in canon law forbidding the funeral service for a suicide. From the open window came birdcalls. The priest even thought he could hear the sound of the valley bottom. A music that climbed up the ravines, entered into the villages, and gathered up the sorrow of each individual, only to scatter it again amongst the rocks and the olive groves, like the ashes of the dead generations, so that the same burden of peace weighed on everyone. In this lay the unhappiness of the South, its untouched privilege. But behold how from Bari came the corpse of a dead girl. A girl who had jumped from sixty-five feet up. The obstinacy, the stubborn individual force of the city people.

A diocesan priest had a duty to investigate the inner dimensions of the tragedy, the monsignor had said over the phone. *Peer into the depths of the heart.* See if somewhere there might have been a flicker of doubt countering the decision to throw herself off the parking structure, even though it was ultimately carried out. And then, while they were at it, the priest had grumbled to himself, try to figure out whether his superior's insistence was bound up with the warp and weft of the world by the double thread of opportunity. Perhaps he knows her relatives, he thought, or owes them something.

"How free to choose, in your opinion, could a young woman befuddled by narcotics really have been?"

Those aren't the effects of cocaine, he thought as he greedily smoked the first Marlboro of the day.

Later the dead woman's family arrived. It was three in the afternoon and the shade of the chestnut tree was stretching over the right side of the church. He saw them pulling back the curtains in the rectory. Father, mother, husband, and two siblings. The car was parked on the crescent of dry grass. He went up to the front door. He grabbed the door handle and pulled it toward him.

They appeared in his presence speaking over each other, disheveled, on edge. "All you had to do was read the map," objected the youngest girl, lowering her voice. He looked at her more closely. She was over twenty, but she was trailed by a heavy childish wake. Someone uttered her name. *Gioia.* She must have been a chubby little girl.

"Our father would like to read from Psalm 40," the older son broke in.

He ushered them in. Their movements slowed. The reason they were there settled back over them. Now they were standing in the small living room, crushed by numbness. He was the priest: what was keeping him from reading from the instruction booklet? The girl was picking at her iPhone case. The dead woman's husband was looking anywhere that he could to avoid meeting another pair of eyes. "Forgive me." The mother. She'd asked for a glass of water. She thanked him and drank, shifting from a blank detachment to a dignified detachment. Her eyes were glistening. The noise of a chair slamming to the floor. The girl had tripped and now she was getting awkwardly to her feet, arrogant and irritated, grateful for the mishap. These were rich people. And even though they didn't know how to behave—at every false step, the assignment of blame elsewhere—through the most unthinkable path, suffering had managed to find its way to them.

"We are in agreement," he'd allowed, "go ahead and read the psalm."

That was then they started quarreling. Gioia said that she

wanted to be one of those carrying the coffin on her shoulder. Her mother took umbrage: "Not this again . . . " as if they'd woken her up from one nightmare only to shove her back into the depths of the one before. Her older brother reiterated that the coffin would be carried by the employees of the funeral parlor. "As we agreed." Gioia began to speak in a slightly angry voice. At a certain point her brother started yelling at her. She burst into tears. Just like a fourteen-year-old girl. The head of the family shook his head. The priest thought to himself that the girl's corpse was drawing closer. Shut up in the back of the hearse, she must have already left the regional capital.

They emerged from the rectory still arguing. Now it was the mother and the daughter who had bones to pick. Five minutes later, from the window, he saw that they were tearfully embracing. Another cigarette. He stretched out on the bed with the book by the competition in his hands. Every so often he'd do it. A way of distracting himself, of shaking off the tension. Woe to those who deal in fraud. Mercy to the smokers. Eighty-Third Surah. He dozed off.

Around five in the afternoon, he saw several powerful cars making their way along the last stretch of the uphill climb. The chestnut leaves presenting themselves over and over in an endless array of new shapes on the enamel of the bodywork. His bad humor roused itself like a dry clod of dirt in the falling rain.

Out of the cars, what emerged were mostly old people. Bent, pale, some with chauffeurs trailing in their wake. They marched forward in dark suits of striped fabrics. They were all over sixty, and almost all males without wives. He thought he'd recognized the chief justice of the Court of Appeals. The chancellor of the university. And that was the deputy mayor of Bari. In the church's small courtyard, they were shaking hands with the dead's woman's father. They were putting on a show of keeping their distance that seemed a product of embarrassment, not delicacy. Stepping out of a midnight-black Maserati was the former undersecretary Buffante—the priest waited for the attention of the attendees to focus on that man, drawn by the wake of scandal and popularity that followed him. But that didn't happen. The ritual of backslapping continued. Every so often, amidst the wrinkles creasing the eyes of those present, there pulsed an annoyance free of abrasions. Then the hearse arrived.

"Behold, I send you forth as sheep in the midst of wolves," said the priest, thinking the exact opposite in mid-Mass.

Vittorio listened to him, not far from the coffin, without taking his eyes off the floor, his face not broken but grim, focused on the voice of the officiant. *The product of my act of will, departed without my having any say in the matter.* The body of his daughter radiated the inexplicable truth of the rooms in houses we haven't lived in for a long time.

The priest theorized: "If thy right eye offend thee."

Alberto lifted three fingers to his forehead. He was pale and exhausted, the body more held up by his jacket than the other way around. When was the last time he had been in a church with her? It was their wedding day, and Clara, in a Vera Wang dress that added to her own allure something unbearable and coarse, had joined him at the foot of the altar, flashing a drunken grin. She had kneeled down next to him. Taking advantage of the fact that the bishop was addressing the rest of the congregation, she had languidly rested her flower-crowned head on his shoulder. "This is the most comical day of my whole life," she had snickered. Which had startled him, in part because he had caught a heavy whiff of alcohol on her breath: Ballantine's or Southern Comfort, clashing totally with the gracefulness of the body that was producing it. Alberto had lifted his eyes to the God in whom he didn't believe and had prayed that Clara hadn't drunk because she needed the liquid courage, though also he found, deep in that fear, a dangerous source of attraction.

Alberto looked at the coffin in front of him. His wife's smooth, spacious forehead, her white hands. The area around the parking structure was as grim as you could imagine. After attacking him so absurdly the day before, the old man had told him how it had happened. The filthy streets in the leaden pallor of morning. He imagined her, ashen and exhausted, walking in the echo of her heels, clutching the lapels of her old trenchcoat around her neck as she passed among the sleeping cars. Then she'd looked over the railing. Alberto felt someone touch his side. Gioia had been sobbing since the coffin had entered the church. She was suffocating her weeping with an effort that was still inferior to that necessary to convince herself that the pain could be mastered. She seemed to stop. Then she peeked at her iPhone and plunged back into a sonorous weeping. Ruggero looked at her with contempt. He was watching the priest's movements with exasperation. He was observing his parents with grimaces of tolerance. He seemed to be doing the same thing with the coffin.

A family of crazy people, thought Alberto, and the craziest one of all didn't even show up.

The priest continued to observe those present. It was clear that the family members had come all the way up here in order to avoid the embarrassment of a ceremony near home. But the fact that he saw not a single person the dead woman's age confirmed his theories. If she had taken her life when she was in high school, for the family there would have been no way out—beautiful, tearful, unstoppable, *by the hundreds*, her friends would have fought their way even through the sempiternal ice.

When a sixteen-year-old died, and sometimes even a twenty-year-old, the churches were invaded by this army of boys and girls. None of them had ventured past a holy water font since the day of their confirmation, and they wouldn't be coming back again anytime soon. A languid, rabid charge of bodies in flower. There wasn't a saint who could match the perfume of fruit and sweat emanating from a fourteen-year-old girl in tears for the death of a girlfriend. *Child of the pure unclouded brow*, the priest recited once again. When it was people in their sixties who passed away, their colleagues from work gathered. People in their nineties were experts at dragging after them whole towns. But the real tragedy was those in their thirties. The thirty-five year olds, not infrequently those in their forties. There were no colleagues from work because there was often no work. And when there was work, then the colleagues were too busy struggling for survival. The friends— the real friends, those who had once been real friends—were far away, lost in the cities up North, mired in the swamps of their lives. Perhaps the news had even reached them, and the condolences (from hundreds, perhaps thousands of miles away) caused tiny twisting flickers in the flames in the electric candles.

And so in those cases the body remained at the mercy of the family. With the result being (the joke being, really, thought the priest as he prepared for communion) that the whole thing was managed by those against whom the deceased must have struggled to emancipate herself when she was still alive—mothers and fathers and grandparents and aunts and uncles whose very teeth, distorted through the curve of the glass from which they were drinking, she couldn't stand the sight of.

Having at your own funeral the people whose funerals you ought to have attended instead. To say nothing of their friends, whom you might never even have met.

So it is for this young woman, he thought, breaking the host over the paten, guessing only in part and never dreaming, for the half he was wrong about, how far he was from the truth.

*

He had no time to give the matter any more thought, because Vittorio leapt to his feet before he'd even called the communion, even before the time had come for the psalm.

The priest's disappointment turned to disbelief when Vittorio turned his back on him, and then apprehension as he saw the man bend over at the waist. Now he needed to turn to the cross. He recited the formula. In the meantime he suspected sudden illness that would only confirm the impossibility of righting a day that had begun badly. He turned to the pews and caught sight of him on his way out of the church. He no longer knew what to think. The first of the communicants answered his call. His fingers picked up another consecrated host and a second mouth opened to his hand. He saw the widower and the young girl step forward. He peered amongst the heads. The line stretched halfway down the nave. The priest searched for a big enough gap through which he might see the figure of Vittorio. Instead, he noticed something else. The hand had been pulled away quickly, which meant that it had been put in just a short while before. The priest thought his eyes must have deceived him. It was absurd to think that's what it could have been. He gave communion to the girl. He gave communion to an old man with an olive complexion. Then the scene repeated itself. The whitish fingers, followed the golden wave of a wristwatch, extended over the dark wooden side, covered by the others stepping forward. The priest stretched his neck to understand. The former undersecretary. Too far away to be him. He looked for him elsewhere, and there he was. The fact that he'd recognized him outside of the church helped. He'd seen him recently on a local TV news broadcast. The round, sagging cheeks, the patch of beard sprouting on his chin to give substance to a boring speech about the university's balance sheet. The university chancellor's eyes were glistening. He seemed to be in a state of despair. Partially concealed by the other men, if in fact what the priest was now certain of actually was taking place, it seemed that the only method he had of calming himself was to come into physical contact with the dead woman. To touch her ankle. The soft fur stitched along the sides of her dress. The arms and then the neck, as the line inched forward. The priest blushed. They'd undressed her and had hastened to break the stiffness of her neck. Same thing for the fingers, the wrists, the jaw. Then, charitably, they pressed down on the urogenital area. Such a pretty young woman. They're turned her onto her side to encourage the discharge of regurgitations from her nose and mouth as well. They'd washed her, shampooed her hair. With the help of a pair of anatomical forceps, they'd inserted strips of absorbent cotton into her various natural orifices. They'd disinfected her, applied makeup, dressed her again. They'd had to drive the needle between her upper lip and her gums, until it poked out through one of the nostrils and the thread could be drawn upward. That was when that grimace had formed. She must have been a very beautiful little girl, he thought to himself. An alert young woman. The chancellor caressed her once again. Though he'd clearly lost his mind, he managed to control himself so as to avoid triggering a scandal. He'd rummage in the coffin, yank his hand away, and immediately clutch at the wooden side, pretending it was a handrail. The priest sought out the body of the deceased woman. Just a few days ago, she might have been sitting down to lunch with a friend. She was still eating, talking. Such a pretty young woman, a magnificent child years and years ago. Then an act of will. The curse of individual impulses. Which had only been the start of the show, the call to break ranks that had led to her body being undressed and manipulated, to his receiving that horrible phone call from the diocesan administrator, and to all those old men showing up here, judges and bankers

and politicos, and now this man, the chancellor of Bari
University, caressing her in the coffin, or palpating her, or
clutching her throat, *and all this absurdity*, the priest intuited;
he watched the chancellor's bewildered eyes and the knot in
his throat finally loosened, he saw, he understood, he was
enlightened, once again he understood, fool of a fool that he
was, and now he could have laughed, danced, *this obsession*,
he told himself, this unbridled frenzy, only the Roman variant
could accomodate and minister to it, bring it on board and
understand it. The weave of the English version was too
loose. The Protestants would have found it implausible. The
Pentecostals would have prohibited it, the Adventists
detested it, Baptists and Congregationalists would only have
let it get close enough so they could wave a noose at it, but
the Roman variant, Catholic and Apostolic, knew how to take
pity on professors who caressed a dead woman in her coffin,
its embrace was broad, its heart boundless, it could feel the
heartbeat of a man when he steals from his brother's pocket,
when he counts the cash, when he cheats on his wife, when
he swears to a falsehood, when he murders and rapes and sets
fires, the Episcopalians would have made sure they came
down with a colic, the worshippers of the crescent moon
would have erected a gallows . . . But nothing could scandal-
ize the Apostolic and Roman variant because everything is
human, thought the priest; he rejoiced, understood, remembered, open and sweet, grateful and compassionate, it could
even accept that a young man of thirty, as he had been,
should have gone with a girl of fourteen, and even managed
to grasp the reasons driving the girl, her expectations, her
foolish mistake of spilling the whole story to her parents so
that the young man swept himself into a fine mystical crisis,
on your knees son! he thought, he understood, suffered,
remembered, north of Rome it was all a matter for the judici-
ary, in Tehran for the executioner, here in the South a mys-

tery, south of London and Mecca, south of Athens and
Jerusalem, her soft, sweet, sweaty hand as she walked up the
hill, her purple leggings and her Peanuts T-shirt.

Vittorio grimaced nastily. He slipped his right hand into his
jacket. He turned sideways to make way for himself. He
bumped his wife and son-in-law and first-born son inconsider-
ately until he had slid out of the pew. He turned his back on
the altar. He walked toward the exit without taking his hand
away from his chest, drilling into the eyes of the men a whiff of
concern for themselves. He walked up the aisle, red-faced. He
went past the confessional. He strode out the door and was
once again in the open air.

The evening wind tossed his hair. Vittorio took a few steps
across the dry grass. A driver was smoking, his back against the
door of a BMW. The sun had dragged the last lingering lumi-
nescences away with it. A foggy blue covered the cow paths,
made the highland, from one moment to the next, an independent profile or one with the sky. The banner of a chain of
supermarkets being towed by an airplane twisted high above
and vanished. Vittorio veered to the right, descended the slope
for a few yards. He placed his hand on the trunk of a tree. He
pulled the cell phone out of the inside pocket of his jacket and
put it to his ear.

"Hello!"

Engineer De Palo informed him that the man from Taranto,
the Tarantine, had emerged from his coma.

He started breathing slowly. He was listening. The voice
repeated the news. Then he added that they had amputated
one of his legs.

Vittorio ran his free hand over his face, trying to ward off
the ridiculous hope that a man with one leg less was in greater
danger of dying than a man in a coma. The amputation of the
leg just made the problem worse. It complicated it terribly.

Vittorio raised his head, observed the way land and sky merged beyond the trees. A gear had started turning two nights ago. The mechanism had gone from one with potential to one that was active, from one that was simple to one that was complex. A universe whose expansion—real and unconscious in the fabric of the world, artificial and well codified beneath the light of his reason—was the most visible manifestation of the concept of ruin that he'd ever beheld.

Engineer De Palo informed him that the first thing the man had demanded was a different room.

"What?" Vittorio thought he must have misunderstood.

"The problem was the patient in the next bed. He was moaning."

He asked what they'd done.

"We gave him a different room. What else were we supposed to do? We cleared out a closet to give him a room all to himself."

Vittorio said that he'd take care of it himself, in person, the next day. The engineer said goodbye. He closed his phone. He adjusted his jacket, shaking the lapels twice. He moved off again in the direction of the church.

They didn't know where to look.

They vanished, hurrying into the underpasses in the railroad station. They brooded, their foreheads pressed against the steering wheels of small cars stuck in traffic after the end of the workday. Outside the Apple Store they lit a cigarette, finding a source of comfort in the first puffs. Via email. Via text. Crimson-red stripes in the reflective plate-glass windows of the Banca di Credito Pugliese. They drank in a bar on Via Crisanzio where they hadn't expected to go. Outside the window, in the shimmering opacity of light pollution, they were following the axis at the end of which it was possible to spot it. With their noses tipped upward, studying the sky. An S, a U, a P on the plastic-coated strip. They were drumming their fingers on the lampposts to kill time while waiting for their dealer. Left alone in the office, they were checking to see if the tweets they'd sent out in the last hour had resulted in new followers, trying to figure out how many of them had been incentivized by the tweets in their own name, how many by the tweets in the newspaper's name, and how many by those tweeted under the nine different fake accounts that they themselves had come up with. Scent of electrostatic shock. The banner reading RICCARDI SUPERMARKETS was done crossing the sky, towed by a plane during the sunset's last convulsions. They lingered to think about it in solitude, or they talked about it with their current girlfriends.

Few of Clara's old friends had seen the obituary in the paper. The news had begun to spread, entrusted to the sovereignty of algorithms. Few if any phone calls. Over the years, they'd all fallen out of touch. The network of contacts blinked on the screens of the smartphones. From the white sea of pixels emerged the old photo of a woman's volleyball team. *This is not a memory.*

They received the news. They clutched their arms about their chests as if they were cold. They tried to figure out which way they'd have to look to be in line with Noci, the small town in the Murge near which, incomprehensibly, the family of their old friend had decided to celebrate the funeral mass.

A mass that, at that time of night, must have been over and done with.

Giuliano Pascucci, thirty-nine years old, head warehouseman at a textiles plant, took a sip of his Negroni and sat there, staring at the lights that exploded and reassembled themselves in the bar's plate-glass window.

Monday and Thursday were practice days.

Back then he'd been working at a car repair shop, after getting his high school diploma from a vo-tech institute. With his first paychecks, he'd bought a used Fiat Panda. On Saturdays he'd round up his friend and drive them to get a pizza in Torre a Mare. His traveling companions, crammed into the car seats—all of them ranging in age from fifteen to eighteen—handed around beers to the tune of idiotic jokes. On the way back, there was always someone who shouted at the whores.

The Panda testified to his self-esteem, and was the launching pad for future feats of virility. But on Mondays and Thursdays, in the late afternoon, after the owner had already left, giving him the keys, Giuliano turned off the lights in the auto repair shop and an additional veil fell over his gaze. Something that wasn't virility but which ran, as it were, parallel to it, made him lower the roller shutter and climb aboard his Panda.

He drove across the city to go see her.

They practiced in a small gym over near Carbonara. A dome-covered facility with a room for the equipment, the showers, and not much else. Outside was the silence of the suburbs. Inside, the girls ran and did push-ups, running their formations and showing off their side rolls. The shouts echoed, sharp and strong. At the end of the big room were two wooden benches upon which friends and would-be boyfriends gathered, only rarely a parent.

He'd met Clara at a birthday party, and then he'd seen her at the Stravinsky: she was dancing at a hardcore punk concert. Their eyes had brushed past each other when she, drenched with sweat, had ordered a Fanta at the counter. Something not completely clear had suggested the span of the social gap between them, and yet it was something else that kept him from feeling up to her level.

Watching her at the gym only confirmed his fears. She was the most interesting girl he'd ever run into. The gym shoes padding softly to the ground, just fractions of a second after the sound of the ball pounding onto the linoleum, ended the aural sequence that he'd have wanted to hear every night in the headphones of his Walkman before falling asleep. The setter lifted the ball into the air, and Clara coordinated her movements so as to hit the sphere just as it reached the highest point. From what he had been able to figure out, there were different ways of lofting the ball to the net, depending on whether the player who was going to spike was on the outside or in the middle. Between Clara and what he liked to call "her favorite setter," there was an understanding that went well beyond the human in its perfection, and well beyond the machine in all that was human passing between them. The setter ensured that the apex of the arc corresponded with the top of the net. A centimeter lower and the spike would bounce off the tape. That allowed Clara—he'd guessed at first, and he understood more clearly now—to strike, each time revealing her nature.

She spiked violently, never maliciously. It hardly even seemed as if the scoring of points were one of her objectives. Her hair flew free, upward, as she dropped, her feet touching ground, the sensation that gravity had enriched itself with something that was not its own. In the surrounding space, the volleyball game became a miniature universe whose deepest ravine had something in common with botany—the slow growth of the blades of grass, the tropism of certain flowers.

He began to dream of her several times a week. When he also dreamed of the owl with eyeglasses, the logo for Berruti Optics that held pride of place on the green-striped team jersey, he understood that it was time to make his move.

One Thursday in late November, after practice, he worked up the nerve and went over to her. He offered to give her a ride home in his car. He hadn't missed a practice in three months, so to Clara he was a familiar face. The girl nodded. Pascucci stood there staring at her in amazement. Clara added that they'd have to take Michele, her kid brother, too (she said the words "my brother" to redact all terms of endearment), and that was how Pascucci took in the most incredible answer he could have imagined with the delay necessary to extract it from the news that undercut its impact.

The girl held out her arm, pointing to the far side of the gym. He followed her finger and saw him.

Motionless on the bench sat a chubby boy aged twelve or thirteen. A heavy sweater and corduroy trousers. A sloppy bowl cut. Cheap glasses. He realized he'd seen him before, more than once. (He raised the glass to his lips, identified the silvery propeller of the gin in the sea of Campari). In fact, he'd seen him *every time* he'd been there. His sister brought him with her and Michele was capable of fading into the background color of someone else's memories. A zebra's head was imprinted on his sweater. The effect was heartbreaking. Clara disappeared into the showers. Pascucci stared at the little boy a few seconds too long. Michele sat there motionless on the bench, his specific gravity increasing.

Twenty minutes later, Pascucci was driving toward the city's south side. Michele was in back. Next to him sat his sister's gym bag. Pascucci struggled to keep from imagining it as a languid treasure chest (filled with balled up socks and women's underwear in fermentation) insofar as she was a treasure without a treasure chest, and all the same more complicated to approach than if she had been locked up tight in a safe. Still, facile fantasies aside, Pascucci felt tense. Since they'd all piled into the car, no one had uttered a word. Clara was looking straight ahead as if the only effort required of her was to confirm the correctness of their route. From the backseat, the little boy was peering straight into the void with such intensity that Pascucci was afraid that it was *he* who couldn't see something obvious. He felt his cell phone vibrate. He ordered his third Negroni at the bar on Via Crisanzio. The lights continued to disintegrate through the plate glass window. The age of confusion. The age of separation. Now he was capable of isolating the components on his palate. And so, already on his way to tipsy, around his head spun the silvery propeller of the gin, the pink rectangle of the Campari, the blood-red square of the vermouth. To reduce things to present day terms, he would have said that brother and sister—in his Panda, that evening—were exchanging an uninterrupted series of mental texts. Question. Answer. Request for explanation. Reassurance. Insinuation. Terse reply. Monosyllable. More extensive explanation. Emoticon.

Once they passed the IP gas station, the girl asked him to turn into the narrow, tree-lined street on the right. After a few minutes they were immersed in darkness. The Panda jolted along, over stones and small potholes. A long line of cypress trees was revealed by the headlights. When the villa appeared, Pascucci thought that, once again, this wasn't what separated him from her.

Now he was thinking about how strange it was that two young people who were so rich should have to ride a bus home. He took the last sip. He peered out through the window in search of the axis at the end of which it was possible to find the church of Noci. In the days that followed, he went back to pick her up at the gym. Clara always accepted his offers of a ride. Every time, Michele came, too. They spent three or four weeks with the torture of those silent rides. Him driving, Clara and Michele sitting still, never speaking so much as a syllable. The more the boy was swept under by some crashing wave of sadness, the more beautiful and focused she became. Pascucci didn't believe he was in the presence of a mystery that he might, with respect and devotion, be able to unveil. He *felt* this the way you feel things when you're young: grandiose, terrible, indivisible, and without explanation. The lens splits the luminous ray and you will not be struck by it. He concluded, very stupidly, that the situation was becoming rather embarrassing. A month, and he hadn't made any progress. His friends would have laughed in his face. In the auto repair shop, as he was disassembling an oil pan, in all those agonizing quarter hours he spent slaving away on a carburetor, out of the grease and the valves, a shadow of resentment was taking shape. He thought of the others his age, enrolled at the university. He stared with the ferocity of his inner eye at the fake Scottish pattern on the seats in the Panda where a woman's back had still never reclined.

One evening, after practice ended, he wedged Clara into a corner of the gym. The dead zone where the equipment was stored. She set down the medicine ball on the floor next to the mats. Pascucci was smiling. (The hot swarm of the other play-ers was dissolving in the steam of the showers.) Clara exhaled as if she'd just finished a tiebreak, tucked a lock of hair behind her ear. Then she took a step forward. Pascucci braced one hand against the wall, cutting off every avenue of escape. She narrowed her eyes imperceptibly.

"I was just thinking," Pascucci improvised, "you were all slower than usual, weren't you? I mean . . . the plays."

"What do you mean?" asked Clara, perplexed.

"Your brother. This evening, if you ask me, he'd be happier if we left him to his own devices. Because, listen . . . " and with-out even finishing the sentence he understood that he'd made a mistake for which he'd never be forgiven. Clara turned pale. Then she scowled. Having forced the issue allowed Pascucci to see her—the shadow of a wound—as she would have started to show herself of her own free will if he'd only been more patient. The extortion of a down payment already reduced to a sale price.

"We'll take the bus."

He was done before he even got started.

Perhaps (Pascucci concluded the few times that he chanced to think back on it) it was a secret calling for failure that made him say those things. The thought distracted him from Clara. He dedicated himself to an inventory of the past few years. He grew gloomier still. He drummed his fingers on the table until his forefinger slipped on something dampish. He told himself he shouldn't order a fourth Negroni, and then proceeded to order a fourth Negroni.

Pietro Giannelli, thirty-seven years old, former clerk in a shoe shop, now Spiderman for the Toy Center at the Mongolfiera shopping center, took a last drag on his cigarette and then he sent it flying with a flick of his fingers. He pulled his back away from the lamppost. He moved away from the lights of the Apple Store on Corso Vittorio Emanuele. He started walking down the sidewalk, hands plunged into his jacket pockets. He squeezed the baggie containing the DMT. Former owner of a Suzuki GSX-400. University enrollment number 16020134, with a grade book into which not a single test result had ever been entered. He blended in among the Friday night crowd. He felt his cell phone vibrate again—having reached the last link in the chain, the information bounced back by mistake to the previous links in that chain. He shut his eyes and walked forward like that a few yards. He stopped before someone could run into him.

The man had invited him to make himself comfortable on the sofa and then he'd asked him pointblank if he was accustomed to walking around at home with eye makeup on. He'd realized that it was a trap while his finger was on the intercom, when he'd heard the rumbling background noise grow in intensity. He'd looked up. Clara's father. Smiling, hair black in spite of his age, green sweater over white trousers.

He'd been coming to see her for a week and they'd never once let him in the house. He'd park the motorcycle and they'd stand outside the villa, talking, for hours. The day before, Clara had come to join him under the willow tree that, extending over the iron fence, made a patch of shade between three and four in the afternoon. She was wearing a light blue, long-sleeved cotton sweater, jeans, and an old pair of Converse All Stars on her feet. At a certain point she had asked him what he thought of the Stravinsky.

"Ever since they reopened, the magic is gone. They can put on all the fucking music they want, but it won't work. The black sofas. That was the secret."

Clara had kneeled, and then stood back up holding a mud-spattered campaign flyer. Then, slowly, she'd torn it to pieces. She'd asked him what he thought of psychiatrists. The wind had tossed the willow tree, opening patches of sunlight on her face. A hair lay stuck on her cheek, looking like the outline of the island of Malta.

Giannelli had thought about the staff of the SERT, the drug addiction center, where he'd been court ordered to sign in on the fifth of every month.

"A bunch of idiots."

He'd seen the patches spread over her and rotate clockwise, but it was just because he was coming down off the acid.

She seemed interested in any word that came out of his mouth. In the shifting group of their friends, Clara had changed her attitude toward him overnight. It had happened after she'd learned about his family situation.

Signor Salvemini gestured and Giannelli started up the drive, finding that the man was now behind him, in a strategically advantageous position. He could hear his buzzing. When they got to the living room—the man was still behind him, saying "go right on in"—he understood how the Persian carpets and the candelabra and all that junk hanging on the walls could be used to make people who came in here feel comfortable or intimidated, depending on how much money they'd glimpsed in their lives.

He gestured for him to sit on the sofa and only then did he pretend to study him carefully, displaying his annoyance at the worn pants and the eyeliner.

Was he accustomed to going around with that mess on his eyes at home, too?

"Yes, Signor Salvemini," he replied, meeting and holding the man's gaze.

He was accustomed to the pettiness of grownups. The fact that people like him existed was useful to the psychiatrists at the SERT because it strengthened their grip on the knife handle. They subjected him to a string of idiotic questions and then sent him off to get papers stamped or schedule urine tests. Every time he pulled out the money for his co-pay at the local health care clinic, he sensed a red-hot tangle of black filaments. The effect vanished instantly. So he'd head back out into the street where he'd drop another tab of acid. The incandescent spiderweb re-exploded all over him, the filaments rising into the air, illuminating the grim face of the legislator, the judge's bench, the cavalcade of law enforcement—the mechanism activated by his act resonated like a flash of lightning that reveals, amidst the clouds, the ghost ship that ensures that in the police appointee's collection plate the annual bonus echoes, as does a sense of purpose the psychiatrists at the SERT, as does life itself for the functionaries at the offices that suspend driver's licenses and travel visas.

"And what does your father think about this disguise?"

"He died last year."

The man was on the verge of making some retort, but his daughter's boots came clacking down the stairs. The buzzing subsided somewhat. Clara made her entrance into the living room. She furrowed her brows, surprised to find her friend sitting there on the sofa. Vittorio picked up a magazine from the glass coffee table and pretended to read. The background noise had vanished entirely. She said: "We're going to be late." Giannelli got back on his feet.

Ten minutes later they were straddling the Suzuki and crossing the main artery of Via Fanelli, heading for the multiplex in Casamassima.

Giannelli had already talked to her little brother a number of times. He was about fifteen years old, in the process of thinning out, unkempt hair and a ravaged green greatcoat that made him look like a deserter from an army that had no particular interest in reclaiming him. He had the air of someone struggling to recover from a particularly hard blow—the physical self a little blurry, the spirit knocked forward by the impact, he seemed to be a prisoner of a future he was struggling to make his way back from. The last time they'd chanced to run into each other in front of the main post office. They'd gone to sit on one of the benches on Piazza Cesare Battisti, hunched over, smoking a cigarette. Michele, too, looked like he spent his afternoons wandering aimlessly around the city. Giannelli had waited until the two university buildings were done intersecting. The mangy laurel hedges had stopped quivering. Before the acid had worn off, he'd felt a new, undefinable sensation. The flick of an eyelid pulled upward. Michele moved the hand with the cigarette back and forth. They'd started a discussion that seemed like the continuation of a dispute begun much later—he'd take a deep drag and then force himself to claw at a concept in the hope of bringing it back into the present. He was saying that, in spite of bad experiences, the most profound part of human beings always expects people to do them good and not harm.

"But that's not the part that gets angry. That's not the part that protests." As far as he could tell, the hurt inflicted below a certain threshold no longer produced a voice that could be heard from the exterior. "In each of us, there's something sacred, but it's not one's personality."

While Michele pursued his line of thought, Giannelli had pulled out the stamp with the face of the Mad Hatter. He'd slipped it under his tongue. He'd waited in vain for the university to split itself in half again. The laurel hedges had convulsed, but the halo of light had maintained a faint intensity. The kid. It was because of him. In his effort to concentrate, like a black hole, Michele absorbed the energy from the world around him. Giannelli would never have realized it if it hadn't been for the acid. The laurel leaves spread their force, but the instant the green light left its source, it was sucked toward the boy. His sister had no reason to be concerned: if they'd decided to drag Michele to see some psychiatrist, they wouldn't be able to wring blood from that stone.

He kept walking down the sidewalk. Grim, dispirited, with

the DMT still in his pocket. Dressing up as Spiderman was better than dressing up as some chicken-man, and that was it as far as consolation went. Every morning, at twenty to seven, he parked his Toyota Yaris in the lot at the shopping center. He'd get an espresso with the security guards. He'd head for the administrative office at the Toy Center, step into the broom closet, take off his shoes and pants, wriggle into the foam rubber costume, and a short while later start handing out flyers. In the past, the eyeliner had helped earn him points for outrageousness, as had the leather jackets and the studded wristbands. If he hadn't tricked himself up like that, he'd have been a scared kid whose father was dead, someone you could think you were depriving of something by revoking his motorcycle license, though on the warm seat of that same bike he had continued to go see Clara without giving it a second thought.

A violent blow to the shoulder spun him a three-quarter turn. A passerby had hit him by accident and now he was walking off.

On the screen in the movie theater, half-empty at eleven at night, the man started slapping the girl around in the bedroom, which was furnished in a Fifties style. The actress put on an ecstatic smile with a bleeding nose. Then the man slammed her flat on her back onto the wall-to-wall carpet. Giannelli's eyes opened wide. Clara had grabbed him by the hand and was squeezing it tight. Her hand was soft and warm, it communicated opposing sensations, of a house deep in the woods and a bottomless fall. They kissed. She took his head in both hands. Giannelli unbuttoned her checked shirt. He touched one of her breasts, delicately, rotated his hand with great care so as to hold it in his palm. Someone coughed from the back of the theater. Giannelli stiffened. Clara lunged at him, half-climbing over the armrest that separated them. Two hours earlier she had seemed worried over this thing with the psychiatrist, where apparently her mother had taken her brother that same afternoon. Now she was furiously alive in the fine, silvery dust of the movie theater. She put a hand under Giannelli's T-shirt. The man on the screen turned off the lamp and started savagely beating the girl. Clara kissed him passionately. Giannelli ran his hand between their two bodies, pressed against each other, caressed the denim of her pants, then rose up and undid the button of her black Wranglers. Clara sighed. He had the distinct sensation of lots of yellow eyes peering out, wide open, from the bushes. He tried to slip his hand into her panties, she pressed on the armrest with one elbow to help him, and when he pulled hard upward he heard Clara's angry moan and saw her white, slender fingers clench into a fist and then extend.

They got ice cream in a café in the center of town and hung around, chatting idly about trivial things. They saw the moon mirrored in the glass-fronted office building of the Banca di Credito Pugliese. They climbed aboard his Suzuki bike, and went for a ride. They went out past the outskirts of the city. They rode up the ramp to the beltway, where the moon was bigger and they could really open up the throttle.

He took her home about two in the morning. At least, at that time of the night, he was sure he wasn't going to have any unpleasant encounters. He went past the gas station with her in the middle of the night. He turned, leaving the lampposts behind him. He started up the narrow potholed lane. The shadows of the cypresses streamed past on either side. The clouds, at the edges of the moon, seemed to curve in an unnatural fashion, toward the roof of the villa.

"Oh fuck!"

Giannelli felt her arms tighten around his hips. He slowed down.

"What's going on?"

"What are you saying, can't you see? Stop the bike and let me off."

The garden was lit up as if it was broad daylight and four

figures were standing on the front steps. A column of black smoke arose from the building, like a giant gallows pointing straight up.

"A fire . . . " he said, open-mouthed.

Clara got off the bike. She pulled off her helmet. She whispered hurriedly: "Go on, get out of here." Beneath Clara's worried gaze, though, a contrary force was pushing. The pebbles alongside the road crackled. Giannelli saw a large lizard dive into the foliage. Then Clara. While she was turning her back to him, walking up the lane toward the villa, he seemed to see a smirk of satisfaction dart across her lips.

"A whore. Half a slut that I fucked before she got married."

Enzo Santangelo—fifty-five years old, a body-building instructor and the proprietor of the Body Empire gym on Via Postiglione, the Extreme Fitness gym on Viale Unità d'Italia, the best stocked store for dietary supplements and sports performance products in Bari (Vitamin Center, Via Calefati)—took a sip of his flavored water and handed over the signed form to the pharmaceutical representative.

"A client?"

"That's right. She'd come into the gym as if she'd just left a fashion show. Then, though, she'd come out of the locker room in these sleeveless tank tops, these Hogan gym shoes, these red exercise shorts that made her look a lot more casual. You see what I mean? I think she was already fed up with her husband-to-be. And you needed to get a look at him. An engineer. He clearly had money."

"Nowhere near as much as her."

"Nowhere near as much as her father, that's right. But every once in while this guy would come to pick her up at the gym and I'd keep an eye on him while he was taking a look around. He got on my nerves. You know those fake-humble types? He'd watch the exercises as if he thought he knew something.

It was obvious that he believed he could buy the whole gym at a discount if he ever felt like it. He pretended to wander around in here with that innocent look on his face. Any minute I expected him to start whistling, and I thought to myself: there isn't a weight bench in here, handsome, not a rowing machine, not an exercise mat, not a treadmill, there might not be a single square yard left in this place where I haven't fucked her."

"You fucked her in the gym?"

"I couldn't help but fuck her in the gym," he said "She wasn't the first and she won't be the last. But listen. This one was a slut. All I had to do was go near her, even if it was only to give her the weekly schedule . . . It wasn't the way she looked at me. The gaze is strictly for beginners. The vibrations. Got it? I'd walk past her, and without her having to move a muscle, I knew she'd go for it. I knew that *I* had to go for it. She was already practically telling me I was a faggot for not having made a move already. Do I seem like a faggot to you?"

"Let me give that some thought . . . " the representative chuckled.

"I'm not a faggot, and what's more, I have a sense for these kinds of things. There were times when she'd get here an hour before closing time, she'd hop up on an exercise bike and get to work, and as soon as I was within earshot, she'd whisper: "This evening I'm having dinner with Alberto." My brain just needed to process the information. I had to stop myself to keep from breaking into a run. I'd open my locker, pull out a packet of Interflon, and slip it into my fanny pack."

"Interflon, the tool lubricant?"

"Interflon is *also* a tool lubricant. I'd take it and go wait for her in the downstairs bathroom. At a quarter to nine, punctual as a rent collector, the engineer would come pick her up. There we'd be, face to face. I'd say hello to him, because by now we knew each other. But especially shake his hand, because I knew that at that exact moment, his future wife was in the shower with an ass I'd bruised black and blue. Well, that was one of the biggest satisfactions I've ever had in my professional life."

He didn't talk about the strange sensation that pierced him straight through one Sunday night, when they remained shut inside the gym until late. Over the course of the years, he'd never stopped thinking about it, but his mind deleted the memory every time it surfaced. So he wound up having a recurring dream about it. And then he'd forget the dreams.

Scared by the motorcycle, the lizard dove into the tufts of grass. It vanished through the branches, tearing, in its flight, the web of the jumping spider, which, having assembled the image of the reptile with its eight eyes, had managed to avoid the impact. The spider jumped. The dry and arid ground registered the information, superimposing it on the alphabet of the ants that were intersecting one another, breaking up and bifurcating and then reassembling a line that was never the same. The law they obeyed modified itself within them, confirming itself in the law of every likeness, receiving new impulses from the depths of the anthill, and then from farther away, from the tremendous force that changes the face of the seasons. The saliva passed from one pair of lips to another and the heart raced in the dark of the movie theater. The curve of the abdomen tensed in on itself and then broke. Under the thrust of the molt, a brand new epidermis emerged from the dead carcass, brownish in color. After letting the cuticle harden in the open air, the cicada took its first flight. It landed on a rosemary leaf. The tymbals under the abdomen began to vibrate, and a sharp sound, like a finger-snap, signaled its presence to the world.

Around Via Bovio the crowds of the city had thinned out

because there were fewer shops. He went on walking with his hands in his pockets. A vertical scrolling billboard shifted from a sunny poster for toothpaste to a nocturnal ad for a lingerie shop. Giannelli turned the corner. He turned right again and saw the parking structure. He remembered when he would walk with Clara, and if they ran into someone, she'd drop her eyes. They'd lost touch after Michele left Bari, one of those sudden changes that only later reveal themselves for the great cataclysms that they are. Her brother had enlisted in the army against all sensible medical advice. Some time later, Giannelli had seen Clara again, outside a restaurant. New hairstyle and a lamé dress. She was laughing, flanked by two men in gray suits.

The sidewalk rippled on both sides of the street, tensed as it curved skyward until an ocean of ink fell on the two errors, the person he'd been then and the person he was now, who moved in solitude through the spring evening.

That Sunday they'd decided to stay in the gym until late. Just to be safe, she'd left before the last few clients and he'd pulled down the steel shutters. An hour later she was waiting for him outside the serviceman's entrance. She was wearing a flimsy jersey dress, open-toed sandals, and nothing else. She tilted her head and said: "Here I am again," and it seemed to him that she was saying the words with such falseness that he had to make a conscious effort to keep from slapping her right in the face. They fucked in the cardio fitness room. Then Clara got back on her feet, leaving a sweat mark on the hardwood floor.

Fucking at the gym after closing time was wonderful. The moans that echoed through all that silence. And then there was the partial darkness. The only lights came from the television sets screwed to the steel bars in front of the exercise bikes, five Sharp monitors turned to music and all-news channels.

At nine o'clock he asked: "You want me to go get a couple of pizzas?"

He slipped back into his tracksuit and track shoes while she, still naked, smoked a cigarette with her back pressed against the glass wall that gave onto the halotherapy room. Salt therapy for the skin. Every time he thought about the money he'd wasted on such bullshit he felt like beating himself silly.

He went out into the street and headed for the pizzeria. He tried to be as unobtrusive as possible, though he certainly wasn't the one who needed to hide. Forty-five minutes later, he came back with piping hot cardboard boxes in his hands. He laid the pizzas on the front desk. He closed the door behind him. The gym was enveloped in a silence that immediately struck him as strange. He called her name. The monitors were turned off. A ray of moonlight descended diagonally, covering the Smith machine with a faint silvery patina. "I'm back!" He caressed the light switch. He stopped. He weighed the possibility that this was some new erotic game. So then he took off his shoes. He tiptoed through the equipment room, then along the short hall that led downstairs to the saunas. He threw open the door and found himself in the most absolute darkness. A noise came up from the floor below.

He thought to himself: why that slut. He started down the stairs, cautiously, one step after the other. He peered down. An extremely faint glow illuminated the floor. Only then did he realize that he was afraid. The knot of the rope, tied just a few minutes ago: he had to admit it had been there from the minute he'd come back in. He chuckled. He descended a few more steps. His heart sped up. This is nuts. He put his hand to the back of his neck: he'd broken out in a cold sweat, and this confused him even more. He set foot on the landing without a clear idea of just where he was. Now the noise had grown louder. He turned his head. A phosphorescent green stripe cut the darkness in two. At first skinny, it swung wide, transforming itself into a luminous wall. His eyes opened wide. An ancient Egyptian deity, preparing to step out of a sarcophagus. He saw the charred black silhouette swing up into a vertical position, first one leg, then the other, and even though he'd just realized that the noise was a whirring fan and that she, Clara, had merely decided to indulge in a short UV sunlamp session in the club's five-thousand-euro Hapro Onyx tanning bed, the sight of her emerging from the capsule and striding toward him in that alien green light convinced him for a moment that the scene wasn't unfolding in the gym's basement, wasn't unfolding in the recesses of his fucking mind, that it hadn't been him luring her to this place for the past several weeks, but actually she who had just dragged him into the exact center of her own private nightmare, whatever that might turn out to be.

The girl's belly shifted from bright green to a more opaque color. Clara turned on the light. She placed a hand on his chest and smiled as she rose on tiptoe.

That episode was on the verge of resurfacing intact in his memory ten years or so later, when he read in the paper that she was dead. Luckily, he was sitting across from a pharmaceutical rep he was on good terms with. He used his voice to cover the weak electric current that was emanating from the depths: "A slut," he said, "half a whore I used to fuck before she got married."

Silvio Reginato, fifty-four years old, hundreds of operations as chief surgeon in the surgical ward at Bari General Hospital, rummaged among the shelves where he kept his records and his art catalogues. He recognized the light blue of the spine, then he touched the stiff shell of the cardboard binder. He pulled out the photo album. He went over to sit down on the sofa. He set the album down on the coffee table. He poured the chilled vodka into the glass. He drank. He'd read the news in the paper. He opened the cover and looked at her. He hadn't done it in months. Dozens of obscene snapshots. A crescendo of increasingly sad perversions, though not for him. Reginato had started taking those pictures of her immediately after meeting her. And he'd continued until just a few months before losing track of her.

Giuseppe Greco, forty-six years old, deputy editor of *Corriere del Mezzogiorno*, the author of a monograph on Rudolph Valentino, five books on the adventure of jazz in Puglia, printed by the regional government's publishing house, divorced, two children, reread the team rosters on his computer screen and sighed. The directories on the website for the Amatori Volley, Bari's amateur volleyball club. A long list of first and last names, including Clara's. The news, on the other hand, he'd just read a short time before in the obituaries.

He lit a cigarette. He watched the smoke dissolve in the empty newsroom. The desks lined up in parallel rows, and then the Xerox machine. He went back to looking at the monitor.

He thought about the Facebook accounts that remained active after the owner was dead. Hundreds of comments immediately after the death and then a shameful dribble. To say nothing of those who posted old pictures trapped in a cell phone's memory.

Every day Giuseppe Greco produced fifty or so tweets, using eleven different identities. The conscious intent was to publicize his column—*Lumière Space*, five hundred words of film criticism, every day—outside of the suffocating basin of the regional boundaries. He used @lumierespace to broadcast to his followers the topic of the day, which he retweeted via the newspaper's account. As himself (@giuseppegreco) he recommended, with a great show of fair play, articles by his better-known colleagues, whose bylines appeared in *La Repubblica* or

Corriere della Sera. Then there were his imaginary identities. @brancaleone was a relentless fan, @nocturama savaged indiscriminately, @magellan reported those takedowns to the subjects of same, while @vivresavie poked directors—but also actors and screenwriters—with questions (a link followed) that came from reading the column. The hope was that sooner or later someone might see fit to answer. And in fact that had actually happened. "Read review. Seems good," was the reply from @wimwenders to a callout from @vivresavie. Giuseppe Greco treasured it deep within himself as a sort of holy relic, after retweeting it over all eleven of his accounts.

There was an imaginary fog to the north of the Tavoliere plain, beyond which the star reporters from the major papers drank their aperitifs on large oval piazzas where the sunsets seemed to last forever. Rome. It was painful to come to terms with his resentment. It hadn't always been like this. (He lifted his fingers from the mouse and thanked fate for the fact that Clara Salvemini didn't possess a Facebook account, or a Twitter account, and that, save for people who had her same name, her online presence was limited to the results of an old sports tournament.) For Giuseppe Greco there had been a time, ever further in the past, when everything worth seeing, hearing, reading, and telling about happened just a short walk from him.

The summer he met Clara and her brother, Giuseppe was working as the culture editor for *La Città*, a tiny daily that pinned its hopes for survival on a virtually imaginary readership. A front-page editorial on the gratuitous act in Gide as part of a commentary on a family massacre made the editors of the rival papers heave a deep sigh of relief. *La Città* folded not long afterward. At the time, though, he was a thirty-year-old full of optimism, and he paid no attention to the storm warnings. He went to small and experimental plays, saw local bands in concert, and while they were playing the encore, he—at a folding table in the back—was just finishing typing the review of the reading he'd attended a few hours before in the Poggiofranco neighborhood, where a poet locked in a dog cage recited Mayakovsky.

He believed in those young people. Naïveté was the protective shell beneath which talent could develop undisturbed. He was convinced that hidden among them was a Fassbinder, or even a Werner Herzog who, one day, after leaving the shadow of the provinces, would take Rome, or even Paris or New York by storm, vindicating them all.

Every night Giuseppe Greco drank his nth cup of espresso and set out in pursuit of them. He made friends with them. He reviewed them with generosity in long, four-column articles. He tried to figure out whether it was worthwhile trying to recruit some of them for the newspaper—who could say? In their midst might be lurking a young Hunter S. Thompson just waiting for the right opportunity.

Michele appeared in his office one afternoon in July.

He was wearing an oilskin jacket that must once have been green. How he kept from sweating remained a mystery. In his hands he was clutching a sheaf of A4 paper that was no more than a Kleenex, it had been folded over on itself so many times.

"I didn't mean. Forgive me. Secretary. An article. But if you have something to do, I can come back another time."

"Please, let's try to calm down," he replied from the unspeakable chaos of his own desk.

Michele suggested he publish a strange religious article, in which he tried to show that Christ's time here on Earth had changed once and for all His Father's facial features. Thus, if Abraham had heard a voice whispering something to him about Isaac now, he would have had to forget about it.

"And what's the current affairs peg?"

In his newspaper, no one was obliged to pass under that kind of humiliating yoke; it was a trick question that Giuseppe Greco used to test the conformism of prospective writers.

"It strikes me as an *extremely* current topic, Signor Greco," the young man replied with dignity.

He liked him immediately. These were the days when people, if they wanted to pitch an article, wouldn't send you a flurry of insipid emails. They had to come to the newspaper in person, climb three or four flights of stairs, and then screw up the courage to present themselves. They had to know what you looked like, or at least they had to have made the effort to try to imagine. And you, in turn, understood whom you had before you. And Michele—he decided first thing—had his reasons.

He gestured for him to hand over the sheets of paper. He gave a quick glance to the opening, the body of the piece, and the last three lines.

"All right," he said, "we'll run it the day after tomorrow."

Thinking back on it now, it was incredible how—in his dealings with him, and later with his sister—he hadn't allowed himself to be intimidated by the weight of that surname. You didn't have to be a good journalist to know who the Salveminis were. On the pylons flanking the entrance to the city pool, there was a bas relief with the company's logo. They had built the city's business district. They'd renovated the last section of the waterfront and expanded the train station. They'd even built the serpentine apartment building on Viale Europa, on the next-to-highest floor of which Giuseppe Greco himself, in a room that smelled vaguely of stubbed-out cigarettes, had had sex ten years ago with a colleague from the university faculty. He knew that the Salveminis counted among their friends the crème de la crème of the city's society. The slightest crumb of their patrimony would allow a small newspaper to limp along taking losses for years.

And yet, none of this had the slightest influence on his decision to publish Michele's pieces. The idea that that young man's strange energy might be linked to a surname hadn't even occurred to him.

Michele showed up another four or five times. He always clutched his rumpled sheets of paper. Giuseppe Greco published them all without problems. Then the boy disappeared. Giuseppe never even had time to wonder why. They were now in the heart of summer and—having ignored them for months—he was forced to give a name to the shadows that were looming over his desk.

One night the publisher invited him to dinner. At Giuseppe's first objections, he held out a sheet of paper with a sales chart for the last quarter, then the fax that he'd received the day before from their advertising sales people.

In response to the advice that he look around for a new job, Giuseppe Greco increased his hours at work from ten to fourteen a day. On certain days he wrote three pieces for the next day's paper, then he'd interview a musician, pop a couple of tabs of methamphetamine, and zip off to the theater to catch a show. Something illusory was persuading him that bleeding his psychophysical energies dry like that might slow the advance of passive interests. Methamphetamine became a habit. The accumulation of articles, an obsession. Right in the middle of his workday, he found himself hunting for traces of the preceding hours, finding himself faced with a sinkhole that reminded him of the Dead Sea as seen in satellite photographs.

One night, while he was editing an article that was likely to see publication only when the paper existed in documents held by a bankruptcy court judge, a noise distracted him from the drift of notes and scattered papers.

He lifted his head from his desk, emitted an inquisitive "Ciao" toward the door.

The girl was looking at him, serious and erect in the dim light. A handful of syllables being typed by the transcription secretary in the room next door came unstuck from her hair the minute she took a few steps forward. She was dressed in jeans, a T-shirt, and a jacket that hugged her hips. She said that she was Michele's sister.

"I'm sorry to bother you. My brother should have sent you some material a few weeks ago. And since he hasn't seen it in print, well . . . " she held her breath.

From the depths of his own confusion, Giuseppe Greco sought, without finding, the information he required: "Ah, of course."

He pointed apathetically to a mountain of large, still unopened envelopes on the shelf. He turned his eyes back to her, taking her measure with a critical eye. He hadn't slept but ten hours in the past three days.

"I'm sorry, but couldn't your brother come and lodge a complaint in person?"

The girl started. Suddenly she seemed mortified. Worse. She seemed quite frightened.

"I assure you in Michele's intentions there was no . . . that is, he *couldn't* come himself."

She explained that her brother was serving in the military at Avellino. She said that Michele respected him, that he thought of him as a father, a precious guide, and that he had sent him this article on Joseph Heller, a "fine article" on Heller, the young woman assured him, even if, she added, she was certainly no expert. If it turned out he'd lost it, she'd bring him another copy. Giuseppe Greco only needed to read it. Read it and judge. And, if and only if he thought it was good enough, publish it.

"Please, my brother cares *very much* about your opinion."

Giuseppe Greco stopped savoring the sensation that the young woman's words were provoking in him. Only when it vanished did he realize what it had been. Complacency. This too was a bad sign.

"Joseph Heller, why of course, certainly . . . " he lied before ushering the young woman out.

More time passed—days, weeks during which the newspaper's crisis became increasingly self-evident. Every so often a desk would disappear, or a photocopier. Individuals he'd never before laid eyes on began lurking in the halls.

When Clara reappeared in his office, the summer was ending. A Friday night. The heat was circulating freely and impetuously from room to room, and at that hour Giuseppe Greco should no longer have been there. Even the editor in chief was somewhere else. But by now, he was living between those four walls, he only went home to sleep. A force that might seem self-destructive—while it was actually an extreme version of every force of self-preservation—was leading him to absorb all that he still could from that life before the death of the newspaper turned the page once and for all. The cleaning ladies were appalled to find him there at the most unthinkable times of night.

Now it was ten at night, and Giuseppe Greco didn't even ask himself how the young woman had been able to get in. He saw the shadow lengthen and shorten, rotating from one wall to another.

"Ah," he said, setting down the X-Acto knife he'd been toying with for the past few minutes.

"Good evening," said Clara.

She was wearing a silver lamé dress and a pair of boots. She seemed different from the last time, but not so different that she was already someone else. A note of sorrow ran up her body, lit as it was by the glow of the table lamp.

"I know," said Giuseppe Greco as if he were smiling into thin air, "the piece on Joseph Heller."

Clara stepped forward, revealing a yellow envelope clutched tight in her hands. Her lips contracted until they formed a tiny zero.

"I believe there's been a change in plans."

She told him that as far as Michele was concerned, the piece on Joseph Heller no longer had any significance. He was still in Avellino. As military life had continued, it had made him change his mind. He considered the previous piece to be obsolete. "I'm going so fast these days that I've already overtaken it a couple of times," he had told her over the phone. So now she had come to ask him not to publish it.

"However I would be very grateful if you'd take this under consideration."

She handed him the envelope. Also by phone, Michele had told her some strange things, saying that, even though he'd put them down in black and white, he was actually composing those thoughts from the future. A long article about the poetry of Georg Trakl. This time the young woman couldn't have sworn that this was a clear piece of journalism. She herself, reading it, wasn't sure she'd understood every passage. What was needed was an expert's eye.

"I'm not sure I'm up to the task," he replied sarcastically.

Clara changed her tone of voice: "Please," she said, clenching her teeth, "my brother's having a rough time. *Really rough*, I tell you. He's not well. It would be important for hi—"

"Just leave it there," he said, cutting her off, and pointing to the pile of papers at the foot of the shelves.

It was a complicated period. It was a complicated period for everyone, though. Giuseppe Greco was starting to reach the conclusion that naiveté was nothing but a smoke screen to conceal the absence of talent. If with all the good will in the world there hadn't emerged a Fassbinder, a Julian Beck, not even a young Oriana Fallaci capable of turning her careerism into a virtue, then it meant that the ferment of the chemical compound that in the lives of great men makes them confidently say "Here," laying their finger on a map to mark the spot from which they set out, was happening somewhere else. A city in the south without great traditions, save its entrepreneurial approach to construction and a particular tenacity among the law firms. That, then, is all that was left in Bari.

He went back to looking straight ahead, and only then did he realize that the dam had collapsed. Clara was bleeding from one hand. The blood was flowing down her arm and dripping onto the floor. Giuseppe Greco shot forward. He opened the fist that was clenching the blade of the X-Acto knife. The girl let him do it, now serious and docile. He took her in his arms and concluded that she was nursing a malaise completely unknown to him. The malaise gripping Giuseppe Greco was a chilly peak in the Apennines, while hers was a Mt. Everest, even a would-be Ararat. The summer was over. The newspaper was dead. An entire archive was crumbling at their feet while the evening heat continued to waft up to them.

And so that same girl, he thought to himself many years later, had thrown herself off the top level of the parking structure on Via Lioce. By now, the members of her family must have returned to their expensive homes. He reentered the details on Google and once again ran into the website of the Amatori Volley team. When someone told him that she had married that guy, it had seemed like the obvious conclusion. Every so often he had stumbled across her brother's byline. He remembered having read an article of his in the back pages of *La Repubblica*. Then another in *La Stampa*, one in *Ciak*, and one in *Panorama*. He would open a daily paper and there he was. Every time he felt the burning sensation of a slap. The fact that he, Giuseppe Greco, had in the meanwhile attained a position of his own was clearly not enough. He felt resentful all the same. Michele had vanished years ago into the jammed streets of the nation's corrupt capital, and even though his mind was fragile—bipolar or schizophrenic or whatever disturbance it was that afflicted him—for the son of Vittorio Salvemini it was quite obviously not a sufficiently large obstacle to prevent him from getting his work published in national papers.

If only Giuseppe Greco had taken the time to think it over, he'd have understood that all told, there were no more than fifteen or so articles in ten years, a very clear sign of failure.

He re-read the team rosters on the screen. He checked the New York *Times* homepage in one of his open windows. He verified the presence of new notifications on two of his accounts. He retyped her first and last name into Twitter. He felt saddened. He reflected on the way that the transmigration of souls was changing the rules of the game. Analog and digital. The transition was transforming the emotions into something for which better-suited adjectives still remained to be coined. Open. Exhilarating. Useful. Friendly. Superficial. Pornographic. Bloody.

Giuseppe Greco sat frozen before the computer screen.

It hadn't existed until just a few seconds ago. But now there it was, before his eyes. You could have touched it, if touching it weren't impossible. The umpteenth grave desecrated by the maniacs on the internet. What a heinous prank. The Twitter account @clarasalvemini loomed, brand new, on the right side of the screen. The picture next to the name showed a girl, naked, from behind. He contemplated in horror the newborn icon. Then he clicked on it. It had zero followers, was following no one, and just one tweet. He held his breath and read it.

"I didn't kill myself."

Every day, at sunset, an adult tiger climbs the steps that lead up to the second story of the Palazzo del Grillo in Rome. For her, the garden door is always open. The tiger wanders silently among the eucalyptus trees and it is in that magnetic instant, balanced among the oil paints, that everyone can see her.

Now he alone was looking at her. The painting was hanging in a small blind vestibule. The visitors went past it without noticing, attracted by the greater fame of Klimt and de Chirico. The gray of the marble and the dark green of the vegetation around that dreamy yellow symmetry. A tiger in a European garden.

The canvas was called *The Evening Visit*, and Michele came to look at it when he wanted to come face to face with a future image. He had read in a catalogue that the animal represented the greed lurking in the homes of the powerful, but he disagreed. The tiger was a reward, and the garden an interior space. If she had already peeked into his own inner space, he thought, things would have gone differently at the notary's office.

He went back through the front hall. He went out through the door. He walked down the grand staircase of the National Gallery of Modern Art. He counted the money in his wallet, gave up the idea of a taxi.

A couple of hours earlier he'd been in the notary's office. A massive mahogany table dominated the room. On the wall was a reproduction of an ideal city concerning which Michele might be in agreement (the absence of other human beings is an excellent remedy for loneliness, he thought, flashing another smile at the notary). There was a paperweight in the shape of a large owl with ruby-red eyes.

The notary Valsecchi read aloud the text of the private agreement. He was a man in his mid-sixties, small and wrinkled, in a navy blue suit from which emerged the snowy sail of a pocket square. It was the second time that Michele had met him in the past few months. Many years ago he'd come down to see them in Bari. Where else had he seen that redhead recently? he thought, staring at the paperweight.

The notary passed him the sheets of paper. Michele lined them up to a sixteenth of an inch to show off. He read his father's signature. He hesitated. Then he started signing as well. The notary was watching the movements of the Parker pen. When it was too late, a smile bloomed on Michele's lips.

"Can I ask you a question?" he said to the notary.

What would have, until just recently, worried the man now filled him with benevolence.

"Anything you like."

Michele looked at the ideal city on the wall. He imagined the foundations in the air, the roofs of the buildings thrust into the soil.

"It has to do with legal rights of inheritance."

"I'm listening."

"Let's say that I draw up a will . . . "

The notary made a perplexed face.

Michele saw him again, sitting on the covered patio in the garden, between a porcelain tureen and the sauce bowls on the hand-embroidered doilies. Many years had passed since then. His father was saying: "You shouldn't pay any attention to that, a good price is never excessive," and the notary's only response was to gleefully seize the bottle of Amarone. He filled the glasses of the other diners around him as well. But the diners vanished from sight. The place settings faded with time. The late-August light tumbled onto the Virginia creeper. At that point, the patio was lit up again with a warmer red. Selam brought the trolley with the cheeses (through the rubber band of time, back into Michele's mind came even the deep blue of the cotton, the white hems on the uniform that his father and Annamaria insisted the young housekeeper had to wear on holidays). The notary spread his hands, simulating the expanse of the land to be auctioned for the public housing plan. Vittorio reiterated: "If that's the margin, then we'll see if I can't find a way of laying my hands on the money." Valsecchi laughed: "All right, let's say you find the money. But with all those construction sites underway, how do you think you're going to come up with the workers to finish it in time? His father shouted: "Pasquale!" as if he'd just come up with the solution to a math problem. After a few seconds, during which Gioia could be heard asking her mother if she could try on her necklace, the voice arrived, deep and low: "Signor Salvemini."

It was then that his memory vivified that part of the garden, too. Two rows of gentian plants emerged from the shadows and Michele remembered about the other table. There was the table with friends and relatives; and, a few yards away, under a large horse chestnut tree, there was the table of construction workers and their wives. (Selam ate alone in the kitchen, even when she was off duty. An apparent privilege, but in fact an exile to which the young Eritrean woman had been sentenced for reasons not otherwise specified.)

An enormous man presented himself before them. He was older than sixty and he smiled, showing a broad mouthful of teeth.

Vittorio rotated his hand around the wrist as if to take in the entire villa: "Pasquale," he smiled with ferocity, "show this poor notary how long we took to renovate this place."

The foreman composed a number with his hands by holding up certain fingers and not others. His curiosity aroused, the notary asked: "Months?" Engineer De Palo snickered. Vittorio shouted triumphantly: "Weeks!" slapping his hand down onto the table. The foreman laughed. Engineer De Palo turned to Engineer Ranieri: "Could someone please ask Cheeta to bring in the profiteroles." "Stop using that name for her!" said Annamaria, out of sorts, but in a loud voice, so everyone could hear her. Gioia was clutching the necklace in her hands. The notary shrugged his shoulders. He said that twenty years ago, the foreman might have finished the renovation work in record time; but now he looked like a retired boxer.

A murder of ravens emerged from the hedges to the west of the garden. It seemed as if they were bursting through the green wall, coming from where the tennis club had once stood.

Vittorio burst out laughing, and made a theatrical show of despair: "Oh, Pasquale! This poor notary from Rome just makes me sad. He breaks my heart, I feel such compassion!" The foreman started unbuttoning his shirt. The ravens kept calling in the sky. Selam brought a tray with the desserts. The foreman in the meantime had also removed his T-shirt, was displaying his bare chest. Whistles of approval went up from the table where the construction workers were dining. The foreman pumped his biceps. The notary was about to raise another objection, but then he reconsidered. Pasquale was on the patio doing push-ups. A number of chairs were pushed back. Someone from the other table started counting out loud. Engineer De Palo said: "Now he'll collapse." The foreman's wife laughed, disgusted, concealed among the wives of the other construction workers. A pitcher full of water fell onto the floor. Selam plunged her face into her open hands. Then came the explosion of voices. The foreman had passed his hundredth push-up. Gioia was riding on his back. It wasn't clear how it had happened, but the little girl was laughing happily. The scene was taking on the appearance of certain nineteenth-century Italian paintings of country vistas (those pieces of artistic claptrap you'll find in civic museums, in which the badness is accentuated because the painter pretends to ignore it), and he, Michele—memory further lowered its shaft of light—couldn't utter so much as half a phrase. Military service had reduced him to a new and disastrous low. On the advice of their psychiatrists, they'd sent him off to Rome. He was sitting next to Engineer Ranieri. Facing him was his father's wife. (Ruggero was pursuing studies in his specialty in Amsterdam, he remembered.) Engineer Ranieri's wife said: "What now, she's even started crying?" "Who?" asked Annamaria. "The girl. What's her name?" She pointed at the Eritrean house-keeper. Someone said: "Cheeta!" Michele was confused. This was the first time he'd come back to Bari since his time in the hospital. He felt crushed by his helplessness, by an astonished sense of shame. Then he saw her.

After handing Gioia back to her parents, Pasquale went back to the table under a torrent of applause. The aroma of coffee started to spread through the air. It was then, at four in the afternoon, that she appeared at the end of the driveway. She was wearing a denim shirt and corduroy trousers tucked into her riding boots. She walked toward the entrance to the villa, careful—but a natural, unforced carefulness—not to get close to any of them. Her figure cut by the curvature of the field. Michele tried to call to her. In fact, he did nothing more than move his lips. Things had changed. After a few minutes, Clara reappeared in the door. Now she was dressed in a T-shirt and gym shoes. She retraced her steps from one side to the other. She was carrying a gym bag with EXTREME FITNESS written on it. It felt to Michele as if a red-hot bar of metal had been jammed into his lungs. To be the only ones who understand that someone else is drowning and the only ones who don't know how to swim. The ravens were cries without bodies, so that that really was the voice of the sky.

The notary said: "Vittorio, you don't know how much I envy you."

And now, years later, after signing the documents that his father had arranged to have drawn up, Michele spoke to the notary about a theoretical will.

"If you would be so good as to notarize my last wishes," he said, "I'd like to leave everything to my father. Do you think that would be possible?"

The man looked at him, more baffled than before. He hesitated. "For the ascendants there would in any case be a forced portion or legitim," he said, trying to divine the young man's intentions, "in the case of the parents the entailed portion is equal to a third. But even if we assume that one wished to expand it . . . "

Six months earlier, that same notary had recorded the deed by which Michele became the owner of a villa on the Gargano coast. A little odd, considering that there was no real estate in Michele's name, and he lived two hundred and fifty miles away. The purchase had been fine-tuned by redeeming the shares that Vittorio had put in Michele's name on the day of his eighteenth birthday, shares of whose nature, issuing institution, and method of access the beneficiary had always been ignorant. Now, an agreement had just been notarized requiring Michele to give back that same villa to the Salvemini Construction Company, within a year. The Bank gives, and the Bank takes back.

"In your particular case," the notary continued, "considering that you're unmarried and you have no children, you're free to leave your father anything you like."

The man paused. He furrowed his brow, as if what he had

just said didn't make the conversation less absurd, and it were up to him to do the dirty work and extract the implicit element: "The siblings have a right to the legitim only in the case in which there is no will," he sighed, "while if instead there is a will, then a person can do as he likes. All the more so for the siblings who only have one parent in common, if that's the meaning of your question."

The thought that the notary believed him capable of excluding Clara from her so splendidly re-proportioned properties—the clothing she could no longer use, the cigarettes that Michele had already smoked, the cheap furniture in his rented basement apartment in Rome—made him feel free to pick up the owl-shaped paperweight and smash it into his face. But that didn't happen. Michele smiled inoffensively: "Why, no, Signor Valsecchi, all I want is to protect my father's interests!"

He needs to understand that I'm a complete idiot. Haven't we just notarized the document attesting to the fact?

The notary faltered. For a moment he was frightened by something he didn't understand. To keep from feeling ridiculous, he hurried straight towards the young man's blissful expression. "Why Michele, what are you talking about!" He threw wide his arms, finally unfurled the gaze of an old family friend. "Aside from the *enormous* unlikelihood of a parent surviving his own children, it hardly seems to me that Vittorio has any need of your financial assistance."

"And what if he were to fall sick?"

"Are you suggesting you take out a health insurance policy for him?" The notary at this point was brushed by the idea that something wasn't right, because he was, after all, an old family friend, and therefore he could hardly be ignorant of the fact that the frequency with which Michele worked was barely enough to allow him to take girls out to a pizzeria. He knew, or at least he could guess, that Michele's father never gave him a penny, since the money always goes to the children who are already making plenty, or to those who follow in the wave of that money, those for example who have a genuine vocation for spending (he thought of the youngest girl: the last time he'd seen her, she'd had, around her throat, a necklace studded with small pink diamonds). He knew that this young man had had some serious problems. Mental problems. But above all, he was certain, since this was his profession, that just a few minutes ago Michele's total assets had been reduced to zero. How could he think of underwriting a health insurance policy for a man in his seventies who was loaded?

Since it wasn't his responsibility to delve into all these absurdities (he was a notary, not a psychiatrist) he resigned himself to finishing the discussion: "It's very noble of you to think of taking out a health insurance policy for Vittorio," he said, "but believe me when I tell you that a man like him can take very good care of his own insurance needs. And, while we're on the subject, your father is in excellent health."

"Offering guarantees about other people's health is never good luck. And in any case, I wasn't thinking of a health insurance policy."

"Then what *were* you thinking of?" The notary Valsecchi noticed the change in Michele's voice. Suddenly, that very skinny young man seemed unreal; he was so sharply defined, not unlike certain criminals.

It was at that moment that Michele's hands shot upward. The notary jumped in his chair.

"I have another agreement in mind that I'd like you to notarize," said Michele with a smile full of ferocity, which dissolved in the afternoon light that suddenly made him want to take a trip over to the National Gallery of Modern Art. "A binding contract," he continued, "an agreement by which I commit myself to donate my liver whenever my father should have need of it, and lungs and prostate in case of cancer. He's always been a heavy smoker, don't forget. We could go as far as the complete removal of my organs, on a strictly preventive basis. I'd imagine that the law allows this."

Now Michele wasn't laughing. He was staring at the owl. And the notary, whose sensations were traveling with a certain delay, was overwhelmed with terror at the thought that Michele meant to smash it into his face.

So Michele went to take a look at his tiger. And now, having reached the center of town, he was about to cross the Sant'Angelo bridge. To pass beneath the angel with the nails. The angel with the spear. The angel with the crown of thorns. There are those who can't wait to be robbed so they can shout, stop thief! Refused to sign the documents and avoided the buffoonery in front of that idiot: that's what he ought to have done. That, yes, would have been a surprise for his father.

He turned down Corso Vittorio. Big buildings and tobacconist's shops. On the third floor of number 141 was the room where St. Philip Neri brought a child back to life. On the ground a flyer was disintegrating in a rivulet of water. He looked at it again. He thought back to the eyes of the owl. The image was on the verge of resurfacing in his memory. A car went past, sirens wailing. He needed to turn the piece in by seven. There's plenty of time, he thought. He turned into Via della Cuccagna. The building's façade was in shadow. He climbed up to the third floor. He rang the bell. The door swung open. Before he could take a step, the door was shut in his face. Two minutes later, the door opened again.

"Maybe I've come at a bad time."

The woman laughed: "If he was here, do you think I would have opened the door again?"

She was wearing a sky-blue dressing gown, with black sandals at the end of her long, skinny legs. How stupid to think of her husband. Those moments had given her the time she needed to make herself presentable. Obviously she wasn't. Aside from her hair—the dishevelment of someone who'd brushed it at the last minute and who is no longer twenty—it was that she kept herself in shape with the expectation that all the effort would go unnoticed which really stripped her of desirability. But that was also what made her so ravenous. Her fingers wrapped themselves around his back and pulled him inside.

An hour later, Michele was back in the street. He reached Piazza Venezia. Here he caught the bus that would take him back home. The sun was setting over the church of the Gesú. The horn honked. The vehicle huffed and puffed. The monument vanished around a curve into the fiery red glare of the afternoon's death throes, and only then did the picture resurface in all its power. I dreamt of a doe that was drowning in her own blood. Michele shuddered. He saw the stoplights blinking, the lights of the shop windows. Shoe stores, delicatessens. Jewelers buying gold. Old rings: shattered pacts. The dream was from the night before. He felt the anguish rise within him. He tried to distract himself. Thirty-four signs lit-up, and I'm thirty-three years old. One block after the other, the shops were thinning out. Already there were just twenty-eight. When I was sixteen, we'd spend hours and hours shut up in my room. I'd take a last drag on my cigarette and then crush out the butt on the star globe, right on top of Ursa Major, where we swore we'd meet again when we were both dead. The time I gave her the articles to deliver to the guy at the newspaper. When I made it clear to her that I was planning to set the house on fire, and she smiled. Michele saw the ancient Roman aqueduct beyond the line of pine trees. The tufa-stone arches were sinking into the grass. Shit. Now he'd have gladly punched his fists into the seat ahead of his.

Every so often it still happened to him. His thoughts wandered off of their own accord and a switch flipped off. He became a sleepwalker. The bus had driven for miles without his noticing the fact. Of the old passengers he didn't recognize a single one. This was the Via Appia in the vicinity of Ciampino, which meant, logically, that he must actually be riding on a different bus. Even though he knew he'd been cured, certain symptoms still surfaced. The aftershocks of an earthquake that had occurred some time ago. That was why the flashbacks made him angry. The bus pushed its way through the hot spring darkness. By now it was too late to deliver the piece. The vehicle was running along the Via Appia. If, by some twist of irony, there were to be no end of the line, in a few hours he'd find himself in Puglia. He got off at the next stop.

He got home a little after midnight. He entered the courtyard. He went down the steps to the small basement apartment and a short while later was in his bed. A soft stroke to his cheek. In the depths of darkness, perfectly mistress of her own motions, the cat had come to say hello to him. Burning bright, in the forests of the night, he recited by heart, chilled, ravaged, convinced that, like all felines, she, too, was capable of reading his mind. A mother. A sister. And now a cat. Michele sank his fingers into the animal's soft fur. He put a hand under her throat, pressed down until he could feel the vibration. He noticed the LED on his cell phone. It had been lying there forgotten on the nightstand since that morning. Michele reached out his hand and checked. Two calls from his father, one from Ruggero, and even one from Annamaria. Four calls in a single day: it had never before happened. Grandma must have died, he thought. The cat started nipping at him. He'd seen a doe in his dream, but it actually should have been a sow. Further proof of how I've lost my powers. He prayed that it wasn't really his grandmother. A funeral would have forced him to stay in Bari for a few days. And when he slept there, he was still tormented by terrifying nightmares.

The cat slipped away, out from under his hands, and slowly disappeared into the dark.

The day after his daughter's funeral, with the streets awash in the sudden heat, Vittorio Salvemini was driving toward Ruggero's clinic.

It would still be several weeks before summer began, the muggy heat recalled to memory old pictures of a city prone to paralysis. Tall palm trees battered by the wind. Voices churned by the whirring fans. The Porto Allegro affair was crying out for revenge thought Vittorio as he turned onto Via Isonzo, wounded by the thought of Clara. His grief at his daughter's death had cracked open a welded seam in him, it shifted the ground upon which the solution to the mess and the girl herself could amount to the same thing.

What had offended him especially wasn't so much the seizure request, but everything that had broken loose even before the request had been filed at the courthouse. The hysteria of the environmental groups. The petitions circulating online. The journalists yammering on about public resources and knowing nothing about hydrogeological and forestry and wilderness zoning restrictions.

"The Vandal King of the Gargano Coast." That's what *Corriere del Sud* had called him. The article reeked of the rancor felt by those who suspect how much talent there is in someone who has achieved success by coming up from nothing. Vittorio knew that kind of hatred. They'd insulted him, provoked him, raised the most fanciful sorts of insinuations, until the heavy eye of the Foggia district attorney's office had blinked open in his direction.

Only then, in defiance of the best legal opinions of two out of the three lawyers he'd consulted, did Vittorio call a press conference.

Disobeying even the last of the three lawyers, he hadn't sent Engineer De Palo to Foggia. Much less had he entrusted the task to Engineer Ranieri, the latter's loyalty devoid of all surges of initiative. He'd gone there himself, appearing in person in the Trident Room at the Jolly Hotel. Here (he'd realized it walking down the carpet that led to the table with the microphone) the fury of the hacks—ready to pounce on any emissary from Salvemini Construction—had begun to waver. From blind rage, the anger all around him had turned more reasonable. *Admiration!* That's what the journalists had been filled with when the owner had, in flesh and blood, offered himself up to them. They couldn't wait for the chance to show him just how good they were at putting him in an awkward situation, and in order to do so, they employed the most disingenuous possible form of camouflage: that of a just cause. And so the match began.

In response to the director of the environmental league, Legambiente, a woman who'd gone from zero to sixty with the destruction of the Mediterranean maquis, Vittorio had countered with the minutes of the Provincial Commission for the Protection of the Landscape.

With the deputy editor of *La Gazzetta del Mezzogiorno*, he'd been more cautious. The journalist had suggested that the judicial proceedings might shake the entire real estate development group to its foundations (a touching error born of optimism: considering their exposure to the banks, the seizure order would bring them to their knees). Vittorio had replied that the sheer number of his employees alone told them all they needed to know about the company's strength and solidity. He'd expressed his confidence that the investigating magistrate would reject the request.

But then the spokesman for a consumers' rights association

had accused him of defrauding the hapless buyers who had purchased their villas before they were finished. Vittorio's face had filled with dismay. "Excuse me, sir, but do you have children?" The man had replied "no" with guilty resentment. Vittorio had suddenly slammed shut the folder that contained the plans and documents of the various building commissions. He'd pulled several sheets of paper from his jacket pocket and started waving them back and forth. Property deeds! Property deeds! he'd repeated. Someone here wants to know who else has tumbled into this trap? My first-born son, a well-known oncologist, bought a villa at Porto Allegro! And in fact, my second-born son did the same thing! Did I defraud them? Did I defraud *them, too*?

Only those who weren't parents could be unaware of how offensive it was to the laws of nature to think that a father would betray his own sons, he'd continued, definitively backing his opponent onto the ropes. Only someone who'd never held them in his arms as newborns—Vittorio had thought to himself—feeling pity for the way the world would reveal itself to their eyes. Only someone who, watching them run themselves ragged on a soccer field (or leap between the Rat King and the Sugar Plum Fairy during a dance recital), had faced up to the fact that those kids would never become soccer stars or ballerinas. Someone who, carrying his own newborn child in his arms, hadn't whispered the well-known prayer: *stay this moment, you are so fair.*

He turned onto Via Innocenzo. He accelerated up Viale de Laurentiis. Rusty playground equipment. His son Ruggero knew the head orthopedic physician at the General Hospital. Good doctors are all members of the same big club. Every patient is a tragedy in his or her own way. This guy from Taranto had busted their chops to get a new room. They'd even bought him a television set. This was nothing but an appetizer.

"Don't you believe that the commitment to urban development is nothing but a shameless trick played in order to pave Puglia over once and for all with cement?"

And you're asking me, you blithering idiots? Your progressive friends have wallowed for years in commitments to urban development. They've constructed conferences on them! Election campaigns! They've sung paeans to the nursery schools, the public parks that the municipalities would build thanks to the taxes levied on builders in return for every construction permit issued. A tenth of total building costs! But was it any fault of his that, instead of building the nursery schools the municipalities chose to use that money (*his* money) to pay back wages to *their own* employees? to renovate the offices that were falling apart? to straighten out budgets that *they themselves* had turned into hellish sinkholes?

The Porto Allegro story was an old one. When the mayor of Sapri Garganico and his urban planning commissioner had welcomed him under the bas reliefs of town hall, Vittorio had no idea whether in their eyes he represented the revival of tourism or a last ditch attempt to avoid bankruptcy. In any case, he'd taken the two of them out for dinner, more than once. He'd invited them to Bari. He'd gone back to see them during the Festival of the Madonna, contemplating in their company the way the fireworks were doubled in the surface of the Adriatic Sea. He'd come to know by heart the shoe sizes, favorite wines, and musical preferences of both. (*Rossini Early Operas*, an exquisite boxed set of thirty CDs he'd given as a gift to the commissioner.) When they'd issued construction permits, Vittorio couldn't have been expected to be able to read their minds, as well. He had no idea whether the 420 acres of coastal pine grove were subject to zoning restrictions. The mayor was behind him, and that was all he needed. It certainly wasn't for him to distrust the man who was guardian of the landscape, it wasn't Vittorio's job to dredge the bottomless well of laws, decrees, and special administrative dispensations necessary to understand in each specific case the fate of a single row of maritime pines.

He needed to solve the problem with the Tarantine, he thought as he waited for the green. The accident had been a mess. Vittorio didn't even want to try to guess at the state of mind of a man who had just had a leg amputated. In the celestial harmony that gives birth to disasters in order to ensure that wonders have a name, the Tarantine hadn't been necessary. He put one hand to his forehead, clenched his teeth. *Clara had been dead three days.* The light turned green and he pressed down on the accelerator.

That morning he'd gotten the phone call from Piscitelli. The assistant district attorney wanted to thank him for sending over the old hospital records. He reported that the case was being closed. Suicide in the aftermath of a serious depressive episode. Vittorio felt as if he were glimpsing the scene through a sheet of pouring rain. He drove past the building that housed the economics and business department.

After the Tarantine, he'd have to settle things with the chancellor of the university. The former undersecretary Buffante and the deputy mayor. The chief justice of the court of appeals. All of them emissaries of chaos.

After he'd passed through the residential district, after he'd gone by the bike racing tracks, the Cancer Institute of the Mediterranean began to loom in the distance. That was where his son worked—the monster of concentration incarnate with whom, during his time at the university, Vittorio had had to struggle for so much as a hello. Bent over his textbooks like a wolf over its prey. The deputy director whose bursts of rage now frightened even the director.

He needed to persuade him to talk with the head orthopedic physician. Convince a man who wouldn't have refrained

from smiling at a diagnosis of cancer of the uterus for the satisfaction of being able to destroy it.

At last Vittorio parked. He unbuckled his seat belt, got out
of the car, and headed toward the front desk. As he slipped his
cell phone into his jacket pocket, he found a call from
Engineer De Palo. A call from his wife. A call from Michele.
He decided, with a touch of resentment, that he wouldn't call
him back. By this time his son must have heard, he was probably on his way to Bari. He was the reason his son had missed
the funeral. He'd basically avoided calling him. But for
Vittorio it would have been impossible to admit to this. If busi-
nessmen failed to keep their thresholds of unawareness high, if
they allowed thoughts to emerge that, once on the surface,
would explode in all their total contradictory essence, then
they'd never be able to rule the world as they do.

And it was therefore not while thinking about these things,
but rather while letting them steam in a pressure cooker, that
Vittorio went to see his first-born son.

S o then the girl was real, Orazio Basile kept repeating to himself, while the others kept changing places for no reason other than to keep the comedy playing.

The head physician had retreated into the background. The fifty-year-old with the brylcreemed hair was reading from the papers on the clipboard. "Via d'Aquino is Taranto's social drawing room," he said. At that point the third man, who seemed the uneasiest of the group, went over to the window. Under his jacket the white hem of a lab coat could be glimpsed. While the engineer finished describing the apartment, Orazio noticed that the other man was closing the shutters, almost as if breaking the light meant keeping the rest of the world in the dark. Stretched out in bed, he could feel the analgesic. He moved the toes of his phantom foot. He saw again in the semidarkness the inflatable puppet that danced like a specter over the gas station. He noticed that the head physician had vanished. The engineer spoke of registration fees paid in advance. The other one kept moving in and out of the darkness, as if on a swing. All to make sure he hadn't seen the girl, even though no one was willing to take responsibility for saying this loud and clear.

All right, he'd keep his mouth shut. But what about them? Were they capable of properly guarding the silence that he was entrusting to their care?

They raised their heads, heard the sound of cars without cars that was arriving from the city's outskirts.

The assistant district attorney laid a hand on the old man's shoulder, and the old man took comfort from this empty gesture. An alligator executing a half turn on the ground, finding in the other's move the missing part of the dance. The lights of the parking structure sparkled in the empty air.

"Signor Salvemini, I'm sorry."

Half an hour ago he'd watched him get out of the car. Vittorio had moved past the flashing dome lights of the cars. The policemen had stiffened. The medical examiner had led the way. Vittorio had identified his daughter's body on the asphalt. The medical examiner's face was long and bony. It looked as if they'd yanked him out of some bed of dubious repute. Then the policemen had started to leave. The squad cars had begun to pull out. They'd turned the corner and had fallen back into somber gravity. After ten minutes, the medical examiner had told him: "Here they come now."

From the end of the road a large black vehicle headed in their direction. It seemed to float in the silence. The bodywork devoured the sound before it could issue from the engine.

Out of the vehicle emerged the three men from the funeral parlor. They pulled the tubular structure out of the back and began assembling it on the asphalt. They pulled out the covered mortuary tray, too. They fastened it to the gurney. They opened the calendered lid, similar to the top of a chafing dish.

They pushed the gurney to where it lined up with the young woman. The driver pulled the handle on the double-scissor frame, the mortuary tray lowered. They loaded the corpse onto it. They closed the lid and the body disappeared. They slid the gurney into the hearse so that the metal legs fit into the grooves inset in the cargo deck. One of them closed the rear hatch. The other went around to the driver's seat. The third waved to the medical examiner. He shook hands with the assistant district attorney. He shook hands with the young woman's father. Vittorio noticed that he was chewing, empty-mouthed. The medical examiner also got into the hearse, and together they set off for the mortuary. The insects continued to slap against the fluorescent lights.

The assistant district attorney decided that he'd put a hand on Signor Salvemini's shoulder, and then he did so.

"Everyone else was sobbing and then this girl starts shouting. The snuffbox. The gold snuffbox is missing. The snuffbox was here before, she says."

"My father-in-law lost his shoes that way."

"Go someday and sit outside the geriatric ward, and get your head down at ground level. Take a look. All the male nurses . . ."

"They're all wearing shoes that don't belong to them. By the time they're ready to retire, they have hundreds of pairs."

"Yes, but this was in the mortuary. I already had the soldering iron in one hand."

"And she goes out of her mind."

The hearse sped through the night. After the public housing projects, the road narrowed. All curves and trees. The tires screeched. They dove under a viaduct. They remerged skidding. Two lines of high red walls lined the roadway. The moon appeared, pale and distant. Another curve rocked the doctor against the hearse's passenger-side window. Now the engine could be heard, the roar of an auger drill at the far end of a cave.

"So she starts accusing her relatives. Thieves, she shouts. The gold snuffbox. She points her finger as if she's going to count them one by one. The son says: Why, where do you think it is, it's in his pocket where you put it when we redressed him. Then she grabs the granddaughter. She grabs her by the wrist and pulls her violently, so the poor girl finds herself face to face with the open casket. The old woman shouts: All right, let's go! Put your hands into your grandfather's pockets! Let's see if it turns up!"

"Last month, the wife of the owner of the hardware store . . . " the guy driving started in.

"The great thing is that the girl *does it*. She's so shocked that she starts rummaging around with the corpse."

A glasses case flew from one end of the dashboard to the other. The tires screeched again. Black trees and low buildings. The doctor grabbed the assist grip. He noticed the gleam on the floor mat. Beyond the buildings the countryside could be sensed, like a white radiation. To pass from a feverish night to a dreamless lethargy. The doctor clenched his jaw. He saw a crane in the shafts of moonlight. Then the city resumed.

When the phone had rung two hours earlier, the doctor had opened his eyes wide with the luminous body of a woman undulating on the screen. While the fifth man came on her face, the numerical sequences had returned to his mind. He'd turned off the television set. The room had been plunged into darkness with the exception of the light from the DVD player. The scene continued in the player's circuits, he thought. His cell phone's ringtone emerged definitively from his state of unconsciousness. Numbers. He'd dreamed of numbers. Combinations that opened electric security gates by remote control. There were numbers behind the animated advertisements on the luminous billboards. A text message: one thousand one hundred and twenty digits. A photograph: a hundred seventeen thousand. A porn DVD: three times ten to the ninth. But then tumblers turned and steel locks were opened. Doors swung open on hinges fastened to nothing but walls, stairs that led to narrow underground passageways. Not even a hundred-digit sequence would be enough. A numerical code of sixteen to the sixth reproduced a lung in a CAT scan. Nine to the twelfth was two minutes of phone conversation. Twelve to the twenty-fourth: all the information contained on planet earth. But for a spider spinning its web, the concept of number was no longer enough. The woman in the porn flick, caressed by a veil of summer light, was now frying an omelet in her home in Van Nuys, California. Now she was a little girl at her desk in a classroom in Wilmington, North Carolina. Now she was dead. Turn to the right in the underground passageway, then to the left. Another door opens wide. The light in the room was so strong that the hairs on the back of the neck were curling. A young woman, naked, on a steel table. The freckles formed a pattern reminiscent of a constellation. He'd held his cell phone up to his ear. *Hello.* Then he'd asked: "Do you want me to go there now, sir?" The director of the local branch of the national health service had given him the address. Necessary to verify that she was dead. He'd thought to himself: I'm not on call tonight. A young woman had committed suicide, the voice had gone on. If the cause of death is known, then what's the use of an external examination in the morgue, he'd thought. "Tonight Palmieri's on call," was all he'd said. The voice had remained silent. Only then had the medical examiner realized. "All right," he'd said. He'd climbed out of bed. He'd put on his slippers. His weakness, their knife gripped firmly by the handle. Walked toward the kitchen. Switched on the light. He'd put on a pot of espresso. Sat at the table. Chewed vacantly. Before the espresso pot came to the boil, he'd stood up. If I have to do it for them, I'll do it first for myself. He'd taken the jar out of the cabinet. Pulled out a ceramic plate. He'd turned the second burner on low. Pulled the baggie out of the jar. Laid it on the plate. Then put the plate on the burner. He'd turned off the flame under the espresso pot. Taken the plate off the burner. Laid it on the cover of the desk diary. Credit card. Chopped the crystals with the edge of the card. First line.

"So one morning the wife of the proprietor of the hardware store comes to see me in person at the undertaker's," says the hearse driver.

The trees grew dense along the sides of the road. Beyond the curve a line of warehouses emerged. The medical examiner wondered why the driver was driving as fast as he was. Beyond the industrial sheds he saw the lights glowing in vertical rows. The driver countersteered, the cemetery vanished.

"She starts in with a roundabout discussion on the economic slowdown that she claims devastated the store after her husband's death. Forced to close, she says. I say: Signora, I'm sorry. She says: Any minute now, they might turn off the electricity.

"They don't throw away anything that belonged to their husbands." The man next to the driver snickers. He knew the rest of the story.

"It's just that this time it wasn't a snuffbox," said the driver, stepping on the gas. "It was the Rolex her husband had wanted to be buried with. A precious one, from the Seventies. The woman bursts into tears. I say to her: Signora, it's been more than a year. It's not as if we can disinter the corpse. She takes her hands away from her face, I look and I say to myself I must not have understood right, then I take another look and I think, here comes trouble. It's clear that she's crying, but basically, she's laughing, too. She smiles through her tears, she slips a finger under the collar of the jacket of her skirt suit. *Oh, yes you can*, she says.

The man next to the driver burst out laughing. The driver

laughed. The man next to the medical examiner laughed. The driver laughed. The man next to the driver grunted. The driver laughed. The night opened out black and diagonal through the windshield. They narrowly missed a dumpster. The medical examiner jerked, startled. Then the trees thinned out. The sky opened out, the road became broad and straight. The cemetery of Bari, with its luminous eyes and its cypresses and the niches and monumental chapels, rose up before them.

They waited while the electric gate swung open. They entered. They skirted the vaults and the horizontal burial crypts. Among the cypresses, the silhouette of a statue, plastic bags full of dead flowers. The vehicle came to a halt in front of the mortuary. The guard greeted them, emerging from the shadows: "Come, bring 'em in, who knows who'll be bringing *you* someday." No one laughed. The guard went to open the mortuary. He came back toward them. He gave the keys to the medical examiner. He said: "Lock up good, after you're done." He headed back to his booth, buried in the perfume of dirt and reinforced concrete.

The medical examiner asked: "Who has a cigarette?"

The three men pulled the stretcher with the girl in it out along the rails, fastened it to the gurney, taking care that the lid didn't open. They pushed the gurney toward the morgue.

The medical examiner thought he heard noises coming through the bushes. He licked his cigarette. He stuck his right hand into his inside jacket pocket. He opened the baggie with his thumb and middle finger. He stuck in his forefinger, then pressed it against the edges of the cigarette. He lit it. Taste of ammonia. A young cat moved circumspectly beyond the leaves. A leap onto the gravestone. The mouse fled. The medical examiner took another drag. The door to the mortuary had opened. The three men from the undertakers came out, one after the other. The last one was pushing the gurney, now empty.

"She's ready," said the driver, "when you're done, we'll be with the guard."

They headed toward the guard's booth.

The medical examiner took another drag. In the distance, the song of night birds. He tossed the cigarette. He picked up his bag and headed off.

He half closed the door, the noises ceased. He closed his eyes and opened them again. The light was so strong that he had to wait for the outlines to take shape. It was a squalid mortuary with tiled walls. The inset wall sink must have considered itself a luxury. He went over and washed his hands. Then he turned off the faucet, pulled a length of paper towel off the roll, dried himself, tossed the towel into the trash. He put on his gloves. Out of the corner of his eye, he glimpsed the trench coat. The skirt, the blouse, the panties and bra. All piled on a chair. He turned away. He had the impression that the light hadn't yet stabilized. The girl was on the steel table next to the window. He stepped closer to the body. He set the bag down on the accessory table. He opened it. He pulled out pen and notepad, and set them on the facing shelf. He leaned over the girl. He felt the hairs rise on the back of his neck. He stood up straight. He adjusted the light of the minispot. He went back and stood over Clara. Even before touching her he felt a slight recoil, as if something about that body had pierced him, depositing itself somewhere he could hardly reach. He clenched and unclenched his jaw. He took the head in his hands. He rotated the neck from one side to the other. The osseous crunch suggested a craniofacial trauma. To establish whether that was due to a fall would require an autopsy. An external examination wouldn't be sufficient. He felt something prick his left forefinger. He pulled the finger away from the earlobe and saw a star-shaped earring, gold-plated, pretty run-of-the-mill. On the other earlobe, the earring was missing.

Torn away. He noticed the location of the freckles. For an instant, he was close to the memory of the Ursa Major he'd dreamed just a short while before. He lost the information. He felt the cheekbones and the forehead. Then it was time for the arms. As he pressed down on the torso with his fingers, he felt the air bubble. As the ribs fractured, they had perforated the pleural sacs. There could be multiple causes for that too. He wasn't there to find that out. He chewed empty-mouthed. Subcutaneous emphysema. He wrote that finding down on his notepad. He turned back to look at her. Her breasts were full and firm. The pale skin on her thighs was riddled with large brownish bruises. A layman would have associated them with Rorschach blots. But it was only blood effusion. He turned her on her side. He tried rotating her. He pressed one hand down near where her kidneys would be. He found something. He felt the back of his neck sizzle. He asked how this could still be possible. He adjusted the light of the minispot. He turned back to Clara. Something stirred in his memory. Who in Bari didn't know the Salveminis? Even the Physical Therapy Institute on Via Camillo Rosalba existed thanks to that family. On a few occasions, he'd run into her when she was alive, lovely and pale in an evening gown, outside some club. She cheated on her husband. That was something people said. A friend of his had told him about some kind of affair with the chancellor of the university. Still, there's something else, the doctor told himself. The mortuary room was steeped in silence. He went back to palpating the corpse. He clenched and unclenched his jaw. With renewed determination, he inserted his fingers under her kidneys. He pressed, until he recognized the compression of the vertebrae. Lumbar fracture. He felt the frozen drop of cocaine in his throat. He set the corpse straight again. He bent over her again. If she were alive, he'd have felt her breath on his forehead. He felt her sternum. He pressed on her pelvis. With one hand he gripped her right ankle, then slipped the other hand under the bend in her knee. No fractures. He braced the left leg. The whiteness of her flesh was a frequency intercepted by the antenna that had been activated in him as soon as he'd glimpsed her. He started to bend the other leg. *Oh, Christ.* The blow hit him direct and violent and now all it was doing was spreading through his head. Like a shot, he dropped the corpse's leg. He looked behind him. Instinctively, he made for the door. He locked it. Slowly, he caught his breath. He went back to the anatomy table. Now the glare from the spotlight burned on him like the reflection from a polar ice cap. It was the girl in the pictures. But of course. He hadn't noticed it at the time because the subject wasn't looking directly into the lens. But he realized it now. He put his hands on the corpse's knees, touched the thighs. He opened the legs. The thing dated back to less than a year ago. Dozens of obscene photos in the hardcover binder. Stuff that demanded a strong stomach. He spread her legs with renewed vigor. He remained stunned for a few seconds. Vittorio Salvemini's daughter. He turned her back onto her side. He recoiled from the corpse as if it were a bag of garbage. He went back to the door. He flipped the light switch. The room plunged into darkness. Now he could hear his heart beat. Little by little, the light of the moon took possession of the room, spread over the floor and onto the anatomy table. The corpse's body became visible again, but this time it emerged from a farther-away place. The medical examiner ground his teeth. He felt an urgent need for a blast of cocaine fired right up his nostrils.

The operation last time."

"A quadra . . . "

"The quadrantectomy," she corrected herself, beating him to it, then blushed.

She was aware of the correct terminology. She consulted the Garzanti encyclopedias, the articles that came out in the popular publications on the subject. A woman in her early fifties. The oncologist's presence threatened to keep her from thinking straight.

"A quadrantectomy of the left breast, with a biopsy of the lymph node," the professor went on, without taking his eyes off the report, "performed on February 15, 1997 at the San Carlo hospital in Potenza."

"Fifteen years ago," the woman said to herself.

The doctor restrained his impulse to sigh. He entrusted the gesture to a cocked eyebrow. His assistant, sitting beside him, stopped typing on the keyboard of her computer.

"Mamma, if it was 1997 that means *fourteen* years ago," the young man broke in, irritated.

The woman and her son looked at each other with all the love, all the hate for the destiny that brings certain bodies to clash with each other just when it attracts them to each other.

They turned back to concentrate on the doctor. Now they were looking at him as if their submissiveness might foster the transformation that everyone hopes to witness in cases like these, in order that, from the eyes of the man of science, a

Christ might emerge, marching across the cornea's aqueous surface. Radiant. Beaming. That he might utter the word.

"We cannot entirely exclude the metastatic infiltration of the regional lymph nodes, Signora."

They knew that he had won the Swiss Cancer League's Robert Wenner Prize at an age when other doctors are going in search of their first fellowship. His fame had filled them with hope in the previous weeks. The young man had searched the online forums where patients exchanged advice about medicines and treatments. They'd even calculated his astrological sign. April 20, 1963. It was written on the Institute's website. They had no idea that his sister had been buried the day before.

Ruggero checked the data on the medical report. With his other eye, he was checking his desk diary. The woman was the third of sixteen patients he'd need to see before going home. No one could have said a thing if he'd simply canceled all his appointments right through to the end of the week.

"What do you mean, the lymph nodes are at risk?" the woman asked.

The Cancer Institute of the Mediterranean had been founded with objective of providing an alternative to the major medical centers in the north. They came from all over Campania, from Molise, to be examined there. They would board a bus, leaving the mountains of Basilicata behind them at the first light of dawn.

"It means that our examination of the axillary cavities revealed the presence of lymph nodes with a diameter greater than three centimeters. Which ought to put us on alert."

"In Potenza they told us that that's a normal by-product of the operation," said the young man, hardening his tone.

This was how they began to lose faith. Ruggero knew how

it worked. In order to quash a doubt, they'd bring a report from another oncologist, who'd say something that didn't perfectly match the words of the first one. This made it advisable to go to a third oncologist for yet another opinion. Only then the third oncologist would say something *completely* different from the first two. Tamoxifen instead of Arimidex. A bone scintigraphy was absolutely necessary. What! No one had recommended it?

"Listen," Ruggero suffocated a still-nascent instinct, "the situation will become clearer in a couple of months, when your mother . . . when you, Signora," he shifted his gaze over to the woman, "are strong enough to undergo another . . . "

The phone started ringing. The young assistant looked up, startled. Everyone at the Institute knew that Professor Salvemini wasn't to be disturbed while he was with patients. Except in a very grave emergency. Ruggero wondered how it could be that a man who could rely on a thousand bulldozers always seemed to need a hand. He lifted the receiver.

The switchboard operator informed him that his father was waiting for him at the reception desk. The day before, after the funeral, Vittorio had announced that he'd come by to see him. "In a week or so," he'd said.

"All right." Ruggero put down the receiver. "What were we saying?" He tried to smile, but some strange expression must have appeared on his face, given the way that mother and son had started looking at him.

In the reception area, he found Vittorio.

He was sitting among the patients. His hands on his knees, wearing a cotton sweater. Ruggero studied him from the receptionists' desk, like someone laboring under the illusion that watching people in their sleep is the same as learning their secrets.

Then the old man saw him. He lifted a corner of his lips. He got up, accentuating the fatigue involved, and walked toward him. Two male nurses walked in front of him. Vittorio had a grim expression on display. He was brandishing the black power of grief as if Clara had had a father and never a mother, never an older brother.

They spoke next to a beverage vending machine, their cheeks brushing, extending their necks toward each other. From the reception area, two patients elbowed each other. The doctor seemed angry. At a certain point he got upset. As he spoke, his face reddened. He leveled his forefinger at his father.

Half an hour later Ruggero was speeding through the streets of Bari in his BMW convertible. He was cursing. He slammed a fist down on the steering wheel. On his left, the Sheraton loomed. On the opposite side of the street, the apartment buildings of the various quarters of the city streamed past, orderly, sand-colored constructions, cleansed by the spring light. He turned onto Viale De Laurentiis. Rusty playground equipment, kids in the public park. When he'd asked Dr. Spagnulo to stand in for him, he'd sensed confusion all around him. He'd recovered now, hitting the steering wheel like that.

It hadn't taken much for Vittorio to talk him into it. Ruggero had felt the blood pulse in his head when it became clear that he was going to have to sacrifice the day. He'd verbally assaulted his father, and only when the old man took the punishment without reacting had it dawned on Ruggero that what he himself was experiencing was pleasure, not anger. Let his son blow off some steam, accept the dressing down. If the old man had gotten in his face, underlining the weight of the interests at play (not even a Nobel Prize in medicine could have reversed Salvemini Construction's priorities in this situation), then his son's fury would have been authentic. Breaking down an unlocked door, Ruggero had instead heard his footsteps echo in an enormous empty space. Dead leaves in dead afternoon light. A weight not unlike regret, or a sense of guilt. The remote, always postponed chance of embracing his father, of curling up with him in a cold grave. "All right," he'd hissed. Then he'd felt an even stronger blow to the head, the sensation of three mornings ago, when Vittorio had come to tell him about Clara. He'd asked Dr. Spagnulo to stand in for him. Without really knowing exactly what was happening, he'd found himself on the phone with the head of orthopedics at the general hospital. He'd walked through the automatic doors, the hot sunlight after the artificial bulbs, fooling himself into thinking that haste might erase the error, much like a sin you abjure by staining yourself with it.

So now he was going to pick up Engineer Ranieri. Together they'd go to the general hospital. There, apparently, the engineer was supposed to meet with a patient who'd had one of his legs amputated. Ruggero looked around. The city was streaming past him as if from another dimension. A large silent house surrounded by greenery. A wooden table amidst the weeds. Beneath it, an obscure, formless world was moving, twisted roots, tiny blind insects, the phosphorescent presence of his sister Clara. Michele was coming home. Motionless in the train compartment, his head resting against the glass of the Eurostar window.

Ruggero turned at Viale Gandhi. A chaotic mess of tiny shops, mopeds, and double-parked delivery vans. His father asked for help and everyone came running. Vittorio knew what to do. He could give the impression of a loser who needed a hand even when the company was bursting with health. Never mind now, with the Porto Allegro problems.

Thirty years ago, when you crossed through Bari, the sense of plenty was tangible. The windows of the boutiques were cleaned and polished three times a day. The terraces outlined in the rich summer skies where the green of the ferns seemed to burn with a life of its own. Many of those steel shutters now were closed, or rusty. The streets half shattered. So, Ruggero thought, this time the threat is real.

He drove past Via Petroni. He turned right again. He remembered when he was a medical student. In bed before midnight. He'd fall asleep thinking about the next exam. He looked forward to the moment when the professor would admit his astonishment at how well he had studied. The mechanisms of ventricular fibrillation. Acute and chronic pericarditis. Eyes closed, tucked under the sheets. The textbook stamped clearly in his head. A noise from the bathroom of the master bedroom. The perfection of those pages crumbled under the blows of his *real* cardiac acceleration. For days his father had been complaining about a delay on a major payment. His face dark, his mouth a macabre fissure. Maybe no one really had overturned the medicine chest in the bathroom. Ruggero felt Vittorio's anxiety inside him, the violence of his father's insomnia. He was endangering Ruggero's university career.

Ruggero would wake up in the middle of the night, knocking his histology textbook off the bed. (He'd breathe slowly, observing the chilly winter lights through the half-closed shutters). In early June, he'd knock over the molecular biology textbook. He'd find himself in his underwear in the small bathroom, clammy with sweat at three in the morning, the volume on forensic medicine hurled against the wall, staring at himself in the mirror in the deadly muggy heat of the summer night. His folks were on holiday in Tunisia. Michele and Clara were on a camping trip. The city was half-deserted, the house was empty. Which meant that no one could have turned on the television set downstairs. No one had broken a plate in the kitchen, and yet that plate had shattered into a thousand pieces. His father's ghost had become very cunning, now it was active even when the old man wasn't there, sabotaging the exam that Ruggero was scheduled to take in early September. Technical consultation at criminal trials, autopsy and external examination, the notion of mental competency, the putrefaction, maceration, and mummification of a corpse, instigation to suicide, gang rape, fingerprinting, the cooling of bodies, the professor wouldn't even have time to fully frame his question before he was halfway through his answer, but that was only provided that the seven hundred seventy pages of forensic medicine were absorbed according to schedule, twelve hours a day, two and a half pages an hour, plus two hours of general review, which was unlikely if he wasn't getting sleep. Ruggero would throw open the window, feeling the hot wind on his skin, observing the hedges in the garden below, the fountain surrounded by the eucalyptus trees. There's something more, he told himself, something I can't even imagine.

No one was moving furniture in the living room. No one was driving nails into the wall after midnight. Ruggero stared wide-eyed in November. He bit his pillow on February nights. He'd wake up coughing at a quarter to two in the morning. Through the crack in the door placental gleams were moving. A thunderous noise forced him fully awake. Ruggero leapt out of bed, hurried out into the hallway, and was overwhelmed by the billowing cloud of smoke. He braved the stairs, two shadows shot past amid the sparks and all around him he felt the desire for their deaths, his parents burnt alive. But a short while later, safe and sound, outside the villa's front door, when he noticed Michele emerging from the bushes with a gas can in one hand, and Clara following behind, at the moment he saw his sister and half-brother walking toward the house, only then did he realize that it was their desire, not his, it had belonged to Ruggero only the way that someone else's music played at full blast does, he was full of a filial love, it was they who hated.

He accelerated down Via Fanelli. The buildings thinned out. Tennis courts popped up, brief untilled stretches. He passed a gas pump. Two young African women flooded with light in the parking area. He continued toward Mungivacca.

Engineer Ranieri was waiting for him outside a tobacconist's shop. A light-blue suit, brylcreemed hair. Ruggero pulled the BMW to a halt. The man walked toward him, then embraced him. "Try to be strong." He'd already said it at the funeral.

Now they were again heading toward the center of town. The engineer gestured toward the sky.

"Spring has returned."

Though he was only two years older than him, Engineer Ranieri had been working for his father since Ruggero was in high school. That established a boundary that Ruggero felt incapable of crossing. Engineer De Palo and Engineer Ranieri. The subtlety of the older man. The passionate adulation of the younger. Ruggero remembered his smile as he congratulated him on graduating from high school, before vanishing into his father's office. Electrified by the 4.0 GPA he'd just earned, Ruggero felt he could talk about the future as if he were the legal representative of a major cement manufacturer.

"Give this idiot a listen," said Vittorio, smiling at him from behind the desk.

The university was important. But it was important for the children of newsagents. "From today to the day you graduate from medical school with a specialization, you'd make more money than a good doctor will earn in his first ten years practicing." To join him at the company, right away. To spend the summer learning the ropes, going back and forth to the provincial urban planning offices. That's what his father proposed, as he stubbed out his Marlboro in the crystal ashtray. He had realized that the summons to sacrifice—celebrating the completion of his secondary education by getting to work—was for a first-born son at once a knightly challenge, and a twisted proof of love. For Vittorio, the matter came down to something much simpler. The timing was good. The size of the company at this point demanded perhaps not so much actual effectiveness as the idea of an heir who was up to the task.

"Give this idiot a listen." And even though Ruggero had only just legally become an adult, the hidden dangers of the wordplay didn't elude him.

One day his father unrolled on his desk plans for a small shopping center that the company had recently finished building. Those plans were the playing field on which Ruggero would have a chance to test his valor.

"You're a smart, reliable, motivated young man. How much are you willing to bet?" asked Vittorio lighting a cigarette. He stood up, his face dappled with the shadow of the kentia palm in whose vase dozens of cold cigarette butts lay scattered. "Do you want to bet that if I entrust you with the industrial sheds, you can get them all rented in a month? If you can't rent them in thirty days, I'll give you a car. You've got a driver's license, you need a car. A nice Porsche. What do you think? But I'll tell you this: If you come to work for the company you'll never get that car out of me!"

He burst out laughing, drowning in optimism and sincerity, a man at the height of his powers.

The light turned green. Ruggero jammed his foot down on the accelerator pedal. With a quick zigzagging maneuver he shot past the other vehicles in line ahead of him. Engineer Ranieri instinctively grabbed for the assist grip.

Ruggero had spent the summer ricocheting from one office to another, his briefcase filled with land registry certificates and permits for mid-project variations. He never set foot on a beach except on Sundays, when he went to Monopoli to see a former high school classmate, a girl, not especially good look-ing, with whom he had sex until the first rains began to fall. Then, in September, without a word to a soul, he enrolled in medical school.

He strode into Vittorio's office full of the energy that had coursed into him the moment he'd handed his form to the department secretary. He was ready to take his father on. The old man's face hardened for an moment or two. Then his cheeks relaxed. "You'll have to study hard. But a doctor in the family might always come in handy. I'm sure you'll acquit your-self honorably." He invited him downstairs for a drink at the bar.

He'd won without fighting. And yet, as he rode down in the elevator with him, he had a strange sensation. He couldn't prove it, but he would have sworn that for Vittorio, in the space between one floor and another, something was moving back into place. He noticed the curl of the lip that he knew so well, as if his enrolment at the university had laid waste to his father's plans but all the same, Vittorio was picking up the bro-ken shards in such a way as to visualize then and there an even more reckless project.

On Via Scipione l'Africano, they saw the four palm trees that surrounded the fountain in the piazza. Then the general hospital appeared. Engineer Ranieri put on a worried face. He coughed. He recovered his joviality, but built atop his previous state of mind.

After he finished training in his medical specialty, Ruggero was awarded a clinical fellowship at the Netherlands Cancer Institute in Amsterdam. Three wonderful years, far away from everything, under the tutelage of a giant in the field, Professor Aron Helmerhorst. Whole days spent observing the TIC10 molecule at work. It wasn't so much the distance from Bari as the brand new atmosphere that protected him. The nightly phantoms no longer came to bother him, and he came close to forgetting them entirely. The obsession with his father wasn't the only one to vanish. The times he spoke to Clara on the phone, his sister's calm and radiant voice was reabsorbed by the banality of the words she spoke, and not by what her physical presence communicated. Michele was a young man full of problems and Gioia was a girl with too few, but at last the boundaries were clear. At night, he'd stroll past the Nieuwe Kerk feeling something approaching happiness.

A residue of the old furor surfaced in the long hours of work. Under Helmerhorst's supervision, he was studying the effects of dacarbazine on mammary carcinomas. It gave Ruggero an animal-like pleasure to see the compound acting on the DNA, preventing it from duplicating itself. A feeling of revenge. They'd spend Saturday afternoons in the half-empty laboratories. They'd check their progress on the apoptotic drugs. Programmed cell suicide. He'd read about it in his textbooks. But when he actually *observed* the tissue sections from the mice whose tumoral cells he'd inoculated, it left him breathless. The less resistant cells began to vibrate, the chromatin went into crisis and, at a certain point, like balloons, the cells burst, leaving behind a fragile luminescence.

They realized that the drug worked on pulmonary tumors. It was effective on colon cancer. As they continued their research they discovered (to even Helmerhorst's surprise) that the molecule was capable of bypassing the blood-brain barrier, arriving virtually intact on the other side.

Weeks passed. The guinea pigs' survival curve lengthened. Ruggero was exhausted, proud, sleepless, and fearless when he signed the article that appeared in *The Lancet*, together with the others. The summer passed. From Zurich came the news that they had won the Swiss Cancer League's Robert Wenner Prize.

He stopped the BMW in a no-parking area in front of the general hospital.

Engineer Ranieri rummaged through his pockets, put together the change for the parking attendant. Ruggero got out of the car.

Five young men and one old man on the podium of the little Zurich Stadtspital. They received the certificates of merit from the mayor. The professor waved his eighty thousand dollar check before an anemic audience of other doctors, researchers, and a few journalists who applauded sincerely, free of the ferocity with which down south it is thought necessary to assert oneself, even through the recognition of the achievements of others. This prize is my safe conduct pass, thought Ruggero. In five or at most ten years, I'll be where I want to be, he thought as a big girl in a blouse and a black calf-length skirt (a girl who, where he came from, would have been mocked even at a gathering of magistrates) gave Professor Helmerhorst a bunch of orchids wrapped in pink cellophane. In five, ten years. Two weeks later he received a phone call. The managing director of Bari's national health care clinic was offering him the position of deputy director at the Cancer Institute of the Mediterranean.

They went through the front gate. There was a hustle and bustle of white and green lab coats. Ruggero gestured: "This way." They walked into pavilion number six.

Amidst the dirty damp walls of the orthopedics ward of the general hospital, on the filthy floors, sensing the encrusted dust on the radiators before seeing it, submitting to the demands of the nurse practitioners on the bulletin board without reading them, in the grim darkness of the hallway, the head physician walked toward them, soberly waving his right hand. A tall man, old and very pale.

He patted Ruggero on the back. He introduced himself to Engineer Ranieri. He invited them to follow him. At the end of the hall, before the exit, after the broken vending machine. In the elevator, as they were riding up to the fourth floor, if one of three had so much as lifted his head, he would have seen the other two staring at their shoes. In the force that frees us, the remains of the force that puts us back in chains. The managing director of the health care clinic had spoken of it as the first alternative to the major cancer treatment centers in the north. Entirely without precedent. They would have a TrueBeam linear accelerator, the tumor-burning machine of which there were only nine in all of Europe. It meant going back to Bari. But it meant going back in triumph. Crossing the finish line before he turned thirty-five. The elevator door slid open.

The room, large and airy, gave the sense of having been cleared out just a few days earlier. The eucalyptus trees waved through the open window. The head physician stood flattened against the door. So there he was, the patient. The off-white blanket followed humps and valleys where the one or the other ought not to have been. The man was nodding from the bed. He seemed tired, disgusted. The engineer described the apartment on Via D'Aquino. "Taranto's social drawing room." Ruggero went over to the window. He closed the shutters. He pulled too hard. The room was plunged into darkness. He pushed them back open, slightly, and the head physician was no longer there. In the semidarkness, he met the patient's half-lidded eyes. The patient closed his eyes, opened them again, flushed with the pain medicine, showing that everything (said the cunning, that is, the patience in those eyes) rested on a pre-supposition analogous to the force of gravity. Too obvious to speak of it in explicit terms in the presence of body shattered on the ground.

Back on Via Fanelli, in the car with the engineer, Ruggero tried to reassemble his impressions. He had to answer quickly to prevent the questions from going someplace where the words hadn't yet organized a proper defense. Why did you interrupt your patient consultations? He talked me into it. Did you understand what you were doing with that man?

Every time he came back from Amsterdam—short stays of three or four days—his father would tell him about the situation. The company was many companies bound up together. A welter of interlocking ownerships, investments, corporate subsidiaries. The company, therefore, was in good health. But the company was going through a terribly difficult time. The company was stagnating. And yet, there was a major opportunity taking shape on the horizon. That was what his father told him. Then, just as he did with Clara and Michele—as he would have done with Gioia, if she hadn't been a minor at the time—he would put some papers before him and ask him to sign.

They passed the tennis courts again. Engineer Ranieri stuck his elbow out the car window. He lifted the cigarette to his lips. His hair tousled by the wind.

Papers to sign were a Salvemini tradition. Over the years, he and his siblings had been summoned for dozens of family meetings. Before Michele left for Rome. Before Ruggero came back from Amsterdam. After Clara married Alberto. Before she married him. They would gather in the villa's large living room. Here, the head of the family, sitting in his armchair, his legs wrapped in an innocuous looking Scottish plaid blanket, would lay out the situation. Lengthy talks that neither he nor his siblings understood in the slightest. Vittorio talked about shareholder resolutions, or acting partners. Ruggero wondered how it could be possible that the pathogenesis of Hodgkin's lymphoma concealed fewer pitfalls than an ordinary deed of sale. He looked to his siblings for their reactions. Michele was looking at the trees outside the window. Clara was crossing and uncrossing her long legs, barely covered by a Mila Schön skirt, taking a drag on a cigarette, a sarcastic smile offered in passive resistance to the show. Vittorio was talking about medium-term leasing, about tax loopholes.

They also drove past the auto dealership, the gas station. The two whores were still there. Ruggero clenched the steering wheel. He resisted the temptation to swerve in their direction and run them over.

One Christmas Eve, his father dragged him in front of the fireplace. The banks were demanding supplementary collateral for a newly founded company. Just a small LLC, but strategically important. I named it Cla.ru.mi. "Cla what?" "It's an acronym, based on your names." While Vittorio went on talking, Ruggero visualized the auditorium at the Zurich Stadtspital. He thought about the conference on the efficacy of pamidronate at Cornell University where he would be in just two weeks. That was his life. Talking to him about the umpteenth corporate emergency was just wasting his time. Vittorio said: "They're asking for all three of you to guarantee the line of credit." Ruggero was ready to grab a fountain pen even before his father had finished talking. Anything, just to be done with it.

"Look out for that asshole!" Engineer Ranieri transferred Ruggero's recklessness to the small compact traveling in the opposite direction.

So this was it, then? Suretyships? Letters of guarantee? Was it the papers that made him feel he was trapped again? Over the years they'd allowed themselves to be dragged into a fair number of messes. The last one had been faking the purchase of a villa in Porto Allegro and then making him sign a contract guaranteeing he would return it. His father had done the same thing with Michele. The situations weren't comparable. What did his brother have to lose? Did he own any real estate of his own? Had there ever been any assets in Michele's life that a creditor could seize? Michele didn't know, didn't care, had never dreamed of taking stock of the situation. Otherwise he'd have come to the conclusion that the sum total of the guarantees they'd all underwritten was greater than the estate that not a low-profile journalist but a respected physician, someone who earned real money, could hope to accumulate in a lifetime of work. Three million euros? Four? How much were they on the hook for? Among other things, it had never passed through Michele's mind that criminal consequences could ever emerge from all those sheets of paper. One day they'd find a couple of marshals on their doorsteps. Oh, Michele wouldn't have given a hoot. His sister would actually have found it flattering! Clara would have flashed a dazzling smile as she proffered her crossed wrists to the finance police. (He caught himself faulting her as if she were still alive. Once again, the feeling of uneasiness.)

So it was for this? This is what you came back for? Or was it the position as deputy director? He knew that voice.

They pulled into Mungivacca. Low houses, small hardware stores. More than once in the last few months, during family meetings, he had noticed a faint, powdery white trace on the tip of Clara's cigarette. It wasn't hard to figure out what she had gone to do in the bathroom. Every so often his sister's legs were crisscrossed with strange hematomas. Deep dark patches on that unnaturally white flesh. Even clusters of bruises that appeared and disappeared as she uncrossed her legs and recrossed them in the other direction. His sister reduced to a minimum the grinding of her jaws *and smiled*. A triumphant happiness, that would send shivers down your back. Then she'd look at her father and shoot Ruggero a wink. Vittorio was talking about the villas that would be put in all their names. He said that Michele was fine with it, he'd meet with the notary Valsecchi up in Rome. "It's all taken care of," he hastened to conclude. (Every time their half brother was mentioned in his absence, the members of the family all rearranged themselves on their various armchairs and sofas, to ensure that the subtle electric slippage could pass by without leaving a trace). His sister would lift an eyebrow. Annamaria, sitting back straight in her chair, would do nothing more than shake her bracelets, looking at her spouse and biological children as if they were the Windsors during a domestic interlude. Clara would imperceptibly tug the hem of her skirt downward, a provocation more than a concealment. Vittorio went on weaving the web of his extremely intricate lecture. Then the sound of galloping footsteps. Gioia would burst into the living room, displaying a necklace studded with tiny pink diamonds that Annamaria had given her, without informing her father. She was shouting: "Surprise!"

Now the BMW was parked in front of the tobacconist. "Then we're clear," Engineer Ranieri said again. Ruggero said goodbye. He heard the door slam. He saw himself turn the car around. The small shops passed from the front windshield to the rear windshield and vanished. Ruggero took a right. He turned down Via Fanelli again. Is this why he'd gone to the general hospital? Tell him no, and tomorrow the banks will come asking for the sums you guaranteed. Disobey him, and the illicit actions for which you're unknowingly responsible will fall from the sky of inactive guilt and come to hurt you. Is that it? Do you really believe it? Do you remember what happened with the archive?

He knew that voice. The voice knew him. The voice *knew* what happened to him every time Vittorio camouflaged very specific demands inside an incomprehensible explanation. The world around him gradually dimmed, his throat tightened. Vittorio presented himself as if defenseless, crushed by his problems, he pretended until he convinced himself that he was a child (a sad, sad child). But this was the technique he employed to ensure that what happened was the very opposite. It was Ruggero who regressed, and the only way to stop the process was to do as Vittorio wished.

"Papà, that's something I can't do."

In Bari, a few months after he'd accepted the position of deputy director of the Cancer Institute of the Mediterranean, Vittorio had come to see him at the clinic. He'd invited him to dinner the week before. He wouldn't give up. He'd even cropped up at the benefit gala for the fight against childhood leukemia held by the AIL. After chatting with the mayor, Vittorio had gone over to the donations table. He'd filled out his check, he'd let it drop into the large transparent bowl. Then he'd headed for Ruggero. Half an hour later, they were strolling in the hotel's gardens. Flooded by the artificial light, the azaleas were bursting with life.

"Papà, I can't," Ruggero had said for the second time.

He crossed Via Amendola again. On either side fields stretched out, colored yellow and green. Similar to a sun, concealed somewhere on the horizon, beyond the olive trees, on the far side of the towns and the adjoining cities. The voice. Ruggero accelerated as if to keep it from catching up with him. He saw the gas station heave into view. He downshifted from fifth gear to fourth. He shot past the gas station, the carwash. Suddenly, he swerved to the right. The girls saw him pull up at a speed that could easily have killed them. They leapt backward, stumbling on their heels, spinning halfway around.

The BMW screeched to a halt just inches from where they would still have been if they'd not moved. The first of the two was wearing a miniskirt that left bare her long and muscular legs. The other one was wearing a tank top and white shorts. For the whole last week, his father hadn't stopped pestering him about the documents in the Regional Medical Archives. The girls, recovered from their initial fright, were now looking in his direction. No tinted glass. One of them stopped scratching her head. She smiled. They started to come closer. The tall one came over to his side of the car. The other one moved to the opposite side (that way, if he did tear out of there, he wouldn't hit them both). Stupid African bitch, he thought to himself. He turned off the motor to reassure them. He opened the door. The tall girl leaned forward. "Ciao ciao." Her eyes were dark, her large lips daubed with transparent lipstick. The wind was moving the trees on the far side of the parking lot. Ruggero said: "Let's go." In reply, the girl arched her back, opened her right hand wide. For seventy euros, her girlfriend would get in the car too. Ruggero rummaged in his pockets. His white labcoat peeked out from under his jacket. The girl put on a obliging expression. "The extra money is so that she doesn't come with you." The girl failed to pick up on the nuance, but the concept was clear. She gestured to her friend. The other girl stood there with her fingers gripping the car door. Then she released her grasp. The first girl went around the BMW while the second one went back to the edge of the parking area. The girl opened the door, got in the seat next to him. Ruggero pulled out.

Five minutes later they were on a narrow side street surrounded by fields. A stand of cherry trees blossomed beyond the metal fence. They were still in the car and it was still the day after his sister's funeral. The girl started to recline her seat. Ruggero admonished her, lifting his forefinger in midair. He looked down. He was tempted to smash her face in. The girl ran her hand through her hair. She slipped her other hand into the pocket of her skirt. She looked at him. Ruggero remained motionless. So then the girl leaned forward. She undid his trousers. She lifted her hand to her mouth, tore the wrapping with her teeth. With her hands free, she pulled down his underwear. The gnats hovered in the air. The girl tilted her head, laid a cheek on Ruggero's thigh, and when she sensed that the time was right, aiding herself with her tongue, slid the condom on. Ruggero had to stop himself from spitting on her. The girl must have sensed something because she grabbed his legs for a moment. The scene shifted definitively to the other end, like a film projector that continues to beam its shaft of light somewhere other than the screen, so that the memories streamed past without Ruggero being able to see them. After hearing that he couldn't give him access to the archive, his father, in the garden at the Sheraton, had slowed his pace.

"You're the deputy director," he protested.

"The Archive of Medical Reports doesn't come under my jurisdiction."

Ruggero understood that his father had understood that he was lying. Small white dots whirled around the azaleas. Vittorio shrugged, filled with bitterness. Ruggero felt his throat closing up.

He put a hand on her head. He whispered: "You cow."

After the time at the Sheraton, his father had invited him out to dinner at the restaurant. They'd talked for no good reason about the renovation of a house. A small villa on the coast. Then Vittorio had resumed his attack. He'd explained that the documentation was needed for a statistical study being undertaken by the National Builders' Association.

"What does the National Builders' Association want with our archives?"

"How should I know?" Vittorio had flashed him a comradely smile. "The president just asked me. He's a close friend. He's done us a lot of favors."

"A formal request should be submitted to the health director. A public institution should make the request."

"You can also do it yourself."

His fingers touched the girl's fingers. She instinctively closed the space between forefinger and middle finger, her thumb hooked around the button of his trousers. She found herself with another fifty-euro note in her fist.

So his father had come to see him personally at the institute. Ruggero ushered him into his office. He had a couple of espressos brought in.

"Papà, do you feel all right?"

Vittorio was pacing back and forth in the room, he was upset. He talked of sums of money on which the Ministry of Public Works had accumulated unbelievable delays in payment, construction projects that were having trouble getting off the ground, and taxes, taxes on corporate incomes, and how when it came to collecting those back taxes the highest officials of those same insolvent public agencies were suddenly transformed into ferocious creditors. He leapt from one topic to another, and when he no longer saw in his son the irascible oncologist with extensive international experience, and perhaps not even the whoremonger, but the simple creature terrified by another's fragility, the quavering grownup child faced with a picture of paternal helplessness, that's when he drove the knife in. He asked him again. The papers from the archive. The medical reports for all the cancer patients in Puglia and Basilicata. The girl felt something on her head. As if he were, absurdly, patting her, delivering small taps, tiny slaps, a series of humiliating reprimands with his knuckles. She looked up, bewildered more than indignant, ready to complain. And yet Ruggero knew. He had realized that Vittorio was himself lying. There was no president of the National Builders' Association. He remembered the file folders in the administrative offices of Salvemini Construction. The file boxes lined up on the shelves that contained the announcements of bare legal titles to property, updated every week. The countryside was gleaming in the glory of early afternoon. This time the girl definitely noticed the slap to the head. Her eyes filled with hatred. She took her lips off her work and looked at him. And then, as if sight had substituted for touch, she understood that he had spat on her. She felt her hair. She was ready to berate him, maybe to hit him. But he let more cash fall. And when more banknotes rained over her, like stones, the situation in which pride might have a price above which more pride is required, and it's not always easy to feel up to it, certain you're not mixing pride up with haughtiness, when he tossed that money onto her, the girl went back to kneeling over something that finally had become a man. It was clear what would happen if the two archives happened to be cross-referenced. The medical reports on cancer patients and the list of bare property titles. Ruggero did as his father wished. A doctor in the family can always come in handy.

Once he'd done something like that, over the years that followed anything became possible.

Is that why you went to the general hospital this morning?

Blood relatives never weary of questioning us. They leave their voices inside us. That's what goes on talking when they're absent. But the proprietor of that voice is drawing closer, thought Ruggero in his BMW. Beyond the curve, beyond the almond trees in bloom, after the gray buildings and the half-empty stores. The red façade of the Bari train station, where a row of rails zipped glittering northward. Michele.

S ix ounces of aged caciocavallo," he said, examining the deli counter with the expert eye of a physician studying an X-ray.

Engineer De Palo had them pack up the olives. He asked them to show him the Parma prosciutto through the glass—like a newborn baby or an artwork—and before the blade of the slicer had even touched the ham, he added: "Thinner." He bought smoked salmon, two bottles of Amarone. He snapped his fingers at the stock boy to get him the quince jelly. Sitting behind the cash register, white and heavy as a Roman consul, the proprietor reiterated the point loudly: "Get the jelly for Engineer De Palo!"

He had them add in some burrata and fior di latte mozzarellas. This was the finest delicatessen in the city. Buying something extra, even if they were products that might wind up being tossed in the garbage, meant helping it maintain that status. Outside, the unemployed might be shouting, the students without a future might be spinning out of control. Where until just yesterday there had been a fine clothing shop it was not out of the question that overnight someone might come along and put up a "For Rent" sign. Poverty was disgusting, but nothing was more disgusting than the needy themselves. And even if that shop was weathering the storm—the garlands around the bars of chocolate and the beluga on display that seemed neither blackmail nor a threat were proof—there was no guarantee that at the first sign of trouble the owner wouldn't give in to the temptation to slip in some average foods amongst the fine delicacies, something that would attract the small-time professionals, the white-collar workers, with all their horrible complaints. He paid. The elderly proprietor leaned out past the cash register. He brought his lips close to the engineer's ear. He whispered to extend his condolences to the Salvemini family.

Engineer De Palo arranged the shopping bags on the rear seat. He got into his Ford Focus. He pulled out, drove away from the city center. He slowed down a few yards away from a men's clothing store. He double-parked. He went into the store. He examined the overcoats on display. He purchased the cheapest one. He left the store. He got back into his car. He drove past even the outskirts of town. After the IP gas station, he turned off onto the narrow tree-lined street on the right. It was a tremendous blow, but the Salvemini backbone should hold. He drove through the villa's front gate. He observed the oleanders and the hedges he cared more about than his own personal possessions. The engineer remembered when they'd sent him out in the middle of the night to retrieve her, one Christmas many years ago. She'd been sixteen at the time. There'd been a fight with her mother over some trifle that concealed the eternal reason: the half-brother, as always. The engineer found her after midnight, wandering all alone on the edge of a road leading out of town. The engineer pulled over. Clara looked up, got in the car without uttering a word. She sat next to him, docile in a way that failed to deceive him. Little viper. Acting like a little saint might be enough to fool her father, helped perhaps by his sense of guilt over Michele, but the girl wasn't about to pull the wool over his eyes. Silent in the passenger seat, so studiedly placid that the underlying arrogance became unmistakable. Obvious that she's hot to trot, he'd thought as he took her home. Even though she was barely a teenager, in spite of the fact that no boy had yet (though when it come to that detail, the engineer would have bet no more than three hundred-euro bills) punctured a hymen whose value at age sixteen Clara must have been smart enough to understand was multiplied by the fact that it would one day be gone, he could sense it baking in the space between her and the car seat. She thought she was who knows who. She felt superior to her mother, for example. Ridiculous! A woman she'd never come close to equaling. Her love for the bastard was absurd, too. The whole thing was a farce. They'd been too kind to the little slut. They should have brought her up on a steady diet of slaps in the face. In fact, now, with her death (which the engineer interpreted as one final insult to a family over which it was his duty to watch as if he were a guard entrusted with the gold of a church), she'd finally found a way of getting her folks into trouble.

But certain troubles are propitious, they arise so that other kinds of problems can be solved, he thought, at last, as he parked on the stretch of gravel.

He switched off the engine of the Focus. He got out of the car, walked around it. He pulled out the shopping bags. For the thousandth time, he failed to see the tiny star-shaped earring that had gotten stuck between the cushion and the back of the rear seat. He heard the twittering of birds. He climbed the stairs. He set down the shopping bags by the doormat, rang the bell. He hoped that the housekeeper would answer the door, to keep himself from hoping for something better. Instead the door swung open and Annamaria appeared. Signora Salvemini emerged from the shadow of the living room, an expression of sadness, of heroic decorum on her face. She was wearing a peach-colored dressing gown and gilt slippers, her naked ankles all angles like lintels capable of warding off attacks. Even if her makeup might smudge in the hot noonday wind, in spite of the fact that her sixty-six years had been assaulted by the selfishness and madness of that degenerate daughter, to him she was still a stunningly beautiful woman.

"Ah, Pasquale, thank you. Leave them there," she said, her voice hoarse.

"Signora, I ventured to get some burrata as well."

"That was smart of you," said Annamaria, with a hint of a smile that pierced the engineer through and through, while she looked at him as she would a play of light or some inert object—he considered her the guarantee that everything was going to turn out for the better.

He went back to the car. He pulled out his cell phone and read the address on the message that Signor Salvemini had sent him a few hours earlier. Before he'd even turned the key in the ignition he heard a shout. He looked up. The lady had vanished. The housekeeper, at the front door, was waving her fist threateningly in the air. The cat dove into the bushes. The shopping bags still next to the doormat. Idiot woman, thought Engineer De Palo.

"There's no such thing as a steady job. There's no such thing even as a steady profession anymore. China. Brazil. Everything happens so fast. So don't get scandalized when I say that academic knowledge isn't per se a professional quali-fication."

" . . . "

"That's not what I said."

" . . . "

"I'd try to turn that question around. Let's try taking a look at the financing enjoyed by the top hundred universities in the ranking that you cite."

Different in their sameness, the questions blew about in the wind of that season's agenda. Briefly, he had been allowed to pursue excellence. This was the long process of decline that he'd have to learn to live with. For that matter, the young interviewer looked like someone who'd be out on the street, unemployed, in three months. He shook the boy's hand. Then Renato Costantini, sixty-four years old, with a master's degree in economics from Chicago, a major figure in local periodical publishing and the chancellor of the University of Bari, got ready to go out.

Noise in the hallways of the departments, students on the move from one lecture hall to another, the tongue ever turns to the missing tooth, heading for the café, the library, the copy center, and no place where sense could be made. Students when they could have just been kids. Crazy that they kept on enrolling. The prize for failing to find a job was learning to be servile. Of course, Professor. After you, Professor. What little they learned they'd lose in the years they spent begging for jobs as baristas.

He went through the gates and he was back out in the street. The prettiest girl on the advertising posters wasn't good enough for him, he mused at the peak of sadness as he thought back on the funeral. A pedestrian bumped into him. A bus braked to a halt right on the crosswalk. A pair of butterflies seemed to spawn out of the blackness of the asphalt. Spring was everywhere. But all this because something inside him had recognized the diminutive silhouette coming straight at him in the distance. The man approached him circumspectly, now they were face-to-face, no way to sidestep him.

"Hello, Mr. Chancellor."

A dreary, gray gentleman, dressed like an office clerk from thirty years ago. Narrow, slumping shoulders. Folded under his arm, he was carrying an ugly camelhair coat.

"Hello," the chancellor replied, shaking hands and trying to understand, guessing, not realizing. Then—in the space of time necessary to associate a name with that face—he felt his stomach clench. Without quite knowing how, he saw her again as she emerged from the shower, wrapped a towel around her head, and then stretched out, belly down, on the bed in the hotel room. "Go on, get the lotion," Clara had said. I'm sixty-one years old. I have a wife. Two children. An ownership share in a number of local newspapers. I don't give a good goddamn anymore.

"We saw each other yesterday, at the funeral," said Engineer De Palo.

"Oh . . . " said the chancellor as he felt his legs go, closed his eyes to block out the sun, "oh . . . "

"You forgot this at the church. I came by to bring it to you."

He held up the overcoat.

"That's not mine," said the chancellor.

"What's not yours?"

"The overcoat. It's not mine. I didn't forget anything."

Touching her yesterday, in the coffin. Sometimes she just wanted me to give her a nice massage. If, after I spread the lotion on her legs, I tried slipping two fingers inside her, she got upset. So odd. Hard to figure out, every time. She'd appeared out of nowhere at the region of Puglia newspaper guild party. Christmas 2008. Paul Newman dead. Charlton Heston dead. She came, arm in arm with her husband. A dreary little man. Then the engineer had left. Who, looking at her there all on her own, hadn't felt at that point as if a light was radiating out of a box newly thrown open? But it was she who had approached him.

"You shouldn't have allowed that Sangirardi to insult my father in your newspaper," Clara had said, walking toward him with a glass in her hand.

"Forgive me if I insist, but I'm afraid you're mistaken," said Engineer De Palo.

They were still standing in the street. On the one side a line of shops, on the other the university building. When the dream ends, what you were prepared to lose suddenly becomes, once again, all that matters.

"We can talk about it in my office," said the chancellor.

Taking her to the Hotel Covo dei Saraceni in Positano. The Hassler Hotel in Rome. The time she made him drive all the way to Avellino. Or when she reserved a suite at the Sheraton, right there in Bari. They stayed in their suite for nearly two days, just a stone's throw from their everyday lives—Clara's husband, the chancellor's wife, the faculty conferences, the meetings of the shareholders of the publishing house EdiPuglia, all fatally within reach, and all shut out of their hotel room. There was something intolerably lovely about a body close to old age that had the good fortune to be gratified by a girl in the flower of her years. Something so unjust that the chancellor thought he could sense in her breath a puff of the divine. The way that Clara got annoyed when he tried to kiss her in the mouth. And the completely unexpected, deeply moving, inexplicable way that, five minutes later, he was in contact with her flesh (he had to do his best to keep from thinking he'd dreamed his own forearms motionless, opening her legs) and she, hoarse-voiced, thrilling with pleasure and baring her teeth in a smile.

"The Vandal King of the Gargano Coast," said Engineer De Palo in the office, grim-faced, "that's what they called Signor Salvemini in *Corriere del Sud* last week. It's the fourth article in six months. Enough to believe that it's not a campaign being waged by a single journalist. There was a different byline. It's not a pretty thing."

"I'm not the editor of *Corriere del Sud*," he said.

"It's owned by the EdiPuglia group."

"Along with everyone else who's involved."

"You could be considered the publisher."

"Oh, listen," she'd said, slipping into the informal voice after not even five minutes, shifting her glass from her right hand to her left, "the article was disgraceful. I felt ill all day. My father described as a criminal." Clara had smiled.

At the time, it was the tourist marina at Manfredonia that was at issue. The accusation was that he'd inflated the costs.

"You must think it's worse to feel bad for your father than

to charge the taxpayers for the Empire State Building and deliver a dinky little marina."

Did she want the journalist who wrote the piece to apologize? Did she want him fired outright? Anything, as long as he could see her laugh like that. Or did she prefer that, in addition to his wife, he be willing to betray a friend as well? One of his children?

"Listen," said Engineer De Palo, "the Porto Allegro complex is one of the biggest projects to have been built recently in this godforsaken part of the world. It's creating jobs. Thousands of tourists will flock here. These days, who else would invest even half of what Signor Salvemini is committing? You ought to build a monument to him. Instead you attack him. So I start to wonder what this is really about. Maybe there's the jealousy of some competitor at work here."

What could be nicer than to screw her at ten in the morning, with her looking at you at a certain point, letting you glimpse the possibility that this wasn't anything yet? "Renato, come here." What more do we really want, aside from a chance to take to bed a girl who could be our daughter? What else could she make us do, that girl? What primary image would she be capable of showing us? Beyond her body as it pants miraculously beneath ours, isn't there by chance some deeper and more primitive pleasure at play? Of course there's something else. "Renato . . . Knock down that wall. Open up that trapdoor."

"That poor girl died such a horrible death," said Engineer De Palo.

Now everything is clear, thought the chancellor, turning his eyes elsewhere.

"I'm not promising you anything," he said a quarter hour later, bidding his guest farewell at the office door, "and thanks again for bringing me the overcoat."

He couldn't stop talking about it. He told his coworkers about it. At dinner with friends. The night before, at a table in a restaurant not far from the newspaper. Look. He passed the smartphone around. This girl must have gotten herself into some kind of serious trouble, he said. What kind of trouble? asked one of his fellow diners. The waiters emerged from the kitchen bearing pizzas. Giuseppe Greco started to reply. Two texts from a fake number are nothing, said another. You ought to see what happens to public figures. People are lunatics. Giuseppe Greco picked up his glass of wine. He took a drink. "I didn't kill myself." "I'm still alive." Between the first and the second message, less than twenty-four hours had passed. Newspaper websites seethed with psychotic messages. Death threats among YouTube users. A price list for prostate massages, divided by city. Invitations to commit suicide, offhand insults that arose from narrow fissures of interest. To call it the unconscious, a century earlier, was even then a mistake, a way of forcing into a single linguistic canon diametrically opposing forces. From the asphalt. From the sewers. A force welled up from wherever it had been confined. One of his tablemates lifted a chunk of sausage to his mouth. Giuseppe Greco turned away. A car shot past with the music blasting.

Her girlfriends did their best to console her. Gioia, sitting among them on the sofa in the living room, went on singing her dead sister's praises. How pretty she had been. She reminded everyone of the unmistakable way she had of entering a room. A line removed from the undifferentiated acoustic cage that surrounds us—that was how you knew that Clara was just a few steps away. Gioia lifted her head toward the credenza: "The wedding," she said, "the wedding pictures." Her four friends twisted on the sofa, as if it were their duty to know where the photo album was. But they couldn't possibly know. So Gioia leapt to her feet. If she had told them that it was a habit of her sister's to levitate at every winter solstice, they'd have had to believe her.

She pulled the photo album out of one of the drawers. She went back and sat down. "Look how happy they were," she said, pointing at Alberto being hit by a cloud of rice.

At noon she texted her boyfriend.

She saw him arrive an hour later, as Engineer De Palo was leaving. She took him by both hands. She embraced him. She wept for some minutes on his chest, standing, under the veranda, in the hot light on the transparent windows. A disorderly, furious weeping. Then she said: "Come." They headed out into the garden. They strolled through the bushes, in the cool shade of the eucalyptus trees, by the stone fountain with green stripes where rivulets of water ran. They ventured past the gazebo and the swing, toward the hedges that transformed the garden into a vast stretch of shade. The porcelain-berry vine emanated its reddish force. They walked down the steps cut into the living rock. A small cockroach fled before she could crush it underfoot. It seemed to him that now Gioia's power had become boundless. The play of light through the leaves formed a large transparent fish. Then they heard a noise. They looked in the other direction. The taxi pulled away. The silhouette came through the gate, like a cart with the head of a man. His roller suitcase in one hand, a cage of some sort in the other.

"Your brother," he said.

It was Michele, and Gioia remained motionless. Michele was home. She forced herself to conceal the blush blooming beneath her skin, as if her reputation as a conscientious young woman prevented her from feeling disappointment at the injustice of a problem coming on the heels of the one before it.

A sliver of moon persisted in the early morning sky. The Chicken Man was hawking gym shoes. The Pig Man was handing out discount coupons for legs of prosciutto. The spotlights of the Mongolfiera shopping center swept through the alphabetized areas of the paid parking lot. On the opposite side, two plexiglass clouds described the paradox of a provisional universe governed by a firm hand. Pietro Giannelli, sheathed in his frog costume, was peeling flyers for the Toy Center from the stack. He was handing them out to the first customers of the day. Baby Control, with special sensors for under the child's bed. Healthy-DinDins, baby food that you steamed. Kiss the frog. The arriving customers disappeared, swallowed up by the stairs of the shopping center.

At ten-fifteen he decided that the time had come for a break. He stuck the flyers back into his fanny pack. He pulled his arm out of the sleeve. He reached one hand behind his neck. He hooked the zipper, slid it down. The frog's head split in half, and from between the two foam rubber hemispheres emerged Giannelli's overheated face. He took a deep breath. He hopped over to the vending machine. He slipped two coins into the slot. He bent over with some effort to pick up the Gatorade. At ten in the morning he was already bathed in sweat. He drank in big gulps. He hopped toward the payment booth in the parking lot. He passed sector H. Still hopping, he went down the ramp that led to an isolated row of garages with their metal gates pulled down. Here there was some shade. Peace and silence. Raising his eyes, he could see the rail line from a distance.

He leaned his back against the cement pillar. He stuck his hand into the fanny pack. He pulled out the pipe. He grabbed the aluminum foil. He tore off a section. He folded it over until he'd made it into a tiny hood. He tucked the aluminum foil into the spout of the pipe. He reached into the fanny pack for the baggie. He pulled out the DMT crystals. He put them on the aluminum hood and lit it. He took a drag. The garage's roller gates became an obsidian wall. There was a high frequency whistle. It expanded. The light regressed toward colors that the sun might have produced in the long Precambrian slumber, before life appeared on earth. The movement of the birds created what were to his eyes perfect polygons. Squares. Wonderful ocean-blue rectangles. Then the geometric concept underwent an evolution. Pietro Giannelli felt on his skin something analogous to a divine wind that began to caress him. An incorporeal tide. Between him and a snow-covered peak there was no longer any more distance than that which separated him from his own nose.

The whistle's intensity grew, then it vanished.

Pietro Giannelli opened his eyes again, stunned. The obsidian of the garage had turned back into steel. The patina that had covered the trees and the road—and the train, that was now rocketing past in front of him—was rapidly beginning to retreat. It was as if *some other* energy source were sucking down the effects of the dimethyltryptamine, like a bathtub draining. If he'd checked his watch, he'd have seen that not five minutes had passed since that first drag. But he didn't need a watch. He remembered that sensation.

They could build the industrial sheds of major agribusiness concerns on it, privacy fences for greenhouses and nurseries, thought Michele, in the carriage of the Eurostar, with his head against the glass of the window. He looked out at the countryside as it ran south with him. On his knees sat balanced the carrier inside which the cat had been riding quietly since the start of the trip. They could build cement plants. The wind turbines that he'd seen earlier. Human ingenuity was free to dream up the oddest pieces of architecture, whatever most convinced man that he was lifting the shadow off the land that had first engendered them. But the foundation of things (the damp soil beneath the wind turbines, the worm in the greenhouse, the white dust that kicked up everywhere) remained enclosed in its mystery. They were the woods they had always been. Mouse follows pied piper. Coach turns into pumpkin. Wolf eats little pig. Girl at the bottom of the well. Mirror mirror . . .

He pushed a finger through the mesh of the little cage. He felt the damp nose.

He petted the cat. A certain kind of sorrow doesn't cause tears. I could be bounded in a nutshell, he recited by heart. He showed his ticket to the conductor again. He got a Coca-Cola when they were around Molfetta.

T he young stray cat gathered itself, concealed amongst the ferns. It lunged forward and buried its face in the shopping bag. It fled with a slice of prosciutto in its teeth.

By the time the housekeeper waved her fist in the air, the cat had already darted into the bushes.

But the screams, the lunge of the beast, Engineer De Palo's Focus on the front driveway, were point, line, and surface in an abstract drawing compared to those who, turning their backs on them, were already facing the credenza in the front hall. Annamaria started up the stairs. She observed the scenes of war that familiarity had transformed into patches of color. The grief of the past few days had turned them back into the unsightly paintings that they'd purchased years ago, when auctions at resorts were all the rage. Cortina 1976. The auctioneer had lowered the gavel on the walnut sound block. Clara had just been born, she was moving her tiny hands in the white lace of the cradle as she and Vittorio sat in their dressing gowns, buttering their melba toast amid the moldings of the hotel suite overlooking the Tofane mountains. Those weren't the good old days, she thought, turning down the second-story hallway.

Annamaria went past the closed door of what had once been Michele's bedroom (now reduced to a never sufficiently dead storage room), went past Clara's bedroom, Ruggero's. Those had been the terrible days. She entered the master bedroom. She collapsed on the bed. She bent her head and ran the palm of her hand over her neck. Through the cracks in the shutters the heat wafted in like the crystals of a kaleidoscope diving into the water. The days full of hope had been the ones while she'd been expecting her first son. Soon after, Vittorio bought the house they were living in, and the energy he devoted to renovating it was already tucked away in her belly like a sun taking shape week by week.

Being pregnant with Ruggero was wonderful. Annamaria felt her belly stretch, her tummy was covered with small brown spots while the veins on her legs became visible. In the morning she'd throw the windows open in the apartment that Vittorio had rented and feel the warmth hit her face.

Men make women happy. And she, every time the baby gave a start (even amidst the waves of nausea in the first few weeks), received confirmation of how right she had been to marry Vittorio. A question of instinct. When she'd been in high school, stealing time from her books at a table in a café with her girlfriends, she'd seen plenty of young men who were capable of rescuing her from a future as a teacher. The son of the lawyer who was defending a former cabinet minister. The son of one commissioner or another. When one of these good-looking scions of important families stopped nearby, Annamaria caught a whiff of large landholdings and corpses. Those young men might have plenty of property but they lacked drive, and in order to get their hands on the former they'd have to ask permission. Annamaria had looked up from her martini and then she'd immediately glanced down again, but in the space between the one thing and the other, she'd already made up her mind. The lunatic who, after circling the block a few times without finding a place, had parked his Citroën DS on the sidewalk and run straight toward the Chamber of Commerce might have been one of those losers who were trying their luck only to fall back on a civil service position a year later, but he wasn't.

The first time that he sat down at the table with them, it seemed to her that he was thinking on several levels at once. Charcoal gray jacket and lovely safecracker's hands.

"This is the third day I've seen you sitting here at the bar. Since you're clearly not that interested in spending time with your books, I've come to study you from a little closer up. But if I'm interrupting something impo—"

"*Caro*, nothing could be more important here than these three empty glasses," one of the girls interrupted him with a laugh.

Vittorio bought a round of drinks. He smiled at them all, but especially at her. He returned the glance with which Annamaria had pierced him without his even noticing. At the same time, he darted his pupils from one side to the other in pursuit of the precious time that those exceedingly pleasant minutes were costing him. A young businessman with aspirations to a great fortune and beginnings in the gutter is obliged to cram fifty or so hours into the normal twenty-four. But he wasn't dull.

They wound up in bed, and she felt nothing. Between the sheets, she studied the apartment, trying to understand. A two-bedroom apartment, barely furnished. Empty boxes and invoices.

The second time, they had fun. The sweat glistening on their naked bodies would influence many of her dreams over the years that followed. That night, they went to a party. The birthday party of some mover and shaker in the food distribution sector. Annamaria saw Vittorio laugh and chat with the guests, he asked her to dance, he introduced her to men and other young women and old matrons whom she could barely remember the next time around. In every move that Vittorio made, there was affability and courtesy, but—she noticed—every facial muscle was employed in pursuit of profit.

The fourth or perhaps the fifth time that they made love,

Annamaria felt a surge of emotion and a depth that she'd never imagined descend on top of her. As soon as they were done, she smoked a cigarette over it. Vittorio, sitting on the edge of the bed, tossed back half a bottle of Sangemini mineral water in a single gulp. Then he got to his feet and, in his underwear, in the middle of the room, he began to pour out his soul, leaving her thunderstruck. He was worried. Even worse, he was terrified at the idea of financial ruin. He had a great many construction projects underway at the same time, he said. But he'd also run up debts, a complicated network of financing that a simple hitch would unravel. "A rise in the cost of steel. All it would take is for the United States to be successful in their trade negotiations. All payments with foreign suppliers are in dollars." He shook his head. He kept repeating the same expression: "You don't understand." In this premature imitation of a married couple, all that was missing was for him to put his hands in his hair.

"Hey, come on, bring me another cigarette." Annamaria called him back to bed in a firm voice. Men were so stupid, even when they were also intelligent. It was clear that he wasn't going to be ruined. It was so spectacularly obvious that he was going to make a pile of money! Only he just didn't know it yet. Annamaria had seen him at work. If two or three deals went south, there were other tables at which he could bring his talents to bear. What could stop a man like him? The only prayer that Annamaria caught herself whispering was for the Almighty to protect him from some cruel disease.

By the time, not even a year later, she found out she was pregnant, Vittorio's wealth had doubled. The airy beachfront apartment that he rented after their wedding was below their means. The skin on Annamaria's abdomen was tautening. The situation was so redolent with promise (Vittorio was flying to Spain, he was engaged in negotiations for a spa in some far-flung corner of the Côte d'Azur) that she felt obliged to spend as much money as they were bound to have a few months later if luck stayed on their side.

When the time came to move to the villa, they could already have afforded an even larger one.

And the way they laughed when Vittorio took her out to dinner? she recalled without moving from the bed, in the half-light, her fingers dug into the sheets, suffering as she sat in the muggy heat that stagnated in the bedroom. The insane dresses that he bought when, just a few months after giving birth, she was already back in shape? The jewelry, she thought, closed in the gloom of her mind. The Tiffany bracelet, the waterfall necklace that filled her with light. The vacations in New York. The cheap bottle of nail polish that might, by way of a macabre prank, pop out of his suitcase after a work trip. Phone numbers on a piece of paper crumpled up in his trouser pocket. All mixed together.

Annamaria's feelings weren't too badly hurt when Vittorio cheated on her, which, for that matter, he did rarely. Great men, in order to keep from turning into monsters, ought to preserve a childish part of themselves. Vittorio might even, every so often, so to speak betray her, the important thing was that *he* not suspect a thing when he returned home. Annamaria found herself eliminating the asterisk of a fine strand of blonde hair from the collar of a jacket she was handing her husband. She felt pity for the nameless young slut, and for Vittorio she felt the blame she had reserved for Ruggero when it still occasionally happened that he wet the bed.

Then she'd go take a sauna, or spend hours in the sweet-smelling shell of a beauty spa.

There's always the chance that within the loveliest bud lurks a filthy worm. But that a nice juicy worm might thrive within the chemistry of Chanel perfume she never would have imagined. When she became pregnant with Clara, the gestation proved, from the beginning, rather unpleasant. The dizzy spells would catch her by surprise. The waves of nausea were more intense than they had been with Ruggero. It seemed to her that a cork had popped, sending a whiff of sewer rot straight into the center of her brain. In the afternoon, alone in the kitchen, she'd burst into tears for no good reason.

At night, Vittorio would tenderly take her face in his hands. "What is it, what's going on?" She felt dispossessed, run through by other people's dreams.

Was it conceivable that a fetus in its twentieth week was doing this? Annamaria knew that at the end of the first trimester they develop a sense of smell, in the second trimester they swim with confidence in the amniotic fluid, start kicking in response to otherwise unspecified stimuli. But this little girl was destroying her. She seemed to inhabit her flesh with a natural hostility. Her presence is malevolent, Annamaria was surprised to catch herself thinking. She had the impression that to the fetus's intelligence (an archaic box of wonders that become nightmares on contact with the outside world) she was simply a nude shell to exploit without pity. However absurd the thought might be, it was as if Clara were the daughter not of another father, but a different mother, a remote female principle that—knowing, indeed, approving of the baby girl's ferocity—had placed her in a womb toward which she need show no clemency.

Acting weak is fine. But beware of becoming weak. Especially if you're married to a successful man who's capable of seeing in other people's problems the basis for his own. It wasn't the chromatic variety of the dead hairs found on an overcoat. On the contrary, the chestnut hue of a very specific head of hair (which she learned to recognize as wavy, glossy, vaguely tumid) began to be the same every time.

Annamaria realized before the evidence brought her confirmation. At home, Vittorio was strangely kind to her. Then, around the thirty-fourth week, he took her to the gynecologist for a vaginal swab test.

They were both in the waiting room. At a certain point Vittorio leapt to his feet. He walked briskly toward the reception desk. Watching him from behind, it seemed to Annamaria that he was saying one thing with the intention of saying something else. He came back to her with a studiously (oh, disgustingly!) vexed expression, denounced the "absurdity" of the fact that in a doctor's officer where a sonogram cost an arm and a leg they didn't have a phone that patients could use. He needed to make a call for work. "I'm sorry, it's pretty urgent. I'll be back in fifteen minutes." Annamaria sat there, waiting for him to get back, tapping the index finger of one beringed hand on the other. The minutes crept by. Three quarters of an hour later, even the last patient before her (a young woman of color accompanied by her boyfriend) was summoned for her examination. Annamaria leaned forward in her chair, both arms wrapped around her abdomen. She felt the steel cable, with which Vittorio had always made her feel safe, snap. And so, when her turn came and Vittorio still had not reappeared, Annamaria got to her feet and went into the office in a slightly disorientated state.

The door closed behind her. The gynecologist, a woman, seemed to be enveloped in a disk of light. She said something in an offhand manner about streptococcus in pregnant women, but by that point Annamaria was observing the scene from somewhere outside of herself. She watched herself take off her shoes, skirt, and panties and then place herself, legs wide, on the gynecological examination chair. The doctor put on her gloves. She placed an exploratory finger in her vulva. She took the speculum. She lubricated it with gel. She inserted the speculum in her vagina. She slowly began to widen it until the pink body of the cervix became visible. Annamaria felt the burning sensation between her legs and returned to her senses. She felt the first and then the second cotton swab being inserted all the way to the cervix (the doctor unhurriedly placed the sample in the test tube, placed the test tube in the refrigerator, and only then did she tear the cellophane containing the second packet and extract another swab to insert inside her), wondered to herself where Vittorio had just seen that slut while the thin thread of a tear streaked the space between her cheekbone and her ear. Maybe they'd met downstairs. They'd chatted in a bar, or perhaps they'd just hurried to a hotel. She assumed (as in fact happened) that she'd find Vittorio in the waiting room when the examination was over, and that that same evening, when she would make the first jealous scene of their relationship, he would deny it with the force of a confession, attacking her like a little boy caught red-handed torturing a dog.

Thirty-six years later, she got to her feet, breathing softly. Now, after her daughter's funeral, with the circle closed (not entirely, she thought with anger, with contrition), she walked slowly toward the window. She peeked into the narrow dotted openings in the heavy, half-shut wooden roller blinds. The garden with its flowers. To the left, beyond the small vegetable garden, the space in front of the kitchen where the veranda had been built.

A few weeks before giving birth she felt as heavy as an astronaut, exhausted like a sack that had been kicked repeatedly. She couldn't sleep except for brief stretches that made her reopen her eyes more agitated than before. Her back hurt, from her nipples issued a yellowish liquid of whose normality even the inane illustrated textbooks she consulted reassured her. It was six in the evening in early spring. Clara would soon be born. Color: white. Dominant planet: the moon. She'd read that too. Ruggero was over at the house of a friend from school. She was alone in the kitchen, making a cup of chamomile tea. Vittorio was in Spain. Salvemini Construction had won a contract to widen a stretch of the highway between Cadiz and Seville. He'd be back before the weekend. Annamaria removed the chamomile teabag from the cup. She twisted the string around it and tossed it into the trash. Lately, she'd come to be ashamed of the thoughts she'd had about her little girl. All the more so because in the past few weeks Clara had been as good as gold in her belly. She kicked very little, if at all. During the last sonogram, she'd remained so still that for a moment the gynecologist had furrowed her brow in an odd manner.

She took the steaming mug in her hands. She went to set it down on the little table on the veranda. She went back into the kitchen, got the melba toast and a jar of jam. She went back out onto the veranda and practically collapsed onto the wooden chaise longue. She felt exhausted. She gnawed on a couple slices of melba toast. She stretched her legs out in front of her. Through the french doors came the wind of the summer to be. On this side of the house, the garden was turning wild. The light of sunset made the myrtle and the tall grass quiver, transforming the tangles of the bay laurel branches into a vortex of light and shadow that came toward her as her eyelids grew heavy. Annamaria reopened her eyes. It was already evening. She saw the darkness between the branches. How long have I slept? She noticed that her hand was itching. The weightless brownish body took to the air. Annamaria looked around her in fright. She started to get up, felt the weight of her big belly. Butterflies. The veranda was full of them. A whirling of furry-winged moths, large insects with brush-like antennae, coats like clouds of dust fluttered from wall to wall, stopped on the little table, or else grazed in groups in the jam, while other animals, like long winged ants, continued to come in through the french doors. Annamaria felt the nausea of the first few weeks come back. She thought that her body was, in that way, translating something that was otherwise unnamable. Before emerging from her drowsiness, and realizing that nothing at all was happening, she once again feared that this was all the little girl's handiwork.

How horrible, she thought in amazement, continuing to observe the butterflies all around her.

Then she recovered. She got up from the chaise longue, and went into the bathroom in search of an insecticide.

From the window she watched Gioia walking in the garden with her boyfriend until they disappeared behind the porcelain-berry hedges. She sat motionless in front of the half-closed shutter. It was a terrible thing that Clara had killed herself. Terrible. At sixty-six, Annamaria had a harder, more elementary vision of things. All she could do was think about it. And yet she knew that was pointless. She could barely touch the reasons that could have pushed her first daughter to do such a thing. A wall that was impossible to climb, after all she and Clara had misunderstood each other over the years. Voices that didn't call, doors that didn't open. But it had been the ground underneath their feet that had grown soft. The Porto Allegro deal. This time, Vittorio might not come out on top. It wasn't so much his age. Her husband was still a strong man. The effects were like those of a massive low-pressure system: it seemed to Annamaria more as if their slice of the world had entered into some cone of shadow inside which the old laws simply no longer applied.

As a newborn, did Clara really exert a malevolent influence?

How absurd! Only the stupid thirty-year-old she had been, the woman terrorized by the idea that her husband might leave her, could have believed it, not the woman she was now.

Had it been painful then?

It had been ravaging, humiliating, terrifying. The birth of the baby girl had forced her on bed rest for two months. A childlike state that Vittorio and Micaela had feasted on unreservedly. Because now she even knew that slut's name, she thought to herself with undiminished hatred as she gazed down into the garden. Gioia and her boyfriend were turning their attention toward the front drive. Annamaria watched as the taxi drove off. It had to happen, she mused. The blameless fruit of stupidity and human frailty was coming once again to scuff the soles of his shoes on the doormat of her home. She knew the name, she recalled, and also the age of her hatred's target, she knew that she worked in a boutique on Via Calefati. She had no trouble guessing that Vittorio had met her on account of the renewal of the lease (she could have pinpointed the exact day on which her husband, due to Engineer Ranieri's being indisposed, had been obliged to take care of the matter in person), and this was because the building on the ground floor of which the boutique was located—"Satú" was the name on the sign out front, whatever that idiotic name was supposed to mean—belonged to him, to Vittorio. That is, to them, which only shook the salt of insult onto the injury.

Annamaria had been forced into the humiliating position of gathering information from her girlfriends. Phone calls from whose heights she had formerly exercised queenly benevolence suddenly became mortifying exhibitions. "Are you sure you really want to know?" Investigative, pleading phone calls. "All right, then I'll tell you." Annamaria understood that, with every detail extorted, the informant of the day would consider public what had until that moment reeked of gossip. In this way, she undermined herself socially at the very moment in which she extracted from the voice on the phone something that gave her at first relief and, seconds later, redoubled agony.

But once she hung up, she felt as if she were being surrounded by the warm exhalations of her enemy, and this was a good thing. To know that Micaela was younger than her (twenty-four years to her thirty as a mother of two), to know she was pretty (at her own request, Annamaria had been provided with the truth), to know she was capable and well dressed, to see not only the way in which she was manipulating Vittorio but also the fact that he glimpsed in this young woman a determination, perhaps even a value that his wife did not possess, turned her into the perfect enemy. Oh, not the kind of enemy that men have, one they might fight to the last blood, reassured by an idea of circumstance. Annamaria knew that Micaela had been promised to her long before she ever laid eyes on Vittorio, long before even Annamaria, and therefore Micaela herself, had been born.

On certain days, the hatred reached such heights of intensity that Vittorio himself became a detail. Those were the only moments in which, strangely, Annamaria had the feeling that she was entering into contact with the little girl. As if Clara lived in a dimension that Annamaria could reach only at the price of excruciating pain.

The little girl, she remembered, saddened, moved as she stepped away from the window and returned to the dim half-light of the bedroom. This is the moment, as she calculated Michele's route from the driveway to the front door. Now I'll turn away and he'll ring the doorbell. Product of chance. Blameless bequest of idiocy.

The baby girl, newborn, cried. As good as she had been right up until birth, now she wouldn't give her a moment of peace. Ten days after her return home from the hospital, Annamaria found herself in an absolutely unexpected situation. She felt tired, benumbed. Her bones ached. Because the tissues had slackened, she suffered from urinary incontinence. And she was alone, abandoned in the villa's enormous master bedroom, with only the housekeeper, and occasionally her mother, when she came to help her, for company. Vittorio would phone to tell her he'd be home late because of vaguely described business meetings. On Sundays, he'd vanish for the whole day.

If the situation had been different, Annamaria would have put her in her place. She'd have gone straight to see Micaela in her piece-of-shit store. She'd have confronted her, kicking phantoms that would, touched by the pointy tip of a Pollini shoe, usually have turned into poor, frightened girls. But she couldn't. She was the one who was frightened now. Stuck in bed, incontinent, held hostage by a baby girl just a few weeks old. Micaela's toned body—she worried as she looked at herself in the mirror—would have incinerated Annamaria just walking by her.

And then there was the night that she feared she was going insane.

She was watching Clara by herself. The week before she'd found a plane ticket in Vittorio's trouser pocket. "The inauguration of the Tour Areva, the tallest skyscraper in France. Valéry Giscard d'Estaing and everyone else who matters in the construction business in Europe will be in attendance," he'd explained. Ruggero was sleeping downstairs. He'd started middle school by articulating with austere logic the system thanks to which he could escape his baby sister's wails. Clara was crying tonight, too. Annamaria had tried to rock her. To hold her in her arms. To lay her in the cradle above which hung the bee mobile. The baby girl fell silent for two minutes. Then she'd start howling again. Annamaria picked her up from the crib, and went to sit down with her in front of the television at the foot of the bed. She turned it on. Clara was wailing. She was sobbing as if she'd been separated from someone fundamental or, better yet, as if she were awaiting some gigantic event set in the future that only she could perceive. Then Annamaria saw him. On the screen, just a glimpse, during the evening news. The coronation of Juan Carlos in the church of

San Jerónimo el Real in Madrid. At the far end of the nave, the new king was shaking hands with foreign leaders. Giovanni Leone of Italy. German Chancellor Helmut Schmidt. Then came the pear-shaped face of Valéry Giscard d'Estaing, the president of France. Annamaria felt the pee run between her legs, watched it stain the sheets and drip onto the hardwood floor. Deep down she'd known it. But until then she'd been able to lock Vittorio's lie away in a deep freeze. It wasn't the fact of imagining him with Micaela per se, but rather the fact that they were together in Paris, whatever the evocative power that the name of this city continues to exert over certain women. Now the two of them were strolling through the Jardin du Luxembourg. Hand in hand before the Medici Fountain, riding over in a taxi to the boutiques on the Champs-Élysées. Imagining the two of them like that was worse than actually catching them between the sheets of her bed at home. Tears streamed down her face. They were in Paris and she was stuck here on account of the baby girl.

Annamaria hissed: "Shut up." Clara did not obey. She was crying defiantly, irresponsibly. There was nothing in her that could be identified as loving kindness toward a mother who had just pissed herself in despair. At that point, Annamaria shot to her feet. The baby was surprised. Annamaria smiled. "Would you shut up, for fuck's sake?" The little girl gave her an irritated glare and Annamaria hurled her onto the bed. Clara burst into tears. Annamaria picked her up with both hands. She lifted her in the air, straight in front of her. Then, with all the might she had in her arms, she hurled her down once more. The baby girl bounced on the mattress and landed on her back. She opened her eyes wide, as if she couldn't catch her breath. She turned purple, then almost black. Then, thank heavens, she burst out crying. Annamaria, through her own tears, took her back into her arms, and started saying Forgive me Forgive me Forgive me, wondering why, in that grand villa where there was no lack of plenty, there wasn't a bottle of sleeping pills so she could put an end to it all, the way they do in the movies.

And then it was even worse, she thought as she waited for the doorbell to ring, and the doorbell in fact did ring. Annamaria crossed the bedroom, walked out through the door, and headed for the stairs. *It was worse*, she was forced to remember.

The period of postpartum recovery came to an end. She got back in shape. The baby girl kept on crying, but Annamaria gradually regained control of the situation. Now she knew what was happening. Vittorio was getting ready to leave her for Micaela. He was on the verge of doing it. He wasn't doing it now, but he'd do it eventually. His children were the one thing stopping him, the fake sense of guilt typical of southern Italians, which is a convenience disguised as a disadvantage. As a result, Vittorio was spending less and less time at home. Gone for two days, or a week. Fights broke out all the time. In the middle of one of these, one Saturday at lunch, in Ruggero's presence, Vittorio unexpectedly burst into tears.

Standing at the head of table, his hair tousled and unkempt. A wealthy businessman behaving like a little boy.

"But you don't understand," he bawled, "I love her!"

Ruggero sat there petrified (it was the following week that his academic performance began its dizzying climb). Annamaria was disgusted. That girl had pushed Vittorio into the absurdity of a declaration that the legitimate Signora Salvemini would have rejected had it regarded her, because it would have meant that her husband had turned into an idiot. It meant that he had become a weakling, as mediocre as the rest of them.

More months passed. More still, and then: Micaela was pregnant. The final blow, the blow that had been expected. Clara was two years old. Annamaria figured it out from

Vittorio's irritability. Confirmation came from the usual rumors that came to her via her girlfriends who no longer found it amusing to fire at heights where it was by now impossible to think of her. It's the end, Annamaria told herself coldly at the time. Vittorio was going to ask for a divorce. Annamaria would be forced into a legal battle she knew nothing about. At night, leaving Clara with a babysitter, she'd go out and spend time with new girlfriends she'd have been ashamed to be seen with just a couple of years earlier. Cheap pizzerias. Absurd Tupperware parties. Slim hopes. One chance out of a thousand. That's what she saw in the coffee grounds that she found herself reading when Micaela's pregnancy was in its eighth month.

And then, like a drumstick hitting the taut skin of a snare drum, it happened, she remembered as she walked downstairs, feeling rejuvenated at the thought of the miracle—that time is over, she thought, it happens only once in a lifetime, she told herself as she headed for the front door, ready to greet Michele, perhaps even to hug him, the guiltless idiot it was her lot to love like a son, she had to love him and love him she did, I love him, she thought.

That night Vittorio was at home. By now he only came to get a change of underwear. The phone rang before dinner. He answered. He stiffened. After a couple of minutes, he started talking again. Annamaria heard the tremor in his voice. She drew closer to look at him. Pale as a corpse. Vittorio ended the call. He grabbed his overcoat. He strode quickly toward the front entrance. He disappeared out the door. Annamaria felt a thrill of pleasure race through her, from head to toe. She didn't dare to think of it, it was such a remote possibility. It was only out of superstitious dread that she refrained from praying on her knees in her bedroom when, three hours later, and then long after midnight, she still hadn't heard a thing from him. What made her think that that's what it could be? Against what ferocious desire would she have to battle to keep from undermining the loom of fate if this, ridiculously, was about to unfold per the plot of a bodice-ripper? In 1978, in Italy, one woman out of every ten thousand died in childbirth. Absurd! Magnificent! She needed to calm down. She smoked a cigarette. She turned on the radio in the living room. She turned it off. She tried leafing through a magazine. At a certain point— by this point it was three in the morning—she heard the sound of crying from the bedroom. She went to get Clara. She lifted her to her shoulder without even feeling the weight. She put her on her shoulders, and she took her around the house, dancing. If the little girl went on crying, Annamaria didn't notice.

At a quarter to six, she heard the key turn in the front door lock. The lights of dawn were illuminating the garden, spreading through the house in such a way that from the far end of the living room it was possible to see the other side. Annamaria lay Clara gently on the sofa. She stayed still, waiting. She saw Vittorio. Her husband was angled away from her as he entered the room, his back hunched as if protecting something. Then he turned toward her and she knew that the woman was dead. But what gave her confirmation was something that, stupidly, had never occurred to Annamaria. Wrapped in a towel, a newborn baby was in Vittorio's arms. Then the doctor came in, too. Annamaria realized that something in the air had changed, as if the universe had chosen to emphasize the scene by changing the background noise. But the universe had nothing to do with it. It was Clara. Now she had finally stopped crying. Motionless on the sofa, she was staring at the newborn baby, wide-eyed.

So now I'm going to have to hug him, she thought, thirty-three years later, reaching her hand out to the door handle, not sparing herself the absurd consideration of how unjust it was that the half-brother should outlive his sister. She opened the door and saw him. It had been a couple of years since Michele had last come home. He looked a little beaten down, unshaven, black pants and a light-blue shirt, from which the tip of his sternum jutted. He was carrying something in his right hand, a pet carrier inside which Annamaria glimpsed the cat. Before Annamaria had time to do anything, Michele reached out his left hand. He shook her hand vigorously, as if they were work colleagues from at a conference in some exotic locale.

"Ciao, Annamaria."

His teeth opened in a smile that scared her.

Michele walked past, without taking his hand off his pet carrier. He introduced himself into the villa as if it were his home, even though it hadn't been for twenty years now. Annamaria heard him climb the stairs. The idea that he could be heading toward his old bedroom sent shivers down her back.

"Home at last!" she heard him shout from the stairwell.

PART TWO

*I went mad, with long intervals
of horrible mental sanity*

He climbed the steps, carrying his luggage. He walked into the large storage room that had been his bedroom. He felt the weight in the pet carrier slip off balance. The cat's ear twitched through the cracks. Michele let go of the rolling suitcase, delicately set the pet carrier down on the terrazzo floor. He went to close the door. As he did so, he wondered whether the cat would feel she had been abandoned. And in fact the cat meowed. He bent back over the plastic pet carrier, undid the fasteners.

The room smelled closed off and stale. During his trips back to Bari he had always avoided going upstairs. Caution mistaken for arrogance. The cat slipped out of the carrier. She sniffed the air of an unknown world. The last time I slept here I couldn't shut my eyes without the nightmares attacking. The cat crept forward until she reached the dresser. She swiveled her ears. To Michele, it seemed as if she were measuring the forces capable of destabilizing her. He looked at the sofa where all sorts of things were heaped. Faded trousers, evening gowns that no one would ever wear again. On a heap of old sweaters he recognized the owl with the eyeglasses. Berruti Optics. Printed on the volleyball team jersey. The cat wriggled under the armoire, vanishing fearfully into the darkness.

That was when Michele felt the blow. Back again in the house where he'd grown up, the Rationalist-designed villa that he'd learned to despise before that which was in it grew capable of destroying him, he was torn apart by the idea of his sister Clara's death, horrible, impossible to accept because, once the central load-bearing beam was gone, the rest of the building ought to have already collapsed into dust and instead there he still stood, and that is how he registered the shock that undercut the false idea of chronological succession upon which we organize our life and our days. The illusion of that bridge dissolved as it had when he was a child, and it seemed to him to have thrown open the field of vision. Not unlike a presentiment, he sensed above him his father's face (and in fact, a few hours later, Vittorio emerged slowly through the front door, advancing as if retreating so that Michele would come towards him, son leaning forward and father offended, as if his absence at the funeral could actually be blamed on Michele; he sensed him arriving in that manner, and so it happened), he sensed the awkward reluctance of his sister Gioia (the minute he stepped out of the storage room he found her in front of him. She threw her arms around him with abandon, a dramatic entrance she must have rehearsed. Undecided as to whether she ought to knock on the door while he was unpacking his bags, on edge at the threshold, retreating into the hallway. Him, in my home. She touched his cheek. She said: "Let's go downstairs." She walked ahead, showing him the way, as if he were some first-time guest. In the living room she introduced him to her boyfriend. The young man extended his hand; he seemed uneasy. That, too, was in the previous sensation, when he'd imagined Gioia in search of a system for making him feel at home. In the hand that strokes me, the harrow that draws a boundary), and Michele then sensed a more complicated distaste, something he broke down as he ran the zipper on the suitcase, savoring the sensation, finding it identical at dinner (the cold roast on the tray, the old overhead lamp, and the hand-embroidered tablecloth aside, there was the same impatience in the way that Ruggero got up from his seat, made a phone call, and came back looking at everyone as if eating without having to worry about anything else were a privilege they could enjoy thanks to him—the family reunited, thought Michele in the storage room, and the family that evening did in fact reunite).

As they were eating, Ruggero mentioned Engineer Ranieri. He told Vittorio that they had gone together to visit the head of the orthopedics ward at the general hospital. Michele swallowed. He hadn't seen the engineer in years. Ruggero went on talking. It seemed to Michele that he was bearing down on everything he said, impressing it onto a sheet of carbon paper to make sure the words came out identical to those he would have uttered if Michele hadn't been there. As if I had come here to interrupt something. The sensation was so intense in the storage room—and so faithful, when Michele sat down at the table—that now he could hardly tell whether he was still imagining it.

Gioia askied: "Would you pass me the water?"

Ruggero lifted the pitcher. Vittorio announced that the meat was tough. The Bari health care service now had the longest waiting lists in southern Italy, which is to say in Europe. That from Ruggero. From under the tablecloth, Gioia typed something on her iPhone. Annamaria got up from the table. She returned carrying the pan with the asparagus. Gioia spoke to her mother about a subscription that needed to be renewed. Swimming lessons. Annamaria hardened. She lifted the asparagus to her mouth. She chewed rapidly, still and silent. Gioia dropped her eyes. Ruggero, too, stopped talking. Annamaria's gaze grew drier and drier, suggesting to everyone how each grimace merely corresponded to the mere physical effort that had generated it. Clara's death had broken the first line of fencing and now a new one was being built in its place. Michele clenched the knife in his fist. He'd gladly have driven it into any of their ribs. Ruggero gestured. Annamaria passed him the bottle of olive oil. He dribbled it over his asparagus. Without a word, Vittorio speared another slice of pork. Gioia started checking something else on her iPhone. Vittorio coughed. Ruggero stifled a cough. Michele let go of the knife. The cat was still upstairs. He imagined her coming out of her hiding place, getting acquainted with her new surroundings. Leaping onto the sofa. From the sofa to the mirrored vanity and from there to the floor so that the old shapes could come back to life. And there, rematerializing after all these years, the night stand. The bed on which Clara would sit on Sunday afternoons. These are Alioth and Mizar, he'd told her, pressing the half-smoked cigarette onto the star globe. Annamaria rose from the table. She came back with the fruit cocktail and served out the portions. Ruggero was eating, head low. Vittorio said: "Tomorrow will be a complicated day." Michele opened his eyes wide. His palm was soft and damp. Gioia had just grabbed his hand under the table and now she was holding it tight. The thief begs his victim to participate in the theft. But there is nothing in nature that truly needs to be destroyed, he thought, not even this small infamous act. Time will pass, and other words, other actions will overlay these ones, no more making them vanish than a fresh coat of paint can eliminate an obscene drawing before yet another rainstorm brings it all back into the light. Every insult avenged. Michele steeled himself. He understood that in just an hour, he'd ask Annamaria if he could sleep in the storage room, instead of the guest bedroom. I'll tell her to have a bed put in my old room.

So he returned the grip under the table. Gioia smiled, deceived by his fakery. He swallowed. He saw in advance the uneasiness on his relatives' faces, then he did what was bound to provoke awkwardness. He coughed. Gripping Gioia's hand still tighter, he looked up and asked: "What is this, a morgue?"

Stretched out in bed. One arm propped behind his neck, the other stretched out in the direction of the armoire.

Jump, don't be afraid.

In the open window, two poplar trees swayed where he once would have seen an industrial shed behind a row of white houses. Twenty years ago, when the trees were newly planted. The cat peered out from the top of the armoire. She leapt into the void and landed on the mattress. Michele smiled. Out of the scent of jasmine he'd extracted a hint of lead wrapped in a whiff of hairspray and Styrofoam. Beauty parlor, appliance store. The smell of the city wafted all the way out here.

He'd been back home for three days. Sadness acted on him like a river on rock. Then it was he who became water. Down below, on the ground floor, his father's wife was chatting on the phone. The cat was sinking its claws into the carpet after eluding an attempted tackle. Annamaria was talking, and the timbre of her voice became that of a woman still young. The red plastic table. The old Grundig with the luminous dials. Denim shirt and shorts that left her bronzed legs bare.

"Half crazy. Luckily I never had to meet her. Though I would have paid good money for a picture of her."

She lets the phone line wrap itself around her wrist. A body that two pregnancies haven't robbed of appeal. Michele comes down the stairs. He's four years old. A rag-doll wolf clutched in his hand.

"He was in a mixed-up phase, I just had the level head to wait it out. I wouldn't be able to tough it out another time."

Annamaria does a half pirouette. She frees her wrist from the phone cord. She drops some ice into her grapefruit juice and shakes the glass. Michele watches her as he walks from the living room to the sofa. He hurls the wolf into the cushions and throws himself after it. He keeps eavesdropping. She says that certain women are worse than sharks. Attracted by the smell of money. She says that the children shouldn't inherit the sins of the mothers. She pauses. "I'm honestly doing my best."

Michele feels a film of cold sweat settle over his back. He

understands that Annamaria isn't talking about Clara or Ruggero. He pricks up his ears, convinced he's caught her out. It doesn't occur to him that the woman might actually be raising her voice to make sure he can hear, too. *What is it that's so terrible about me of all people?*

"A misfortune."

And so in the end Annamaria tells that story, too. She's clearly talking to someone who hasn't kept up on the events of recent years. She utters the word "deceased." She says that the woman was leading a wild life. That's why she died bringing the child into the world. Reckless. Maybe taking drugs, who knows. Annamaria thanks her lucky stars. As she does she hits a false note, identical and contrary to the one Michele is convinced he's detected in the vowels of "misfortune." "Luckily, the child survived," she says.

Michele lies there with his head among the pillows. He's stunned. He thinks about Ruggero and Clara. He intuits that he ought to play with them, that every once in a while they ought to roughhouse, the way siblings do around the world. But those two keep their fighting to themselves. "You damned idiot!" Ruggero had shouted just the other day, slamming his fist down onto the table. Michele would give anything to be included in these fights, but that desire is just a protective shell to keep from now having to touch the other end of the problem. Annamaria. Michele calls her "Annamaria": while Ruggero and Clara have always called her "Mamma." He'd never thought about it. *But if I call her "Annamaria," that means I knew. At a certain point they must have told me. How can it be that I'm only realizing it now?*

(No one had ever explained anything to me, he'll realize years later. *If they had, I would remember it.* As long as he's a child he's incapable of understanding, the problem doesn't really exist, they must have thought, and when things finally come into focus for him, it will be as if it had always been that way. Ruggero and Clara, for their part, will always feel the presence of a boundary beyond which lie dangerous territories, unknown sorrow and shame. They won't cross that boundary).

Annamaria hangs up the phone. She's not my mother, the child thinks again, perplexed. If he tries to imagine her now, the woman who brought him into the world, he can't associate her with anything human. Not a mouth, not a pair of hands. Annamaria emerges from the kitchen. Her footsteps move away. Impossible that she didn't see me. A malevolent black shape remains carved into the air for a number of seconds, and then vanishes. It reappears inside him. Michele feels his head fill with voices, sounds. They say strange things, phrases so atrocious that he could never bring himself to repeat them. Michele is disconcerted. What ought to glitter in a steady and constant stream of light begins to slide downward. Something is getting turned around in the wrong direction.

On a sunny day a few years later I disappeared from circulation, he thought, looking at the cat on the other end of the bed.

Second grade. After the bell rings, all he has to do is wait for Engineer Ranieri outside the teachers' lounge. When the engineer doesn't come, all Michele needs to do is walk through the courtyard and climb onto the school bus. Instead, that day Michele vanishes. When Vittorio phones the school, they tell him that his son never boarded the bus. Engineer De Palo and Engineer Ranieri are unleashed to pound the pavement inch by inch, searching the city in their station wagon.

Michele reappears at four in the afternoon. His father is at work. Annamaria walks from one room to the next in the villa. She's carrying two gym weights. After her last pregnancy, she's getting back in shape. Gioia is upstairs with the nanny. Annamaria puffs, lifting the weights toward her one after the other. At a certain point she freezes. Something there, outside the screen. Motionless among the calla lilies, emerging from the still-warm autumn light. And he's wet. Completely drenched, right in the middle of the garden, as if someone had dumped buckets and buckets of water over him. Annamaria drops her weights. She goes over to the french doors. She opens the screen. To her surprise, she catches herself calling him as she would some wild animal.

"Michele," she rubs her thumb between the tips of her middle and index finger.

The child turns around. He walks toward her.

"What happened to you?"

"I don't know."

He really doesn't know. He can remember neither exactly what drove him not to board the school bus, nor why he is in that state. He *did* know just a little while ago, but a sudden surge of thoughts must have pushed the information somewhere beyond reach.

That night his father scolds him.

"You frightened us," he says. "Annamaria spent the whole afternoon trying to find out where you were."

That's not true, thinks the boy, avoiding his eyes.

One afternoon Michele forgets to convey the message that his father's father has been rushed to the hospital for appendicitis. (He picked up the phone before dinner, before anyone else was home.) Another time, he found an address book full of phone numbers in his hands, while Vittorio searched the house for hours, investigating every nook and cranny. He'd be likely to walk away from his own birthday party, if they ever held one for him. It's clear that the child has a complicated relationship with reality, to say the least.

Certain school assignments are there to prove it. Classroom dictations. When he turns the paper in to the teacher, it's impossible to say what he's done. He started writing only after the voice had already been pronouncing the words for some time. Or the opposite: he starts out just fine but breaks off halfway through. Certain times from his papers there emerges a single phrase transcribed faultlessly, something that in any other situation might perhaps have a bizarre oracular value, but which is incomprehensible if the purpose is to evaluate a second grader.

The fact is that his teacher's voice reaches him from another world. A ghost that you can hear before it returns to its own dimension. Then, quiet falls again, Michele shouts "I'm coming!" to the other voice that calls him from downstairs. Certain afternoons, the sky begins to turn to liquid. High above, holes open, larger and larger, so he can look through them, seeing the rows of desks and, further back, the teacher's desk. There it's always morning, while here the sun is close to setting. The sky closes up again, the teacher disappears. Michele finds himself back by the open window. His mother has called him for his snack (a voice so sweet and full of life that it seems brand new to him every time he hears it). As he closes the shutters, Michele reviews the serialized stories that he's dreamed up in the past few days. That one time his character didn't board the school bus and walked to the park instead. After stretching out on the grass, he was caught off guard by the sprinklers. Another time he risked his life for having hidden a powerful mafia boss's desk diary. Fantastic stories. Adventures.

It would all be fine, except that occasionally Michele remembers that he's also invented a gray classroom as the sky swings open and that classroom actually reappears. Aside from the shivers from the short circuit, the child is also touched by a suspicion. The afternoons pass, but he's never once gone downstairs for his snack. His mother has called him, he's always been right on the verge of leaving the room, but he's never done it. He hasn't gone to her, he hasn't plunged his face into her soft hair. If someone asked him to describe her physically, he'd actually have a hard time. Is her nose pointed or tip-tilted? Are her eyebrows dense or elongated like doll eyebrows? And then, come to think of it, the voice. This wave of warmth that calls his name every day, if it's not clear to what physical body it belongs, doesn't it therefore resemble a silence that expands like wine in a pond? A slender body runs in the garden. A black silhouette against the October sun leans over him when Michele turns his gaze elsewhere.

Clara.

And then there was the episode with the shit.

One afternoon his mother calls him for his snack. He shouts: "Coming!" and looks at the sky through the open window. The swallows disappear into the blue belly. Michele turns, sees the teacher's desk. The room is elongated like the accordion-folded sleeves of certain old cameras. The desks are jumbled together. Salvemini. The teacher has called his name for the second time. Michele raises his hand and says "Present" and immediately regrets it because every action he undertakes on this side threatens to take him away from the other side. He feels something under his shoes. The teacher pronounces other surnames. The girl in the row ahead of him raises her hand. Before lowering it, she turns in his direction. Michele pulls his pens out of their case. There it is again, a strange lump on the footrest. Another little boy turns uneasily in his direction. Michele looks down and is frozen to the spot. He splits the next instant into ten parts, and each of those into ten more to better handle the catastrophe. He's stepped on an enormous piece of shit and carried it into the classroom with him. They're all about to notice it and he, watching the progress of events in slow motion, reconstructs the emotional slap in the face that's about to hit him just before it can happen, a secret sorrow that comes before the full-blown one and defeats it, leaving a part of him inviolate.

When the first type of sorrow is reproduced, Michele releases his grip. Time once again flows normally. A classmate pinches his nose shut with the tips of his fingers. The little girl in the desk ahead of him stares wide-eyed. More heads turn. Michele stares insistently at the footrest. Now it's as if time were accelerating, because it is he who reveals to the student body a few seconds early the source of the smell. A robust, nauseating stench.

The little girl in the desk ahead of him starts shouting: "Ahhh!"

A little boy says: "That's disgusting!" He does it in the way that Michele had foreseen and already defused a few seconds earlier.

The bodies of the other pupils rise and fall. The fat boy in the fourth row is seized by an attack of hysterical laughter.

Someone cries: "Salvemini!"

The teacher, too, cries out: "Salvemini!" Then she shouts: "Cristina!" speaking to a little girl running for no good reason toward the door. The chairs screech across the floor. A notebook flies through the air. Then a satchel takes flight, too. "Something *stinks!*" A boy with red hair clutches his throat with both hands, pretending he's being strangled. The janitor walks into the classroom. The teacher raises her voice to be heard over the general bedlam. She asks the janitor to bring some sawdust.

"Salvemini!—Salvemini!—Salvemini!"

He'll come out of it alive. The pain no one else knows anything about possesses furrows in which it's possible to hide. But all the same, something else is going on. The colors of the classroom are coagulating. Michele looks up at the sky through the big windows. He looks straight ahead and again finds the teacher's desk. This can't be. The children are still there, and so is the teacher. So he looks outside, and then he looks straight ahead again. The scene hasn't changed. He feels a sense of anguish throttling him. He shuts his eyes, reopens them. He's in despair. If this is reality, then he's only been imagining (for weeks? Months? Or has it lasted a year?) his mother calling him for his snack on a warm and endless afternoon. With the added problem that the sky, glimpsed through the classroom windows, has no intention of throwing itself open the way that other sky did. A closed, metallic blue. An entire mechanism has inverted the marching order. My mother doesn't exist. I've never seen her, nor will I in the future. That is the reality. The world without nuances.

The cat leapt off the armoire. Michele took another drag on his cigarette. The small ears peeped up over the edge of the sheet. If he had tried to grab her, she would have run away. So he turned over onto his side. As soon as he stopped looking at her, the cat traced a crescent moon on the mattress. She crept nearer in silence. After a few seconds he felt her on his back. Without stroking her yet, just thinking of doing it, and therefore doing it, reaching his arm back, into the animal's shiny black fur, he sensed his father and Annamaria on a territory that, more than obscene was brutal, more than noisy, mute, and chilly and bare. *What happened afterward*, he remembered.

What happens in the months that follow is enveloped in the mists of uncertainty. You might say that Vittorio starts to detest him. He tolerates his son's awkwardness less and less. His shyness fills him with rage. It seems as if Michele is always about to say something but then the way he doesn't say it is artfully contrived to inflict a form of damage the blame for which falls on them. To say nothing of his apathy, the lack of anything in him that can be ascribed however vaguely to ambition, or to self-respect. It is as if he is building scale models of a far-off indictment so that they can't tear their eyes away from it.

Vittorio is forced to scold Michele every evening for how late he is to come to the table, when Ruggero and Clara have been sitting before their steaming dishes for some time already.

"I didn't hear."

This child is lying. His father called him in a loud voice a couple of times and then was forced to shout up the stairwell. When he at last takes his place at the table with the others, Michele eats with downcast eyes, making everyone feel awkward with an absurdly submissive attitude that defies interference. Gioia, in her high chair, claps her hands and laughs.

His grades, though, those are subjects for discussion. There's plenty of arguing about them. Michele drops from outstanding to satisfactory. Then unsatisfactory, needs improvement, gravely unsatisfactory.

So one day, Vittorio tells him to get in the car and drives him out into the nearby countryside. He turns off the engine and asks him what's wrong.

"Go on, spit it out."

"Spit what out?"

Maybe he thinks he's found some ingenious way to defy them, says Vittorio. Maybe he has problems with Annamaria, or with his brother, something more general that he can't digest about a family that is remarkably considerate toward him, whose patience is inexhaustible.

"No," Michele objects.

"Feel free to talk."

"Really, Papà. It's . . . nothing," he says, staring down at the car's floor mat.

It is in these moments that Vittorio is tempted to slap him silly. His son summons the ghost of the woman who brought him into the world, the fork in the road beyond which Vittorio's own life would have gone in a different direction. No one ever talks about these things. Lines that have been erased. Even Vittorio can't bring himself to think about it when he's alone. But since there's someone who seems to exist only to refresh his memory, he should get to the bottom of it. That's why Vittorio wishes his son would tell him there's something wrong. That he'd back him up against the wall and make clear to him—piti-lessly, incontrovertibly—the long sequence of mistakes that keeps their lives standing upright, if that's really the case. Instead, Michele remains silent.

"All right." Vittorio feels overwhelmed by an unconquer-able weariness, starts the car up again. "All right," he says, "let's go back home."

Everyday life. When he looks at his siblings in the morning, Michele feels admiration. He watches them in the bathroom struggling with the dental floss. The nonchalance with which they occupy space, the absolute mastery that they possess as they move from one floor to another in the villa—these things lead him to reflect on the fact that he cannot do all the things that they can. Not with the same natural ease.

On sunny Sundays, Clara doesn't even think twice before hopping on her father's old bike if she feels like going for a ride. Every time, Michele feels obliged to ask permission. He knows that it will just expose him to an even worse humiliation ("Why, what kind of questions are these? Just take it, no?" Vittorio would reply), so most of the time he just does nothing.

Circumspection, prudence. Then, one afternoon, it could have been at the end of spring, Annamaria is having tea in the living room with some new girlfriends. One is the wife of a magistrate. Another comes from a family that has a coffee monopoly in Puglia. These are all solid, educated women, with enough of a sense of humor to either establish intimacy or raise the drawbridge without regrets. There are times when Annamaria finds herself at a loss. When they talk about art, or the books they're reading. She understands that their money is worth more than hers, even if they have less of it. These acquaintances nonetheless are the threshold beyond which she can glimpse herself the way she's always imagined. And after all, it's not as if the crème de la crème of the city's high society only talk about art exhibits or old classics. Right now, for instance, they're talking about film, a topic about which Annamaria knows a thing or two.

"The leather sandals and all that white linen. Milena Canonero did an incredible job on her," she says about Meryl Streep in *Out of Africa*.

"The safari vests with all the pockets that you see in the film."

"Apparently Karen Blixen had a whole collection of them," this from the magistrate's wife.

At that point she hears the sound of a car on the front drive. Through the curtains, Annamaria glimpses Engineer Ranieri's station wagon. She furrows her brow. She has no way of knowing that Michele's catechism has been canceled at the last minute. So the car drives off, and a few moments later the child comes into the living room.

"Hello . . . "

All the women turn to look at him. Annamaria goes white as a sheet. The other women make an effort to appear nonchalant. One of them seems unable to tear her eyes away. There's something not right about this little boy. First of all, he shouldn't be dressed so sloppily. To say nothing of his glasses. Where did they get them? And then the rolls of fat. Here there's no shadow of any rudimentary attempt to encourage physical fitness, no sign of a dentist's touch, paid to correct the overlapping of his incisors. His smile. Even that is different from what it ought to be. Some very strange things seem to be happening in this house.

Michele sees the veil of disapproval settle over his father's wife. It's clear that Annamaria has committed a serious mistake. Michele actually begins to suspect that she's even concealed his existence. Could it be that she's been so reckless, so foolish and naïve, as never to speak of a child born out of wedlock?

"I'm going upstairs," Michele mumbles.

The other women smile, frozen-faced. Annamaria waves her hand: "Ciao, Michele." He shoots up the stairs. The thought of what happened makes him feel like sobbing his heart out. He'd laugh like a lunatic. He can feel his heart speed up. In order to let off the tension, he's ready to slam his fist against the wall, he could head-butt it. He lengthens his stride. Then a gray shadow. It happens before he reaches the end of the hall. He feels the misery subside, the anxiety drain away, sucked away into the vibrant black rectangle that is the open door of his sister's bedroom. Clara is looking at him.

The period between the ages of nine and ten is a mystery that not even the adult of thirty will be capable of fathoming. Few are the sensations that remain intact over time. Like geologists with the center of the earth, he will reconstruct that year by process of induction. He will believe that he was in the depth of things in a way he'll never again approach for the rest of his life. Crushed by an absolute darkness, like the centipedes, like the termites, creatures unchanged over millions of years, capable of picking up on information without needing to translate it.

The adult will perhaps be the laborious result of the child aged seven or twelve. But it's the nine year old who has a one-way ticket.

One Sunday morning, for absolutely no reason, he makes a girl fall down the stairs, the daughter of a steel supplier who's there on a courtesy call. He trips her. The little girl gets a cut to her eyebrow. Vittorio doesn't know how to beg his guests' forgiveness. Michele is sent to his room for the rest of the day.

Another time a wall collapses just inches from him without his noticing.

"To make a long story short, this bulldozer crashes into our classroom and I don't bat an eyelash," he'll tell the story years

later, in Rome, in bed with an older woman. "They were supposed to demolish an old building nearby and they must have
read the documents wrong. That'll tell you what kind of shape
the school where they sent me was in." Nine in the morning.
The schoolteacher hasn't finished calling roll. There is a
tremendous roar. The other children are the ones who heard it.
The teacher screams. The children instinctively run for the
door. "And I . . . do you know what I find myself thinking at a
time like that?" he'll confide to his lover. "I ask myself: isn't it
a little early for recess? All this while the wall behind me collapses. Do you see the level of alienation I was capable of? In
any case, at a certain point I do turn around, and there where
the wall used to be is a whirlwind of dust. By now I'm alone in
the classroom, I can see the bulldozer, too. A huge yellow beast
with the shovel in plain sight and two big shafts of light."

"And afterwards?" she'll ask. "What happened afterwards?"

As if it were the most natural thing in the world, the child
turns his back to the bulldozer. He leaves the classroom and
heads down the hallway. Silence all around. The doors of the
other classes are open and the classrooms are all empty.
Michele walks past the teachers' lounge. He passes another
hallway. Now there's a sound of voices. He goes out into the
courtyard. That's where they've all gone. A tide of light-blue
and white smocks. A few children sob in terror. The school-
teachers count them with their ledgers in hand. A short distance away, the principal is talking animatedly with a man in
jeans and a yellow T-shirt. The man gesticulates, tries to jus-
tify what's happened. The second the principal lowers her
eyes, she starts in surprise. She strides away from the construction foreman. She runs over to Michele and bends over
him. She puts both hands on his head. She asks: "Are you all
right?" He says nothing. Suddenly the principal is worried. If
he was left behind, then someone else might have been left

further behind. "Were there other children?" she asks. "Yes. Another little boy." The principal goes pale. "I turned around and I saw him. A little hand, opening and closing under the rubble."

"I didn't have the faintest idea that I was lying."

"Because it wasn't a lie," the woman will say, running a hand through her hair, "it's obvious that the child under the rubble was you."

She'll turn in the bed, displaying the nudity of her breasts, the too taut flesh of a forty-seven-year-old body subjected to nine hours in the gym every week. The afternoon light will immerse the room in the salmon pink that is the red of eighteenth-century apartment buildings risen to the third floor through the smog of Rome. Michele will think: it's true, I was that child. The trail of his semen on the woman's neck will become one with her husband's sadness were he to see her now.

"I was punished that time, too," he'll say, caressing her chin; he'll rotate his wrist downward, touching his mouth with the tips of his fingers.

That night, the little boy is sent to eat all alone. Vittorio asks Selam to bring in a folding table, and to set Michele's place so that the boy can see them all together at the other end of the living room. His father, Annamaria, Clara, Ruggero, and Gioia. The dinner is eaten in general silence. Someone makes a half-hearted attempt at conversation. There's something comical about it, as well as something painful and awkward. As he eats in silence, the child notices something at the other table. Sitting between Gioia and Annamaria, she seems sad. With her thumbnail she's tormenting another finger's cuticle. She's carved open a wound. In the wound there's a light. Someone is suffering for me.

He grabbed the cat by her rear paws; the cat struggled to

get loose but finally gave up. He hugged her. Then he got up from the bed.

At three in the morning, everyone was asleep. Michele threw open the window, felt the wind on his face. The cool of springtime mingling with the muggy heat of the impending summer.

He slipped on a shirt, and left the room, taking care to close the door behind him so the cat wouldn't run away. Then he went downstairs. He felt like a burglar. When he reached the living room, he ran a finger over the silver platter sitting in the middle of the table as a decorative centerpiece. Touching this thing that's not mine. Having discovered a portion of his face on the opaque surface, he received confirmation of the opposite. A right of usucapion on anything a person has survived. If I were to go and awaken my father and start talking to him, he'd look at me in bafflement. Annamaria would recoil in fright. They wouldn't understand. And yet, they'd understand something. From the usual incredulity, the expressions on their faces would turn tragically incredulous. This so-intimate stranger is once again in our midst. If I spoke to them, if they reflected on the fact that since the day of the funeral, a greenish patch has sprouted on Clara's chest, has started to spread, her belly has swollen, her eye sockets have begun to collapse, her flesh corroded by intestinal bacteria is now emitting a devastating stench, if they were to imagine what the dark of the grave is like, the loneliness of the tuff in which she's decomposing. They'd understand that I'm talking about from down there.

He went back to his room. He stretched out on the bed and went back to sleep.

The next day, Alberto came to see them.

He had an appointment with Vittorio to take care of a number of bureaucratic matters. Burdens that fell to the surviving spouse. Returning her driver's license to the department of motor vehicles, her passport to police headquarters. Shutting down various accounts, finding the originals of old contracts. More than ten years of marriage. But the documents were all still there. As if Clara, when she went to live with her husband, had just been loaning herself out.

Michele saw him come in. He observed the scene from the upper floor. In Vittorio's presence, Alberto almost bowed his head. Annamaria greeted with condescension this son-in-law who, though he was widely considered one of the finest engineers in the city, was treated as an errand boy by everyone in that house. The two men went into Vittorio's study. An hour later, Michele heard voices echo. At that point, he emerged from his room. Alberto and his father were downstairs. Standing there talking. Still, it seemed like the one was eager to see the other to the front door. Michele waved his arms out over the railing.

"Alberto!"

Alberto raised his eyes; his face lit up. He smiled, puffy with sadness. His features hadn't changed over the course of the years. Now he looked like an aged child. Someone who, instead of facing his sorrows head on, had tucked them under his skin like so much Botox.

Michele came down the stairs, went toward him. He seemed to sense Vittorio's disappointment, which told him he was doing the right thing.

Alberto held out one hand, placed the other on his shoulder: "How are you?" Then he pulled him toward him.

Recognizing embraces. Michele had been practicing it for a lifetime. He was an expert in the discipline. In the clutch with Alberto he recognized a sincere enthusiasm. Immediately after, though, he sensed an excessively emphatic note, the hint of misdirection. The background noise was trying to distract him from his sister's voice. I dreamed of a doe. Alberto was looking at him. The last time they'd met, Clara had been twenty-four. Alberto and his sister had just recently gotten married.

Even then she was cheating on him with anyone she could, thought Michele.

Alberto took his arms off Michele's body.

"It's so good to see you again." His voice rose half a note, rediscovered a fluent cordiality. "How long will you be staying in Bari?"

Just then Annamaria joined them. Michele felt the expectation that Alberto would get out from underfoot suddenly double. That's when he made his move.

"Why don't you stay for a cup of tea?"

He sunk his gaze into Annamaria's own, so that the woman, forced to return his smile, had no time to improvise an excuse. His father seemed too caught off guard to react. Michele saw him look down in irritation.

They had tea on the veranda. The atmosphere was strange. Even though no one spoke about Clara, Alberto's presence ensured that his sister's death pressed against the background in a way that was different from the previous days. Two opposing falsehoods give a true reading. Things take shape. In the intricate forest of grief, a path emerges.

"What are you up to in Rome?" asked Alberto. The effect was ridiculous.

Michele glimpsed the opportunity and seized it. There was at least half an hour to be earned. "I'm working with newspapers," he said. He started talking about himself the way Annamaria would have done about Gioia if his sister had just started working. As he was citing *La Repubblica* and *Il Messaggero*—attributing to himself an importance that was absolutely nonexistent, but without the exaggerations that would have justified a request to show his cards—he sensed that the trick was working. For minutes on end he held them in his grasp with a succession of commonplaces.

Then Gioia arrived.

"Oh, ciao."

She was dressed in a short skirt and a tight-fitting little T-shirt. Surprised to find them all there together, she took a half a step back.

Michele was quick: "Come, sit down with us."

Gioia ventured closer, circumspectly. In the end she gave in, overcome by the force of gravity. She set her handbag and her cell phone down on the table. Michele went back to talking with Alberto. Annamaria seemed uneasy. Vittorio was tapping his foot nervously on the floor. Michele's sister gave a start. She reached out a hand, dragged the iPhone toward her. She started typing a phrase into it. Or perhaps deleting one. Michele noticed something. That's when he stretched out his hand. He reached under the table and grabbed Gioia's free hand, started squeezing it. His sister smiled nervously. He squeezed tighter, more intensely. Gioia responded by pushing her sweaty palm obtusely against his. After ten minutes or so, they heard a car engine coming closer and closer.

That was when his father leapt to his feet and headed toward the interior of the villa. Freed of the invisible ties with which Michele was binding them, he went to welcome the guests at the front door. But instead they went around to the back. Before Vittorio returned, the new arrivals appeared on the veranda. His brother Ruggero. Behind him, an old man. A long gray face. Black jacket, sky-blue shirt. He raised one hand slowly. Michele saw, on Alberto's face, the chasm open and then close back up. Clearly, the two of them ought never to have met.

The old man said: "Good evening."

Michele and Annamaria replied with a nod. Ruggero led the way indoors. As the guest was walking past the table where they were all seated, Michele saw for the second time the agony, obvious and then hidden, on Alberto's face. He couldn't know that the two men had met at the funeral. But he did know the truth behind that contraction. The same that—so many years before—had deformed Alberto's face when he saw Clara returning from the gym with her bag in hand.

Later Michele learned that the guest was Valentino Buffante. Former Undersecretary of Justice. He'd gotten in trouble for something related to rigged civil service competitions. Acquitted. Now the chairman of a foundation for economic development in southern Italy. The business of the pre-emptive seizure of his father's tourist complex. This sort of disaster foretold to which Vittorio was devoting all his efforts. Over the past few days, Michele had heard doors opening and voices talking, men's voices, strangers' voices. This Buffante wasn't the only one who'd showed up in person.

After dinner, Michele went in the garden for a smoke. He walked past the fountain. Now he could relax. He thought of Gioia. He couldn't believe he'd seen *that* of all things on her phone's screen. He walked through the tall grass, noticed a slight drop in temperature. He felt then that he could sense the city. The traffic lights. The buildings in the center of town. The electric curve of the lights along the waterfront. The places where he still hadn't set foot since his return. There, another image of Clara awaited him. A more fluid shape, he thought, different from the adulterated memories from in here. The glowing lights on a sign that changes continuously.

After the incident with the child buried under the rubble, Michele starts taking long walks in the fallow fields that lie not far from the villa. He gets home from school, eats quickly, and hurries outside. He takes the dirt lane. He jumps over the dry-stone wall and ventures out into the fields.

He walks among the daisies. Then the red of the poppies. He lowers himself down among the leaves, makes his way over the ground using his elbows to push himself forward. Line dot, line dot, line dot line. In the beginning were the ants.

He follows the broken line. The tiny creatures travel over

rocks, dead leaves. Each individual insect rhythmically taps its antennae against those of its fellow creature, passing each other information then scooting away in opposite directions. Further on, the line becomes a large clustering black fist. They're swarming over a swallow's corpse. That which in heaven now here on earth. Michele leaps to his feet. He starts running, trips. Another day. He lifts his head among the mallows, sees the moon striped with silver. Shift in focus. The moon loses distinctness, the silver thread is here under his nose. A spiderweb. The transparent veil tosses in the wind. At the outskirts of the orbicular structure he notices the silk cocoons. He looks around. He carefully places a finger on the ground. He waits until an ant climbs onto his fingernail. He lifts the finger, raises it to the height of the spiderweb. With his forefinger, from below, he flicks sharply at the base of his middle finger. After describing a small parabola in the void, the ant lands on the spiderweb. The threads undulate. That's when the spider comes out. It descends and very quickly climbs up from one end to the other. It lunges at its prey. It's all a convulsive agitation of bodies. The predator tries to immobilize the ant before the ant has a chance to wound it with a swipe of its mandible. And yet there is no passion in this battle. As if the breath of a single god were channeled into two different shells, transforming itself into opposing thrusts. Before Michele has a chance to recover from his fright, the ant is all wrapped up.

At nightfall, Michele returns home. He comes up the drive, passes the rose bushes. He doesn't have time to take more steps. He feels a dark red imprint on his head. She's watching him. Maybe her eyes are following him from the second-story window. Or else she's hidden among the trees. Silence and a few clouds in the sky. Soon this summer will be over.

Another time. Michele ventures out among the spikes of the Bermuda grass. Out of the smell of gasoline and mosquito

coils, the impalpable scent of fruit popsicles that lingered in
the air until just a few days ago, has already started to fade. It's
colder than it was yesterday. Beyond the last trees there's the
line of traffic. Glowing lights. Michele brushes off his trousers.
He continues in the opposite direction. After a few yards, the
vegetation starts to grow again. A dragonfly. The moon bigger
than on other days. On the right, the stripe of a stand of cane.
Michele stops. He's never been here. He looks around. He
crouches down in this sort of peat bog. Protected by the tufts
of rush, he immerses himself in the basin of late summer. A
sensation of well being, of calm. He feels the pressure on his
hand. He might have slept. He focuses and he sees it.

A tree frog has landed on his wrist. Emerald green, with a
black stripe running from the eyes all the way to the rear
limbs.

Michele is careful to breathe. The little animal seems as if
it's about to leap away. Instead, without his feeling a thing, the
tree frog gets more comfortable on its platform. It makes a half
turn, steps forward a few centimeters.

Still sitting in the grass, as if checking his watch, Michele
slowly bends the angle of his elbow. He brings the frog
beneath his eyes. He observes it. The frog observes him. Never
seen such a brilliant green. Inside the throat of the tiny
amphibian, something pulsates continuously. The frog goes on
staring at him, imperturbably. So beautiful. One evening, in my
presence, a tiger will reveal itself.

Something explodes on his hand.

Michele feels the burning sensation. He sees the frog leap
away. A violent gray-green spurt shoots in the opposite direction.

"Got him!"

Michele leaps to his feet. For a few seconds he doesn't
understand. Then he notices the two boys among the ferns.
They're probably his age. He lowers his eyes. He sees the frog

struggling to move across the ground, pushing with a single leg. No. Damn it, no.

"Don't you even try it," says one of the boys.

The other one aims an oversized rubber band in his direction.

Without giving it a second thought, Michele puts his head down and takes off. With one absolutely precise movement, he snags the frog from the ground and lunges forward.

"Ah!"

He hits the two boys. He makes an opening for himself and starts to run.

"Come on! Come on!"

They chase him, but their bodies preserve a memory of the impact. This child is strange. Michele runs like a lunatic. Branches. Lashes against his ankles. Everything's green. He can hear them talking amongst themselves. A sign that they're slowing down. I can't stop. His fingers delicately clenched in fists. Please. I'm begging you. If I run fast, if I'm in danger of making my heart explode, then the frog won't die.

The façade of the villa appears amidst the tops of the pine trees. Michele has no idea how he even managed to find the way back. He goes through the gate. He starts up the drive. A terrible burning in his spleen. Only then does he begin to slow down. The frog, far too relaxed in his fist. He passes the oleanders. The sound of leaves underfoot. Close to the vases with the ferns, a female shape. Michele feels the anguish grow. Annamaria. A part of him has already understood, tries to find a way to persuade the other half. He stumbles over his own footsteps. The frog slips from his fingers. He watches as it falls into the grass. A leg extends and folds back in on itself. Involuntary reflex. But I ran. I really did try to make my heart explode. Evening will fall. It will be day again. The ants will arrive. The gardener will gather one thing among the others. Michele passes Annamaria. He goes through the front door.

From the contrasting shadows of the living room he sees the interior stairs emerge and, further on, the sofa. Inside the armoire's mirror, his dead figure.

So it happens. He senses the shift. The clamp around his throat. As if a wild animal, patiently lying in ambush in the dark, had lunged at him. For an instant he believes that the boys with rubber bands have followed him right into the house. Then the scent of fruit mixed with something heavier, rougher. His sister. She's thrown her arms around his neck. And she squeezes, squeezes tight. The brownish warmth of her body. Michele feels like sobbing. The first shaft of light. Things at the bottom of the well start to take on a shape.

In bed, the cat still on his belly. Michele woke up once again in the middle of the night. He went downstairs to the living room. He stopped for a few minutes at the exact spot where it happened. But not as if in prayer. He sensed her. She was still there. Michele went back to his room. As if it was only from that moment on that I had the tools to understand, he remembered. He patted the nightstand in search of the cigarettes. You have to receive some good before you can separate it from that which is not. If no one loves you, you'll never know where to begin. That's where everything begins, even hatred. He put the cigarette into his mouth, but he didn't light it. He stroked the cat's head.

Beginning that night, he and Clara start to see each other, so to speak. Absurd, considering that they've lived in the same house since she was three. And yet that is what happens. At five in the evening, before Engineer Ranieri comes to get her, Clara worms her way into her brother's room. Every time, she brings a little gift with her. Michele is bent over his games. He hears the door swing open. The artificial light is stripped bare and then destroyed by the glare from the outside world. Clara

sets her sports bag on the floor. Amatori Volley. Still not satisfied, she crosses the room and throws open the window.

"What were you doing in the dark like that."

She impresses the question with a faint timber of parody, as
if she knew perfectly well the uses of darkness, approved them,
and just wanted to let him know.

"You've just killed them," he says, making the two robots,
who are now less convincing than ever, fall theatrically onto the
floor.

"Look what I brought you."

Clara climbs up onto the bed, drawing a semicircle. She
rapidly crosses her legs on the mattress. She shifts the bound
volumes from her right hand to her left, hiding them behind
her back.

Michele draws closer. He comes over and sits on the bed.
Right across from her. Clara smiles in amusement.

"What's that behind your back?"

"*The Hidden Vall* . . . Oh, what do you care about it."

"Let me see."

She's hopeless when it comes to comic books. *The Hidden
Valley*. When Clara saw the cover with the cowboy on horse-
back, it seemed like a good idea. Now she realizes it that it's a
mediocre editorial product. She hands him the Little Ranger
comic. What an idiot I've been. Her brother has a mind out of
the ordinary. As quick as a thousand hands simultaneously
searching for a needle in a dark room. Only an idiot could fail
to see that she had something precious right in front of her.
How could I have gotten him this stupid thing?

"Oh, thank you," he says, seriously.

A shadow passes over him, changes the shape of his lips. It's
unclear whether he's making fun of her. Clara wishes she could
drop through the floor. Luckily the difference in age comes to
her rescue. There are secrets that fourteen-year-olds possess
that are unknown to the experiences of eleven-year-olds.

Clara smiles again, her face slightly pointy: "And that's not all . . . "

Still facing him, motionless, legs crossed, he sees her rummage around her back. She hands him the slim volume.

Songs of Experience.

"I'll read it all," he says.

"There's a really nice one about a tiger."

"A tiger hunt."

"Tyger tyger . . . " she recites. "More than anything else, the poet wonders whether he who made the tiger also created the lamb."

Michele looks at her in silence, looks at her big toes, which are sticking out of her terry cloth socks. Then he says: "No."

"No, what?"

"One creates the other."

A small vertical crease between Clara's eyes.

"How do you mean?"

"The lamb created the tiger by letting herself be eaten by him."

The mark on her forehead vanished. Clara opens her mouth and bares her teeth: "Like this? Like this?" She lunges at him.

"Ahhh!"

Michele shouts amid his laughter. Clara sinks a knee into his stomach, with the other knee pressed against the base of his neck. She lifts her arms, spreads her fingers as if they were claws. Matching make-believe for make-believe, Michele slows the movement that might have staved off the attack. Clara is on top of him. Her fingers in his ribs. She tickles him. Michele delivers a slap to the back of the head that comes dangerously close to being a real and proper smack. Clara opens her eyes wide in astonishment. Now, he thinks. He grabs her by the hair, yanks just enough to cause her pain. Clara launches herself forward, stretching. For an instant, they're belly to belly. Michele lets one leg slide between hers, he pushes, he grabs her by the arms. He kicks hard enough to fling her away.

They laugh. They're about to hurl themselves at one another again. Then he looks down at the bag on the floor. Soon Engineer Ranieri will come to pick her up. Clara is panting. Michele, too, is catching his breath. They snicker nervously. For a few moments they remain there, as if they had suddenly become aware of what surrounds them. An evil aura. Clara tucks her hair over her ear. Michele stays motionless in his place. She gets cautiously out of the bed, first one foot then the other.

Michele watches her lift the Amatori Volley gym bag. His sister raises her other hand, torso rigid, backlit by the September light.

She turns her back and leaves the room.

What really counts, in that autumn of 1989, is the industrially reproduced artwork on the covers of certain records, comics, books, and art catalogues, affordably priced at five thousand lire apiece. The lovely oil painting, a landscape, that appeared in the De Agostini offprint that Clara purchased, swayed by the institutional authoritativeness of the title (*The Masters of Modernity*), and which Michele peruses passionately during the afternoons that follow, when she isn't home.

He's impressed by what he sees in those low quality reproductions on cheap paper. The paintings done by this Pierre Bonnard are magnificent. He feels as if he's arriving at a party to which he was invited years earlier. Everything moves dizzyingly. You need only open a window and the shadowy part of an interior in the Midi of France thins out, revealing a comb, a cup of tea, all the way up to a bathtub inside which a girl starts to disintegrate, hit by the too-strong light. If Michele hadn't spent the summer getting lost in the fields, perhaps he wouldn't have felt such intense joy in these sensations. But if, when looking at the images, he hadn't undergone the incredible experience of passing from perceptible reality to its rethinking, nature would have remained to him merely a brute force without purpose.

Michele closes the catalogue. He goes downstairs to get a glass of water. Gioia is on the carpet playing with her Legos. She sees him go by, she sticks her tongue out at him. Again on the stairs. Annamaria. They brush past each other. Then each of them on different steps. A different density in the air.

For the past few weeks, the woman has started looking at him in an odd way. As if he, for the first time since his mother's death, were the potential danger forever lurking on the other side of the curve.

Terrace at Vernon. Spring Landscape. Nude in the Bath and Small Dog.

Pleasure sharpens the senses and demands more pleasure. And so, the more time that Clara spends with him, the more she chats with him, the more she showers him with attention, the more clearly Michele can reflect on the state of things. Only those who have never had anything are willing to settle.

On certain afternoons, coming back from her German lessons, Clara gets out of her overcoat, takes off her sneakers, and makes an effort to throttle her joy. She walks cautiously through the living room. But once she's upstairs, she starts running. Last stretch of hallway. She plunges into her brother's room as if it were a tree house.

Michele's pupils dart from right to left to hook onto the next line. The door is thrown open, a dense autumnal shadow interrupts his reading. "Ciao." He finds her curled up on the other side of the bed, fists clenched, legs tucked up to her neck, smelling of rain.

"There was a girl who couldn't pronounce the word *Karfreitagskind*. She was spitting everywhere," she snickers.

Michele doesn't respond. He looks at her harshly, and then

he conceals that same gaze to keep the message from becoming explicit. Clara is disoriented. She's the one who brought him back to life, but by so doing she has exposed herself to what happens when a seal is broken. So she tries to change the subject. "Did you see the ridiculous girl that Ruggero brought home the other night?" Her hand reaches out for his. Michele recoils. Clara's feelings are hurt. Now the blow has been delivered clearly. After all, what does his sister want? Does she fool herself into thinking that she can go on visiting him as if he only sprang into being when that door was thrown open? Is it possible that she doesn't look around? Open your eyes good and wide. Count the differences.

Because they're there, the differences, Michele thinks as he sits on the bed after Clara leaves, his gaze veiled with sorrow. He knows that now the bite is hurting her. Slow-release venom. He imagines her in the days that follow, burdened by a grief that wasn't there before. He feels he can see her as she comes home from school in a fine drizzle, Clara's eyes in just a few weeks, as though they were his, which burn right now with anger.

Because my big sister goes to one of the most famous private high schools in the city. Why was it that Ruggero was, in his time, enrolled in an elementary school where the fees were higher than the worker's compensation checks received by the laborers for their injuries while employed by our father. Because Clara had braces. Because they shower Gioia with gifts. Aside from playing volleyball, Clara takes swimming lessons, studies German. My brother did swimming, too. National junior championships. Gioia knows what the word *tournesol* means, what the word *Sonnenblume* means. Experimental school. *Sunflower.* In the mantelpiece in the living room are the trophies marking Ruggero's triumphs. Third place, backstroke. First prize, butterfly. I have slumping shoulders. I could call myself fat, for that matter. Levi's, Calvin

Klein, Emporio Armani. I've never seen myself dressed in an article of designer clothing. And yet everywhere I look in this house, I see nothing but Levi's, Calvin Klein, Emporio Armani.

Middle of the night. Eleven days since his sister's death. Standing motionless in front of the window. Those who weep don't listen, now he was listening. The cat leapt up onto the windowsill, rubbed against his arm. She sneezed. Bothered by the smoke. She shook her head again, turned to go. Michele petted her. A mewing. He petted again, his hands ever heavier. He was forcing her to stay.

On the Feast of the Immaculate Conception, stretched out in the bed side by side, together they read Oscar Wilde's fairy-tales. The nightingale and the rose. The happy prince. During the tragic parts, Michele bursts out laughing to keep a tear from appearing on her cheek. Meeting her halfway. Increasing the credit due.

Then suddenly reversing course.

The following Wednesday they're reading a biography of Maradona when the doorbell rings. Engineer Ranieri. Down in the courtyard, the car is running. She doesn't even have time to get down out of bed.

"Don't go to volleyball today," Michele says out of the blue.

"What did you say?" Clara asks, stupefied.

"No practice," he insists, "let's just go for a walk downtown."

"But he's waiting!" Clara replies, dropping into a squat.

"Tell him to leave."

His sister stiffens. Michele is unfazed. Even though Engineer Ranieri is only Engineer De Palo's deputy, Clara acknowledges his importance. Michele watches her struggle against a principle of authority that evidently still means something to her.

"Go downstairs and tell him to beat it."

"Listen . . . "

He sees her hesitate, uncertain, he senses her suffering before she catches her breath: "Listen," his sister says again, "I'll see you later."

Michele looks at her with contempt. Clara disappears timidly through the door, taking care not to close it entirely hoping that at the very last second he'll say something. Michele doesn't speak. When he hears the station wagon driving off, he hurtles himself off the bed. He smiles with satisfaction. The part of him that Clara now has inside of her is too big for a certain thing that's rolling downhill to stop.

December twenty-fifth, after Christmas dinner. Michele is unwrapping his gift. Annamaria is sitting on the sofa with Clara. Vittorio is in the kitchen, on the phone. The dark green of the box containing foot soldiers, cavalrymen, and cannons placed one after the other in horizontal sequence. The boxed game of Risk that he'd requested. Michele lifts his eyes to Annamaria: "Fantastic . . . " He smiles, sincerely grateful. Ruggero is standing with a glass of wine in his hand. The Rolex Daytona with the stainless steel case glitters on his wrist. Clara shivered while her older brother extracted the watch from the inner box embossed with the tiny gold crown. But Ruggero is almost fifteen years older than Michele. Clara seeks clues in the black hole of previous Christmases. The rule of proportions. It is then that Gioia calls her. Sitting under the tree that is bedecked with colorful balls, she repeats the name on the card. Clara smiles. She reaches forward, takes the present from her sister's hands. Annamaria uncrosses her legs on the sofa. But it's Michele that Clara watches as she unties the satin ribbon. He's reading the instructions for Risk. Suddenly he seems defenseless again, as if the presence of all the others intimidated him, made him plunge back into last year.

Clara finishes unwrapping her gift. She opens the box slowly, in a way that—she will realize later—will serve to delay acknowledgment. She pulls out the first earring, remains open-mouthed. This doesn't come from a costume jewelry shop. A miniature candelabrum encrusted with diamonds with five tanzanites for contrast. The beauty of the jewelry disconcerts her. Clara bites her lip. She's filled with shame for being happy to hold it in her hands. Desiring that object as the expression of hebetude with which Michele looks at her enflames the other part of him within her.

"Clara!"

Annamaria has leapt forward on the sofa. Her legs are bent in an x while her arms form the half-swastika that in cartoons mean that a character is running as fast as they can. This, immediately after the box containing the earrings grazes her head and hits the wall.

The woman flops onto the cushion and immediately regains self-control, but she doesn't have time to lift a finger before Clara starts shouting at her.

"Filthy pigs," she says.

Red-faced, hands shaking. They'll never see her like that again. Gioia, sitting under the tree, slams together two large blocks of wood, over and over again. Michele awakens from his torpor. It seems to him that his sister's slim, straight body, filled with rage, is casting a terrifying reddish shadow beyond the visible surface of the wall.

You're a bunch of filthy pigs.

Vittorio sticks his head out of the kitchen with the telephone receiver clamped to his ear: "Who's that shouting?"

Now Clara is at the front door. She opens it. She walks through. She slams it behind her so loudly that for a moment her mother clenches her fists and closes her eyes the way kids do when they're frightened.

(It's past midnight when, after searching for five hours,

Engineer De Palo spots her on state route 16. Alone. She walks along, with her back to the oncoming traffic. She's not clutching herself. She's not hunched over. Admirable the way she tolerates the cold, if you take into account the fact that in her fury to be gone she didn't even think to put on a pair of tights. When the station wagon pulls up next to her, Clara raises her head. She gets into the car without a word. "You should have seen how he looked at me," she'll tell Michele the next day. "He was waiting for me to talk but I just stared at the windshield. I kept my eyes on the road to keep from giving him the satisfaction. Maybe he expected me to start objecting, or thought that I was going to cry." Then something else happened. It was clear from the way his jawbone protruded on his cheek as he drove. Unload onto her the disgust that belongs to him, a sea of filth that, if Clara only believed in it for an instant, she would make the mistake of attributing to herself. "Engineer De Palo isn't Engineer Ranieri," laughter, "Engineer De Palo is some kind of pervert.")

When she comes home at a quarter to two in the morning, escorted by Engineer De Palo, it's a different girl that passes under the eyes of Vittorio and Annamaria.

"Ciao," she greets her parents with a smile that's about to fall apart.

Her face slapped by the cold. Her legs purple under the woolen skirt. She looks like the mug shots of certain movie stars immortalized in police stations, triumphant in the immediate aftermath of arrest. Embarrassment. That's the feeling Vittorio experiences when his daughter walks past him. "I'm going to sleep." They ought to scold her. They'd be within their rights if they slapped her. The problem (as suggested by the weakness of the electric interaction running through her) is that right now Clara could do or say something that would prove unbearable for them. As if she'd come into possession of some terrible secret concerning them, but about which

Vittorio and Annamaria—aside from the knowledge that the secret exists—no longer remember a thing. She strides past her mother, too. She heads up the stairs, lifts her hands to her mouth. She blows into them to warm up.

"Get dressed. And try to hurry."
"All the great minds, wherever they're seen . . . "
". . . none can explain the mysteries of the nineteen."

After finishing this idiotic nursery rhyme that they'd invented, Clara lifts her gym bag to her shoulder to emphasize her point.

For the past several weeks she's started dragging him with her to the gym. With the confidence of a grownup, she's informed Engineer Ranieri that she no longer requires his services.

"You've been too kind. You've given me so many of those rides that I'll be forever grateful to you."

(The engineer searched the girl's face for the slightest hint of sarcasm that would give him leverage for a retort, found nothing.)

They take the bus to practice. When they head out (she in sweats and leggings, Michele more bundled up than if he were heading out to walk through a snowy wood), even when there's no one in the house, they feel a small sea of habit open up, a space free of the intrusions of Vittorio and Annamaria, as if they'd scored that point once and for all.

Near the barracks, standing in the light of the streetlamps, they bet on how late the number nineteen is going to be. In the winter haze, the streets seem even more deserted because of a sandwich stand where there are never more than two customers sitting. Their breath forms clouds that quickly disappear. The box that is the bus appears jolting in the black of night.

In the gym, Michele watches her practice. The spikes with

the jumps are nice. He's fascinated by the synchronization with which the players switch places after the defender responds to a spike. But it's when his sister is smashing a spike that Michele seeks an alternative time within which to spread out those instants. The jump. And then the smash. A high-pitched shout resounds, after the thud of the ball slamming into the floor.

"Sco-o-o-ore!"

There's a violence, in the successful shots, that seems all the more surprising given the fact that Clara seems alien to any vindictive impulse. There with her, Michele is at peace. She's not one of those stupid girls who score the winning point just so she can dedicate it to her little brother who's come to watch. In the fractions of a second that extend from the set to the spike, he and Clara are like those little temples that have stood face to face for millennia in certain Mediterranean valleys, motionless, gazing at one another without ever having felt the slightest need to come together.

Then Michele finds himself in some guy's car, an older boy who works in an auto repair shop and who's asked his sister if he can take her home.

Michele is in the back seat and the two of them are separated by nothing but the handle of the handbrake. He realizes it the second time he gets in, a sign that he's not entirely healed. The car is an old khaki green Fiat Panda with a sticker reading CHANNEL FOUR? YES, PLEASE! next to the license plate. He realizes it while he's staring at the backs of the necks of the two people in the front seat—which necessarily means that he's remembering the other time he's been here. He's on edge. But he got over that anxiety, too, the last time, when his sister had smiled in the dark, admonishing him on the uselessness of an emotion as stupid as jealousy.

Then why does he mix up the chronology? Why does he feel the disappointment he already filed away days ago? His head isn't working the way it ought to. The progress made isn't enough to forestall backsliding. The girls vanish into the showers after practice. He might be remembering it while he's in the Panda. Or else he really is in the gym. Michele feels bewildered. The axis of time spins out of control in his head. At certain moments he finds himself in places where he and Clara are by no means at peace. They're unhappy. They're in a terrible mess. She's crying. He climbs the steps of the National Gallery of Modern Art. He's in a notary's office signing papers. He enters into a woman's body, and this woman later runs her hands through her hair and says: "Clearly the child buried under the rubble was you." Michele goes off for his military service and five days later thinks of killing himself. He looks at the painting of a tiger. In Avellino, he's sitting on a pile of old phone books, hunched over his typewriter, in a tiny room where the light beats down like the sun on the tiles of certain public latrines, clack clack clack clack, if the poet, describing ravens and tree branches, illustrates the emotion of the Great War without ever having to name it, and we, looking at real ravens and real trees, take from his verse not a sense of relief at the narrowly averted danger but rather the pain of an occasion lost, clack clack clack clack, if we understood, before forgetting it, if we grasped something in these verses dedicated to Grete that is trees and ravens and war together, greater than war, more luminous and dark than the passing of the years, clack clack clack clack. Michele sees the future in the past, will send the sheets of paper to his sister who promised him that she would take them to the newspaper. Gone completely crazy. Hospitalized. He's getting better in Rome. He looks out over the San Lorenzo station, drags on his cigarette until he reaches the filter, observes the traffic, and feels within himself the trace of an opposing movement. Out of nowhere. An overcrowded space is now completely empty. The din has stopped. The orchestra has stopped playing. Healed. Suddenly he's aware of it. As it retreats, the tide takes with it something precious. Then he's holding a pet carrier and in it a cat with no name.

So every time that one of these things actually does happen, Michele will feel a stabbing sensation. An object whose shape and purpose he'd identified years earlier (a blind man who says "knife" as he runs his finger over the blade) will come to light in its ultimate meaning at the very moment it finds the place it's to be plunged into.

And his sister? Can he see Clara, too? Drunk on her wedding day. Feverish with excitement as she hooks up with a publisher at the journalists' guild party. Stuffed with sleeping pills. Wrecked on coke in her old trench coat as she contemplates the city from high atop the parking structure. Slapped around in a hotel. Observed in an obscene photo by the medical examiner who will certify her death a year later.

Despite the fact that just one of these images is false, Michele at age twelve sees nothing of all this. He *senses* the significance of all this. Whether in the Panda, or at the gym, or in Rome before his complete recovery, he senses, he knows that, at the moment when she finally emerges from their ideal dimension (the ball spiked to the floor, the gym shoes still floating in mid-air), troubles will ensue. They have. Something unpleasant. Something terrible, he thinks as the young assistant mechanic slouches off, head down.

A few minutes later, his sister emerges from the shower.

"Come on, let's go home."

The winter loosens its grip, the sun shines bright on the windshields of the parked cars.

Michele has started going around the city on his own. The previous months have filled him with a courage that he doesn't clearly recognize. Parks. Video arcades. He talks to people he doesn't know. He spontaneously makes friends with people he doesn't see again for days. He runs into them again outside a record store. He finds Clara at home when he returns. He goes with her to practice. Then he stops. He runs into her on the street on Saturday afternoon while she's standing in line outside the Stravinsky.

At home, Gioia has started looking at him strangely. For some time now, Annamaria has been treating Clara with mistrust. Vittorio flies to Berlin. He flies to Seville. Apparently, this is another golden age for Salvemini Construction. After every trip, his father returns home electrified. Michele wouldn't bet on business having a mind of its own. If, however, it does, it's not particularly well disposed toward him and Clara. Certain afternoons she bursts into his room and finds him smoking one of his first cigarettes. Michele sucks greedily on his Lucky Strike. Without taking the last drag, he crushes the cigarette against the star globe sitting on the nightstand.

"Alioth!" he tells her. "After we die, that's where we'll meet."

"As soon as possible," his sister smiles.

I didn't kill myself.

I'm still alive.

Michele had gotten hold of the demented, nonsensical sequences of words at night through Inagist. Not on Twitter, where the tweets had been deleted. The account was still active. But the photo had been changed. Clara's bare back. When he'd had the impression the other day that he'd seen it on the display—before Gioia could grab back the iPhone—he'd allowed himself a margin of error. I was dreaming. It can't be. He remembered that photo in its original version, taken by Giannelli on the Monopoli beach—she was changing her top—and then dumped with some others in a cookie tin. But now he had to accept the evidence. The cat was looking at him from the chair.

@ClaraSalvemini.

The new picture showed two butterflies overlapping their wings to form a little heart. The graphic design infuriated him. It seemed that superficiality had definitively branded the indecency of creating an account for a young, dead woman. He pressed his fingers onto the screen. The false account wasn't following anyone. So he opened up the list of the account's followers. @guillaman. @herself. @max1084. He jotted down each name on a sheet of paper. Then he recognized one of them. @giuseppegreco. He clicked on the picture. There he was, ten years older. He wondered why the journalist was one of the followers of that despicable prank. He thought back to Gioia. The presence of the cat, motionless, staring at him, in the circle of light from the lamp, helped calm him. Still, thinking in the dark. If I left this room and kicked her right out of bed, the hoax would be over. She'd shout, beg forgiveness. She certainly wouldn't get the itch anymore for these kinds of exploits. The account would be closed. The fingerprints erased.

But with this prank, the right thing is to see it through to the end.

Michele turned off the lamp. He turned over in the bed. And yet, he thought, however absurd, you had to admit the presence of something true in it. As if the messages written and deleted, the images of the followers (an owl, a Beardsley nude, a pair of red slippers) and the incessant anarchic indecent traffic of messages that continued to stream past behind the online platform, were, taken together—shifted onto a different plane—the most faithful imitation of Clara that he could imagine.

The next morning, while shaving, he listened to his father talking on the phone downstairs.

"He said that he wants an elevator?"

He was pacing back and forth in the living room.

"We ought to slam him back into that cesspool where he lived in old town Taranto!"

Michele emerged from the bathroom, flattened himself against the wall. Now he was eavesdropping, as he had so many years ago.

"Do your best to make the man listen to reas . . . " Vittorio lowered his voice. " . . . Find him a caregiver, a nurse . . . " Five minutes later he ended the call.

After lunch, Gioia's boyfriend showed up. Michele ran into him on the veranda. Handshake. The same sensation as that other time. Staring at him he felt certain that, as soon as he turned his gaze away, the young man's face would relax.

"*Buongiorno*, Signor Salvemini."

Vittorio came out onto the veranda with the cordless in hand. He tossed a hasty wave in his daughter's boyfriend's direction. He poured a few drops of espresso into the demitasse. Still talking, he walked away down the hall. Gioia's boyfriend vanished upstairs.

Twenty minutes later, Michele still hadn't moved from the veranda. He was listening. His father was still just a few yards away, talking on the phone. He made one call after the other. From his tone of voice, Michele tried to guess the identity of the person on the other end of the line. Irascible (Engineer Ranieri). Exasperated, and then conciliatory and resolute (Ruggero). He was talking about the former undersecretary Buffante. More about this guy from Taranto ("Fine, agreed, with one le . . . sure, sure, but do you understand how many damn obstacles you're going to have to get around to build an elevator in a building of that kind?") He heard his father move away. Then Vittorio came closer again. Once more, he uttered Buffante's name. The words Porto Allegro. Drawled out. Gravely. Opaque and nauseated. It seemed he was speaking with Engineer De Palo. "The chief justice of the Bari Court of Appeals," he said. The chief justice, apparently, was key to the investigating magistrate. The university chancellor could be key to the chief justice of the Court of Appeals. The tone seemed to thicken every time he failed to properly distance himself. The equivalent of a piece of mud that had to be swallowed, thought Michele, as he heard his father's footsteps moving away toward the front door.

Michele made himself an espresso. Then he went upstairs. He gripped the handle of the door to his room. He relaxed his grip. A squeak. He went back, his curiosity piqued. Gioia's bedroom. Ridiculous that they'd left the door ajar. More than a provocation, it struck him as a form of carelessness, as if it were something they were used to doing, a house within that house that had long since collapsed, with them thriving in the disorder, in the absence of authority. Gioia was whispering something in a low voice. She was moaning. She was giggling. He couldn't keep himself from looking at her.

Michele went back to his bedroom. He started to lie down on the bed. He stopped himself. From right to left. The nightstand. The armoire. He looked around with a worried expression. The half-open window. His heartbeat accelerated. Stay calm. She can't have jumped out the window. He sat down on the edge of the bed. He took off his shoes without making any noise. He picked one up off the floor. He gripped the end of the lace. He pulled it out. He leaned forward, started moving his wrist so that the lace undulated across the floor like a snake. Another couple of seconds and the cat shot out from behind one of the doors of the armoire, hurled herself onto the shoelace, and started to play.

Four patches of light. They ran over the edge of the fountain, rose up to the leaves. Vanished. Five in the afternoon.

Michele went downstairs again. He stepped out onto the veranda. He saw her rosy cheeks while, as if she were still a little girl, she drank her milk, holding the cup with both hands. She was alone. He noticed that she had noticed him. His sister set the cup down on the table. From her fixed gaze (and also from the unreality, the evanescence that anyone pretending nothing has happened can confer upon their features), he understood that she was hoping he wouldn't approach.

Michele approached. He sat down facing her.

"Ciao, Gioia."

She was wearing a light cotton blouse and pajama bottoms, sky blue with small white clouds. It wasn't clear whether she was dressed to go out or to go to bed. The afternoon light smoothed out the star of her twenty-five years. On the table, a large book, closed. *Introduction to the Philosophy of Language.* Michele smiled, pointed to the textbook.

"I've started studying again," Gioia sighed. He didn't stop looking at her. She added: "Sooner or later I was going to have to do it. Return to normality. I open it in the morning and it's like reading a book in Chinese. I don't understand a thing. Shit . . . " she shook her head.

It was always strange to talk to someone who had just finished fucking. It meant recognizing in the person before you the mark of a door thrown open and, at the same time, a sign barring entry, all while that body, until just recently heated and abandoned, was now hastening to tidy itself up, to regain so to speak the normal equilibrium between doors closed and thrown open. But to find oneself face to face with one's little sister, well aware that she had just finished fucking, and, what's more, knowing that she knew that you were conscious of the fact (since she'd done everything within her power to ensure that you could see it), this transmuted a vague intellectual seduction into a pleasure that smacked of rot, a pleasure taken from suffocation, since the same body that lay sprawled between the bedclothes and later debated in your presence university exams and grief to be processed might as well have been still writhing, might as well have been molesting you (it obliged you, that is, to imagine its own sex while pretending not to allow you to imagine a thing, since it was you, now, who was forced to find the sum of the moment in which it had allowed you to understand what was happening and the present moment), so that you were able to catch even its odor (though no odor strong enough to be perceptible was produced by that body), so that you found movements, contractions, bent to her wishes.

Her wishes, in this case, were taking form in the expectation that Michele would abstain from asking unwelcome questions.

But Michele did not intend to give in. He made a concerted effort to distance himself. He smiled without dropping his gaze.

"They didn't stop for a second," he said, trying to cast the lure. He was alluding to Vittorio and Annamaria.

Gioia understood immediately. "They're always in a hurry," she said, "they're constantly busy, ever since . . . " she paused. "This Porto Allegro thing . . . I'm not saying it isn't important . . ."

"Everyone reacts the way they can."

"You just say that because you haven't had to put up with them all these years. You weren't the one who had to deal with them every damn day. Instead, they react in a way that *no* mother and father who still have children ought to."

Something satanic truly is pulsating in this sea of stupidity, thought Michele as he looked at her, because right now she was managing to complain while remaining securely lodged in a groove, pretending to be on Michele's side, pretending to raise a small objection against him, while she was in fact on a completely different side.

"Every time one of us had a problem, they always had something else to do," Gioia continued. "They had something else to do even when *they* were the ones who had problems, even major problems. I mean private problems, maybe emotional problems. They can't bring themselves to appear vulnerable. They can't even manage to be affectionate. It's stronger than them. If only they had bee—"

"Do you miss her?"

"Oh, fuck, Michele!" His sister turned pale; her eyes glistened. "From drinking a glass of water to the simple fact of looking at myself in the mirror in the morning. I can't do anything without there being a picture of her right in front of me."

"She was beautiful," he said, stifling the temptation to smack her.

"She was stunning. She had something that ninety-nine people out of a hundred lack. She'd walk into a room and everyone would notice her, even though she'd do nothing to attract attention. For that matter, she was the most generous person on ear—"

"Why do you think she killed herself?"

"Why do you . . . Oh, thank you!" a tear raced down one cheek. "Thank you for asking me these things. Thank you for coming back."

Michele reached a hand out toward hers. She grabbed it.

"Does this seem normal to you?" said Gioia, continuing to cry. "Does this seem . . . oh fuck, Michele!" she broke off, sobbed, blew her nose. "Does it seem possible to you that she's been dead for twenty days and no one in this house even talks about it? Clara's no longer with us, and everyone pretends she's gone off on a little jaunt to Rome." A shiver ran through Michele, Gioia's grip was the artificial light that dimmed the moon's splendor. "There are days when I feel like I'm losing my mind," she went on, "I understand that no one reacts to these things the way they ought to. No one acts like they do in the movies, I understand. But here we're doing the opposite. Look at Mamma," *Annamaria* he thought, making a mental correction, "have you heard her say Clara's name since you came home? Papà has all his troubles with those fucking villas down in the Foggia area. Ruggero. You know what they say about certain doctors, don't you? They save other people at the hospital so they have an excuse not to give a fuck the rest of the time. Even you and me," and here it was as if the tears were solidifying on her cheeks, "why are we only talking about this now?"

Stupefying, thought Michele. She puts a part of the problem in front of you and that's how she neutralizes it, she conceals it by slapping you in the face with it.

"Why do you think she killed herself?" he asked again.

"Ah, Michele, why do people kill themselves?" As she talked, Gioia bared her teeth. "Loneliness. A sense of emptiness. Do you realize the lives we lead?"

"Her marriage," he said.

"Alberto loved her. He's still in love. It breaks my—"

"That wasn't a happy marriage."

"Even happy marriages aren't," she said, "especially not the ones that aim at love. For Clara love was important. She sought it in the ridiculous way we hunt for things that don't exist. We know they don't exist. And yet we keep banging our noses up against them all the time. You know what it's like when you're waiting to meet the one, the moment that will change the way you see things, that will make you put work on the back burner, make you want to get married and maybe have children? What happens when you wait for it and it never comes? And maybe the reason it never comes is that it doesn't exist in the first place, that kind of love was invented by an advertising executive to sell perfume."

Now she was talking as if she were in a TV series. Loosen your grip, he told himself. He pulled his hand away from Gioia's.

After dinner, Michele went for a walk in the garden.

The moon, almost full in the May sky. He stood there looking at it, as if doing so cleansed Clara's voice within him. The wind through the leaves. Then he turned to walk toward the villa. Beyond the front steps, a shadow. Tall, pallid. Annamaria. She's watching me, he thought, she was here waiting for me to come back. He looked at her warily.

"Excuse me," the woman said, "there was something I wanted to ask you."

That's the way she always was. When there's something important, she always dives right in, thought Michele admiringly.

"I wanted to know whether you had plans for Saturday. If you were planning to stay home. Or else . . . "

Twenty days. Twenty days he'd spent without once setting foot outside the villa. Why would he think of going out on Saturday, of all days?

"*Or else?*" asked Michele, embedding the question with the emphasis that forces the interlocutor to voice the thought that follows without having time to disguise it.

"No, nothing," said Annamaria with a hint of embarrassment, "I was just wondering if you would still be . . . or else, if you're staying, I wanted to tell you . . . "

It had slipped out. She had been extremely swift at turning a possible insult inside out, but for an instant Michele managed to glimpse beneath. Her expectation. The desire to have him go back to Rome.

"I wanted to tell you that there's going to be an important dinner and it would make sense for you to be there, that's all," she continued after reading on Michele's face the will to stay on.

"What dinner?"

"Oh, he organized it." The conversation had jumped back onto the tracks of their customary code of communication. "He's invited the chief justice of the court of appeals to dinner. He wants to get a better understanding of this whole thing with the tourism complex. You know what your father's like. He's convinced there's a plot, and in fact, unless I'm mistaken, we might be in real trouble. Obviously he's talked to the chief justice. Having him over to dinner is just one more thing. Human warmth. Your father is convinced that this, too, will turn out to be useful. I'd like it if we were all there," she concluded.

SEP: Student Exchange Program.

That summer, his father and Annamaria decide to enroll Clara in a study abroad program in England. Three months in Eastbourne, where she'll stay with a local family. From blouses to gray pullovers in virgin wool. *Light lunch*, *cream tea*. Brushing up on her language skills. Mingling with young people from all over the world.

Clara tries on an overcoat in a shop downtown. She asks, in a worried voice: "How do I look?"

Photo IDs and new luggage. It all happens so quickly that at first Michele doesn't understand. He takes the danger for enthusiasm, and he allows himself to be infected. When they need to renew the exit visa on Clara's ID card, he offers to take care of getting the documents stamped. In the weeks that follow, he manages to all but forget about it. Clara doesn't mention it when they're together. They pretend nothing's wrong. More time passes.

The day before the departure is a Sunday. Michele wakes up early. He eats breakfast. Then he leaves the house, catches the bus. He stays downtown for a few hours with his friends. They go into a coffee shop. They chat, smoke cigarettes. At a certain point he stops talking. He sets his demitasse of espresso down on the table. A disaster. A horrible premeditated catastrophe. Suddenly it's all clear. He stands up. He leaves without a word.

An hour later he comes running through the villa's front

gate. He's out of breath. He leapt from one bus to another. He goes in the house. He finds Gioia in the front hall sniffling all by herself. His father shouts in irritation: "I can't find it!" The words are aimed upstairs. "Will you help me with the puzzle?" Still Gioia. Michele ignores her. Instead he notices a long line of dresses on the sofa, in their plastic covers, one next to the other. So he gallops furiously up the stairs. He runs down the hall. He resolutely grabs the handle as something grips his stomach.

"Hey! Wait!"

He closes the door again immediately. The long profile sheathed in the white of the panties. It remains impressed for another instant on the retina. The rosy-tipped breasts hurled up to the ceiling as if in a Cubist painting. He's afraid she did it intentionally. Sat there, half-naked, waiting, so that she could reject him in that way. Michele takes a deep breath, opens the door again. He walks forward into his sister's bedroom.

Now Clara is in short shorts, back to the window. The same striped sweater she had in her photo ID. She tips her head back. Michele looks around. On the bed, the open suitcase. From the suitcase, the handle of a hairdryer sticks out. He clenches his teeth to keep from crying.

"You're leaving."

"Michele . . . " Clara comes toward him, it doesn't seem like her.

When she's about to hug him she stops, as if the show threatens to go to pieces if she takes it past a certain point.

"Michele," she tries again, "we won't even notice it. I'll be home again before Christmas."

His sister is sitting on the bed. It seems to him that she's about to start crying, too. Michele doesn't understand how it can be. How they could have failed to realize. The ambush was not only foretold, it actually required their involvement. The form stuffed into the files of the St. Giles International School of Eastbourne. The British pounds exchanged. The tutor over here is already in touch with the tutor over there. Everything has been set up.

"Come on, help me pack my suitcase."

Clara gets back up. The light cuts through her as it slants diagonally into the room and it seems to Michele that his sister is about to dissolve or die, pierced by a sorrow less painful than the dedication it takes her to keep from showing it to him, while still showing it.

"Are you going to be able to fit in all the clothes I saw downstairs?" asks Michele, inflicting the same treatment on himself.

"That's exactly what we're going to find out. Go on, run and get them."

A few minutes later, Michele comes back into the room with the bags stacked one on top of the other. "I'm going to drop them!" Clara lends a hand. Dresses. Sweatshirts. Dusters. One of them grabs an item. The other places it in the suitcase, taking care not to wrinkle it. Buckingham Palace. Driving on the left. Their avatars talk about this nonsense all afternoon. Even the Beatles. They continue over dinner. They say goodnight without looking each other in the eye.

But when Michele wakes up the next morning—the puddle of light on the floor testament to ten hours of sleep—it's not the avatar that finds itself in bed with scalding temples. What reemerges from the sheets is a blinded body. She's not there. They must have taken her to the airport.

Michele drags himself out of bed. He goes down to the kitchen. Three empty mugs. The glitter of the stove top in the glare of the late-August light.

The months without Clara are a sort of fake nightmare. As if the nightmare were being dreamed by a Xerox machine. Which is even worse. Michele goes to school. He comes back home. He does his homework. He plays soccer. But it all takes place in the silence of a vibration without which there's nothing left but the naked material world. If as a child he fell down wells that put him in touch with something so powerful it couldn't be remembered, now the opposite is happening. He'd be able to catalogue the writings on the walls, the license plates on the cars that he sees in the street. Except it's all fake. Roads without a road. Trees without a tree. He misses his sister. He misses her in a stabbing, hallucinatory way. The sense of annihilation is so intense that certain afternoons he forgets what her face is like. How her features change when she laughs. Her lips, rounded, as she says no. So he rushes into the living room and stares at a photograph.

At night, he sleeps poorly. He wakes up with a start, covered in a layer of tar that was the same as in the dream.

In class, she recited the poetry of Ben Jonson. Then there was choir. Standing erect in the blazer with lions embroidered on the breast pocket, she intoned, along with the other girls *Jesu, as Thou art our Saviour*.

In the morning, Michele wakes up as usual in his bedroom. That is, if the days are actually passing. If that really is his room and not the arid space between walls that would look the same to anyone if time were to collapse in on itself. Perhaps he's still going to school. Perhaps he's listening to his math teacher and understanding everything she says. Perhaps, on his way home, he runs into that strange young man with the eyeliner he met some time ago. He says: "It's me, Pietro, do you remember?" Perhaps he shouts: "Hey, I'm talking to you. Can't you hear me? Hey, stop!" On the afternoon of that same day, he's lying in his bed with the pillow over his head. He's mulling things over. Something that could happen when he's home happens precisely when he's not there. Clara phones. Or they call her. Why haven't they spoken since she left? Perhaps Michele is going to school. Perhaps, after lunch, he does his homework. After studying, he picks up the books that she gave him. It's been a while since he last did it. Tyger tyger. *Die Raben*. Where you go, it turns to autumn and to evening. Between one line and the next, one has the impression that time once again begins to flow.

She stepped out of the Jaguar's back door, re-buttoning her blouse to the neck. Whipped by the rains of East Sussex, she readjusted her skirt at the waist. She started down Longstone Road on foot, touched by the lights of dawn.

Michele's eyes open wide. He looks at the clock. Four in the morning. He rolls over in bed.

The next day is Sunday. He wakes up early. Vittorio and Annamaria have gone out. He jumps out of bed, washes up in a hurry, and goes into the kitchen. He puts the espresso pot on the stove. He pulls out the phone book. He opens and closes drawers. The form. He pulls the big dictionary with the red cover down off the shelf. He pours the espresso into the demi-tasse. Then he takes the form, the list, and the dictionary, carries them all over to the phone. He looks up the country code. How do you say "urgenza" in English. He calls the St. Giles School, leafing through the dictionary. A strange prolonged sound. Wrong number. The pressure. So he calls back. Stay calm. They have to believe everything you say.

When the voice responds, he explains everything coolly. The switchboard operator seems quite matter of fact.

"Please, hold on."

As he's waiting, deep inside the receiver he thinks he can hear the fluttering of wings echoing in a tower. Then another voice. All the imaginary sorrow swept away by a sea of reality.

"Clara!"

"Michele! What the hell . . . "

His sister's voice is excited, frightened, embarrassed, wonderfully on the verge of a hysterical fit.

"What's happened? They told me something about an emergency.

"Forget about that. I just said it to be sure . . . "

"You scared me. But Michele, why haven't I heard anything from you these past few weeks?"

"That's the point! It's exactly . . . "

"Every time that Mamma and Papà called me, you weren't there. And then, the other day, when I called, they told me . . . "

"Clara. Listen to me. Now you're going to board a plane and come straight back here to Bari."

"What are you talk . . . "

"Pack your bags and get out of there."

"It's not like I could . . . Have you lost your mind?"

"Never been saner in my life," he says, raising his voice. "Drop everything and leave now. Away from that shitty island. Don't you realize that they're screwing us? That they're doing it on purpose?"

"That who are, for Pete's sake? Who is it that you think is screwing us?"

"It's in their interest to keep us apart. They're . . . Wait! Shut up for a second!"

" . . . "

"What's that sound?"

"What sound?"

"Voices. Voices singing."

"Ah. It's the St. Giles choir."

"And what are they singing?"

"What are they . . . *In Freezing Winter Night*, is what they're singing."

"I knew it! You see?"

"See what?"

"Clara, come back to Bari and do it now."

"Michele, but even if I wanted to . . . " says his sister, and in that hesitation he thinks he's found confirmation of all his suspicions. "Even if I wanted to, I can't very well just leave overnight. If I didn't finish the quarter, when I got home they wouldn't accept the credits. I'd lose the year. And I'd look like an ass. The family I'm staying with . . . "

"The Wilsons!"

"They're called Thompson. And anyway, they're so sweet and all. What would they think if I just left without a word of explanation?"

"So sweet and all? What the hell are you saying? Clara!"

"Listen. In mid-December I'll be in Bari. You only have to . . . we only have to hold out another month and a ha . . . Hello? Hello, Michele!"

(In a certain sense I was right, he'll think seventeen years later, as he finishes taking a long drag on a cigarette at the San Lorenzo station, a year before she dies, just a few seconds after realizing he himself has recovered. He'll look at all the cars on the bypass as if it was the first time he'd seen them. It's obvious that his father and Annamaria didn't send her to England with the specific intent of separating them. It's clear however that they did it—as if they'd foreseen danger, a day of reckoning—because we're not ourselves, he'll think, as he coughs, because we're guided by forces of which we're unaware, we act without knowledge, we say things whose motive is unclear, crimes without guilt and deaths without any apparent cause).

When, on December 12, at Bari Palese airport, as she walks down the steps of the 767 in her short sky-blue overcoat—red-cheeked, but nothing compared to the cold in England—and sees her mother and Gioia frantically waving their arms on the other side of the plate glass, Clara is not surprised. Their bodies adhere to the figure she'd cut out while watching the clouds out the plane window.

As soon as she gets home, she drops her suitcase and catches up with her own mental image, which has been immobile out-side Michele's door for a while now. But when she opens the door and searches for the boy's shape, presumably stretched out on the bed with a comic book in hand, that shape Clara doesn't find.

"Mamma, where's Michele?" she asks later, nonchalantly, at lunch, when her father's there too.

Vittorio mutters something. Gioia has her head bent over her Game Boy.

"Lately, we can't pin your brother down for a minute," says Annamaria, "he's always off somewhere."

"Somewhere where?"

"You tell me. Listen," Annamaria changes the subject, "later let's go with your sister to run some errands downtown."

"No, thanks, Mamma."

"Oh, come on-n-n-n," moans Gioia, lifting her head from the screen.

"No, really, I'm exhausted."

So Clara stays home. She dreams up excuses to put off the girlfriends who call her every half hour. They're anxious to see her again. But she doesn't want to miss Michele's return. She checks her watch. At a certain point, she hears footsteps at the front door. Clara holds her breath. But it's only her mother and Gioia on their way back from shopping.

After dinner, around eleven thirty, Michele finally shows up. She hears him open the front door, she leaps to her feet. But when she sees him emerge from the hallway, she's taken aback.

"Ciao, Clara."

"Ciao, Michele.

They ought to hug, but they hover at a distance. Her brother waves one hand in her direction. He starts up the stairs. Clara follows him submissively up to his bedroom. He's lost weight. He's wearing a strange tattered green jacket. His hair has grown. His face is pale. "Do you have a light?" Even the room has changed. Very neat. A stack of new books. On the wall a poster depicts a vitrified forest. "What is that?" *Europe After the Rain*," he says, "don't you know it?" His face isn't pale, it's actually white, Clara thinks, looking at him more carefully. A ghost. Or an insomniac.

"Well. The lighter?"

He hasn't stopped loving me. But he's a different person now, she thinks. The person he used to be, I've lost him for good.

In the days that follow, Clara studies the situation. She goes back to school. She's brilliant in her meeting with her tutor. She lets her girlfriends celebrate her return. Meanwhile, her gaze is elsewhere. It's vaulting over the walls of the school, pushing through the streets, going into bars and clubs.

In less than a week it has all become reasonably clear. Her brother has a social life. He's hanging out with a group attached to an older boy. A guy who's always in ridiculous getups. He wears makeup, maybe he's on drugs. Pietro Giannelli. It's not hard to spot him racing down Via Amendola on a Sukuzi GSX 400. Michele likes being with him. School. That's the real problem. For a couple of months her brother's performance improved. Then (more or less starting with their phone call in November) his grades started collapsing the way they did a few years ago. Vittorio and Annamaria say they're worried. Her mother insinuates that Michele is suffering from some kind of attention deficit disorder. Over the course of a few days, this disorder is transformed. Without anything significant happening, as if a young man's state of mental health could change according to the chitchat of his parents (of his father and his father's wife, Clara corrects herself), Michele's problem turns into a bipolar disorder. Perhaps a mild form of schizophrenia.

Clara listens to what the two grownups have to say. She sees

Michele come home at night. She observes him carefully. There are times when he actually does have a somewhat hallucinatory gaze. All things considered, though, it's the face of someone in full possession of his faculties. One afternoon she runs into him in the center of town. She went to buy an LP that they played for her in England. She sees him in front of the record store with his new friends. Michele looks up, goes over to her. He makes the introductions. This is Nicola. This is Domenico. Valentina. Pietro Giannelli, thinks Clara before her hand grasps the hand of the guy with the eyeliner. Meanwhile, she's been keeping an eye on Michele. He's laughing. It even seems as if he's sort of playing the fool with that girl Valentina. My brother's doing all right.

"Them," says Michele one Saturday night.

He and Clara have gone out to the movies together. Afterward they've gone to get something to drink. They're sipping a milkshake.

"They need to be stopped," he goes on, "not with words, not with recriminations. They're innocuous only in appearance, but there's nothing innocuous, not even in their silences. If we give them more space, it will be too late."

Clara looks at him without understanding. She decides that she cannot touch him the way she did before. She can't hug him to her. The new understanding doesn't entail physical contact.

Michele stops playing with his straw: "You should know that these are phrases uttered by Adolf Hitler. Taken from his speeches. You should read them. From the beer halls to his official rallies. If their progression had a shape, it would be a funnel. The situation becomes increasingly irreversible. But instead," and here he impulsively lights a cigarette, "what would happen if these phrases were placed instead in the mouth of one of his victims? The words of the most evil man on earth adopted by a truly good person. Not, however, a victim determined to take vengeance, but an innocent, someone who feels pity for him. Cleansed. Transfigured. Don't you believe then that History would retrace its own footsteps? As if another dimension were to open, the light on the path that we rejected when we chose the path of catastrophe."

"Oh shit!" Clara bursts out laughing, slaps a hand down on the table, almost knocking the glass with the milkshake over. "Shit, Michele, are these the kind of things you're saying at school? That's why they lowered all your grades!"

"No. These are things I say at home," he replies seriously.

At home, Vittorio and Annamaria continue to speak of Michele's alleged problems. One day, in the kitchen, while Clara's brother is away, Vittorio asks his wife whether she's noticed anything that's gotten worse recently. His tone is very serious.

"Well," Annamaria replies, "I was hoping to talk to you about it when there was time."

The woman stands up. She vanishes into the living room. She comes back with a half-open envelope. The letter from the vice principal summoning "the parents of Michele Salvemini." As soon as she's finished reading the letter, and before Vittorio can ask "Could you take care of this?" and Annamaria can reply "Certainly, I'll go in and talk to him," it seems to Clara that her folks are showing signs of a solid bond, as if they found the news comforting more than it could be worrisome.

Them, she thinks.

She pushes back her chair. She gets up. She looks at Vittorio and Annamaria. She pushes back a lock of hair with a quick swipe of her hand: "What on earth are you talking about," she smiles incredulously, "my brother isn't sick." She turns her back on them and leaves the room. She's furious. In the hallway, she notices something. Gioia is staring at her aghast. So Clara walks over and leans over her. She gives her a kiss on the forehead, closes her eyes. *Them*, she thinks, *and you, too.*

(It shouldn't be assumed that Annamaria tells Vittorio everything that the high school teachers told her. The Italian teacher confesses she's perplexed. The history teacher speaks of a "scholastic achievement" that is "indeterminable." "A psychological collapse?" Annamaria ventures. The man throws his arms wide. To the English teacher, Michele is "a mystery." To the Latin teacher, "some kind of ghost." The math substitute, though, says it's something else. In fact, Michele started the year out well and then he collapsed. But there is one important thing that the substitute teacher noticed. The classwork that the regular math teacher gave a D minus—classwork that this not yet twenty-eight year-old woman had the stubbornness to go and fish out of the file cabinets in the teachers' lounge—if examined carefully, might lend itself to a different interpretation. At first glance, the problem of calculating the perimeter and area of a square with a side congruent to the height of a rectangle whose area and the proportions between whose base and height are known seems to have been addressed by Michele in an incoherent manner. "You see?" asks the substitute, displaying a sheet of paper covered with incomprehensible marks: first Michele tried to set up an equation, then he gave the effort up entirely and started dividing the base of the rectangle into seven equal parts. "In reality, however," the substitute teacher raises her eyebrows in a way that Annamaria doesn't like one bit, "this is just an alternative system for arriving at the same conclusions. At the correct solution of the problem. I just think that he didn't manage to finish in time. The surprising thing is that the kids hadn't yet studied this alternative method. Do you see what initiative?" And in the subsequent exercises, the substitute realized, something very similar took place. "You might

264 · NICOLA LAGIOIA

not believe it. I didn't believe it at first either. Michele doesn't actually arrive at the solution of the problem, caught up as he is by the anxiety of attacking it in so many different ways, all of them equally correct." "Does that mean that he's mentally confused?" Annamaria interrupts her. "Well, I certainly wouldn't say that," says the substitute with a shrug, "if anything I'd say suspicious. If I were really forced to ascribe it all to a specific state of mind, I'd have to say that he doesn't trust what we teach him. He hasn't, so to speak, taken into account the official version of the truth. He must have considered it to be suspect. Or dangerous. So he went off in search of a method all his own. And, surprisingly, he almost succeeded," and now she laughs, full-throated, "maybe I'm overstating things, but as I review his classwork I get the impression that he's discovering mathematical laws all on his own as he proceeds. And though these are theorems of a certain simplicity, each time it must have taken a tremendous effort. Which is why none of his classwork is finished." "A tremendous effort," Annamaria repeats, "like when someone is on the verge of a nervous breakdown." "I'd have to say no, Signora. To say nothing is hardly to lie if what you omit would only complicate matters needlessly." And so, Annamaria will choose not to report a syllable of this conversation with the somewhat flighty young substitute teacher who won't be there in just a few weeks' time." What do you think we ought to do?" asks Vittorio once his wife is done speaking).

"Ever since they reopened, the magic is gone. They can put on all the fucking music they want on, but it won't work. The black sofas. That was the secret," says Pietro Giannelli.

Clara kneels, stands back up having picked a mud-spattered flyer up off the ground. Then, slowly, she tears it to pieces. The wind tosses the leaves of the willow trees that extend onto the road from the garden, throwing open luminous patches. Giannelli sees them rotating clockwise, but it's just because he's coming down off the acid.

That's when the girl says: "What do you think of psychiatrists?"

Today she's wearing a light blue, long-sleeved cotton sweater, jeans, and a pair of old All Stars on her feet. If he could indulge their shared happiness, he'd kiss her right then and there.

"A bunch of idiots."

"That's what I thought. Same for me."

Naturally, Clara hasn't talked to Pietro about it. She couldn't say exactly when it was that she and Michele decided it. Maybe it started with that song where the singer invited everyone to burn down the disco. An interplay of allusions. A game of Scrabble in which everyone has inserted a letter in such a way that the word forms itself.

Vittorio and Annamaria have decided to have him examined by a psychiatrist.

They can't be stupid enough to pull this move, thinks Clara as Giannelli, after almost brushing against her cheek, takes a step back and says: "See you tomorrow."

It's not clear how the gas can first appeared in the house.

Hidden for the past week in my dresser, thinks Clara. She returns to the living room. She'll stay long enough to take a shower and she'll go out again. She's always off somewhere. Her father has tried to scold her, but she knows how to make him give ground. But then, the following afternoon, Clara goes down into the living room and finds Giannelli sitting on the sofa next to her father. Vittorio invited him in. Clara clutches tight to the last length of railing. Her father picks up a magazine from the glass coffee table and pretends to read. "We'll be late for the movie." In the meantime, she thinks it over. Clearly, something has happened. She can tell from Giannelli's face.

Clara stares for a moment at her father. Vittorio avoids looking up. So then she blesses the gas can. Materializing out of nowhere like the paintings of the physician saints that appeared overnight in the wells of the churches.

"You can't do it."

Clara chuckles on the living room floor, after taking another tug on the bottle. They're half drunk. Ruggero has just won a very important fellowship. Apparently, he'll be going to study in Amsterdam. Vittorio and Annamaria took him and Gioia out to dinner to celebrate. Clara and Michele were left home alone. At first, she was planning to cook. Somehow the bottle of Barbaresco found its way into her hands.

"Do what?" he says with a wink, sitting with his back against the television cabinet.

Clara stretches out on the carpet, like a cat stretching. She looks at him, an unkempt mess, her back on the floor. She takes another drink and turns her head to one side, opens her mouth wide, her teeth bluish, wine-stained.

"Do what," she repeats her brother's words with her eyes closed.

The next week, Vittorio sees her emerge from the darkness of the hallway. Blocky checked shirt and black Wranglers. But she's like a ghost, a presence that hails from some future disaster. She stands in front of him so he can't get past her.

"Is it true that later Mamma is going to take Michele to the psychiatrist?"

"I wouldn't recommend it," she adds before he has a chance to reply.

That night, at the movies with Giannelli, as she kisses him with ferocity, she realizes that it's going to happen again. Very soon. After the man she met in England, she's going to make love with this young man.

But when Giannelli takes her home, the plan goes sideways once again. Two in the morning. Clara sees the cloud of black smoke rising from the villa. Ridiculous that she'd stopped thinking about it. She walks through the gate at a brisk pace, then she slows. Her father comes toward her. "Where have you been until now." A dark, credible voice. As if the seriousness of what has happened opened her up to insinuations (that which, deep in some unattainable depths, he'd like to be justified in thinking of his daughter) that until tonight had never brushed up against her. Clara holds Vittorio's gaze. She wonders what she'd actually wished would happen. That the house would collapse, devoured by the flames? That Vittorio and Annamaria would die?

He walked out of the bathroom with the towel wrapped around his waist. Meowing. The cat performed a complimentary half-turn around his ankles. After extorting a stroke, she leapt up onto the bed. At a quarter to eight, seen through the window, the sunset presented itself as a glass of water into which a few drops of wine had been poured. Twenty days to the start of summer. The cat tensed with the muscles of her posterior. Then she leapt onto the top of the dresser. The love that he felt for the little beast, so different from the love she felt for him. Michele looked at himself in the mirror. He sought on his own face traces of change. Grief excavates along paths that are difficult to comprehend, and to him, just an hour earlier, it had seemed he was dying when in the garden he had recognized the nick on the edge of the fountain. Clara had fallen on it by accident. She'd chipped a tooth.

He undid the towel. He pulled open the dresser drawer. He got out a pair of underpants. He put them on. He put on the socks as well. He took the striped shirt, pulled it on, first one arm then the other. From downstairs came the noise of major operations. Tables being moved, crockery stacked. Soon the chief justice of the court of appeals would arrive. The plates arranged on the table like a flower pushing out petals from nowhere. Michele smiled into the mirror. The signs of disgust, so much quicker to show themselves. He wondered whether with her prodigious sense of hearing the cat would hear the red-hot coils in the stove, cooking the sea bass in its salt crust.

Idiot wind, a rain of leaves on the record stores. All my problems seemed so far away. The clouds were scudding over the waterfront and my brother had the indecipherable smile of lead on newsprint.

Not even when she cheats on Alberto with the owner of the gym, or when she enters the Palace Hotel for the newspaper guild party, not even at the moment she swallowed all those sleeping pills will Clara be able to forget the afternoon she rushed out to the newsstand to buy the copy of *La Città* that featured Michele's first piece.

At the time, he went everywhere dressed in a horrible oil-skin jacket. Clara has enrolled, without enthusiasm, in the School of Architecture. Though she considers him capable of winning an argument with a university professor, reading his name at the end of the article still stirs her deeply. The third newsstand she went to. The first two had never even heard of the paper.

She rips out the page with the article, and tosses the rest in the trash. She turns on her heels and strides off, clutching her trench coat shut to ward off the wind.

Since the night of the fire, things had been getting steadily worse. You couldn't say that she and Michele had drifted apart on purpose. Maybe they'd suffered some sort of blowback from which they'd never managed to recover. The disappointment. Maybe they deserved no better than what happened. Neither of the two was, perhaps, the innocent, pure-hearted soul Michele talked about that time after the movies.

At night they cross paths around the Black Drone (ex Stravinsky Club). She's downed a couple of vodkas. These days, alcohol doesn't seem to have any effect on her. Michele is hunched over in a black jacket with a couple of guys she's never seen before. Brother and sister exchange a smile. They have a hard time talking. She tries to strike up a conversation. He looks at her, says nothing. Intermittent explosive disorder. A mild form of schizophrenia, the psychiatrist had said. Should Clara believe it? The fact is that lately he's been so strange, all closed up inside himself. As if he were doing his best to fit into the groove of the diagnosis.

At home, in the middle of dinner, Michele stands up without warning and say: "Fine. I'm going for a smoke in the garden."

Vittorio and Annamaria don't so much as bat an eye. Even if he smoked at the table, they wouldn't scold him. They let him do what he wants. In turn, he lets them do what they want, but they're getting the better of the exchange. Clara carves at her finger with a fingernail. As if things, for some time now, had reached a point where doing nothing leads to inevitable consequences.

A few minutes later, she catches up with him in the garden.

Michele takes a drag on his cigarette, looks up at the stars shining against the November sky. The cinder turns an intense red. At least his second, Clara reckons.

"Why are you staring at me?"

"I'm not staring at you."

"Before you got here, I thought I could hear the garden seething."

"You . . . you what?" she asks, touching her forefinger to her teeth.

"The plants. The flowers. As if they were talking."

"And, excuse me . . . what were they saying?"

"They were dying," he takes another drag, "they were alive

270 · NICOLA LAGIOIA

a long time ago. Now it's as if they were circumscribed by a square. In nature, you'll never find two identical ladybugs. A square is an abstraction. Besieged by something that doesn't exist. The truth is too delicate, too haughty not to allow itself to die in the presence of such a grave insult. This, before you got here."

"And now that I'm here?"

"Now the garden has been dead for centuries."

"Do you want me to go away?"

"No, no, you can stay."

In the past few weeks, Clara has started having sex with other boys. Pietro Giannelli is in the dark about it. In a rather reckless way, he's presumed that he's her boyfriend now. If only he'd stop to think for a second, she tells herself, then he'd easily be able to figure it out. It's as if at a certain point her olfactory tracts had gone off kilter. All the places she used to hang out in strike her as pathetic now. Giannelli's leather jackets make her feel like laughing in his face, and then giving him a hug for the sadness he inspires.

So, one afternoon, leaving the university late, she casts her eyes on a stranger at the bus stop. He must be younger than thirty. Curly hair, an athlete's physique. He runs his eyes over her. Clara meets his gaze before he has time to look away. The young man smiles at her. "Ciao." His physical beauty strikes her then as even more obvious. "How are you?" Clara responds. Half an hour later, they're at his place. As they're making love, she brings herself pleasure as if she were skinning an animal. That night, she'll go to the movies with Giannelli. That afternoon, in the meantime, she walks alone through the streets of the city center. She feels pity for the university students who stand crumbling hash into joints near Piazza Umberto. The glowing sign of the Macondo bar serves only to run up the electric bill. A lower degree of hypocrisy in the Prada and Armani signs. The new spiral parking structures.

Buildings being renovated along the waterfront. She feels as if she can see written text superimposed over them. As if a caption were popping out from behind every corner. Giannelli is at the entrance to the Odeon. While they watch the movie, he takes her hand. If only he understood what reality is actually made up of, she thinks, if he knew that this very hand is still warm from another man. End credits. On the one hand, Clara feels as if she understands things with a clarity she's never before possessed. On the other, she is forced to admit that the direction in which her life is moving is not at all clear. The university. Since enrolling, she's spent maybe one or two days with her books.

But then, every time one of her brother's articles comes out, she rushes to the newsstand to get a copy of the paper. She reads hungrily, in search of hidden meanings. One Sunday morning, sipping a cappuccino in a café. One night, after a fight with Giannelli. She runs her finger over the lines from left to right. They're obscure, fascinating pieces. At the very best moments, she feels as if she understands without understanding anything. She talks herself into believing that Michele is developing a secret code to stay in contact with her. As if their relationship were continuing undercover. He might have found a way of sending her messages, a distant place into which they can retreat to talk, to tell each other things that outside of there would sound ridiculous or implausible.

One afternoon in early December, Clara finds Michele talking to himself in the garden. She is coming home. She's wrapped in an overcoat, bundled in a cashmere sweater that keeps her warm. She walks through the gate. She walks past the fountain, too, heading for the steps. I'm not really sure I got that. Clara stops. She retraces her steps.

He's standing against the large terracotta vase, bent over the ferns.

"Michele, is everything all right?"

"Ciao."

Clara stands there for a moment, taken aback. Her brother's eyes drill right through her. His lips alternately relaxed and puckered as if he were about to say "no" but then didn't say it. A room where the drawers have all been rummaged through and then everything has been put back and tidied by a hand paid to do so. Even his clothing seems to fall off him.

"Hey, seriously, are you okay?"

"Yes, everything's fine."

She nods goodbye. She heads toward the front door. As soon as she turns her back on him, she hears the whispering again. So she goes back a second time. She puts an arm around his neck. The compliance with which Michele lets her do this makes her feel bad. She hugs him to her. They head toward the house. And, still side by side, holding him as if he were five, she leads him up the stairs.

Once upstairs, Michele wriggles free. He walks down the hall. He enters his room. Clara has the impression she hears the key turn in the lock. And so she lengthens her stride, leans against the doorjamb. After a few seconds, she takes her ear away from the door. The hem of her overcoat hangs over her calves, then folds like the pleats of an accordion. Now she's sitting on the floor. She shuts her eyes and tries hard not to cry.

"A general. Or otherwise, I don't know, a warrant officer from the carabinieri. Or maybe a doctor, a cardiologist. He could diagnose him with a heart murmur."

"You're saying I need to get someone to put in a good word for him."

Clara is in Vittorio's office, sitting across from him. It's eight at night. No one's home. The hotel with the golf course built in the Salento in the Sixties. A crew of construction workers on the stretch of highway running from Cadiz to Seville. Clara turns her gaze away from the pictures hanging on the wall, turns her eyes on Vittorio again. Separating them is a desk diary and a large paperweight in the shape of an airplane.

"Papà, it's so obvious that we need to get someone to put in a good word for him, and in a hurry! That certificate of fitness is the stupidest thing I've ever seen in my life." For a moment it seems as if she's about to violently rip herself away from the chair. "Do you have any idea the condition he was in after his draft examination?"

"He's always been a young man with in his own particular w—"

"Papà, he was *talking to himself.*"

"All he'd need to do is enroll in the university."

"Only he *doesn't want* to enroll."

Vittorio has an incredulous look on his face. His expression seems swept clean of defensive intention. He slowly rotates his hands on the desk, as if he were shaping the small god of justifications.

"But didn't you tell me—"

"I don't know exactly what happened during his draft exam," she interrupts him again, "maybe they noticed he was odd. In other words . . . he's different from all those . . . when they're doing draft exams at the barracks, all kinds of people show up, don't they?"

"I served in the military."

"They must have seen how introverted he was . . . maybe they ganged up on him. Oh, come on, everyone knows the kind of fucked up pranks . . . " she heaves a sigh. "I'm not saying they did anything to him. Maybe they did nothing more than to *say something* to him. But that's all the more reason, if that's all it took. The fact remains that he was a mess that day. I don't understand how we can even think of . . . "

"It seems to me that he's okay now."

"I stood there for a half an hour listening at that door. The things he was saying aren't the things someone who's okay would say."

"Now, let me point out, it strikes me that your brother behaves in a fairly normal way. He goes out at night. At school he's passing. As far as I can tell, he's going to graduate without problems. He doesn't seem to me to be in danger of losing his mind. He was talking to himself, you say . . . "

Vittorio hesitates, furrows his brow, as if he were seized by some preventive regret, the suspicion that this is the last opportunity to change course. Michele, his mother's death, making peace with what happened. To confront it before the error becomes irreversible. A presentiment. Vittorio decides to ignore it.

"Come on, Clara," he smiles, "who doesn't talk to themselves every so often? You should have heard me the day after the finance police came to see me. Monologues an hour long, the whole time staring at that little airplane there," and he points to the paperweight in the shape of a bomber.

"Papà, the fact that he *seems* normal doesn't mean that he is. Even if for certain periods he manages to achieve an apparent state of equilibr—"

"But you're the one who said your brother wasn't ill."

Vittorio now has his hands clasped, an even more baffled expression on his face. A wrestler, a rock crusher. How could it be that someone like him suddenly appears so ill equipped? Clara feels a slight dizziness.

"Papà," she presses her thumb against her forefinger as if she were crushing a pencil, "I'm begging you to make an effort of the imagination. Think of Michele in a barracks. A whole year far from home. Thrown into a place where every instant is regulated by a concept as rational as only the will of superior officers can be. At worst, though, it's the will of the strongest, the most violent. So there you are. Just tell me what you see.

Because what I see is something I don't like one bit. Some friend of yours in the army. A cooperative doctor, maybe some colleague of Ruggero's. Whoever it was who put his signature on that certificate had no idea what he was doing. You *have* to get him a deferment."

"Get him a deferment," Vittorio picks up a pencil, starts drawing circles on a blank sheet of paper, "but just think, if he was rated unfit, he'd lose a whole series of rights. Faking myopia would mean he could never be an airline pilot, if that's what he decided he wanted to do one day. Aside from the fact that finding someone to give him a deferment in cases like this isn't exactly as easy as drinking a glass of water."

This is where Clara's dizziness turns into nausea. There's something foul in Vittorio's languor, at least as marked as determination when he decides to shove aside an adversary. He may not be able to force her to come home early at night if she doesn't want to. But there's nothing that Clara can do to convince him, if he's opposed.

"Oh, who gives a damn if he can never become an airline pilot," she says, exasperated, discomfited, hollowed out. "Who cares if he can't join the civil service on account of a heart murmur he doesn't have. Don't you even understand that what's at stake here is something . . . " her voice catches in her throat.

"I promise you," he says firmly, "I promise that we'll do everything within our power."

Clara tries talking about it with her mother, too. But the distance that's grown up between them ensures that the woman dismisses all objections with even greater facility.

"Do you think that if there was any real danger your father wouldn't have done something?" is all that Annamaria has to say a week before Michele's departure.

These are days when her brother is, anyway, impossible to track down. He leaves the house first thing in the morning. At night no one knows exactly what he does. Clara finds him unexpectedly at home long after midnight. She's alone, watching TV with a can of beer when she hears the footsteps in the front hall. A slow shadow, then him. But at that hour, all Michele wants is to sleep. He greets her with the same gesture a traffic cop might use to order a driver to halt.

The day before his departure, Clara enters his room as he's packing his bags.

"Ciao."

She finds him on his feet, folding a pair of pants. The suitcase on the floor. A pile of underwear on the bed. He looks skinnier than usual, less substantial. But the room, too, is strange. It gives the impression of losing weight as the seconds tick by. "Ciao," he responds. His face is so distant that Clara can feel herself vacillate. If the roles were reversed, it could be the scene of her departure for England. But now there's something else. Clara can't know that this will be the last time Michele ever occupies his room. She also doesn't know that she, in less than a year's time, will leave this house. And yet the untranslated language of the imminent future swells the walls.

At that point Clara sits down on the edge of the bed. With a confidence that she can feel draining away, she holds her hands out to Michele. Michele stares at her, dumbfounded. She persists, motionless, arms extended, until he finally has no choice but to take her hands.

"If you don't want to leave, you can stay here."

Michele smiles.

"If you don't want to take that stupid train to Avellino," and she clenches her brother's hands a second after he starts trying to wriggle free, feeling ridiculous, "then just don't set your alarm tomorrow. Or else go out and don't come home."

"You've been drinking."

"What?"

"You've been drinking. Your breath."

"Oh, two stupid glasses just to get rid of the . . . Michele, don't leave if you don't want to go."

"What on earth are you talking about? It's not as if I can," and he looks at her as if she were his baby sister.

"We aren't at war," Clara resumes her grip, and he lets her, "it's not as if we're under martial law. If leaving right now strikes you as nonsense, and it strikes me as a huge pile of nonsense, don't get on that train, and the worst that can happen to you is some kind of administrative sanction. And anyway, probably, with Papà's help—"

"It seems to me if I don't go, I'll be looking at something worse than a simple fine."

He untwists his hands from hers. He steps back. The unruffled look on Michele's face is unbearable. He turns his back to her. Clara sees him rummage through the drawers. He pulls something out. He turns and comes toward her. He has some stapled sheets of paper in his hand.

"But I did want to ask you a favor."

He entrusts her with the new article he's written for *La Città*. A lengthy refutation of Joseph Heller and his novel about military life. He tells her that he mailed it to the paper a couple of weeks ago, but that strangely the piece still hasn't been published. He asks her if she'll take it to the senior editor in person.

The first day without Michele, Clara feels as if she's going crazy.

She wanders through the house like certain pets when they're deprived without warning of some crucial point of reference. She goes out before lunch, skips a series of appointments, drives alone around the streets of the city. Even though she hasn't spent all that much time with her brother in the past few months, it still felt to her as if she were picking up his signal. She might not have had any idea of exactly where he was, but in every instant of the day she felt the imprint of a tiny dot that turned off and on, echoing through the void. Now that signal has vanished.

The second day without Michele, as soon as she wakes up, she goes downstairs and immediately feels as if she's been thrown off balance by the sheer act of looking around. The objects. She has the impression that nothing is related to anything else anymore. A chair. The tea kettle. The cooktop. The kitchen no longer exists as a whole, only the objects in and of themselves. She clutches the mug of hot milk as if it were a handle without which she would fall into the void.

A sound behind her. Gioia, too, walks into the kitchen. Clara catches her breath. She stops clenching her teeth. She realizes that she's just stifled the instinct to hurl the scalding milk in her sister's face. She greets her. She abandons the mug on the table. Then she leaves the kitchen, exhausted. She goes upstairs to her room. She puts on a pair of jeans, a T-shirt. She puts her wallet, a pair of sunglasses, the stapled pages, and her driver's license into her bag.

In the city center, she walks four times around the block without being able to make up her mind to go in. Stalling for time, she enters a record store. She stands looking at the display window of a jewelry shop. She eats a grilled cheese sandwich. She wastes more time. Hours later, she goes back and surveys the area around the corner of Via Cairoli and Via Dante. It occurs to her to call Giannelli. But it's a desperate thought, and she knows it. At last, she heads for number 127 on Via Cairoli. She climbs the stairs to the newsroom of *La Città*.

As she talks to the senior editor, that is, while she implores him to publish Michele's piece, she thinks for a moment that she's heard his signal. Extremely faint. But once out on the street, the signal has vanished.

The next day, she phones the barracks. A young man with

the voice of a castrato tells her that he's answering from the regimental office. He informs her that today it's not possible to speak with enlisted men, but then (as if it were the logical consequence of what he'd just said) he asks her to call back in two hours. Clara calls back, the phone rings and rings, but no one picks up. That evening she tells her father that he must, "absolutely," let her know when they hear from him.

Two days later, Annamaria summons her from downstairs because "Michele's on the phone."

"No, yes. Everything's fine. It's just that it's kind of cold here. At night, more than anything else."

That's what Michele's voice says through the receiver before she even has a chance to ask him how he is. The tone is dull, slightly metallic. Clara repeats: "Cold?" and overcomes the gazes of her parents who are watching her attentively because of the strange expression that must have surfaced on her face. She folds her hand into a shell in front of her mouth.

"Would you rather we talked when I'm alone?" she whispers.

"Yes. Thanks for the phone call."

"But just tell me what time I can call you there in the barrac—"

He's hung up.

In the days that follow, Clara telephones a number of times. She's worried. Michele's tone evokes images that ought normally to be sad, but that seem to her like the normality behind which something else lies hidden. At the barracks, the same voice as the last time answers. A different voice answers, but it's still the voice of someone who seems to have no idea what she's saying. A couple of days later, a third voice tells her: "Clara Salvemini. Michele's sister?" "Yes, that's right," she replies. "Well, listen, your brother left a message. He says to call him at 7:30, even if what he wrote right here is 7:27." Clara is about to hang up. "Excuse me!" she reconsiders. "Yes, I'm listening." "Did he write thirty or twenty-seven?" "Twenty-seven . . . and, listen . . . " he says this time. "Yes?" "It's just that I wanted to understand. Because maybe you, being his sister . . . " "Yes, what is it?" asks Clara, suddenly alarmed. She hears other voices overlapping. "Then just call back later," the young man says, cutting her off.

At a quarter past seven, surrounded by the palm trees of Piazza Umberto, Clara occupies a phone booth across from a stand selling drinks and sandwiches. To keep the two men standing in line from complaining, she pretends to talk into the receiver. After a few minutes, she dials the number for the barracks. She drops her eyes, stares at the metal grate. The switchboard operator's voice says: "Hello?" She asks to talk to her brother.

"Difficult to communicate. Anyway, yesterday I was fine," he's saying at a certain point.

"Michele!"

"Yesterday a magnificent day. The sunlight. As if through the sunlight I were able travel back to certain afternoons from the past. Back then you were there, too. You understand. But this is exactly what . . . "

"What . . . But how are things up there? What's life like in the barracks?"

"Down here, you mean. Avellino is actually just a little south of Bari."

"Sure, all right. What I meant to say . . . "

"That's what doesn't work. If yesterday I was feeling so well in the past, today it's as if I were stuck there. As if I were looking at myself right now from back there. You're there with me, on that long-ago afternoon, and at the same time, I'm being watched by the both of us while I'm here in this barracks. So I wondered whether at the time when it seemed that I was capable of traveling to the future I wasn't really, basically, already here. As if it had all happened just yesterday. And there it is, the contradiction in terms. And when those boys asked me to come with them to the orderly room because it was over . . . "

"What boys? What orderly room? What are you talking about, Michele!"

"Oh, please. Don't start getting upset. They'd lied. Here we all seem to be a little too upset. But, more importantly," his voice is different, "the piece on Joseph Heller."

"The piece on Heller," Clara repeats, staring furiously at the two gentlemen outside until they stop staring at her. "I went to the paper. I talked to the guy. He told me not to worry. From what I was able to understand, it's just a matter of—"

"Forget about that piece. It's gone."

"What? How do you mean, gone?"

"But Christ Almighty, are you not understanding on purpose?" and what frightened her wasn't the sudden souring of the voice, but the fragility of its harshness. "If I tell you that it's gone, it means it's gone. Dated, obsolete. Kaput. Learn to open your ears when someone talks to you. That piece should never have come out because it already came out."

"Already came out."

"It's like writing a piece that came out ten years ago. You'd have to be arrogant not to see it clearly. You'd have to be a pathetic asshole daddy's boy. Those boys in the orderly room tried to teach me that point."

Clara narrows her eyes. She wants to clap her hands over her ears. Now her brother has burst out laughing.

"Michele! Cut it out! Cut it out, for Christ's sake!" she wishes she could punch the plastic dome of the phone booth.

"No, you cut it out!" he snarls. "And do exactly what I tell you."

"Yes."

"Go back to the newspaper."

"Yes."

"That piece of shit newspaper."

"Okay."

"That good for nothing, Giuseppe Greco. Tell him not to publish the piece about Joseph Heller. To publish it would be a grave error. Like making something happen that had already happened in the past. Blasphemy. But listen. In place of the Heller piece you have to get him to run a different piece. It's a piece about a poet. Possibly the greatest poet of the past hundred years. I'm still writing it. Every time I add two lines, I'm the first to be amazed. As if I were putting something together a few years from now, but none of it is my doing. You understand. Clara, but what are you . . . come on now!"

She's crying.

"Come on, Clara, let's stay calm," his voice is newly kind.

"Please . . . please," she says, unable to stop, "I'm begging you . . tell me when I can . . . What I'm trying to say is I need to see you."

"Well, you could have said so earlier," and now he's actually cheerful. "That is, sorry, I should have told you. What a dope I am. I have some leave. I'll be in Bari next weekend."

But the following Friday, Michele doesn't show up in Bari. He doesn't get there on Saturday either. When Clara asks for explanations, she sees her father's face darken. Annamaria looks away.

"What's happened?" she asks, worried.

"Nothing is what's happened," Vittorio says. "It's just that his leave was revoked and he couldn't come. A problem we're taking care of."

There's no further trace of the man who a few months ago handled her requests with a timid evasion. Now he's the boss, taking charge of operations, and he doesn't want any interference.

"Taking care of what."

"I already told you. A problem."

"Okay, tell me what problem."

"A problem with a military court, if you really want to know," Vittorio snaps, as if it were partly her fault. "A problem of the kind that the other day your brother pressed another soldier's hand down onto a kitchen grill. A grill that was on and not, I think, by chance. Apparently he ruined the poor guy's hand only because he couldn't manage to slam his face onto the grill."

"If he did something like that he must have had his . . . " Clara says disjointedly. She's scared, upset.

"We're talking about a crime. A crime committed in a barracks. And for your information this isn't something over which we can convince the victim to withdraw charges. We can't put this thing to rest with a bunch of apologies and a check for damages. They don't even need a criminal complaint from the victim. This is something they're required to prosecute. To get him out of this situation we'd almost have to pray that your brother is out of his mind. And this," says Vittorio, totally illogically, "this is the result of having managed things the way you all insisted."

"I want to talk to him."

"What is it you want to do?"

"I want to talk to him on the phone. I want to talk to Michele."

"Oh, certainly. Your brother practically murdered some poor guy and now you'd like to call him on the phone. Fine. Be my guest. Ask the judge in charge of detention."

Clara spends the next few days phoning the barracks and going around town.

Having received an invitation from a former high school classmate that she would have trashed just a few months ago, she shows up alone at a party for young lawyers at the Yacht Club. She moves in her evening gown past silver buckets full of iced wine. "Clara! What a surprise!" The next morning, she phones the barracks. Later, at the Teatro Piccinni, she buys a ticket for Peter Brook's production of *The Tempest*. In the afternoon, she phones the barracks. The usual voice informs her that it's not possible to talk to Michele. "All right, I'll call back," she replies. That night, squeezed between two bejeweled matrons, she's watching Caliban's antics on the theater's stage. She realizes she's being observed. Three rows ahead. A man in his forties. His face skinny, polished, pleasing in its way if it weren't entirely expressionless. The glances seem to her so shameless that Clara doesn't even feel offended. The next afternoon she manages to snag a spot with the finest hairdresser in the city. "Are you sure, ma'am?" When she goes home, her mother tells her that she looks like Jacqueline Kennedy. They go out together in the center of town. They spend five million lire on clothing. That same evening, Clara goes with her parents to dinner. They eat at the restaurant with the director of the Banca di Credito Pugliese. Together with him are his wife and his thirty-five-year-old daughter. When they leave the restaurant, Clara says goodnight and leaves. She spends a few hours at the Blue Velvet. She comes home drunk. The next afternoon she calls the barracks. "I can't believe you don't know where the hell my brother has gone!" she shouts at the young man who has the voice of a castrato. The young man tells her to call back. Later Clara drinks an aperitif with the bank director's daughter. They talk about holidays, the wedding of a friend they have in common. She's a little tipsy. That evening she takes her new friend to a party being thrown in honor of an academic. She's bored to death. She doesn't touch a drop of alcohol. In the morning she phones the barracks. That evening she has a fight with her father.

Vittorio sees her come into his study, in a short silk sleeveless dress and high black boots. On her earlobes, she's wearing the earrings encrusted with diamonds and tanzanites that her mother gave her many Christmases ago.

"Why am I unable to talk with Michele?" she asks without so much as saying hello.

Vittorio lays the pen down on his desk diary, raises his head.

"Oh, well, you see . . . " he says, making an effort to conceal his satisfaction at her new appearance, of which he instinctively approves, "that's exactly the problem I've been working on these past few days. We're getting everything squared away."

"Yes, but I make phone calls to the barracks, and they never put me through to him. Where is he now?"

"Good question," Vittorio sighs. "He is, so to speak, in a juridical void at the moment. He's where he shouldn't be. Which is a way of saying that he isn't where he ought to be. He's not in solitary confinement. And he's even not in prison, thank heavens."

Vittorio stands up. He walks over to the bookshelf. He pulls a file folder out of a cabinet. He comes back to the desk. Now he's in the exact place where he'll be fifteen years from now, when they call him to say that she's dead. He pops open the binder rings. He pulls the sheet of paper out of a plastic sleeve.

"The request to be filed with the detention judge," he says. "Greatest possible impact in the briefest possible space. Thanks to this, your brother will soon be set free."

The following morning Clara phones the barracks. They tell her to call back in the afternoon. In the afternoon, no one answers. In the evening, she goes alone to the Yacht Club. Dance music. A man in his fifties dressed all in white tries to chat her up. He pays her a series of vague compliments. Clara stares at him. The man smiles. She ditches him by the buffet table. *Giannelli*, she thinks for the last time, on her way home. The next morning she phones the barracks. They tell her to call back. Clara chokes back the tears. That evening she's in her room, staring at the ceiling. She's taken a tranquilizer. At nine thirty, she decides to go do something. She gets up from the bed. Without bothering to shower, she slips into the dress she wore the night before. She leaves home. She gets in her car and heads into town. Half an hour later, she makes her entrance onto the roof garden of the Oriente Hotel. It's a ninetieth birthday party for one of the city's old mayors. From what she can tell when she gets there, the birthday boy has already blown out his candles, delivered a brief speech, and gone to sleep, urging the guests to continue to enjoy themselves. Clara wanders around the buffet tables. She serves herself: first and second glass of cold white wine. She greets an acquaintance. When she's about to grab the bottle again, the waiter beats her to the punch. He slips it out of her hand. "Allow me," he smiles. An overgrown boy with red hair, cropped short. He can't be any older than twenty. She intentionally moves her glass so that the wine splashes onto the tablecloth. She stares at the boy, until she sees the blush spread across his face. Now the wine is once again being poured in the right place. Now Clara's arm is still. She's noticed something out of the corner of her eye. She waits until the waiter is done pouring. She turns. She smiles sarcastically.

"Are you in the habit of staring at people like that?"

Charcoal gray suit, black shoes, white shirt. Small blue eyes. Solid-color tie. He doesn't smile, not even as he watches her approach him with a badass swagger.

"At the theater the other night you wouldn't stop staring at me. And now even when I had my back to you."

"Clearly in both cases I was enjoying the show," he says without a hint of irony.

"Oh, is that right? And what type of show do you think I am?"

"I was just looking at you because I know your brother."

"Michele?" Clara's eyes open wide.

"No, the oncologist. Ruggero."

The man's gaze is so level and expressionless that Clara feels as if she's been run through like the other night. No pain. No attraction. Nothing.

"Silvio Reginato, I'm a surgeon," he introduces himself, shaking her hand, "and it strikes me that tonight you've overdone it a bit with the wine."

Clara bursts out laughing: "Ah! Exactly the kind of thing you'd expect from a—"

"You're right, a stupid thing to say," and he puts a hand on her back. "How about we both go get a cup of coffee."

He gives her a brief shove. Clara starts walking. They go past the table with the pastries. Her head swivels slightly. His footsteps behind her. Clara stiffens. She does it just enough so this man will take his hand off her back. He doesn't. So they go past the table with the espresso machine. The scene seems to glow at its center, blur at the edges. Curtain, tied back. They leave the room. They go through the atrium. Then a black door. At last, he takes his hand off her back, opens the door, and ushers her through. Now it's all white. A long marble table with blue veins. Three faucets, one after the other.

"But this is the bathroom," Clara points out in a fairly obvious way.

She hears the key turn in the lock. She doesn't have a chance to turn around in time. He's walked past her again. He slips a hand into his jacket pocket. He bends over the marble counter. He dries the space between the faucets. He starts laying the coke on the surface. It all seems to happen very quickly. At the same time, the man doesn't seem to be in any hurry.

"Be my guest."

Clara takes the banknote out of his hands. She bends over the counter. She closes her right eye. She positions the rolled-up banknote over the small white trail, and snorts. A cold drop glitters in the eye still open. She feels the man's hand. It slips without hesitation under her skirt. It slips under her panties, makes way, enters.

The next morning, Clara wakes up with tremendous headache. She's convinced that it must be past noon. She throws open the windows. She half-shuts her eyes. She reaches out and picks up the alarm clock from the floor in a corner of the room. She doesn't know how it wound up there. Nine-thirty. She curses herself. She staggers into the bathroom, washes her face. She goes back into the bedroom and starts getting dressed. As she's about to leave she feels something icy grip her temples. She wraps her arms around her belly. She rushes into the bathroom. Ten minutes later she's back in her room. She picks up her purse and leaves.

She drives to the end of Via Fanelli. As soon as she sees a phone booth she pulls over. She phones the barracks. She asks for Michele. "You're the sister, aren't you?" Clara drags out a "yes." The voice is the one from so many phone calls ago. It's not the same one as always. "Yes, certainly, that's me," she confirms, and she feels her legs give beneath her. "Listen," says the voice, "strictly speaking I'm not even authorized to give you certain information." He tells her that Michele isn't in the barracks. He's at the Alma Mater in Salerno. Clara hangs up. Her head still hurts. She gets back in the car. She returns home. She has a quick lunch and goes up to her room. Exhausted. She collapses onto the bed.

She reopens her eyes when it's already the middle of the afternoon. She must have slept for two hours. She yawns, caressing the nape of her neck. Then it's as if her eyes fly wide open, even if they don't. I wasn't dreaming. Ten minutes later, she's back in the car, she presses down on the accelerator. Then she starts to slow down. She gets out of the car. She steps into the phone booth. She dials the switchboard number and asks for the Alma Mater of Salerno. Someone tells her that it's a psychiatric clinic. She asks for the phone number and hangs up. Now she's breathing slowly. She looks through the glass at her parked car. Other vehicles go sailing past on the road. Clara opens and shuts her right hand, as if she were about to give blood. She lifts the receiver and calls the Alma Mater. She asks for her brother. They put her on hold. The switchboard operator again. She tells her to call back in half an hour.

Half an hour passes, Clara phones again. She asks for Michele. She's told to hold. A piece of music starts playing. Five minutes later, the music stops.

"Clara."

"Michele, thank heavens!" she swings a weak punch against the phone booth wall. "But what did you get up to? Jesus . . . And how did you wind up . . . How are you?" she catches her breath.

"I've really messed things up. I understand that."

Understand what? The voice strikes her as even stranger than it was a couple of weeks ago, far too calm.

"But when are you getting out of there? When are you coming home?"

"Come on, now we'll see. Let's do things nice and calmly. We need to stay calm and collected. You know . . . "

A very tired voice, a voice Clara might find common ground with when she's asleep, not now.

"You know," he resumes, "I even broke a tooth."

"A tooth?"

"I thought I was the only one, but luckily that's not the case. It happens to lots of guys. The rubber mouthpiece. At a certain point you clench so hard that you run the risk of breaking a few teeth. It's really tough at first."

"Yes," Clara looks out again at the traffic in the street, afraid that now she understands.

"The first day, there are times when you can't remember

who you are. Who your family is, who your friends are. Just think, I couldn't even remember you. Total void."

"Yes," she nods again. She'd feel she were dying if it weren't for the fact that in order to hold his hand, virtually, she has to hurl herself into a dimension where listening to these things leaves one indifferent. "Yes." She observes the trees, the blue sky.

"That's the way it is," says Michele, "and just to have something to hold onto I immediately asked for something to read. They gave me a copy of *Il Mattino*. I'd get past the first few lines and forget what the piece was talking about. So then I had to start over."

"And now?" she asks.

"This kind of thing is all right again," his voice is even calmer now than it was before, puffed up with hot air, "and after the first few days the other things come back to mind, too. Slowly, then increasingly quickly, and before you have time to wonder what it is that's happening, you already remember everything perfectly. The time to absorb the shock."

"When are they going to let you out?"

"You have to be patient. In any case, it's much better here than you'd ever imagine. There's ping-pong. There are cats. The cats are fantastic."

"I'll come visit you. I'm totally dying to see you again," she gets the tone completely wrong.

"Oh no. No, dear. That can't be done." He'd never said "dear" to her like that.

"What do you mean? Since when aren't relatives allowed to come—"

"Oh, no no no," he chuckles, embarrassed, "I wasn't trying to insinuate . . . the people at the clinic have nothing to do with it. They're wonderful. Of course relatives are free to visit. Why on earth wouldn't they. But if I wanted to turn my brain into total mush, then I'd just let you do as you please."

"You don't want to see me."

"It's better that I don't, Clara," he says, maintaining the same tone of voice throughout the conversation, as if it were a system for remaining faithful to the imperative not to lie. "It's much better if we don't see each other. And now maybe I'm supposed to add that I'm sorry. In fact, though, I'd be sorry if we saw each other. You understand. We'll see each other, don't worry. We just need to stay calm. I mean to say," and as she listens to him, Clara observes the summer sky, "in other words, that time, it seems to me, is over now," he concludes.

That very same evening, Clara is on the terrace at the Sheraton. Inside, people are eating and cutting loose on the dance floor. White flashes behind her. Every so often she hears the music. Then the glass doors are closed, and once again the only noise is from the traffic on the street below. Earlier her father came by, too. There was the director of the Banca di Credito Pugliese. The mayor, the Public Works Commissioner. A group of engineers. She drinks her first glass. From the geraniums on the top floor she looks out over the lights in the neighborhood all around her. The trelliswork with the climbing vines. To jump. She dries her tears, doesn't even have the strength to regain her composure when the man appears before her. Light-blue suit, unbuttoned white shirt. Nice hands, long and gnarled. A kind face, all things considered. At first, he seems to have to overcome his embarrassment, but then something gives him strength and he extends his hand toward hers. She shakes his hand. He says his name is Alberto.

Three weeks later they'll be engaged.

Clara will see Michele months later. The psychiatrists will recommend against any contact with his family. Apparently he'd threatened to kill himself, or to kill someone else, if they made him see any of their faces, even from a distance. And so his father rented him a small apartment in Rome. It turned out to be an intelligent decision. So much so that over the course of the next few months, the situation improved. He even came to see them for Easter. They ate lunch together in the garden. A Sunday afternoon. The construction workers were there. Lots of ravens in the sky. The notary Valsecchi was there, too.

But she was screwing that guy from the gym and actually I was sick as a dog, thought Michele, smoking at the window.

The cat leapt up onto the windowsill, mewed. Michele put out his cigarette. It was sad to see her sneeze when the smoke curled in between her whiskers. He stroked her head, the cat multiplied her pleasure, opening her mouth slightly. Ecstasy and a dull daze. Then the invisible thread broke and the animal shot away. A voice called out from the floor below.

"Michele!"

The big metallic Audi. He'd seen it from the window. The dark of night through the tree branches, pierced by the beam of the headlights. The driver had walked around the car to open the door. He'd seen the man walk confidently down the driveway.

He carefully closed the bedroom door. He went downstairs.

"Hey, wait for me!"

Hurrying footsteps. Michele stopped and Gioia caught up with him. "Hold on, let's go together." She was wearing a peach-colored satin dress that would have been perfect for a debutante ball. Ringlets and color. She's even gone to the beautician's, he thinks, nauseated. Now all they needed to do to complete the picture was lock arms. In this slightly ridiculous manner, as if they were a pair of sweethearts, they made their entrance into the dining room.

Michele saw his father sitting in the armchair next to the fireplace. Decorative logs of firewood. Then the other man. The minute he noticed their presence, the chief justice of the Bari Court of Appeals got to his feet and came toward them.

He introduced himself. His sister made an imperceptible curt-
sey, the way a ballerina flexes her legs. The judge held out his
hand.

"Mimmo Russo."

"Michele."

"Ah, Michele. Your father told me all about you. You're living in Rome. The capital. Pleasure to meet you, a pleasure," he
mumbled.

Michele had to wait for the handshake to relax before he
realized that this was actually the judge. However implausible,
he'd assumed this was the driver.

"Let's not stand here. What are we standing for. Let's sit
down, let's sit down," said the man, standing in for the hosts
for a moment.

Michele went and sat on the sofa. The judge resumed his
seat in the armchair next to Vittorio's. Michele felt uncomfortable. The guest's handshake had left him ill at ease. He tried to
observe him more carefully.

He was a powerfully built man with a slightly hunched
back, about sixty-five years old. Despite the tufts of white hair
that stuck out of his eyebrows and ears, his hair was black and
combed over on the right, which didn't keep a part of his cranium from revealing its nakedness, as if some diseased form of
vanity had pushed him to dye his hair but not get a transplant.
His teeth seemed to have some problem with tartar. His manner of speech, all speed and half-uttered words, was evidence
of a passion that Michele believed inappropriate at the summit
of the judicial system. But his clothing was the tell. His camel-
colored suit with the frayed hems would have looked old-fash-
ioned fifteen years ago. The whole package gave the impression of a peasant who'd made money.

"Mr. Chief Justice, good evening!"

Annamaria came into the dining room. At her side, the
housekeeper was carrying a tray with glasses full of non-alco-

holic drinks and an array of canapés. The chief justice of the court of appeals beamed a broad smile.

"Signora, how are you?"

The man slapped his hands energetically on his thighs. He got up a second time, and went to greet Annamaria. He staged an impromptu kiss of her hand. He took a glass from the tray. "Let's be careful not to spill." Gioia broke into a confidential little giggle.

The judge went back to his spot. The housekeeper walked by with the tray. Vittorio took a sip. "And so these were charity dinners," he said to the judge. They resumed whatever conversation had been interrupted.

"Charity dinners. But now it's not like you can just go about organizing soirees for Haitian refugees with the region's money," and having bitten down on one canapé, he popped a second into his mouth whole, "it's not as if you can just ignore the constraints of the budget," he was chomping open-mouthed, brushing his hands over his trousers to get rid of the crumbs.

"Forgive the delay."

Ruggero arrived, too. The judge made to get to his feet. His brother lengthened his stride. "Mr. Chief Justice, please don't trouble yourself." He leaned toward him and shook his hand. Serious, not deferential.

"Well, then, I'd say we can go in to dinner," said Annamaria.

The table, you had to admit, was magnificently set. Hand-embroidered white linen tablecloth. Damask linen napkins. In a wicker basket sat the breadsticks and the olive bread. The gold thread of the placemats glittered in the candlelight and when Vittorio picked up the bottle of Amarone and began to pour, the ruby red spun in the eyes of those present.

"Mr. Chief Justice, the cuttlefish will just melt in your mouth," Vittorio proclaimed.

"You say I'm sure to like them?"

Ruggero asked for the serving dish with the raw fish. He bit into a slice of cheese. Vittorio and the judge, meanwhile, had launched into a discussion of a complicated case involving urban development funding. Every now and then Ruggero would join in the conversation. Annamaria smiled, her chin propped on her hand. Gioia watched them talk, and when the judge's eyes met hers, his sister would nod. But aside from Vittorio and the chief justice, and perhaps his brother on one or two points, no one had the slightest idea what they were talking about. The tone. The gestures. Those, though, were important. And the gestures—including the mere act of nodding, the mere act of smiling—served the purpose of rendering the surface solid and impenetrable, so that the river could flow along underground. The salt-roasted bass came to the table. Michele looked with disgust at the white tufts of hair on the fingers of the old judge. Annamaria nodded. No one mentioned Porto Allegro. Gioia yawned. She rested her head on Michele's shoulder. He tried to stay calm. Then his sister shook herself, and resumed eating.

After five more minutes, Michele said: "Excuse me, I need to go to the bathroom."

He left the dining room. He walked down the hall. It seemed impossible to him even to think of Clara, as if the conversation had constructed all around the place a leaden shell through which ghosts could not pass. He passed the built-in bookcases, the little table with the telephone. He went into the bathroom. He shut and locked the door. He turned the faucet. He went over to stand before the toilet. He lifted the seat and cover. Kneeled. Shut his eyes and vomited. He got back up on his feet. He went back to the toilet. He vomited again. He flushed, cleaned carefully with toilet paper. He went to the sink, rinsed his face and shut off the water. He left the bathroom.

In the hallway, he heard the phone ringing. He was about to walk past it. Then he stopped. He lifted the receiver.

"Hello."

It was Engineer Ranieri. He was asking for his father.

"He can't come to the phone right now."

"But it's urgent, Michele, urgent," whined the engineer.

"I know," said Michele, overwhelmed by distaste, by nausea, with no idea of what they were even talking about. "My father said you were to report to me. How far along are we?" he ventured.

"No further than we were last week," the engineer said after a moment's hesitation. "The Tarantine wants an answer about the matter of the elevator. I wanted to find out from your father what we should tell him."

Fury, nausea. He tossed an imaginary coin into the air.

"The answer is no," said Michele.

He went back to the dining room. He resumed his seat at the table. The judge and his father were discussing tourism in the Salento.

Around half past midnight, after the judge had left, Michele sat smoking in the garden the way he used to do when he was a kid. The moon was pale and full. Swarms of gnats were whirling around the floodlights over the front door. The nausea wasn't going away. He heard a noise in the hedges. He had a hunch, but it was itself wrapped up inside something else that needed deciphering, so he didn't turn to look. He took a drag on his cigarette. He coughed. He headed back to the villa.

He walked through the front door. Annamaria and the housekeeper were tidying up. Ruggero had gone home. Gioia had gone out. Michele started up the stairs. As soon he reached the upper floor, he stopped. He was breathing slowly, as if struggling to overcome the sensation of incredulity. The door to his room was open. He bit the inside of his cheek, strode quickly into the room. Immediately switched on the light. The bed. The armoire. He had the impression he'd glimpsed something out of the corner of his eye. For an infinitesimal fraction of a second, he relaxed. Then he understood. Nothing but a pillow tossed in the corner. He started whistling nervously, under his breath. He stretched out on the floor, peered under the bed. Back on his feet. He pulled open the armoire and started rummaging through the clothes. Suddenly he felt very agitated. He grabbed the chair, set it down next to the armoire. He climbed onto it. He checked the top of the armoire. He got down off the chair. He left the room. He looked in the bathroom, and then in Gioia's room. He walked down the hall to the master bedroom. He threw open the door without knocking. His father turned over, under the covers. "What on earth is going on?" Michele didn't answer. He turned on the light. (He thought he could detect his father curling his toes, it disgusted him). He paced the room from one end to the other. He opened the armoire, pointless though it was. "What's going on? What's going on?" Michele switched off the light and left. He rushed downstairs. A sister, a mother. He started calling in a loud voice. He whistled repeatedly. Annamaria's head poked out of the kitchen.

"What's going on?"

"What's going on is that you need to keep that fucking door closed!" shouted Michele, glaring at her with open hatred, and suddenly everything came bobbing back to the surface, everything was clear, transparent, resplendent.

He advanced toward her. Annamaria stepped back. Michele looked around in the kitchen. Of course the cat wasn't there. He hurried out into the garden. He cupped his hands in front of his mouth and started calling her. "Fuck, fuck!" he shouted, stamping his feet, after five minutes. In spite of the moon, it was hard to see through the darkness. So he hurried back into the house. He came back out with a flashlight, already switched on, in his hand. He aimed it at the bushes, the plants, he raised the beam of light all the way up into the trees. While he went on calling her. A mother. A sister. And now a cat.

After an hour of fruitless searching, he started toying with the idea that she had retraced her steps and returned to the house of her own accord. And so he headed back in to his bedroom. He climbed the stairs, nurturing the absurd hope that the whole thing had just been a nightmare. The cat wasn't there. Michele sat down on the bed. He was exhausted. He put his hands on his head. Then he relaxed. Two minutes. I'm just going to rest for two minutes, he said aloud in the hope that he'd awaken from the nightmare.

He woke up with a start. He'd slept fully dressed. On his feet, the tight clamp of his shoes. He looked at the window. The dim, grainy luminosity that comes just before dawn began to spread. He got to his feet. He ran a hand through his hair. He went into the bathroom to splash water on his face. The house was immersed in silence.

He went down the stairs. He opened the front door and went out into the garden. The light was more intense. The blades of grass and the trees and the fountain and the rose bushes. He looked both right and left. He shook his head. Two magpies landed on the lawn. The thought of the cat on a paved road stunned him. The total unawareness of evil, and the fact of unexpectedly finding ourselves right in front of it. That's all it ever was or had been, deep down. He walked up the front drive. His clothing was all rumpled and creased, his hair was a mess. He reached the gate. He clicked it open. With a vigorous shove, he opened one of the gates. He stood there, looking. And then, as if someone had pushed him, he took a step forward. Another, and then yet another.

In this way, at six forty-five on a morning in mid-June, thirty-two days after returning to Bari, Michele started walking back to a city he hadn't seen in ten years.

PART THREE

All cities stink in the summer

An army of rotary fans churned the heat from one room to the next, defeated by the majesty of June on the Adriatic. Ninety-five degrees in the shade. Palm trees in the muggy breeze. This year, once again, it had happened without warning. Yesterday people were taking the steps two at a time and now just leaving the house wore you out. An airplane's contrail cut through the pure turquoise of the sky. And for that matter even those who, with the help of an air conditioner, went from night to morning without suffering the sudden change in temperature, could hear as they awakened the buzz of the mopeds on which kids were deserting school for their first dips into the sea. They zipped down along the state highway, past the gas station's inflatable puppet, heading straight for the beaches of Mola and San Vito. And so, if you were a grown up, the thought of summer arrived swollen with regrets, dissolving memory in envy.

Signora Grazioli woke up at seven thirty. She breakfasted on an ounce of oat flakes in a cup of skim yogurt. She allowed herself an espresso. She went back to her bedroom. She turned on her smartphone and waited in vain for a text from her daughter. She smoked a cigarette. Looking out the window, she saw the pool: it possessed the splendor of certain paintings from the school of American realism. Youth really was a paltry thing without a bundle of equity funds. The woman let her nightgown slip onto the hardwood floor. She unhooked her bra, kicked off her panties. She bent over the dresser. She got out the two pieces of her swimsuit and put them on. She went into the bathroom. She put on her slippers, grabbed her bathrobe. She picked up her pack of cigarettes and the latest issue of *Astra*. She put on her sunglasses, ready for the morning swim.

Before going out, she turned off the exterior lights. Wall-mounted floodlights. Large oval polyurethane lights. Her husband insisted on leaving them on all night long, because he was convinced they scared away burglars. How stupid. The woman went out into the garden. After a couple of steps she noticed the torn plastic bag, the remains of dinner on the grassy lawn. God only knew what kinds of wild animals were roaming around the area, and he just dropped the garbage outside the door. As if the heaps of dead moths at the foot of the floodlights weren't bad enough already. The housekeeper would tend to them, but in the meantime, she'd seen them.

She walked to the lounger. For an instant, she defied the sun from behind her dark glasses. She removed the sunglasses, took a few steps, and dove in. The blue basin. Slivers of light sparkled on the bottom. Deterioration began with a poorly maintained pool, but the chemical balance of the water that morning was perfect.

After twenty laps, Signora Grazioli decided that she'd had enough. She used the ladder to climb out. Her bent, wrinkled body, struck by the light of a star millions of miles away, was the only image of vulnerability offered to the imaginary witness.

She stretched out on the lounger. She undid the top of her suit and disposed herself to receive the sun. Then she luxuriated in the pleasure of a Marlboro Red.

Once she was done reading the horoscope, she cinched her bathrobe and got back to her feet. It was time to review the roses.

Cherry Brandy. Dame de l'Étoile. Cross breeding worked

miracles. Proof if it was needed was that the poor Albertines (a variety that would have looked no different when her grandparents' great-grandparents had admired them) were already sagging and withered in the heat. As she gazed at them pensively, the woman heard a door slam on the other side of the hedge. At that point she stiffened. The next-door neighbor's villa. How unfortunate. Now she'd be forced to say hello.

If only she'd run into him anytime up until a month and a half ago—she thought, stung with remorse—she'd have scolded him for the all the uproar at night. Since the ex-undersecretary was a widower, it wasn't hard to guess its cause. Not just music. Not just lights from the carefully curtained windows. Women's laughter. Raucous cries. But now it had been weeks since the last sign of life from the villa. So when her neighbor's long, grayish face appeared through the leaves of the mastic bushes, Signora Grazioli forced herself to flash him a nice smile.

"*Buongiorno*, Signor Buffante."

"*Buongiorno*, Signora Grazioli."

The woman went back to the swimming pool. The old man walked through the garden gate. He got into his midnight-black Maserati and pulled out.

Valentino Buffante was driving down the State Highway 100 on his way into the city center. He had an appointment to meet with his colleagues at VersoSud, the foundation for the development of southern Italy's Mezzogiorno region, a foundation he'd been chairing since he'd lost his positions at the ministry. He was in a lousy mood, sweating under his shirt. The problems had started when old Salvemini had called him up to tell him about the funeral. Invited him to join a father to share in his grief, which gave him a chance to brandish his daughter, a corpse, as a tool of persuasion. He'd been forced to shake hands with Costantini. He'd successfully avoided the engineer.

A few weeks later had come the phone call from the eldest son. "Signor Buffante, I'm so sorry to bother you. Knowing as we do of your experience in matters of public administration, we'd be very interested in getting your opinion concerning a problem we're trying to solve."

They wanted to get his opinion on the hydrogeological reports that were meant to persuade the judge to reject the seizure request. To save the tourist complex with which they were gutting a section of the Gargano coast.

Official stamps. Resolutions. Maybe a couple of backdated records. Opinion my ass. They were clearly blackmailing him.

"How much shall I put in today?"

"Fill it up, please."

Or maybe they could guess, he thought as he drove away from the gas station. He watched as the inflatable puppet vanished in his rearview mirror. They suspected that he'd had a hand in it last time, too, when it was a matter of getting approval for the zoning variances concerning the geomorphological risks in the Val di Noto. A resolution tailor-made for the residential complex that Salvemini Construction was just finishing work on down there. At the time, Buffante was still undersecretary. More importantly, she was alive.

He remembered very clearly when Clara had told him about the residential complex, because that had also been the time she had demanded he drive her to Avellino. Enveloped in a translucent gauze of thoughts as she climbed into the car. Motionless and silent for a hundred twenty-five miles. Then she'd started to talk. Also at her request, they'd slept in Salerno.

Even though Buffante's villa was available, she preferred to hide out in hotels. Even small bed-and-breakfasts outside of town. Hotels offered the proper degree of anonymity. The undecorated rooms. The wallpaper peppered with ugly heraldic crests. Clara sat on the edge of the bed, crossed her legs so she could easily take off the first shoe, and when she stood back up, usually in an undergarment, or naked under the electric light, he felt as if he held in his arms a body emptied of memories. White as wax, not dissimilar from the figures in certain old canvases in which all it takes is a second glance to turn the height of familiarity into the height of estrangement.

Helping her father with the residential complex, all right, that was a request that made sense. But why force him to cross Italy from coast to coast? Buffante couldn't figure out if it was a passing whim. He still didn't know her well. That surgeon had introduced her to him. A young married woman who at the first attempt allowed herself to be seduced by a man twice her age. He hadn't had to fight to get her. And when, not even twenty-four hours after watching her vanish into the crowd, he'd kidded himself that he was being daring by texting her ("It would be nice to see you again"), it was only a handful of minutes before he got an answer back: "Sure, tonight."

A young woman, not even thirty years old. Even though his familiarity with power fostered illusions about the allure of maturity, it didn't escape Buffante what it meant to sense on oneself the smell of an old man who in ten years might perfectly well be dead in accordance with the laws of nature. And yet it happened. He'd send the signal, and Clara would come running. When he'd see her in the place where they'd arranged to meet, usually near the corner of Via Fresa and Via Lenoci—serious and modest in her skirt suit, underneath which lurked the only reason for the hours they were about to spend together—the impulse that made her walk toward his Maserati undermined all the rhetoric on the need for courtship. Clara would get into the car and immediately ask at what hotel he'd made reservations. It seemed as if that technical detail was the crux of the matter as far as she was concerned, or perhaps the real pleasure lay in the ability to imagine between which walls she would no longer have a personal history.

Buffante would drive toward a restaurant. In certain cases, directly to a hotel. The total absence of obstacles was the sole actual obstacle to a full understanding of what was happening. Clara talked very little. Never about her husband. And when the time came to stretch out in bed, she completed the task, becoming a complete stranger. A girl met by chance. A call girl or a streetwalker.

One time they'd stayed out until four in the morning. The tranquility with which she pretended she had no home to return to was almost embarrassing. And now she was asking him to take her to Avellino.

As they were taking the hairpin curves of Irpinia, the young woman's inspired, attentive face had persuaded him to ask no more questions. Clara observed with obstinacy the dark and solid reliefs through the windshield as if outside there were a magnet of terrifying strength.

In Avellino, they ate near the municipal gardens. After lunch, she went off for a walk on her own. It was a nice February day. Buffante watched her walk off past the ugly apartment buildings of the quarter. He assumed she just wanted a bit of privacy so she could make a phone call to her husband, and he went to get a newspaper. But Clara had no intention of calling Alberto. She made a beeline for the barracks. Even if Buffante had tailed her, he wouldn't have understood.

The red walls within whose perimeter Michele had been enclosed during his months in the military. Motionless and silent, the young woman stood watching for several minutes. The oblong specter once again filled with flesh. The fragile hands. The skinny, skinny torso. The young man typed away all afternoon, shut up in a small room, sitting on a pile of old phone books. He was writing his piece tomorrow, *tomorrow*.

Well, that day had finally come. He wasn't seeking a memory but a beginning. She'd talked to Michele recently to wish him a merry Christmas. She'd phoned Rome. But Clara wasn't looking for that Michele. She was waiting for the other one. Just as she herself must clearly be somewhere else, because otherwise the Clara that went to bed with a repulsive old man would have no explanation. She caught a flash in the window opened and then closed on the watchtower. Now Clara could feel him. She was convinced that Michele's shining demon—the trace left behind after spending enough time with a person that their primary characteristics recombine inside us in an increasingly complex manner, until they take on a life of their own—sparkled in those who had known him as a boy. And so it necessarily sparkled inside the other one, the Michele who was in Rome. The one who was becoming an adult, who was trying laboriously to heal, maybe forget. But she, his sister, was now summoning him to her. *Michele.* A tiny dot. A small dark patch in the young adult who every Friday would go to the National Gallery to watch his tiger, hopeful, unaware of the little flower that it had caused to blossom inside him.

Clara turned her back to the barracks. She went back to Buffante.

A few minutes later she asked him to take her to Salerno. At that point it was four in the afternoon. However senseless the request might have seemed, Buffante turned his car southward. Impossible to contradict her, they still hadn't had sex today. Taking her to bed one more time meant splitting into further units the time he had left to live (a time that Buffante now thought he could glimpse in its entirety), so that even a second itself, split up into tenths, then hundredths and thousandths, would last into infinity.

While Michele had done his military service in Avellino, Salerno was where the psychiatric clinic was. The minute they got to the city, Clara insisted they stop at the first hotel they chanced to come across. "Here," she said, pointing to an unattractive *pensione*, its roof covered with gray wooden shake shingles. The caricature of a mountain chalet. He tried to dissuade her. But the vise that held her in its grip was so powerful, so unequivocally intense that Buffante was forced to yield. They went into the room. They handed over their IDs. They went up to the room. Fast, unsentimental. Then the girl got dressed again. She slipped on pantyhose and skirt and shoes and sweater, and then the overcoat, too, while he lay naked on the bed, recovering his strength.

"I'm going to go for a walk," she said.

She went down to the ground floor. She left the hotel. Ten minutes later she had left the city center. Night was falling among the buildings on the outskirts of town. The sea glittered less and less, while the city lights were still off. In just a few minutes, the long drive that led up to the psychiatric clinic became a deserted track, infested by the shadows that became denser where the welter of branches extended. Clara lengthened her stride. The cars framed her in their headlights at the last moment. A few drivers flashed their brights. Others whistled. A compact car driving in her direction slowed down before it passed her. Clara wrapped herself tighter in her overcoat. The car window rolled down, someone whispered an obscene phrase to her. Then the car sped up and vanished. They could have raped her and no one would have noticed. For her, it wouldn't have been any different from what had just happened in the hotel room half an hour ago.

She saw the lights of the Alma Mater after what seemed like the thousandth curve. She drove to the end of the long lane. She came out on the large clearing that served as a parking area. The last blazes in the sky, thin bloody strips, were descending vertically over the two buildings separated symmetrically by a long gravel driveway. It was from one of these two parallelepipeds that Michele had spoken to her that day, when he'd told her it would be best if she didn't come to see him. Well, now his sister was here anyway. Clara walked over to the gate. She slipped her hand through the floral vortices of wrought iron. Michele was in there. The one who'd been talked into starting a new life was gone. But the boy determined to burn his whole family alive, the one who stubbed out cigarettes on the star globe while alluding to a meeting someday in a place beyond death that only now could Clara fully sense, that boy was there, he was moving all around her with the slow breathing of evening. Over the roofs of the clinic. Through the branches of the trees. In the deep rooms where she awaited him. Clara put a silver coin into his hands. So now he was committed. She'd go back to the hotel. Buffante. The surgeon. Then someone else. She knew that was the lead to follow. The black forest in the depths of which the long figure of Michele, white and silent in the morning mists, awaited her. It would be the other part of him, the one that was in Rome, that would bring him back to her.

Clara returned to the hotel. She let the undersecretary undress her. She let him caress her. Right now, he was probably inside her. He was pushing. Getting himself excited. A poor old naked man, immersed in a sea whose expanse was unknown to him. And when Clara closed her eyes, she let her smile be interpreted as a response to the determination the man was putting into it. Poor idiots. When they were pushing into a corpse, only then were they convinced they were worth something.

A wonderful night, Buffante remembered.

And now it would never happen again. He passed a truck, and then a BMW. On his right appeared the Ikea tower. Talk to the analysts from the Commission on Environmental Impact. Convince them of the validity of those technical studies. Then arrange for the administrator of the provincial office to backdate the Commission's opinion. It wouldn't be easy. And that was just one front in the battle. Then there was the matter of timing the hearings. Slip the opinion into the files of a trial already underway. But old Salvemini would take care of that. He drove under an overpass plastered with posters layered one atop the other. He left behind the five-a-side soccer pitches and two minutes later he was in the traffic of Bari. Seafood shops. Bakeries. Laborers unloading merchandise from double-parked semitrailers. The Odeon movie theater. Then the Gardenia café. Buffante tried to keep from looking at it. But the traffic was creeping.

That had been another time. An evening in late April. He and Clara were sitting outside. The girl was drinking one Negroni after another. They were talking about the journalist she'd gotten fired. It had been five years since he'd driven her to Salerno. An eternity. As if time weighed down twice as heavily on Buffante because he was seeing her, but ten times as heavily on Clara, seeing that she was the epicenter of the tremor.

"Certain people can't control themselves," she'd said, shaking her head. She'd had her hair cut. She'd bleached it in a way that on the whole made her look a little bit savage.

"The journalist?" asked Buffante.

"Who else?" she'd answered, dragging out the words, then dropped her eyes. "After he was fired, he continued to slander us. In the pages of *Puglia Oggi*. He accused my father of having pushed the mayor to appoint I don't know which of our employees to a position in I don't know what agency. But do you want to know something?"

"Yes?" Buffante would have to be careful to nurse the wine, serve it with an eyedropper.

"I managed to get him fired at *Puglia Oggi*, too!" The girl burst out in a cavernous laugh. Her voice was coming from the depths of a well.

"Can you guess what I have in here?" she asked, tapping her red-enameled fingernail against the purse.

Perfection, thought Buffante as he looked at her. At thirty-four, she could as easily be sixty as sixteen. When he'd met her the vice that was inside her was an undemanding tenant. Unsullied at twenty-nine. Uncorrupted at thirty-one. But now the habits were beginning to tell. The bags under her eyes. That put-off smile. The imminence of decline made her even more desirable. The cocaine. Cocaine was a blessing.

At that point Clara noticed something. She got to her feet. She staggered in place. She turned her back to him, looking toward the crowd coming down Via Re David. A moment later, Buffante saw her in the arms of a man. She was literally sinking into the dark suit of this stranger. The undersecretary didn't understand. Clara turned around. Without needing to take him by the hand, she dragged the man toward the café table. It seemed as if she were laughing and crying and was amused and wanted to die. The surviving portion of a slow process of destruction. So she crushed that part, too.

"My husband," she said.

Her husband, the engineer, nodded his head uncertainly. A partial motion of the hand. Then he vanished among the pedestrians who kept streaming past along the street.

At that point, Buffante, too, got to his feet. Inebriated by the same force he'd perceived when she'd burst out laughing. He took Clara's arms in his hands. "Let's go to the restroom." Even he couldn't say whether or not he was drunk.

He gave the young man tending bar a hundred-euro tip to make sure no one bothered them.

Shut up together in the restroom, the old man plunged his hands into her hair. He wrapped his arms around her hips. The narrow, barren room. The toilet a white altar. Everything unfolding in an absurd, chaotic manner. Clara opened her handbag. She pulled out the plastic baggie. Buffante grabbed it out of her hand. Then, after kissing her on the mouth—as if the baggie was something he'd stolen only to give it back to her for a price—he waved it back and forth in the air. Clara reached out her hands. He yanked back his arm, snickering. At that point the girl slipped. She landed with both knees on the filthy floor. "Fuck!" It felt as if she were in the belly of a ship during a tempest at sea. Buffante showed her the baggie with the coke. "Give it to me!" she said. Driven by the power of the music he could hear echoing all around him, the ex undersecretary stepped back. He lifted the lid of the toilet. He laid out a line of coke on the rim. At this point even he didn't know what he was doing. He saw her lunge toward the toilet bowl. She snorted the coke hungrily. But at the center of her being she was tranquil. In a part that no longer required any contact with the exterior, she knew that the process was irreversible. She was happy to have finally arrived. The certainty that a rock tossed into a pond would kick up a spurt of water. The rock was in midair. Only God could have stopped it. Deep down, amidst the chilly currents, when her body touched the slimy green surface, then Michele's eye would snap open, mirroring itself in hers.

Once past the traffic jam on Via Amendola, Buffante turned left into Via Capruzzi. He drove down into the underground garage. It was a quarter to ten when he made his entrance into the headquarters of VersoSud.

At a quarter past noon his secretary informed him that Engineer De Palo had arrived. Buffante closed the file folder containing the Salvemini documents. He went to welcome his guest.

"Let's go get an espresso."

They went down to the street. They strolled down Via Carulli, turned onto Via Melo. They went into the Café Riviera.

"Dottore, *buongiorno!*"

The proprietor was a powerful-looking man in his early fifties, his forehead dotted with sweat. Next to him was a man in overalls, ten years his younger, his face devastated by acne.

Buffante and Engineer De Palo drank an espresso. The engineer ate an ice cream. The proprietor of the bar and his friend complained about the heat. "Arrivederci, Dottore!"

They went back out into the street. They walked silently down Via Melo. They returned to the foundation. Buffante headed back toward his office. He shut the door. He waited for his guest to make himself comfortable. He sat down across from him. He opened the file folder. He pulled out the technical reports. He said: "Now then."

"Thick as thieves," said the pockmarked guy after the other two had left.

"Shut up," said the proprietor.

"Do you know how much that guy's pension pays?"

"Still, he had to resign his position."

"He lives in a three-story villa. He drives a Maserati that costs more in upkeep than you and I make in a year."

"You don't know how much this thing costs in upkeep," he said, pointing at the espresso machine behind him.

The pockmarked guy checked something on his smartphone. The proprietor served other customers. He went on chatting, mopping his brow, and cursing the two fans that were failing to keep the place cool enough.

Then the pockmarked guy went home. The proprietor ate lunch alone, a tea sandwich. He sat there, reading the newspaper behind the cash register. After an hour of no business, a few university students came in. The bar started to fill up again.

At a quarter to four a young man, around thirty, came in. An odd duck. Skinny, angular. He pointed to the glass-paneled display case where announcements could be posted. He wanted to add his own. It wasn't an advertisement, he added. His courteousness seemed as if it might snap from one moment to the next. Just like certain criminals. But he was clearly no criminal. He said that he was handing out these flyers to all the businesses in the neighborhood.

"A cat?" asked the proprietor, as if he were struggling to process the concept. Or maybe it was because the young man was talking in too low a voice.

The man told him that he could put up the notice himself. He handed him the adhesive tape. He went back to sorting the bottles on the counter. A lost cat. As if citizens didn't already have enough problems already.

Michele left the bar. He headed down to the sea with his fists jammed into his pockets. The heat wasn't letting up. It struck him that the apartment buildings were shimmering before his eyes. But it was sheer determination. Teeth clenched. Like clutching an amulet in his fingers, the silver coin to pay for the journey into the shadows. The cold wrath. This force led him toward the newsroom of *Corriere del Mezzogiorno*, where he intended to ask Giuseppe Greco why he was following a dead girl's Twitter account.

He told you *what*?"

"To say no, Signor Salvemini. He assured me that it was you who had made that decision."

"And when was it that he would have told you such a thing, excuse me?"

"On the phone. The other night. I called to find out what we were supposed to do and your son answered. He said that you'd said to tell me that we were supposed to turn down the request—"

"My son *expressly* told you that I'd discussed it with him?"

"Yes. That is, no. Signor Salvemini, right now it's not as if I can remember every single wor—"

It was in that very moment that Engineer Ranieri raised his right hand to his temple, and the mild state of panic that he'd managed to keep tucked out of sight, in a dignified manner, until just a short while before, suddenly began to moisten the groove of his upper lip.

"Did Michele tell you *expressly* about an elevator to be built in an apartment house on Via d'Aquino?"

"Well, to tell the truth . . . you see, it came out at a certain point in the—"

"Did he tell you about it, yes or no?"

"I don't think so, but—"

"Did he speak to you *expressly* about a truck driver from Taranto?"

"Here too, while we were talk—"

"Did he speak to you *expressly* about an invalid?"

"No. I'm certain about that part. The thing about the leg didn't come out at all."

"Well then . . . " Vittorio took a long, deep breath, as if storing up oxygen would help to dissipate the purple color that had taken possession of his face, ". . . if he wasn't the first to mention Taranto, if he didn't talk to you about a man with an amputated leg, if he never said anything about an elevator, then how can you!"—fist brought down hard on the table—"Even say!" —second fist—"That he told you that it had been *my* decision!"—yet another fist—"Not to have that damned elevator built?"

"Signor Salvemini—"

"What did you say to him?" he asked with his voice kept intentionally low, so that the engineer would have to make an effort to understand.

"What did I say to him . . . about what?" he seemed confused.

"To the Tarantine. What answer did you give the Tarantine."

"That we weren't going to have the elevator built."

"Call him back."

"What?"

"Call the Tarantine back. Tell him that you made a mistake."

"Well, sir. I'm afraid that's not going to be possible."

"And for what reason."

"Because he doesn't have a cell phone. I know that it's strange . . . He always called me."

Vittorio whispered something.

"What did you say, Signor Salvemini?"

"Taranto," he said again, in a louder voice. "*Now.*"

"Taranto?"

"Don't bother going home. Don't go take a shower. If you

could only concentrate properly you'd realize that you're not even talking with me anymore. You're already in your station wagon. You're already driving to Taranto."

If he'd never entered that lovely, freshly painted apartment, with the plaster crenelated molding along the ceiling and the hardwood flooring, overcoming his own disbelief at the fact that it was his and not someone else's (he wasn't there as part of the moving crew, it was actually his home), then the effort necessary to reach the seventh floor would never have kindled all that resentment in him. He felt it the second time he came in.

He reached the landing. He felt the ache under his armpits. He opened the door. He closed it with a shove of his crutch. He caught his breath. He saw the lights glitter through the windows in the living room. Because the apartment faced west—though he didn't even need to know this—the glow came from the Aragonese Castle, then there was the luminous arc of the floating cranes and the grainy nebula of light-blue flares and white dwarfs that were the flames from the petrochemical plant and the steel mill. He wasn't used to seeing them from afar.

He took a few steps forward. He let himself drop onto the sofa. He found it more comfortable than he'd imagined. He dropped the crutches. He laid his head on the cushion and felt the unmistakable sensation of progressive recovery. Immediately after that came the anger.

He'd have had a hard time trying to calculate how many lifetimes it would have taken him to buy an apartment like this one, but he understood all too clearly how much trouble the person who had gotten it for him must have gone through. And so, what ought to have been a sensation of danger averted, if not an actual stroke of good luck, turned into mere humiliation. Orazio Basile wouldn't have felt that if it hadn't been for that brief quivering sensation of privilege. Even dignity sprang out of an abuse of power. Due to the circumstances under which the accident had occurred (he'd happened to be in the wrong place, with his headlights trained on the wrongest of all the girls, who seemed to be in the habit of strolling down the state highway naked and smeared with blood), someone had nonchalantly offered him what would have been for many the dream of a lifetime, and they hadn't even bothered to see whether the building had an elevator.

In the neighborhoods around the steel mill, young men in their early thirties died. Twelve-year-old girls fell ill. Tumors of the stomach, of the lungs. Healthy family men folded over at the waist and in the course of a few months were dead. Hollowed-out faces. Bald heads. One out of every eighteen people was sick, a rate akin to that of a biblical plague. And this was, deep down, what Orazio Basile had been afraid of until just a split second earlier, what even those who emerged from the distant era of the union battles were afraid of. That there was something supernatural at work here. Some cruel and invincible god. Investigations were undertaken, the investigations ran aground. Entire plants were seized by the state, yet the plants went on running. Enormous fortunes were frozen, the fortunes were returned. Meanwhile the hospitals were full to bursting. The surgeons opened chest cavities, sawed through brainpans. Small knots of people wept in rooms that grew ever grayer and more run down. If something happened that was capable of reversing this cycle, then perhaps tens of thousands would gain the awareness that they were alone on the earth. They'd arm themselves with rocks and clubs.

But now Orazio Basile, fifty-six years old, former truck driver and legally disabled, had been given a nice apartment in the city center, and it wasn't the inscrutable cruelty of some distant entity but rather the petty cruelty of men together with the gift itself that had inflicted the insult. The one rendered the other visible. He decided that he would demand the elevator.

The response that his request was not going to be fulfilled had been conveyed to him by the most idiotic of all the boot-lickers he'd had to deal with while in the hospital. Orazio Basile stepped out of the phone booth swaying with rage.

That evening it took twice the effort. He was getting used to the stairs, he could even foresee every individual move. He knew that he'd have to place the right crutch on the step, push-ing himself with his body against the railing. To press on one side, regain his balance immediately after using the second crutch. The anticipatory thought was every bit as odious as the effort itself.

Descending to the ground floor was no less complicated. The next morning, when he found himself opening the door to the street, he was already drenched with sweat. At the height of his fury, he headed for the swing bridge. By noon he was in the old town. He cursed. He hobbled along behind a line of parked cars, careful to keep from being seen outside the rec center. The sun was beating straight down, perpendicular rays hitting the devastated asphalt. With aching forearms and armpits, he saw the two girls on the pedestrian mall. Pink miniskirt. Cheap, tight dress. The one in the miniskirt was bet-ter. It would be the first time since the accident. But he'd also feel it was his duty to crush a couple of her ribs with a few blows of his crutch. He kept walking.

An hour later, he entered the train station. Sitting in the waiting room, his hands intertwined on the plastic arm cuffs, he stared down at the fake-marble floor. He grabbed the crutches again. He'd make that gaggle of idiots pay for the stairs in the underpass, too. He boarded the first train for Bari.

He finished editing the piece. Then he went online to check the impact of yesterday's article. A long think piece about the films of Arthur Penn. It had taken him three days of hard work. All the same, he realized as he gazed at his reflection in the screen, the piece hadn't gotten more than thirty likes.

At that time of night there was still a fair amount of activity at the newspaper. He went to get a glass from the water-cooler. He came back into his office. What did he expect, after all? That his work would circulate so widely that it might eventually come to the attention of the arts editors at *Corriere della Sera* or *La Repubblica*? That the editor in chief of *Ciak* might notice him? Or that he might wind up catching the eye of a Tornatore, a Benigni, someone who might mention his name to the executive staff of some international festival?

Well, yes, that's exactly what he'd been hoping.

Giuseppe Greco contemplated the empty desks on a Thursday evening. The important things were happening elsewhere. Certainly not in Bari. He went back to his desk. He had to write a long article about the delegation from the department of tourism now visiting Beijing.

He heard someone chatting in the other room. Night owls like him. After another fifteen minutes of typing, he ordered a pizza. In the office that was home to the travel supplement, three editors were sweating out the issue around a desk.

Giuseppe Greco went to the bathroom. He took a piss. He washed his hands. He came back out into the hallway.

He realized that he'd walked past his own office. He turned around and went back. He hadn't registered his own office because when he'd left the lights were still on, and now, strangely, they were all off. He entered the room. Suddenly he stopped.

"Excuse me, who were you looking for?"

The slender figure turned in his direction. Giuseppe Greco felt an inexplicable sensation of sorrow flood through him. As if he were touching the hull of a sunken ship lying abandoned on the ocean floor. The memory of youth. He turned on the light.

The silhouette revealed a young man in jeans and a black shirt. Dark hair, jutting cheekbones, and one eyelid slightly lower than the other.

"What are you doing in my office?"

"No, you see . . . " the stranger smiled, and Giuseppe Greco once again felt the same sensation, "please forgive me for the time of night, it's just that I wanted to purchase a space . . . "

"For advertising you'd have to go up to the sixth floor. And anyway, at this time of night, the offices are . . . "

"Actually," with a sudden leap, the young man sat on the edge of the desk, "it's that I've lost my cat and I wanted to place an advertisement with all the details and contacts."

"It's just that this isn't the advertising office. This is the entertainment page."

He was surprised to find himself offering all those explanations. As if his objective wasn't to kick out some stranger who had snuck into his office and, to make things worse, was taking the liberty of sitting on his desk like that, but rather to defend himself from something.

"Oh, and do you also cover culture?"

"Now and then," he said dismissively, "but I hope you'll excuse me because I have to finish editing a . . . "

The young man did another strange thing. He jumped down off the desk. He pulled one of the wheeled chairs toward himself and sat on it. He gave a good hard shove with his feet and skated all the way around *behind* the desk.

It wasn't just the arrogance of the gestures. Rather it was the ease that was, in a certain sense, amputated. As if moving with that presumption wasn't in fact something that came easy, and he, the young man, were obliged to overcome invisible obstacles even just to get from one point in the room to another, obstacles that in the past might perhaps have conditioned his life in no uncertain terms, but that were now tucked away in some corner of his inner map. Giuseppe Greco knew that way of moving. It was this ineffable sensation of familiarity that kept him from calling the security guard, while his conscious memory was working at full steam to dredge up the rest.

But once again it was the young man who beat him to the punch.

"Maybe you'd be interested in a nice long article about Joseph Heller and the art of war."

Why of course, thought the senior editor.

"My youthful misdeeds have come to pay me a visit."

He regretted the wisecrack. He'd said it to cushion his guilt at having failed to recognize him, not in order to put him at ease. The Salveminis, he thought without restraining his dislike. He pulled up his own chair and sat down across from him. Michele wasn't smiling now. If anything, Giuseppe Greco would have said he was looking at him with disregard. He's looking at me with *arrogance*, with *contempt*. He observed the face more closely. Where he remembered a curve there was a sharp angle. He'd lost the disarming impracticality of adolescence. After a certain age, the true nature emerges. They thought of themselves as the masters of the city. They came strolling into your office at all hours because they were used to doing as they pleased.

"Like I was saying, I'm just finishing up something important," he hissed, fed by the antagonism that burned in the young man's eyes, so that a perfect hostility glittered between them, the kind that exists between those who detest each other for different reasons, each of them unaware of the other's. "There are some of us who have to work late," he continued, "and I'm not even clear on whether this whole thing with the cat is true. In any case, if there's anything else you want to ask me, I think you'd better get to it."

"Just one thing I'm curious about."

"Let's hear it."

"Why are you following my sister on Twitter? Clara has been dead for more than a month."

You make the first move. Now the passage of time really weighed on them both. Aside from the physical changes in each, what hadn't happened to him in the last decade, and what, in contrast, was Giuseppe Greco convinced had happened to the scion of the Salvemini clan. A daddy's boy. A young man who'd only needed to snap his fingers to sit down to dinner with the editor of some major newspaper. And now, the very incarnation of social injustice had the nerve to come and lecture him for some minor peccadillo.

"There's something I'm curious about myself," the senior editor replied coldly. "I'd like to know how it's possible for someone like you to rise so high."

Michele furrowed his brow. He didn't understand if the man was serious.

"I open the pages of *Corriere della Sera* and I read an article you wrote about Flannery O'Connor's peacocks," the senior editor continued, "then, again in *Corriere*, a piece about Ellison. I leaf through *Ciak* and who do I find? Michele Salvemini holding forth on Herzog as if he were a family friend. *The Madness of Fitzcarraldo.* A piece that, among other things, is riddled with fairly serious inaccuracies."

Now Michele was taken aback. He could barely even remember those pieces. He'd transformed his habit of failure into a faithful and protective traveling companion. He preferred to forget the few times his name had appeared in a major publication, as if those notches in his biography were a threat rather than an encouragement. Apparently, though, there was someone who remembered everything right down to the slightest detail. The world certainly was a strange place.

"How is it possible, I've asked myself all these years," the senior editor tried to reverse once and for all the ownership of the element of surprise, "for a young man with all your problems to make his way in the world? Everyone knows how important it is to be able to deal with other people in this line of work. To know what moves to make. A young man who's actually mentally ill," he continued shamelessly, "someone who's never even taken a class in journalism and whose only experience, before heading off to Rome, the *big city*," he emphasized, full of resentment, "consisted of writing articles that only someone like me could have taken seriously. Articles that no one else would have dreamed of publishing. How is it possible that I now find the work of this misfit in *Corriere della Sera*, in *La Repubblica*, in *Ciak*?

"I often ask myself the same thing," Michele replied, toughing it out.

"Your surname," Giuseppe Greco smiled malevolently, "the importance of being a Salvemini. And then, once you've entered the clique of renowned journalists, the habit you have of protecting each other."

"I see that you know everything about me," the young man said, careful to remain impassive, "while I still haven't been able to figure out why you're following a dead woman's fake Twitter account."

"To put the profession on alert," the senior editor surprised him once again. "Because your sister, dead or alive, had a habit of getting rid of journalists that didn't suit her purposes."

Giuseppe Greco lowered his gaze. That's the rumor that was circulating. And anyway, he didn't have it in for that poor girl. It was *him* he couldn't stand.

"What are you talking about?"

"Oh no? *Oh no?*" Giuseppe Greco reacted as if Michele had denied something. "Oh no!" he raised his voice, and his excitement make him tear a page out of his notepad, grab a pen and write, on that same sheet of paper, someone's name, with all the heat of someone completing an evil spell, as if the exact sequence of letters were about to destroy Michele, immediately incinerate him.

But Michele wasn't incinerated. The most remote part of him, which was also the most dangerous, protected him this time. It breathed inside him much like an underwater sea monster in whose belly lies sleeping the little sandman of our dreams. For an instant, Michele glimpsed himself at sixteen. He saw Clara too. He was afraid. Then the sensation vanished.

Giuseppe Greco handed him the sheet of paper.

"Ask him if what I say is true or not."

"Coming to ask me. That took some courage on your part . . ."

It was a beautiful afternoon. They'd been sitting together for the past hour in the old Ford Fiesta parked under a walnut tree. Untilled fields. Reddish dirt between one tree and the next. Then there was the sea, the blue line. On the other side were the first few buildings of Mola. Collapsing rents and good food. It was here that history slowed down. But this was also a place where someone like Danilo Sangirardi could find a haven in which to lick his wounds between one investigative piece and the next.

"But I love this sort of thing," the journalist went on, "I adore ungrateful children."

He was rattling on and on. Since they'd gotten into the car, he hadn't stopped for a moment. He was doing and undoing. An overgrown boy of around forty. His curly head of hair undermined by the beginnings of a bald spot. His stout physique communicated an idea of inexhaustibility, as if being overweight had put at his disposal a stock of resources he could afford to burn through.

"It took more courage to find out how to get in touch with you," said Michele.

But the guy wasn't even listening to him. He was talking about a shipping container full of toxic waste. "The system of flipping waybills. They just change the codes on the form and at that point industrial waste can become agricultural after-products. From Germany to Foggia, then straight into Campania and Albania. But some of the shit stays right here, don't kid yourself. A month or so ago a piece was published in the *Frankfurter Allgemeine*. And guess who wrote about it here in Italy, aside from me. No one. Did you hear anything about it? You couldn't have," he said, answering his own question, "because they published the piece in *Daunia Oggi*. The weekly parish bulletin, more or less. And as soon as they did, we were notified that the lab that did the chemical analysis had filed a lawsuit. And now that you mention it, yes, if I think about who gave you my contact information, I feel a little ill."

Instead he listened to everything. He stockpiled every piece of information. "Giuseppe Greco is an imbecile," he added, "one of those reporters who interview Peter Gabriel when he does a concert at Melpignano and think they've cleansed their conscience."

A truck loaded with watermelons passed by. It kicked up a cloud of dust and vanished.

Giuseppe Greco, Sangirardi continued, hadn't had the simple courage to defend him when he'd been sued by the Mangimi Mediterranei feed company, nor had he carried the news that the lawsuit had been dismissed out of hand. And as for letting him, Sangirardi, ever write in his paper, forget about it. Anyway, he'd probably given him the contact just because he owed Michele's family.

"After all, who doesn't owe you Salveminis?" he said, as he lit a cigarette. "They fear you or they hate you. When they're not dependent on you. I don't hate you. It's much more interesting to study you. You're one of the natural consequences of this land. When you don't plough a field properly, then of course what happens is that weeds proliferate. If it hadn't been you, it would have been some other family of entrepreneurs."

Michele, too, lit a cigarette. He looked at Sangirardi. He admired him. He had the impression that the quest for truth in this man went hand in hand with personal glorification. As if the urgency sprang not from a wound but from a challenge, a desperate competition to which he'd summoned himself.

"That's right, precisely," said Michele, "but let's go back to my sister."

Sangirardi ashed out his window. In the distance a tiny dot appeared, moving in their direction. Slow, wobbling. An unidentified object in the stifling June heat.

"So you want to know whether your sister really did get me fired from the newspaper?" Sangirardi turned toward him and smiled. "Absolutely, she did. Twice. First from *Corriere del Sud*, and then from *Puglia Oggi*. But don't think she was the only one."

It seemed to Michele that he could see Clara's face emerging from a pool of water.

"My CV is like a war bulletin," Sangirardi continued with macabre satisfaction. He listed the publications that had fired him. Once again Michele had the sensation that this was some kind of race in which Sangirardi was devoured by the need to come in first, whatever the cost. There was a calendar and there was a trophy shelf, even when the winner was the one who lost.

"If they hadn't tied my hands, I'd have easily proved that your father inflated the costs for the expansion of the port of Manfredonia well beyond the threshold of decency. I'd have shown that the city commissioner for public works was actually on your payroll, and it wouldn't have been hard for me to show that you got away with building the residential complex in Val di Noto by manipulating the coefficients of environmental sustainability. Instead something always happens just when things are coming together. Some important document disappears. Or else I get fired."

The strange moving object proved to be a cart loaded with fruit. It seemed that it was being hauled by a man on a bicycle. A scooter overtook it.

"Why did my sister have you fired?"

The journalist sat with his cigarette poised in midair. His mane of hair waved in the wind.

"What kind of question is that?"

He got a little more comfortable in the seat, as if he wanted to be closer to Michele. Perhaps he felt sorry for this young man who seemed incapable of fully understanding the mechanism, and Michele, in turn, registered how the car shook and staggered under the weight of its owner, shitty shocks, a clattering old jalopy hurtling against an armored world, proof that the journalist was in the right.

"The question, really, is how she managed to get me tossed out on my ear so fast," he continued without ever losing his smile. "Costantini," he said, "your sister was Renato Costantini's lover. The chancellor of the university. One of the big shareholders in EdiPuglia. I was writing a piece attacking your father, Clara went to talk to Costantini, and he called the editor of the paper in the middle of the night."

The object in motion could be seen more clearly now. It was in fact a man on a bicycle.

"I'm sorry she killed herself," said Sangirardi with a fatalistic tone that Michele didn't like. "Every so often I'd see them together in Bari," he scratched his chin, "her and Costantini. I have to say they made a strong and not particularly pleasant impression. It wasn't just the difference in age, or all the cocaine. The thing is that . . . Look. To suddenly come face to face with them on parade along Via Sparano, or see them appear under the porticoes of Via Capruzzi only to disappear immediately after into Costantini's car. They looked as if they'd popped right out of a sewer main. Don't take this the wrong way. It was as if they glittered in a cruel, gruesome light. I don't know how to explain it any better for you. At a certain point, when *La Gazzetta del Mezzogiorno* started publishing the occasional article that raised doubts about whether the construction sites at the airport were being run properly, it appears that the guy in charge of that project went to complain personally to Costantini. If you see what I'm trying to say."

"Alberto," Michele said in astonishment.

"Exactly," said Sangirardi, "so do you see what kind of people your sister got herself mixed up with? Her husband went without a second thought to ask a favor of the man she was going to bed with. Maybe at a certain point she couldn't take it anymore."

Michele nodded. He knew that wasn't it.

Sangirardi stopped talking. He looked through the windshield. Michele did the same. The shadows of the clouds ran along the road, and between the shadows and the sunlight jolted this huge cart. Apricots, bananas. A green pyramid of watermelons. Pulling it was an old man on a bicycle. Now that he was closer, they realized that he might be very old. One of those ancient fifty-year-olds from four or five centuries ago. All muscles and sinews. Canvas trousers, braided plastic sandals. Sticking out of the shirt were the bones of an intensely bronzed torso. Bald cranium. The mouth a horizontal fissure. He was pedaling with all the effort in the world, but never slackening his pace, driven by a force more primitive than that of will. The journalist held his breath in the seat beside him, and Michele felt that there was a narrow but deep groove within which they both loved the South in the same way. Then they began to translate that skinny old man who was hauling a load twenty times his own weight using different dictionaries. He and Sangirardi would never be able to understand each other entirely. Opposite models of orphanhood. They had a better shot at understanding and being understood by their respective adversaries.

In any case, the journalist was kind.

After they were done talking, he drove Michele to the station. Michele fell asleep on the local. By ten that night, he was back in Bari. He emerged from the underpass. He walked along Via Capruzzi. He couldn't help but imagine the scene that the journalist had described to him. His sister and Costantini getting out of the car and disappearing into the mouth of a sewer. He saw a shadow moving under the parked Fiat Punto, and he thought of the cat. But when he remembered that now he was going home to his father's house, he felt even worse. He turned down Via Giulio Petroni. He headed for the number 19 bus stop. The blackened sky overhead. He could feel the thousand pieces of the puzzle moving into place. Iron filings on a sheet of paper under which a magnet is placed.

When, many years later, Gennaro Lopez, former medical examiner for the Bari health clinic ASL 2, found himself extracting from his many if tangled memories the most awful one, that is, the one that could do him the most harm, he would choose the night on which a guy of about thirty knocked on his front door and started showering him with questions about his sister's death certificate.

He dialed Dr. Rosaria Nardoni's number. The cell phone was turned off. He tried the second number he'd been given. The phone rang and rang, but no one picked up. So he phoned the Foggia court directly. He asked to speak to the office of the court clerk for the investigating magistrate. After a short pause, a second operator answered. Vittorio asked to speak to Dr. Nardoni. "Hello?" the woman said two minutes later. "*Buongiorno*, ma'am." There followed an awkward pause. "Are you calling me . . . that is, you're calling . . . " "No, no," Vittorio hastened to reply, "I'm using my wife's cell phone." "Forgive me," the woman said, in relief, "I should have guessed. These have been extremely exhausting days." Vittorio thought how unfortunate it was that he'd called during the so-called Black Week, when at court they sometimes were forced to work for as long as three hours at a stretch. "In any case, however, I'm answering your call in the court clerk's office." The old man got the hint. He gave the woman his wife's cell phone number. She hung up. Ten minutes later the cell phone rang. This time city traffic was the background to her voice. Vittorio informed her that the technical reports on the hydrogeological impact of the villas of Porto Allegro were ready. They'd been countersigned by the administrative offices of the Italian National Institute for Environmental Protection and Research (ISPRA). Dr. Nardoni said: "Certainly." Then she added: "Signor Salvemini, the only reason we're doing this thing is because the approval from the

Ministry of the Environment depends on it." "Of course," Vittorio replied, contemptuously.

He phoned Engineer De Palo. Then he phoned Ruggero. He told him about his sour stomach. Ruggero said that it was because of the stress. He recommended Maalox. Vittorio sighed: "Do you seriously think I haven't already taken it?" Then he said it took him forever to digest these days and his ankles were swollen." "Papà," said Ruggero, "you're seventy-five years old." He added that if he wanted to do some tests, he could swing by the clinic any time he wanted. "Listen," Vittorio stopped him before his son could hang up. "The new technical director for ARPA, the Regional Environmental Protection Agency." Ruggero's silence, so to speak, intensified. The new technical director, Vittorio went on, had managed pharmaceutical services for the Bari health care clinic until two years ago. "Do you know him?" Ruggero had no choice but to confirm. "Well," said Vittorio with a sorrowful voice, feeling his son's growing mistrust. Now of all times, after the Porto Allegro mess was finally getting under control, it was time for ARPA's biannual monitoring of the Gargano district. "Well?" asked Ruggero. "It's not like you have anything to hide." When he was like this, he was intolerable. "Of course we don't have anything to hide," Vittorio humiliated himself, "but given the fact that there's a file open on Porto Allegro, I wouldn't want the ARPA technicians to start digging in their heels." "In other words, you want me to talk to them." Vittorio replied that the economic crisis out there was something awful, that if the tourist village fell apart it would be a catastrophe. "The banks would bleed us dry in an instant." He was sure that his son remembered all the lines of credit he'd co-signed over the years.

After lunch, Vittorio tried to find some pretext to talk with Michele. It had been a month and a half since his son had come back to Bari. The old man would never have bet on such a lengthy stay. In truth—the initial awkwardness aside—the situation gave him a great deal of pleasure. In the last several days he'd been surprised to catch himself feeling tenderness where there had once been nothing but bafflement. In the rare breaks in his work, he reflected on the possibility that they were reestablishing a relationship. With certain children, mutual understanding comes late. He was sincerely sorry that he'd lost his cat. It was a pity he didn't have a steady job. Growing up without a real mother must have been complicated. It might just be that Michele was on the verge of finally finding his path. Vittorio felt the prospects were rosy. And then, after all, Michele was the only one who never asked him for anything. Never a favor, a gift. The only one who was truly selfless, he thought with gratitude as he walked from the living room into the kitchen. He walked out onto the veranda, where he finally found him.

"Ciao, Papà," said Michele.

They drank an espresso together. They talked about summer, which had finally arrived. Michele said that recently, in Europe alone, more than twenty thousand people were dying from the heat every year. "You read that on the internet," said Vittorio, emphasizing his lack of expertise with the medium. As if that weren't enough, he added: "At my age . . . " He said it as if the admission of weakness were a tribute paid to his son's own, convinced that Michele wouldn't catch the innuendo, since Vittorio hadn't entirely caught it himself. Then he asked Michele if he'd spoken recently with Engineer Ranieri. "Yes," said the young man without hesitating. Vittorio was beginning to calm down. In the pot of cyclamens at their feet, two insects were battling savagely. "Last week," Michele added, "when the chief justice of the court of appeals came to dinner." Vittorio asked whether he'd given the engineer any particular instructions. "Concerning what?" The young man avoided the trap. "He mentioned some situation involving elevators to be installed in Taranto. I didn't understand what he was talking about. I told him that he'd have to talk to you." "That's what I thought," the old man replied, shaking his head. In the meantime, one of the two insects was dead.

Half an hour later, Vittorio went upstairs to his bedroom for his afternoon nap.

He awoke at four. He went downstairs. He made himself another espresso. He phoned Engineer Ranieri. The engineer said that he'd been unable to track the man down. He'd been going up and down the streets of the city for three days now. He'd even staked out the apartment building on Via d'Aquino. Of course he'd pressed the buzzer. He'd gone to the rec center. Nothing. He'd vanished into thin air. Vittorio asked him if he was certain he was in Taranto. Engineer Ranieri asked: "What do you mean, Signor Salvemini?" Vittorio was fully convinced that Engineer Ranieri must be turning stupid. He felt a surge of love for his third-born child greater than ever before.

"Because you actually think that at Porto Allegro it really is just a question of a few maritime pines being cut down?"

"The Mediterranean maquis," replied the pockmarked guy, "are you kidding? One time at Castellaneta Marina my mother-in-law dug up two rosemary bushes. She stacked them up behind the garden and burned them. The State Forestry Corps was there immediately. A 2,000-euro fine. And then, anyway, there's the whole issue of the coastline. You can't build a tourist complex fifty feet from the water."

"Do you remember the newspaper ads?"

"The owners went right into their villas in their boats. I seem to remember that the truth-in-advertising standards were brought into play, or something like that."

"It's not just that. For instance, what about Rodi Garganico? There really are villas there with private moorings."

Two customers came in. The proprietor stopped talking.

He served them cappuccinos and pastries. The customers ate. Then they left. The man went on with what he was saying.

"It's not just the Mediterranean maquis. It's not the distance from the sea. In that area they've done crap you can't even begin to imagine. The whole upper Gargano area. Stuff that if you lived there, you'd pack up your whole family and leave in the middle of the night."

A university student came in. The proprietor served him an espresso. The student drank it. He left.

"What kind of crap?" asked the pockmarked guy.

"Waste," replied the proprietor "Special waste buried under the agricultural waste. And even that waste ought to be disposed of differently. Everyone says so. We know who's ended up charge of the area, and for some time now. Stuff that in a couple of years could go up like a bomb—"

"Like Ilva?"

"Even worse."

"Have you by any chance talked to Engineer Ranieri?" the older man asked the younger one in the cool shade of the veranda.

But for the tiny mite clinging to the abdomen of the wasp these were just shadows that distance kept from being transformed into real dangers. Despite the fact that the wasp was ten times its size—its sting capable of causing anaphylactic shock in a small dog—the impersonal force that governed the mite drove it to attack the wasp the minute its presence in the vase of cyclamens was identified. The wasp tried to react, but it was too slow. The mite was able to sink its small sharp fangs into the wasp's abdomen, and then finally insert its powerful tubular appendages. It had no way of knowing that the wasp was old and feeble, and that this was the only reason the mite could hope to best it. The force knew, and that was enough.

E ducated man that he was, Renato Costantini was familiar with the effectiveness of certain re-proposals of the same thing after the crime has been consummated. Voices that rise from underground. Ghosts that only the suspect can see. He also knew that in the real world these things happen at the hands of the ill-intentioned, ready to seek their own gain. Usually blackmailers.

All the same, they preserve their anguishing power. He'd had concrete evidence of the fact just last week. He was striding briskly through the monumental entrance to the university when he'd seen him. Sitting all alone on a bench in Piazza Cesare Battisti. He'd noticed the strangeness of the scarf knotted around his neck. He thought he'd recognized something whose emotional consequences (a sorrow, the grim unfolding of a Good Friday) had kept him from remembering. He hadn't stopped.

Two days later came the shareholders meeting of EdiPuglia. The heat was tremendous. The discussion went on and on. At a certain point Renato Costantini felt the need to step out onto the balcony for a cigarette. From there to the breakwaters the sea was calm and metallic in the summer afternoon. From the conference room came the sound of familiar voices raised. Costantini took a drag. He lowered his head to raze his thoughts to the ground and reconstruct them in a different order. Before this could happen—his mind a temporary open path—he saw him again. About sixty feet away. Sitting at a table of the bar on Piazza Diaz. Jeans and black shirt, hunched over the pages of a newspaper with a demitasse of espresso.

Costantini felt his head spin. The image of the young man, plummeting like a dead weight into the yielding photo archives of his memory, promptly merged with another one, almost identical. The way in which Michele twisted forward, legs crossed. An unsettling geometric figure—the empty triangle of a chain-link fence swollen in the open countryside by a tumultuous wind—that resembled Clara's posture. Unnaturally identical. As if the young man had come all the way there to challenge him but, after entering provocatively into the role of his sister, had in his turn fallen under the thrall of it. The man definitively focused on the scarf, as well. Wrapped around his neck was the neckerchief from the other day, the same one that she had been wearing when Costantini went to pick her up in the dark funnel of a night several months ago, and the girl, in the car, looking at him, with a puffy lip, no seriousness to her, had transformed a page otherwise brimming over with meaning into a mirror.

Costantini was seized by anxiety. It seemed to him that now Michele, bent over the newspaper at the table in the bar, his finger hovering over the porous paper like a pendulum over an alphabetical grid, was reading from that very same page. As if he were talking to himself—a whisper not listened to but nonetheless real—and saying horrible things about Costantini, details that he, first and foremost, would have lacked the courage to admit to himself. *Clara.* Then Costantini became himself again. But the young man was still there, in the street.

Someone called him into the meeting room. It was a lucky thing. A few minutes later he was deep in discussion with the other partners. They were arguing over whether it would be wise to move the very expensive offices of *Corriere del Sud* out to the outskirts of town.

*

Friday night, the third apparition.

This time, Costantini was at the supermarket. He hadn't had a chance to swing by the deli. He'd been forced to fall back on the Conad supermarket on Viale Unità d'Italia, which stayed open until late. In the long aisles drenched with fluorescent light, he felt lost. The hard part was making sure he didn't buy the kind of low-quality food that would earn him a rebuke from his wife. And then the people all around him. The faces. The instant reflex with which their attention would seize on the phosphorescent yellow of a deal of the week. If you were lucky enough to be comfortably off, the last thing on earth you'd want around you was poor people.

He watched anxiously as they sliced his prosciutto. He chose some bread. He headed for the refrigerator case. The long metal tray was packed with yogurts and terrible industrially produced cheeses. He'd just looked up from an unlikely package of frozen croquettes, when there he was before him. Skinny, pale. He was pushing a completely empty shopping cart. His gaze was lost in something that Costantini couldn't seem to entirely uproot from himself.

Pretending he hadn't seen him, Michele brushed past. He vanished behind the refrigerator case. Costantini felt the hairs rise on his forearms, his belly tighten with malaise. They'd forced him to attend the funeral. Then the owner's lackey had showed up with that ridiculous excuse of the overcoat. Trying to extort favors from him. But now the young man had ambushed him for the umpteenth time. Carrying in his face the pallor of his dead sister (in the grotesque twisting of his lips, Clara's tranquility), he was doing something that was completely devoid of logic. Unless he was trying to tell him something else. The hypothesis that there might be aspects of Clara that he'd never even come close to. Entire universes. A story that fluttered all around, pulverized, beyond Costantini's ability

to reconstruct, any more than it is possible to go from a bonfire to a book by putting the ashes back together.

That same night, lying in bed next to his wife, he couldn't
get to sleep. An idiotic prank. The young man was trying to
scare him. In cahoots with the rest of the family. Still, after the
meeting with Engineer De Palo, Costantini had gotten busy.
He alone knew how much effort it had cost him. But had new
pieces hostile to Salvemini Construction come out in *Corriere
del Sud*? Had they appeared in *Puglia Oggi*, in the *Gazzetta del
Levante*, or in any other paper where he had so much as a
friend? What message were they trying to send him through
this young man's apparitions? Perhaps they were demanding
that articles come out actually *in favor* of Salvemini
Construction. But that was impossible. They were still continuing to devastate one of the loveliest areas in the region. In
given circumstances, silence was the most valuable gift that the
local press could offer a company of that kind.

Costantini tossed and turned in the bed. His wife went on
sleeping. Her mouth half open, her features relaxed like a rubber mask. Costantini shut his eyes to keep from penetrating
any further into that unguarded opening. But as soon as darkness enveloped him, allowing the outlines of things to become
a skeleton of light, all at once he saw her again. A sketch
enclosed in itself. Exactly the same as when, after making love,
Clara would get dressed again and he felt he hadn't modified
in her even so much as the mood of the two minutes that followed.

Looking at her for the first time, obscurely nonchalant at
the journalists' party, it had seemed to him that she was summoning him to fill a void. The sensation of some missing piece
(an invitation that provoked pity, and immediately thereafter,
aggression) was something that Clara emanated even when he
wasn't there. This was damned clear. Even when they'd seen

each other just the day before. Even when he caressed her flesh, grabbed her wrists in his fists, tried to impress in her body a lasting impulse.

But none of all this endured in her.

In his travels around the city, it often happened that Costantini would spot her in the company of other men. Never her husband. Leaving a restaurant with Valentino Buffante. Out shopping with the director of the Banca di Credito Pugliese. Then, one night when she'd asked him to swing by and pick her up out front of a club so they could go to dinner together, he'd found her talking in the shadows with some kind of aged chimp in an overcoat and black shoes. To Costantini it seemed (but as if in a nightmare, the intermittence of a premonition) that it was the elderly chief justice of the court of appeals. To stifle the jealousy, they would have had to be in the hotel already, bodies sinking into the bed. Shame and rage prevented him from suggesting the change of plan. And so, after helping her into the car, Costantini limited himself to driving toward the restaurant. Once they emerged onto Via Crisanzio, he even began to wonder whether she hadn't gone to bed with the judge that same night. Maybe only an hour ago. That is, if it really was the judge. He thought it with her sitting beside him, as a whiff of her exceedingly faint scent reached him, flowers mixed with sweat. Even if she hadn't done it, she was certainly capable of it, he told himself. So she'd done it. The indifference of certain beautiful young women. That devastating weapon. If it had fallen to him, to keep two or three lovers on tenterhooks simultaneously, he would have succeeded only through sheer force of will. However brutal and instinctive. The reason he'd never be as successful at such a thing as she was. Clara never put any will into it. In her, there wasn't even the strategic determination to do without will. For Costantini it was a sort of brainteaser that drove him crazy.

That night they dined near Via Amendola. They had sex in a hotel at Torre a Mare. But already, as he watched her get out of bed, walking naked toward the bathroom, it seemed to him that, from a body held firmly in his hands, Clara was turning back into an elusive compound of other people's thoughts. He imagined her as composed of pure energy rendered possible— in her immaterial intensity—by what she did with other men. Exactly what she did with him. If he had been able to peek through a keyhole, he wouldn't have found anyone other than himself.

Being part of the same logic meant not understanding.

If he'd hoped to so much as graze the edge of the problem, he ought to have overturned the plane on which he reasoned. Change his point of view. He would have had to glimpse her immersed in her most concrete pain. The grass up to her calves on summer evenings. When, in an absolutely pathetic manner, after going over to her parents' for dinner, Clara got up from the table and went for a walk through the moonlit fields. Walking past the mulberry bushes, she ventured deeper amongst the spikes of Bermuda grass. Then into the peat bog. She was searching for Michele. There had been, in their lives, one long moment of happiness. Every time she came into the old house, Clara better understood what would otherwise have been for her just a mute force that governed her days. Then it's this, she said to herself after climbing the stairs to the second floor. Seeing Michele's bedroom reduced to a storage room made her feel ill, but it was the sign of the insult. *It's this, of course it is.* Clara managed to fetch it back an instant before the black drop was diluted in the sea inside which it would have become an indistinct malaise, with neither origin nor direction. Instead, there was an origin. There had been an outrage, a crime that now cried out for compensation. Clara imagined herself repeating the phrase under her breath beneath the constellations of summer. Not that she dreamed of vengeance. She liked order. A small ceramic vase to be put back in place. She went past the tufts of the cane plants, then past the trees in the radiant sky of eleven at night. She knew that naming him too explicitly was the opposite of finding him again. It wasn't enough to walk through the places where he had loved to get lost before that wonderful year had begun. It wasn't enough to dig up those comic books she'd given him as a gift. There was something mawkish, something obvious about these attempts. At the same time, they were necessary to ensure that the real grief could surprise her from behind. Point blank, it would happen. Clara felt herself being torn by the same emotion as when she and her brother would wrestle in the bed. The splendid peace of the moments in which Michele observed her while she was spiking over the top of the net. Delirious with joy, she had the confirmation that the world wasn't just made up of naked material objects. It wasn't even made up of people, but of presences. *He and I unleashed the energy of the dead.* In a future as inaccessible yet certain as the sprout of a seed already buried in the dirt, Clara sensed that Michele would mentally unroll the missive, would give it voice. At that point, she fully understood. She remembered that she was a ghost, and wouldn't find peace until things had gone back to the way they were supposed to be.

At last she was heading back toward the villa, ready to say farewell to her parents, get in her car, and go join Alberto. She thought for a moment about her lovers, vague bumpers in a game about whose precise workings she knew no more than what her instincts told her. She moved in a sea of fog, trusting in the fact that going forward was the right thing to do. Even though the fog thickened, and the ground beneath her feet grew chilly and dank. The odor of marsh and rotting leaves before the waters made their presence known, lapping around her waist, lifting her dress like a parachute.

That was when the nighttime phone calls started coming in.

Costantini tossed and turned. He turned his back on his wife, afraid that the woman's slumber might harpoon his secrets. He curled up in the bed. The first time, he remembered, the cell phone rang a little past midnight. He was in a restaurant in the city center, together with the editor-in-chief of *Puglia Oggi*. He answered the phone. He raised one hand in a gesture of apology before a table full of glasses that had already been filled and emptied many times. Half an hour later, he was driving all alone toward Viale Europa. At that time of night the area was completely dead, surrounded by farmland and discount furniture stores and ugly, illegally built houses. He found her where she'd told him. Where the road widens, just past the Q8 gas station. Motionless in the night like a sentinel for a world he didn't have the credentials to access. Costantini slowed down. Clara hopped into the car. He looked her in the face and started in surprise. She said resolutely: "Let's get out of here." Out of an abundance of caution, he drove for a few miles, and then pulled over to the side of the road. He turned off the engine. He turned on the dome light. He turned to look at her.

"So, do you mind telling me what's going on?"

Clara was wearing a leather jacket, a white T-shirt, a silk scarf around her neck. And her upper lip was swollen. She was surrounded by the electric wind of bodies that have ceased to struggle. Costantini imagined that someone had hurled her out of a car after something he couldn't imagine. He tried to contain his anger.

"What happened to you?" he asked again.

"Nothing, really, nothing." Clara shrugged. She gave him a sort of half-smile that made her unapproachable: "Come on, take me home."

He pulled back out onto the road. He tried to say something. He was agitated, confused. Twice he spread his hands out into the air before replacing them responsibly on the steering wheel. He didn't know if she really had been hit. Much less what she was doing in that ridiculous part of town in the first place. He asked her whether she'd had a fight with someone. Clara replied wearily not to worry, that it was all under control. "Was it your husband?" More than a question, Costantini caught himself realizing that it actually constituted a hope. She lit a cigarette. "What are you talking about? Alberto's at home waiting for me." She had the tone of voice of a mother trying to reassure her son about something it's better for him not to know. Costantini went on driving. He was following the reflectors. He asked no more questions because he was starting to feel embarrassed. He was afraid that she might be able to read his thoughts. He tried not to look at her. Why could someone else do this and he couldn't?

What Costantini would have had to know—and he couldn't know it, he was barred from the scene—had nothing to do with the nighttime occurrences. Sooner or later he would have had access to those. But he could never have seen her the next afternoon, at home, immediately after a long warm bath, when Clara got out of the tub with the specific intention of phoning her brother. It had been a month since they'd spoken. She wrapped a towel around her head. She slipped on her bathrobe. She shut the toilet lid, sat down on it and stretched her legs out in front of her, crossing her ankles on the bidet. She lit up a nice cigarette and dialed Michele's number.

"Hello?" he said after a couple of rings.

Ten minutes of conversation without telling each other a thing. They'd been talking like this for years. But she, smoking and chatting, joking about empty shapes, caressed with satisfaction her fist-pounded lip. She sought in the voice of this Michele the unconscious resonance of the other. She thought she could hear it. Much louder than the last few times. An angry breathing grew under the calm, judicious tone.

Then Clara smiled, so happy that no one could see her. She

was waiting for the harvest. She was receiving the confirmation that the journey through the mists was proceeding very well.

The second phone call came a few weeks later.

Costantini was going to bed when his cell phone lit up. He went out onto the balcony to keep from being overheard. His wife put up with his cheating on her, so long as certain duties of courtesy were respected. "Hello, Clara?" The young woman's voice seemed to come from another dimension. She was whimpering. She uttered a few disconnected phrases. Between the fragments of what she said, Costantini thought he understood that she was asking him to come get her at the same place as the other time. He couldn't understand clearly. She ended the call.

A short while later, in the car zipping toward Viale Europa, Costantini tried calling her back. The phone rang and rang. He went past the cemetery, the parking area in Viale Buozzi. Five minutes later he saw the gas station. He pulled over at the wide spot in the road and got out of the car. The girl wasn't there. The hedges along the edge of the road were trembling in the desolate emptiness. So he turned and went back to the car. He got his cell phone. He tried calling her one more time. He heard the ring of the phone behind him. He saw her coming out of the black of night. She was weaving in a strange sleeveless denim dress buttoned up the front. He'd never seen it on her before. That alone was enough to make him feel even more disoriented. Costantini went towards her. He put an arm on her shoulder, the other around her waist. She was burning up. With some effort, he dragged her toward the car. He eased her down onto the passenger seat. Clara shut her eyes. She had another nasty mark on her lip and one on her forehead. Her arms were covered with scratch marks. She was moaning as if she were having a bad dream. Costantini wondered whether they weren't both dreaming. He undid the top buttons of her dress. Scratches on her neck, too. "Clara," he said. After confirming that there was no answer, he stood there, looking at her. She was so still. Not the elusive flash of light he couldn't even dream of chasing, but a young body, physically abandoned on the seat of his car. He undid more buttons until he'd uncovered her sternum, then her brilliantly white breasts and her belly. He looked, and he was left astonished. She was covered with bruises. Deep marks. Costantini touched her. He felt ill. He undid the last buttons, right down to the bottom. He was desperately trying not to take advantage of the situation.

He turned over in the bed again. If he tried to keep calm, to think coldly and logically, it seemed impossible that he'd let himself be swayed like that. Actually set foot at a certain point in Buffante's villa. And yet it had happened. He'd allowed the knife to be rotated 180 degrees. He could feel the blade at his throat. They could make him do whatever they chose.

He looked over at his wife, still asleep. He shut his eyes and fell asleep himself.

The next morning, he loafed wearily from his home over to the university. In the afternoon, he shut himself up in his office. He felt confused, out of sorts. He did his work badly. When he talked on the phone he was preoccupied. He'd catch himself and lose his concentration.

At eight o'clock in the evening he left the headquarters of EdiPuglia. As he was getting his car, he saw him for the fourth time. At the other end of the street. Lit up by white light, standing in front of the Apple Store on Corso Vittorio Emanuele. Costantini closed his eyes to keep from slamming his fist down on the hood of the car. They were trying to drive him crazy. He looked once again at the store's window. Michele was still there. At that point he lunged forward. He crossed the street. The young man stood motionless. By so doing, he prevented the man from grabbing him and shaking him. When he was a yard away, Costantini raised his forefinger to shorten the distance even further. He looked for his sister's posture in the young man. He didn't find it. Nothing was ever the way you might expect it to be. So he said that it was time for them to cut it out. Stop trying to blackmail him. It was disgusting, he added. Then he lowered his voice. He tried to explain himself. He assured him that beyond what he was already doing it would be impossible to come up with anything else.

Michele furrowed his brow.

A few seconds later he nodded as if he'd actually understood every detail.

T hey passed over the chestnut groves, over the limestone sinkholes. They could feel beneath themselves the green force of the Gulf of Manfredonia, which was nothing compared to the emerald green that was drawing them south. The coasts of Libya, then the heart of Africa.

They gave the impression of a giant black hand sailing through the empty air, breaking up into a thousand dots and then condensing into a shape that was equal but never the same, not unlike the astonishment of a man watching them from afar is mutable and perhaps equal. Plovers. In flight over the Gargano. A couple of months early relative to when, after nesting, they ought to have begun their crossing, as if they perceived the arrival (churned up in the hot wind) of a premature winter.

They flew high over the beach of Siponto. Then the Cervaro channel, near Zapponeta. After that they arrived at Lido San Giuseppe and a small cluster of agritourism resorts and tourist villages. Baia Serena. Porto Allegro. Episodic gray shapes on a blue and green map. The children pointed their fingers up into the sky. How did the members of such a huge flock know with every beat of the wing which way to go? What held them together?

The grownup's explanations were always wrong. The leader, they'd say. They're following the leader.

They didn't know that flocks of birds have no commander. Each creature regulates its movements in accordance with those of the ones that fly alongside them, a miracle by which from nothingness, life and motion seem to emerge. A game of mirrors with nothing at the center, similar to that which brings consciousness into existence. That was the reason why men, watching the birds pass in a group, seemed to find, since time out of mind, something of themselves.

Then the plovers arrived on the salt marshes. Veering to the right, as their golden-grey feathers glistened in the sunlight, many of them began to lose altitude. They'd drop and rise in the air, so that the large black hand would return to itself seconds before becoming nothing. It was a zone of small ponds and channels of brackish water. A spectacular succession of basins made it a territory of supreme beauty. For migratory birds these were small oases, the equivalent of intermediate ports where fleets making the journey between continents would lay over. Here the plovers would drink. They'd refresh themselves. They'd mix with teals, snipes, and delicate pink flamingoes engaged in the same operations. Then they'd resume their flight.

A half hour later the flock approached San Ferdinando di Puglia. Since their senses were a surface radar, they recognized the shape of streams and ponds, not what totally alien thing could be concealed beneath them. Here, as at Castel Volturno or Mondragone, stopovers on the previous day's flights. Nor were their senses designed to associate with the blades of grass and the nourishing muddy waters such elements as cobalt, lead, and manganese.

A fair number of plovers suddenly started dropping. They were dying on the wing. One after another. The large black hand, before turning into a smaller hand, took on absurd shapes that fell outside the laws of nature.

Alberto emerged from the supermarket, his arms tense with the weight of the grocery bags. He headed back home. He counted his footsteps, looking around in the hope that he'd find no known faces. They'd called him on the phone. They'd sent him emails and texts that expressed their lukewarm condolences (a sign that these were the rewritings of phrases that at first seemed too original). To say nothing of the cards of condolence. He hadn't replied to a single one.

They'd placed the coffin in a niche five yards off the ground. They'd sealed up the slab with bronze lettering and the ugly oval of the photograph. It couldn't be considered a genuine burial. If anything, a byproduct of urban construction. If the purpose was to lodge the dead in the invisible band where at times the spirit of the living penetrated, it had been a failure. The sun set hot and red between the buildings. Thus, Alberto was the true custodian of his wife. That is why he needed peace and solitude. At every hour of the day and night he was tossing a handful of dirt into the grave.

The concentration of black dots over the shopping center lit up with an intense vermilion red and vanished. A flash of light deformed the plexiglass clouds. Then, once again, reality.

"That was a kick," said Pietro Giannelli.

Michele shook his head, stunned.

They were sitting on the asphalt, their backs against the metal roller gate of a garage.

"That's insane," said Giannelli, massaging the back of his neck, "just like the old days dropping acid in Piazza Cesare Battisti. When you're around, even the effects of DMT only last half as long."

Michele felt the wind of late morning on his face. A few milk-white clouds were in the process of disintegrating in the torrential heat. The sky. When he was small even the fields behind the house had seemed immense to him. To say nothing of the Salento plain, red and green, when, aboard a Southeastern Railway train, he traveled down to the sea at Leuca. Once he'd even gone camping with his sister.

That was the good thing about breathing that air: you rediscovered the memories that were so to speak outside the narrative. He and Clara had tried to pitch the tent until nightfall. She wouldn't give up, kept delivering massive hammer blows to the stakes. She was wearing a terrycloth tank top with white and orange stripes. The South is also this deception, thought

Michele, wounded by the sunlight, a part that is greater than the whole that ought to contain it.

He looked at Giannelli in the frog costume. There was a time when he went everywhere with his eyes made up, his jacket covered with studs. Now the world was in a new phase.

An hour earlier, Pietro Giannelli had been handing out flyers for the Toy Center. He kept his distance from the Chicken Man. Above all, he steered clear of the Great Hog, who was giving out discount coupons. The Hog was a machine. The number of coupons he distributed halved the number of potential customers for those who worked around him, and Giannelli had planned to get rid of his first batch of flyers by ten.

It was horribly hot. Those who hadn't left for the beach were pouring into the shopping center in waves. At ten-thirty Giannelli felt slightly unwell. He grabbed hold of the zipper that closed the large amphibian head. He was suffocating in that foam rubber cage. The zipper wouldn't come down. So he gave a more violent yank, but all that did was to pull the eye-holes out of alignment. Green. That's what he saw now. He felt his heart start to race. He staggered. He saw two dark shadows grow larger on either side of the costume. He felt something squeeze around the ears. Kiss the frog. Immediately afterward he saw the hands that were freeing him from the harness.

When the frog's head came off entirely, he was looking at the skinny smiling face of Michele Salvemini.

"I've been waiting for you for at least a month," said Giannelli, but the other man didn't understand.

He pulled his arms out of the costume, too. He pulled his friend close. Then—half man, half frog—he led him over to the drinks machine.

He drank a Gatorade. He treated Michele to a small bottle

of water. He dried the sweat off his forehead. Without saying a word, he hopped off toward Section H of the parking lot. Michele followed him.

They headed down the ramp that led to the garage. Giannelli sat down in the shaded area. Michele did the same. Giannelli slipped a hand into his fanny pack. He pulled out the pipe and the aluminum foil. Michele got scared. It had been so long since his problems had manifested as anything more than minor relapses. He was afraid that a drug like DMT would reawaken inside him the monsters of permanent disturbance.

Giannelli formed a little inverted hood with the aluminum foil. He inserted it into the pipe. He extracted the crystals and put them into the bowl. He lit it. He inhaled. Before slumping forward, he handed the pipe to Michele. Michele looked at it apprehensively. He put it into his mouth. He closed his eyes. He inhaled.

The world shattered into a billion spots. Michele felt no discomfort. Instead he felt an enormous pair of eyes open wide before him. They scrutinized him, they caressed him lovingly. He, in turn, recognized them and began to be moved. Then the world went back exactly as it had been.

"Insane," said Giannelli, massaging the back of his neck, "just like the old days dropping acid on Piazza Cesare Battisti."

But in reality they were talking about Clara. It was as if they'd been doing it even before Giannelli pulled out the pipe. As if they were still sitting side by side on the benches in the piazza, telling each other what they would say to each other as adults if things were to happen exactly the way they ended up happening.

"After my father's death, it was the hardest thing to take during my adolescence," Giannelli was saying with a smile that still hadn't healed. "At a certain point she just vanished. Just before you left for your military service. She dumped me without a word. You know how things work with kids. You might be together for years and then, at a certain point, it's all over. You suffer, you're miserable as a dog, but the whole alphabet that ought to help you decipher your grief doesn't exist yet. Without warning, your sister wasn't there anymore and I was too much of a mess to even go and ask her what was going on. We never did talk about it."

"I don't remember much about that period."

Michele dropped his gaze. He took a deep breath and tried to tell him what had happened in the past month. He talked about the absurd atmosphere that reigned in his father's house. He told him about Gioia. The way she was running, incomprehensibly, their sister's fake Twitter account. Ruggero, he said, was swallowed up by his work at the clinic. And then there was Annamaria. If she were grieving over Clara's death, she gave no sign of it. Michele touched on the constant bustle at home. There was something sick about all the phone calls going in and out. "I don't know how to explain it to you any more clearly." He held out his hands as if to mime the shape of a giant subterranean worm. He told him about the chief justice of the court of appeals, and how he'd come to dinner at their house.

"That night I threw up."

But Giannelli went on talking about the past. Over their heads wafted the notes of a jingle coming from the clothing department. Pushed and undone by the breeze, it might have been reminiscent of *A Change Is Gonna Come*. Giannelli said that the first little while without Clara he'd lived in a sort of trance. "I realized I'd lost her months after the last time we saw each other." Blinded by a solipsistic delirium, he was convinced they were just taking a break, that any day now Clara would be calling him to talk things over. Giannelli had even gone so far as to *work out*, as he waited for that fateful meeting.

"I joined a gym. I started getting my hair cut by a decent barber. I went so far as to buy myself some *decent clothing*. I wanted to make an impression, in other words."

But instead of the meeting there was that terrifying five-a-side soccer match.

"Five-a-side soccer?" Michele thought he must have missed something.

"Yes, yes, after the match," Giannelli confirmed.

To keep from losing his mind during those months, going to the gym every day was not the only thing Giannelli did. At night he'd go into the first movie theater he happened across. He'd walk endlessly along the waterfront. And he started drugging himself with games of five-a-side soccer. One, two, five matches a week. At the end of every match there was always someone who asked who wanted to play another the next day. Maybe with a different group of people who often went to a different sports facility.

"If you're serious about it, in Italy, through five-a-side soccer alone you could try to climb any kind of social ladder."

Giannelli found himself playing all over the place. On the small ravaged fields of the industrial district and under the elegant tensile structure on Via Camillo Rosalba. In Poggiofranco. In Carbonara. In a sports center on the road to Valenzano. Sometimes his contact canceled at the last minute and he'd run up and down the field with total strangers for an hour. So it was that one night he wound up in a team of lawyers. There was a notary, too. People who were fairly well off. The match was a normal game between middle-aged men. Not a lot of competition, laughter and shouts of encouragement when someone screwed up an easy goal. But afterwards it turned horrendous. In the showers, one of the lawyers started talking about an underage whore that he liked to go see in an apartment in the Libertà quarter. Another one said that there was no way he could start the day without a blowjob from his secretary. "A blowjob from the secretary!" shouted the notary as if it were a newly coined slogan at a meeting of advertising executives. The laughter echoed through the locker room. Pietro Giannelli, covered with body wash, started to feel a little uncomfortable. At a certain point, they were talking about nothing but sluts and whores. "One of these days I'm going to put some arsenic in that old slut's Valium!" The "old sluts" were their wives while "the whores" were the women (usually very young) with whom they went to bed outside of their respective marriages. The game of "who would you fuck" started up, and a few seconds later her name popped out.

Giannelli stopped massaging his soapy hair.

He was certain he must have misunderstood. But the name was repeated. One of the younger lawyers asked: "The daughter of Vittorio Salvemini? But is she hot?" "*Hot?* She's the sexiest whore you're ever likely to see on Via Sparano." "She's a world-class cum bucket!" Amidst the steam of the showers, one of the voices said that she was so hot that he'd gladly fuck her while also kicking her ass black and blue. Another one (maybe it was the notary again) added: "Slam her against the floor until she loses consciousness. Then you can fuck her in the ass." "Until she dies!" More laughter. "Like this? Like thi-i-i-s?" Out of the steam emerged a pale white body with a partially erect dick. He pretended to try to sodomize his showermate. "Cut it out, fuckhead!" Then the voices went back to describing what kind of attentions they'd lavish on Clara.

Paralyzed under the spray of hot water, Giannelli wished he were dead. For a moment, an absurd instinct had suggested he lift his fists in the air and shout: "Me, you miserable idiots! *I* screwed her!" But the pathetic truth was that he had lost her. They knew who she was, but he hadn't seen any of their faces before that night. Clara would never call him again. The girl whose details he'd carved so painstakingly over the past few months didn't exist. In reality there was another person, and she no longer had anything to do with him.

"I had all the confirmation I needed when I ran into her on the street," he told Michele.

One evening, not even a year later, Giannelli had just taken his new girlfriend home. Driving down Via Putignani, he saw her. Standing outside a restaurant, smoking. New haircut and lamé dress. She was laughing, flanked by two men in gray suits. A hundred yards further on he'd lost her even from his rearview mirror.

Michele interrupted him, and stuck his cell phone under his nose.

"Look at this. Can you wrap your head around it?"

On the display were the two butterflies that were intertwined to form a heart. Under the Twitter account, phrases that would have seemed ridiculous if they'd found them when unwrapping a chocolate, but in this case the effect was macabre and senseless.

"I'm struggling for life."

"The truth hurts everyone, everyone but me."

"Everyone loves you when you're six feet under."

"Every so often a new one pops up," said Michele. "The terrible thing is that more and more people are following it."

Michele told him about his encounter with the journalist in Mola. The absurd things that just a few days ago that other guy had said to him in the street. Renato Costantini. *But I know a change is gonna come. Yes, it will*, he sang in his mind, well aware by now that the music coming from the clothing department was some other song.

For the first time, Giannelli seemed to stop wandering off on his own tangents. He joined the conversation. After that time with the five-a-side soccer, he said with a sigh, all he did was run into people who had news of her. Maybe that's what always happens. He was constantly being pelted with rumors and gossip. One day he chanced to cross paths with Vanessa Lovecchio.

"I think you know her. Her father is friends with your father."

"Who's he?"

"Saverio Lovecchio. The director of the Banca di Credito Pugliese."

Michele's pulse started to race.

This Vanessa, said Giannelli, had gone to the same high school as him. The minute she saw him, she practically jumped on him. She dragged him unresisting to the nearest café. "She was out of her mind." Sitting at a table, she'd pointed her finger right at him. "You," she said, "dated Clara Salvemini." He nodded. She shouted that that bitch had ruined her family. "'In what sense?' I asked her," he told Michele. "In the sense that she's been fucking my father, goddamn it!" she retorted, doing her best to keep from breaking something.

Vanessa had met Clara one night many months ago. They'd all gone out to dinner together. Vittorio and Annamaria, Clara, and then Vanessa's father and mother. In the days that followed, Vanessa and Clara had become friends. They met for before-dinner drinks. They gossiped. At night they went to parties. And a few months later, her father was screwing her.

It seemed to Michele that two of the many pieces that were twirling in his head had just popped into place.

"And then," said Giannelli, moving a little closer to him, because the shadow on his side was growing shorter, "at a certain point she said that her mother had had a nervous breakdown and that she herself felt nothing but the foulest disgust: one time, passing by the bank headquarters, she'd even surprised her father chatting with Alberto. Which was obviously the worst thing imaginable."

"Alberto," Michele repeated sadly, sensing two more pieces slipping into place. He looked up at the summer sky.

"I don't know how much truth there is to it. The girl really wasn't in control of herself."

"They're blackmailing them."

"Who is?"

"They're blackmailing them because she was going to bed with them and they're all married."

Michele shook his head, the way you do when the satisfaction of having understood something crumples in the face of the evidence that this half-truth is totally illogical, beyond being pointless, until you have the rest that will complete it.

So Giannelli told him about the last time he'd seen her. It was almost lunchtime now. The buzz overhead had increased. The music had vanished. The sound of shopping carts, cars.

"A night not even a couple of years ago."

He'd happened to run into her in a deli that stayed open until late. Horrendous faux marble walls, neon lights everywhere. He'd stopped in to get a bite before going to bed, and he was sitting on a stool with a hot mozzarella-and-tomato *rustico* in hand when she came in, too. Her hair was super-short. She was wearing a leather skirt and a white T-shirt. Her arms were bare. Skinnier than he'd remembered her. And alone. It was Clara who took the initiative. She slapped him on the back. They said hello with a sort of frozen, but still perceptible, affection. Giannelli bought her a beer. "And," he said to Michele, "you must have figured out that I have a certain experience when it comes to matters of this kind. She was drugged out of her mind."

"I can imagine."

"Anyway, she was standing upright, she was connecting. We talked for a while about pretty much everything."

"Even about me?"

"We must have gone on for a solid twenty minutes," said Giannelli.

She no longer resembled the diva you look at as you leaf through the pages of a magazine. She was now the diva you run into on the street many years after her last hit and you notice how different she looks from her picture in the paper. And so the worst gossip is confirmed. You understand that if you felt like it, you could pull out a knife and disembowel her. Give into the general climate. And so, even though he felt like going to sleep, Giannelli hadn't made the first move. He waited for her to say hello to him. "Because I didn't want to leave her alone in that place at two in the morning."

Michele repeated the question. He asked if they'd talked about him. He was more precise. He asked Giannelli if Clara had talked to him, Giannelli, about him, Michele. He broadened the question before Giannelli had a chance to answer. He asked if Clara, perhaps in other circumstances, had ever talked about him.

"Talked about what?"

"Anything in particular, anything that stuck in your mind," he asked, holding back his tears.

In his frog costume, Giannelli stopped to think for a little while. He, too, was looking up at the immense sky.

"To tell the truth, no."

Once he reached the station, he caught a whiff in the air of the same odor he'd breathed in the hospital every time the nurse opened the windows. His stomach lurched. He grabbed his crutches. He refused the extended hand of a young man who gazed at him through the elegant frames of his sunglasses. He got out of the train. Once on the platform, he followed the strip of light that led to Piazza Aldo Moro.

He moved forward through knots of university students and well dressed women. If you just counted the clothing shops, you'd guess that Bari had twice the number of inhabitants, and the average income of a city in Northern Europe. He saw the sky, more open to the right, beyond the nineteenth-century apartment buildings. He headed in that direction. Leaving behind him a checkerboard full of completely useless symbols and pawns.

After a church reduced to a gray parallelepiped hurled upwards, the landscape became familiar. Isolated gas stations. Old men sitting on blocks of cement. These were people you could talk to. He asked for directions from a tire repairman sitting outside his shop and smoking. He continued along Via Ballestrero. The city was big, and the people he was looking for wouldn't necessarily be easy to find. He put his right crutch forward, and gave a push on both props at once.

After an hour, he was walking along the waterfront on Via Cagno Abbrescia. On the right, a long strip of uncared-for grass. He passed a small dump. At the foot of a ruined build-ing, on the terrace of which was an incomprehensibly new sign (MARINA SPORT), he saw the unmistakable silhouettes.

One of the women was wearing a leather jacket and black panties. The other was wearing hip-high pleather boots.

He was too tired and angry not to take a break.

The one with the hip boots looked up. She understood immediately. Keeping in mind that he only has one leg, she thought, there was even time for a cigarette.

The BMW convertible went off the road after a curve taken badly. Ruggero clenched his teeth. He didn't make the mistake of trying to jerk the wheel around. With a move hardly intu-itive but perfect, he accelerated until the car was accepted into the new trajectory sketched by his mistake. The door brushed against the guardrail. Only then, after downshifting, did he steer leftward. The BMW returned to the ribbon of roadway.

"Fuck! Fuck!" he shouted. Even he couldn't say if he was more angry or more satisfied that he was still in one piece.

He continued along the waterfront. He was getting near Pane e Pomodoro beach. It wasn't far now. There hadn't been time to prepare an appropriate speech. He cursed his father. In his mind, he improvised the words that he'd say to the techni-cal director of ARPA. He went through two stoplights. After a hundred yards or so, he saw the large building of the Regional Environmental Protection Agency heave into view. Ruggero parked.

He entered the building. He told the receptionist that he had an appointment to see the technical director. The young woman asked him to wait. Ruggero went over and took a seat on the sofa facing her desk. He could see the young woman talking on the phone and nodding her head. The young woman, in turn, noticed that the man was ceaselessly tapping his right foot on the floor. She ended the call. She informed him that Dr. Paparella was waiting for him in his office. "Thirteenth floor." She watched him vanish into the elevator.

"Listen, sir, I'd be sorry if this whole ugly episode were to create any prejudice as far as your monitoring in the Gargano region is concerned."

He finished uttering that sentence. He looked the technical director in the eye, wondering whether that was the right approach.

The office was a 325 square-foot room with a terrazzo floor. Two desks. A leather sofa with its back to the oversized windows. On the walls hung large plastic-laminated posters depicting the region's natural beauties. The sea stacks at Mattinata. The grottos at Castellana.

"My father has invested very heavily in that area," he added, "and after everything that's happened, frankly, we're scared."

He wasn't sure whether he'd been right to address the man in the formal voice. He was nervous. He sensed that every action he took, that morning, was slightly ahead of the train of thought that ought to have calibrated it.

"Our work is carried out in complete independence from the pending cases that involve the area being monitored," the technical director said in an exaggeratedly institutional tone. "If we were to try to follow that line, we'd constantly have to shift our objectives and operating strategies. Don't worry about it," he added, reinforcing the distance between them and at the same time doing his best to appear protective, "the agency undertakes its investigations without allowing anything outside of its own scruples and sense of responsibility to influence it."

"No, because in any case I can assure you that the seizure request is going to be rejected," he realized the heat that he was putting into every word, tried to rein himself in. "It's a

matter of days at this point," he said, regaining a certain equa-
nimity.

"That's inconsequential to us." The man reiterated the
point with a smile.

Next to the desk, it was impossible to ignore the standing
ashtray. Ruggero noticed the shape of the lamp, too. The array
suggested the idea of the elegant interior of a ministerial office
in the Seventies that would have depressed anyone, unless it
was on display in a museum in London or New York.

"You know, in Italy you never know how certain things are
going to turn out," Ruggero tried to shuffle the deck again,
"when I think about the number of jobs that my father—"

"I'm sure that what you say is true," the technical director
interrupted, lowering his eyes. "Your father has certainly
respected all the zoning restrictions and the villas won't be
taken over by the state. In any case, we'll proceed as usual.
There's no reason to think, for that matter, that the surface area
of the tourist village will form part of the sample that we'll be
examining. Leaving aside the areas that are sensitive by defini-
tion, the monitoring stations are placed each time in different
locations. Listen, I haven't even checked to see whether in this
case—"

"They're very nice villas, you know?"

The director stopped talking. He raised his head. He stared
him right in the eyes.

"I have no doubt," he finally replied.

Ruggero understood that the man had understood. Now he
could quit it with the whole song and dance.

"That one there was designed by Gae Aulenti," he said,
pointing to the bat-shaped lamp.

The technical director nodded. He said that the furnishings
were the only thing that the economic crisis had spared in
those offices. Then he added: "By the way, the service at the
agency's café is terrible. Why don't we go out for an espresso?"

The hot wind swept over them as if it were exhaust from an industrial air conditioner. Once they were out in the street, instead of heading for a café, the technical director started walking toward the sea. Ruggero followed him. Beyond the sidewalk were the planters with their succulents, then a parking area without an attendant. They passed that, too. The noises of the city faded into the distance. The technical director took the narrow path leading down to the beach.

Five minutes later they were walking among black pebbles and papers blowing in the wind. Straight ahead of them the Adriatic: choppy and blue. The beach, if you could call it that, was no bigger than a basketball court. About fifty feet away, a man with a fishing rod and rubber boots was standing in the water, ankle-deep. The waves covered up all sounds other than their voices.

"Listen," said the technical director, "I want to be as frank as possible. I'm not interested in your villas."

Ruggero said nothing. He sensed that his father had pushed him into the arms of a colossal error.

"The fact that you've come to talk to me at all means that the seizure issue is nothing compared to what would happen if we went into the Porto Allegro site with our monitoring stations. Am I right or am I wrong?"

Ruggero still said nothing.

"In any case, it wasn't hard to guess," the man went on in a friendlier tone of voice. "You're not alone in this. In fact, you probably had no real alternatives. We know what's been going on in the district for some time now. This monitoring process will let the cat out of the bag. The other day we received the quarterly report from LIPU, the Italian Society for the Protection of Birds. The chancellor bent over backwards to convince them to delay. There's going to be a joint publication of the documents. Obviously, we can't go over that part of the Gargano with a fine-toothed comb. For the same reason, a complete reclamation would be impossible. We lack the personnel, to say nothing of the funds. Most of the area will always remain ou—"

"Look, I don't have any idea what you're talk—"

"Yes, of course," the technical director interrupted in turn, "you're just an oncologist, you know nothing about it. But your father is well informed on these matters. Ask and you'll be told. In any case, let me say it again, for me the villas are just a complication," he paused. "I need a hundred fifty thousand euros. And, unfortunately, in a bit of a hurry. I'm sorry to have to put it like this. If you have problems with a cash payment, we can come to an agreement on a fake consulting fee. I can point you to a trusted individual. You, or your father. Anyone you like."

He drove twenty miles an hour the whole way home. What do I have to do with any of this? he kept saying to himself. He felt unsettled, depressed.

Half an hour later, he passed the Texaco station. The industrial sheds of Officine Calabrese. The old bowling alleys, closed for years, with a gigantic rusty pin that stuck out over the road. Which is how he realized he was heading in the wrong direction.

When, many years later, Gennaro Lopez, former medical examiner of the ASL 2, the Bari health care clinic, found himself extracting from his many if tangled memories the most awful one, that is, the one that could do him the most harm, he'd choose the night on which a guy of about thirty knocked on his front door and started showering him with questions about his sister's death certificate.

At the time, Lopez was deep in debt and consuming two grams of cocaine a day. He'd managed to dodge a threatened disciplinary proceeding. He was taking Diamet, Lormetazepam, Depakote drops, he was patronizing prostitutes on a regular basis, and all this ensured that he was tormented by an elusive sense of déjà vu—the sensation that he'd read the same page of the newspaper, that he'd experienced a scene the day before the same synesthetic details organized themselves before his eyes.

@ClaraSalvemini:
Everyone loves you when you're six feet under.
4 retweets 2 favorites

@pablito82:
@ClaraSalvemini That depends how your corpse is being preserved.

@ClaraSalvemini:
@pablito82 Very well, I can assure you.
9 retweets 4 favorites

@themoralizer:
@pablito82 @ClaraSalvemini A picture as proof.

@ClaraSalvemini:
@themoralizer @pablito82 30#rt and I'll enclose 3 pictures in a row.
But the loneliness, that's something you can't photograph.

She moved the iPhone away from the tip of her nose, set it down on the nightstand. She finished drinking her grapefruit juice. She set it down on the nightstand, too. She got out of bed. She went into the bathroom. She locked the door behind her. She peed. She pulled up her pajama bottoms. She looked in the mirror. She decided she looked pretty. She went back into her bedroom. She picked the iPhone back up from the nightstand. She counted the retweets. There were *lots* of them.

At that point, Gioia let herself fall onto the bed, overcome by a feeling that was the height of happiness and the height of sadness. She missed everyone. Her boyfriend from high school. Summer ten years ago. Certain cartoons broadcast by a local TV station. She missed her sister. She even missed the anger she used to feel when she'd see Clara and Michele talking intently, excluding the rest of the world from their conversations.

"Clara Clara . . . " she whispered clutching her smartphone as if caressing its head, lovingly scolding it.

T hen Clara would get home in the middle of the night and her husband would pretend not to notice her. Alberto would turn over in bed, close his eyes as soon as the rivulet of light extended under the door. He'd hear footsteps in the living room. Her high heels, then the muffled sound of bare feet. With an extreme imaginative effort (the faithful reconstruction of what happens when the pull tab stops sliding down the zipper), he could bring himself to hear the impalpable rustle of the dress detaching itself from her body and collapsing softly onto the hardwood floor.

She'd been with another man. It was obvious that she had. In her gestures, the memory of the encounter just recently consummated. Over the years, Alberto had learned to recognize the imprint. He'd learned to tame it, manage it. And even if it persisted the morning after, while they ate breakfast, Alberto was able to drive the invisible mark of the offense onto a territory of conjugal life where Clara became his again. Then they'd chat. They'd smile at each other. A test of strength in reverse. But no longer. It had become impossible for some time now.

If he could have seen her now, at three in the morning—her split lip, the bruises, the arms covered with scratches—all his self-control, his backbreaking strategies meant to give shape to something that would otherwise have caused too much pain, would have been upended. That was why he shut his eyes. Pretended she hadn't come home. And for the exact same reason, at a certain point Clara burst into the bedroom.

The door slammed against the frame, he lurched in the bed, and that signaled a fire ready to devour everything.

She didn't come in on tiptoes anymore. She didn't slip silently under the covers, delivering the bomb that it would be his job later to defuse by himself. That piece of ordnance now exploded in the very act with which Clara threw open the door, and there was nothing that Alberto could do about it. She let the light abruptly invade the bedroom. She crossed the room half naked, heading straight for the bathroom. She slipped into the shower and turned on the spray of hot water with a resolute slap of the hand. Ferocious, satisfied. At that point he had no choice but to open those fucking eyes of his. It was no longer credible for him to be asleep. Knowing that she was at the center of his attention, that they were separated only by an insignificant partition, Clara let the water slide over her scratches and bruises.

At this point, Alberto could only take refuge in the rhetoric of a before and an after. What else remained to him, with which to defend the idea of their marriage? He could hypothesize that Clara was no longer herself, that she'd lost her mind or that the cocaine had transformed her. Otherwise how could he explain the fact that he could hear her laughing? Under the shower, Clara was sobbing. Reduced to that state, she made a joke of the situation.

In the first few years, her betrayals had been the carcasses dropped lovingly on the doormat to ensure that Alberto accepted her, and therefore kept her clutched tight to him. So then they could go to dinner. They could leave together on holiday. They could make love. Conjugal life could recover its stability and, in spite of everything, those were genuine gestures of affection that they managed to exchange, the attention paid, the attempt to protect each other, even a certain kind of complicity, these were all real.

There was no hypocrisy in the hard, scrupulous work

through which Alberto prevented himself from detesting her, or even from loving her less. He welcomed her back into his arms thanks to a gesture that—measured in terms of patience, obstinacy—was more expansive than her yanking away. But this state of mind could prove in certain cases to be worse than hypocrisy. Once the shell of everyday life was shattered, when Clara happened to collapse into the epicenter of his life, it no longer worked. There was a time when women tolerated their husbands' flings as a way of preserving domestic peace. The despotism of their men was so crude and idiotic that it never struck them in full. But with a man who put up with betrayals as Alberto did, there could be an even greater oppression: in the apparent reversal of roles, an attempt to abuse power that aspired to the absolute. The political correctness of degradation. The presentable face of violence. That is what Clara saw when she found herself defending not just daily life, but everything precious that came with it.

And so, now, naked and sobbing in the shower, so very vulgar as she laughed, wounded and overexposed, she was destroying in an irretrievable manner all attempts to hold her in check. There was no magnanimity that could re-stitch a tear of that severity.

The water stopped running. Clara ran her hands through her hair. Without even realizing it, she saw herself as a teenage girl again. A physical crossing. Michele. The happy days of their lives together. Her legs trembled. Then the sensation vanished. Once again, the porcelain tiles of the shower. She needed to let herself be fucked that way. She needed to let herself be beaten and kicked. Certainly not to wound her husband. And now that Alberto could no longer hide her beneath blankets of reasonableness, he was forced to contemplate the panorama in its entirety. At that point, he, too, thought he could see in the depths of Clara an opaque and inerasable sign. She had been happy. During a long-ago period of life, a time that Alberto would have been unable to reproduce even in a scale model, his wife had been happy to be in the world in a scandalously pure, disarming fashion. And the worst thing, Alberto mused with growing concern, was the possibility that the recipient of his wife's innermost thoughts—the object of a chant, of a prayer—this unforeseen entity that he recognized pointblank as the *real* enemy, might detach from Clara like an idea taking form and odiously, unexpectedly—he thought again as he girded himself for battle—materialize one day in their home.

Motionless in his chair, struck by the late afternoon light that was pushing the rest of the house toward a past swollen with shades of warmth and neglect, he listened to him talk.

The young man was waving his arms back and forth, like an amateur conductor who can't seem to bring the performance to the proper point of equilibrium.

Was it true that he'd gone to lodge his objections with Renato Costantini over certain articles in which they'd attacked them?

No.

Her lovers.

No.

But he'd actually met the bank director. Her friend's father. Another guy Clara was seeing regularly.

No, Michele, no. You're still way off track.

The young man wouldn't give up. He masked his safe-cracker's intentions under the guise of a courtesy call. On the adjoining table gleamed a vase overflowing with wood anemones. Laid out in plain view, the latest issue of a women's magazine. The porcelain ballerina that Clara had sent away for from London enjoyed pride of place on the crescent-shaped console table. On another piece of furniture—a small desk with gilded edges—sat her purse, and the little perfume samples that she collected with all the tenacity of someone trying to elude melancholy, conscious of the fragility of that effort.

Every object simmered on the low flame of a time out of order. One had the impression that Clara was bound to come back any minute from a shopping trip, smiling and loaded down with bags, as if her death had been the blow capable of thrusting reality inside itself, shoving it back into the dimension where it should have resided from the very start. An alternative past, which just needed time enough to catch up with them.

But now Michele had come along to upset this process of adjustment. He was making insinuations. He was bringing up his wife's habits in an unpleasant way.

"Over the past several days I've met a series of people," he'd said after the usual exchange of courtesies, "at a certain point I found myself pretty confused. So I thought I should come talk to you about it."

He pretended he didn't have things straight in his head. But he actually wanted to extort information from him. Details that, just by passing from one hand to another, would wind up rewriting the whole story.

"I'm glad you came to see me," Alberto had replied at that point. He'd pushed his elbow into the cushion, barely twisting his wrist, as if Michele were some tremulous apparition and he were gripping a handle thanks to which the reception might improve or perhaps even vanish entirely.

Michele had called him the day before, he'd texted him more than once. Alberto had ignored his texts. So, right after lunch, he'd found the young man downstairs.

He was returning from the minimarket where he'd developed the habit of going twice a week, always at the same hour. First he'd passed by the newsstand. Mourning had kept him away from work, and soon it was going to be August. In the fall, he could not go back to work on the construction sites at all, or just do the bare minimum, he thought to himself. Everything in its place. Two packs of beer, three bottles per pack. Chicken breasts. Salad. Fresh milk. Normal actions. Very regular habits. Building a fortress inside which he could wall himself up, together with her.

Turning the corner, he'd recognized him from a distance. Michele had smiled. Alberto had half-closed his eyes, as if to crush the eggs that the apparition seemed to think it had laid inside him simply by showing itself there, in the hot flush of summer.

Alberto had said hello to him. He'd invited him to come up. Michele had offered to help him carry the groceries.

"Make yourself comfortable," Alberto had said five minutes later, noticing with satisfaction the way that Michele's expression had changed. A body that betrays the different density of the environment it's entering, wrong-footed by the atmosphere of expectation more than of contrition. A place where his sister's absence was merely temporary.

"A beer?"

"Thanks."

Alberto had gone into the kitchen. He'd exchanged the bottles in the fridge for the ones just purchased at the supermarket. Calmly, very calmly, to ensure that his guest was left even more at the mercies of the objects that surrounded him. The matrimonial nest. His and Clara's home. He'd come back in balancing a tray with beers and a bowl of popcorn.

He'd sat down across from him and voilà, now they were talking.

"There'd been a certain distance between my sister and me for a while now," said the young man. "No one talks about her at home. It's strange. Before heading back to Rome I wanted to get a better idea. Even though certain things can be explained, up to a point."

"You didn't come to the funeral."

Hard, fast. First blow.

"What?"

"You didn't come to the funeral. That's why they don't talk to you about her."

Alberto lifted the bottle so that it became the board to which he could nail him with his gaze. He took a sip. He hadn't failed to see the young man's strategy, the way he foregrounded a truth to conceal the nuances that this very same statement would have acquired if glimpsed from another angle.

But Michele didn't take the bait.

"I don't think that's the reason," he said. "It's that they're actually having a hard time processing what's happened. Like I was saying, in the past few weeks I've chanced to talk to some people. From what I've been able to gather, lately my sister was having a ton of problems."

"You didn't come to the wedding, either."

This time it was Michele who took a sip: "You know," he replied, "back then I was spending most of my time in psychiatric clinics."

Alberto started in surprise. The way the young man crossed his legs allowed a design to emerge—as lasting as a circle drawn in the water—that belonged to her. The smile with which Clara had lately absolved herself for something that became less serious than the wound that she'd opened with her gaze. A different Clara than the girl evoked by the tidiness of the apartment. A creature who wasn't coming back from shopping but from the grave, to lay waste that other woman.

"Of course my wife was having problems, otherwise she wouldn't have killed herself."

Alberto adjusted his aim, repossessing himself of the memory. Motionless in the armchair, he breathed with perfect mastery the hot air that stagnated between the walls. He continued to exert leverage on the apartment, the place that Clara had shared with him, not with her half-brother, so that the interference would vanish just as it had appeared, and that in fact was what happened. "She was having problems," he repeated, shaking his head, wallowing in the mud of a sorrow that he had cultivated with such dedication that it had made him unapproachable to anyone else, "none of us was able to grasp how serious those problems were. None of us who were close to her, I mean," and he looked up coldly.

"The cocaine," said Michele.

"Certainly, the cocaine," Alberto sensed that the young man had brought up the coke thing to brush against something else, so he said it first, taking possession of it, too, "and also the fact that for a while now she'd been seeing other people," he kept his voice firm, "but this was the effect, not the cause. Clara was going through a complicated time. Your sister was a very sensitive girl. She couldn't tolerate hypocrisy. She didn't protect herself."

"Exactly," said Michele. "Isn't it possible that one of the people she was seeing caused her some problems? Maybe she'd argued with someone."

For the second time, Alberto raised his hand in the young man's direction. He slowly clenched his fingers, as if to crush him. You aren't the one who married her. You don't know of what the flavor of her lips is made, you never saw her cry like that on the terrace of the Sheraton. You may be a son of the same father, and you may have spent your childhood in the house where she too grew up, but what fell to me was the incomparable part. You had to have placed the ring on her finger. You had to have waited for her, awake in the night with your heart in your throat, afraid of an accident, and then hoping for some trivial mishap because now the fear was that she was in the company of another man. You had to have found the strength to put your arms around her shoulders all the same the next day, leaving everything tacitly understood, taking up a position from which not even she would have been able to unseat you.

"That wasn't it," Alberto replied. "She hadn't had any disagreements with anyone. If she'd had troubles of that sort, I'd have been aware of it. As I was saying, she was going through a hard time. She was depressed. I tried to stay close to her. We talked about it constantly. There were no secrets between us."

A flash. The backlash of someone who'd been cornered. Then Michele said it.

"Listen, Alberto, try not to misunderstand me. The last thing I'd want to do is be unpleasant. Going to talk with the men that Clara saw. Actually doing business with them. I really don't understand how that was a way to help my sister."

"Then you should have gotten to know her a little better." Alberto kept his composure. At a certain point you'll get tired, he thought as he looked at him. You'll get up out that chair. You'll disappear out the front door. Disintegrated by your idiocy. Your curiosities shattered by the power of selfless love. You'd have to have had her at the altar, half drunk. You'd have to have dragged her into the hospital after she'd taken all those sleeping pills, not even a year after she'd decided to marry you. To know what one feels. Sitting, head sagging, in the waiting room outside the ER. Butting your head against the obstinate barrier of vanity, of pride. And this, of course, was only the beginning. To find out about her affair with the owner of the gym. A man whose hand you'd shaken many times. Swallow your pride. Lower your head. Keep your anger from gaining the upper hand.

There'd been the period with the bank director. Then Renato Costantini. Undersecretary Buffante. How had he been able to put up with it? There was another wrong question. He shouldn't wonder why he hadn't divorced her. Rather: Why hadn't he ever even conceived of the idea that he could do such a thing? What was he looking for? Or perhaps, what had he already found that was so fundamental that it allowed him to take that sort of humiliation as a necessary evil?

And then one night—Alberto remembered, watching the

young man's reaction; Michele was moving his arm from left to right, all in slow motion—everything become clearer.

It was March. Alberto had come home after spending the day at one of Vittorio's construction sites. He'd talked to Clara on the phone. His wife had told him to go ahead and eat dinner without her. She'd be going to the movies with a friend.

"*The Straight Story*, at the Odeon."

That had been the answer.

He'd asked the question, driven by the desire to catch her red-handed. He realized it only after he was done talking, when Clara's voice had reemerged from the silence with a slight crack in it. They ended the call. Alberto immediately felt his head start to spin. Clutching a lie in his hands. A naked, pulsating heart. Until that point, he'd kept a safe distance. He knew about spouses cheating, the way we know that the sun sets every night over cities where we don't live. He'd never tried to dirty his theoretical understanding through a test. And so, immediately after the phone conversation, he set all hesitation aside and went without shame to get the newspaper out of the trash. Famished. Excited. A rat rummaging through the garbage. He spread out the entertainment pages on the kitchen table. His stomach sank. The atrocious joy of seeing things with your own eyes. Alberto let himself drop onto the chair. What an incredible girl she was! She hadn't even taken the trouble to check it out. But it was at times like these that Clara sparkled in all her splendor. *Costantini.* It wasn't rare for Alberto to know the names of her current lovers. But now things were different. For the first time he could hypothesize that she was cheating on him the very evening that its happening was all but a foregone conclusion. He got up from his chair. He went into the bathroom. He turned on the faucet. He felt as if a giant wedge had been driven into his head. He put his neck under the spray of cold water. Then he lifted his head and looked at himself in the mirror. Devastated, dripping. He clenched his teeth. Then it happened. He felt the tension collapse in on itself and, at that point, he didn't even understand how, he'd already crossed through the mirror. Suddenly there was only peace around him, a mineral silence. Incredible. On this side, everything became so clear. He saw his wife's fingers as she unbuttoned Costantini's shirt, and he recognized them as *his own fingers*. If was his mouth that he was allowing the old man to kiss. And at the very moment that Clara started making love, he, Alberto, was there, in a point in his body so profound that Costantini became nothing more than a mere vehicle of dead flesh.

That's why he would never leave her.

His rebirth. From that night on, Alberto stopped worrying. Being on the other side meant seeing the world for what it was. Recognizing humiliation as an error in perspective. Anger as the weapon of those who crave defeat. Now, at last, he felt strong. In this new garb, Alberto had been able to *consciously* shake Costantini's hand, just as he'd *unconsciously* shaken hands with the owner of the gym. He would even have been able to speak to him. Why not? With Costantini. With the bank director. Revel in the stupefied expressions of his wife's lovers.

Of course it was never painless. You had to know how to suffer in exchange for a reward of that kind. But it was a *different* kind of suffering. A wall to be slammed against violently so he could find himself with her, magically, united like no one else.

"I know Clara," Michele replied, letting his arm fall back on itself.

Just that. Then the young man smiled. Looking at him, once again, the way she would have just a few weeks before her death.

Alberto felt himself blushing. In the last months with Clara, when the cocaine had become an obsession and she had become unrecognizable. When she came home and was covered with bruises. Pale. Scandalously skinny, as if from her thirty-six-year-old skin, stretched tight, a mocking skeleton were emerging. A wicked presence that wanted to tip everything over. Obsessed by a project from which Alberto was excluded. As if this terrifying slippery slope were the last act in a very specific strategy, of which she herself—naked on a Sunday morning in the bathroom at home, her eyes ringed with exhaustion and an expression of deranged triumph between her lacrimal bones—had only now understood. Rereading the years they'd spent together. Convincing him, with her simple presence, that she had always followed a different path. Something prior to him, much more important. The house that had been burning in her dreams every night for years.

But the woman of the last few months had no longer been his wife. She was what might be left of a magnificent young woman when she skids off the road in all directions and the accumulated errors start to be too many. She was a specter. An impostor. The macabre presence that was now emerging from Michele's own flesh.

"Let's say instead that you abandoned her," Alberto replied, to rid himself of the apparition, savoring the young man's wounded look, "let's say that you left just when she needed you most. That with the excuse of your alleged problems, you cast a spotlight on *your* absence above all. Absent from the wedding. Absent from the funeral. Where were you when she took those sleeping pills?" He saw the young man suffer, but Clara's sneer, her mocking smile, remained in its place. "*I* took her to the hospital," Alberto thundered then. "Your father was there to identify the corpse. You were away while she plunged into depression. You left to Engineer Ranieri and Engineer De Palo the task of lifting a corpse you never even saw," and to Michele it seemed that something had been shown to him by accident, he ground his teeth in the effort to understand, then Alberto, frightened, piled on. "Do you think that she never talked to me about it?" he lied, full of rage. "She talked to me about it. We talked about everything. Even about you. Do you know what she used to say to me?" He brought the young man to the depths of misery, Michele was sitting on the sofa, his face twisted, and it was if his most secret horrors were all dancing together, the voices that spoke to him from within, this madness that had never died, while the shadow of the gaze, thought Alberto, was instead still standing, in all its feminine ferocity, independent of the young man but driven into him, as if that were the mission of the *other* Clara: to drag her brother along to this point. "She told me that she was so hurt, that she couldn't wrap her mind around it," Alberto hissed, "a brother that she had helped so many times and that he repaid with such total indifference. How could you blame her? Just do the numbers. When is it that you came to see her since you moved to Rome?" He raised his left forefinger. "Don't think that it was easy for her to accept all this."

Then Alberto heaved a long exhausted sigh, slapping his hands twice on his thighs. He shut his eyes. He reopened them. The spell was broken. It seemed as if a hurricane had roared through the room. Roofs torn off. Branches broken. Michele looked at him in silence. The atmosphere continued to return to normal. Alberto began to feel awkward. Much like when, at the end of a fight in which you've lost control, you start to wonder how on earth you could have made such a scene. You start to feel regret. You consider the consequences. You persuade yourself, in the cool aftermath, that the real mistake was articulating your real position poorly. And in this way—outside of the mystical maelstrom of the tantrum—you fail to fully consider that you might actually have let slip some piece of information that you would have been better advised to keep to yourself. He saw the young man clench the armrests with his fingers. Michele got to his feet.

"I got carried away," said Alberto. "I'm sorry."

The young man dropped his eyes: "Sure, it's okay. We're all a little out of sorts these days."

Alberto walked him to the front door. They said a few more things. Conventional phrases that erased themselves even as they were being uttered. Alberto opened the door. Then, with relief, he watched him disappear.

After the outskirts, he was back in the city.

He'd covered a long stretch of coastline that was completely deserted. Industrial sheds and buildings that had been left unfinished. Then he'd angled inland.

The bushes thinned out. Now it was red dirt in the sunshine. Orazio Basile was sweating on his crutches. He was crossing a no-man's land that he would have found, identical, whether leaving Taranto or venturing into the Calabrian plain. He'd have found it identical in Palestine.

He approached a virtual idiot who was sitting all alone on the grass with a plastic bag in one hand.

Then an older woman, dressed in black, bent over at the edge of the road. She was gripping a small sickle she was using to uproot wild chicory.

Then he stopped a man on a bicycle who didn't look as if he was pedaling for his health.

No one seemed to know what to tell him.

At two o'clock, he found himself in the Japigia neighborhood. The white silhouette of enormous apartment buildings, all identical, emerged around a corner, surrounded him. He asked for directions in a small *pensione* on Via Gentile. Having obtained the address, he went back out. The idea of a taxi, or a bus, irritated him.

At five in the afternoon, he was already hobbling along on the city's southern outskirts. Here the children were kicking a ball around, safe and protected, in the courtyards of the row houses, their voices drowned out by the sound of the sprinklers. Even the sunlight was gentler. The heat that arrived was screened by well-tended trees. Along the road, high-performance cars stood parked. Hoods glittering. A plane flew low overhead. The noise diminished in intensity. Once again, the sloshing of sprinklers.

Orazio Basile resumed his walking. He walked past the IP gas station. He'd understood for some time now that he was approaching his objective. Now he could see it.

I'm doing it for them. They give me the strength.

Vittorio Salvemini was sitting among the patients in the waiting room by the reception desk of the Cancer Institute of the Mediterranean. He was waiting for Ruggero. With the excuse of a doctor's visit for his by now proverbial sour stomach, he'd be able to hear directly from his son's lips what had happened with the technical director of the ARPA.

The video screens in the waiting room—four Samsungs attached to a metal bar—were showing cartoons sponsored by a pharmaceutical company. A cat was left alone at home. It was chasing a fly in the living room. When the master returned, he found the place half wrecked and the cat rolling on the carpet in the front hall.

Vittorio wondered how those images could help a cancer patient. They were part of the new world. Smart phones. Action figures. Childish things that were born on the internet and a few months later were worth millions. In the old days, people built cars. Television sets, toasters, electronic calculators. But now they were making stuff that didn't even exist. You could think it, maybe even see it. Great constellations turned in the night sky, freed from the physical phenomenon that had begat them. All this produced cash. It produced future. Vittorio had been afraid of being cut out of the change. He'd been afraid that a heart attack was the logical consequence of his efforts over the last few months. But after all the back and forth, Valentino Buffante had arranged for the technical reports to be drawn up. Dr. Nardoni had added them to the file to be sent to the investigating magistrate. At last the phone call had come. Mimmo Russo, the chief justice of the Bari Court of Appeals, had heard from the tribunal of Foggia. God bless him, he thought. The invitation to dinner had been decisive. That was what had untangled the situation. Letting him feel the warmth of hearth and home.

"Signor Salvemini."

The girl at the reception desk was smiling. Vittorio got to his feet. A male nurse came out the door of the staff entrance. Behind him was Ruggero. He wore a lab coat. And he was grim faced. "Let's get going." Vittorio was afraid that something irreparable had happened with the technical director.

Now he was walking along behind Ruggero down the long hallway that led to Radiology. They'd give him blood tests. A gastroscopy. Amylase and gastrin. Whatever it meant, it would take all day. Vittorio was sure he didn't need any of it anymore. His pains had vanished the instant he'd heard that the chief justice of the court of appeals had talked to the administrative office of the court of Foggia.

He waited for Ruggero to greet other colleagues. He saw him stop to talk with a male nurse. Or was he a doctor? They started walking again. Before they could get past the dispensary, Vittorio lengthened his stride. He grabbed him by the arm. He lowered his voice.

"Well, how did it go?"

"Damn it, Papà. Can't that wait? We have an appointment at nine thirty at the lab for tests."

Perfect Ruggero style. Angry about one thing, he dredged up another about which he could lecture you more easily and immediately. The trick was to make him angrier still. He couldn't get his blood test without first finding out what had happened at ARPA. The results would come out all skewed.

"Come on, you're the deputy director," Vittorio insisted without releasing his arm. "Who do you think's going to complain if you show up fifteen minutes late with your old father to get a few blood tests? Blame me," he chuckled. "You can always tell them that because of my prostate I had to stop and piss a few times too often."

"But how can you not . . . it's a matter of principle, goddamn it!" Ruggero slowed down as he came even with a sign that said ANTISMOKING CENTER.

Two minutes later, Ruggero had given him the news. The little office consisted of a desk, an exam table, a glass-front cabinet full of documents. On the walls were diagrams illustrating the indices of replacement of precancerous cells, depending on how long it had been since the last cigarette. Twelve months. Two years. Ten years. One hundred fifty thousand euros, said Ruggero with a grimace of disgust. A fake consulting fee would do the trick. He was swollen with rage.

"One hundred fifty—"

"Do you realize? Do you or don't you understand what kind of humiliation you've exposed me to?"

Vittorio couldn't believe it. What he'd feared would be bad news wasn't even good news. It was fantastic news. A man who tells you his price is a problem solved before it's even been examined. One hundred fifty thousand euros was a ridiculous trifle in comparison with the amount at stake. And Ruggero, instead of being gratified, was acting scared. What's more, he was acting angry. He felt mortified, outraged, and he was blaming it on Vittorio.

And yet I did it for them, thought Vittorio, remaining serious, concealing his jubilation to keep from offending his son. For them he had run risks, fought. It had been for Ruggero. And for Gioia. For Clara who was no longer with them. And

Michele. On this point, Vittorio came close to becoming emotional. Lately, when he thought about Michele, he felt as if he was able to go back in time. Once again young and full of energy, bent over the damage, a turning point in his life that was waiting to be put right.

Riccardo Terlizzi, sergeant in the Forestry Service of Margherita di Savoia, stopped his jeep among the blindingly white pyramids. The salt marsh stretched southward for ten thousand acres. Even those who worked here routinely entertained the thought that this beauty was excessive. The pools of water ran one after the other in an uneven succession, and every hundred yards or so they changed color. A shattered mirror, a kaleidoscope that could give you vertigo in the summer.

Riccardo Terlizzi got out of his jeep. He wasn't sure of what he'd seen as he skirted the coastline. It was hard to believe that it was what he thought it was. After the plovers last week, found dead in clusters in the brackish waters, it was reasonable to expect nasty new surprises.

He drove past the gate. He ventured into the wetlands. He tried to calculate the point at which the parabola ought to have come to its conclusion. He saw the canals flowing. Further off in the distance, the ponds like vibrant horizontal lines. He heard the teals flying overhead, the flapping of wings. This was where the canebrakes started. Here the water turned red between the islets breaking the surface. The pigment of the microorganisms that prospered in contact with the salt. The view at a glance was incredible. The light, reflecting between the pools of water and the mountains of salt, took on shades of cobalt and ashy green.

He made his way through the rushes, and when the vegetation opened out, transforming itself into a cornice framing the water, he saw them. Twenty or so specimens. Clouds on long, straight poles. Pink flamingoes. Creatures of an almost unsettling beauty. They were dipping their beaks in the water, tipping their long necks backward and nipping at their plumes. It was here that the guides told children about the mysterious arrival of the birds in the mid-Nineties. Not far away, he saw the canes moving. Exactly the area where, if it had been true, the trajectory would have come to an end.

The Forestry Service sergeant stepped forward. He saw the water rise to his ankles, and then to his thighs. He was moving slowly. He felt the silt beneath the soles of his boots. Irises and ranunculi were bobbing all around. He emerged half drenched on the other side. Mud and foliage. He passed an arrowhead bush. He stopped. The large pink body was writhing in the marsh water. So it had happened. A flamingo in flight fallen out of the sky. The bird's movements were convulsive, desperate. Every so often the beak would open, and out of the curving extremity would protrude a large rough white tongue. The sergeant felt himself caught by a feeling of pity. He took a couple of steps forward. At that point, the flamingo raised its neck. Blinded by whatever it was that was devouring it, it tried to lunge at the intruder. It wriggled in the mud, and even though it was no predator, it seemed to be on verge of rebelling against its nature. The man was paralyzed. The flamingo emitted a deep hoarse cry that no animal behaviorist had ever recorded. It fell back into the wet soil and died.

Vittorio Salvemini was at home when the phone rang. With his customary low, Lenten voice, the tax lawyer announced that the request for a preemptive seizure of the tourist complex of Porto Allegro had been turned down by the investigating magistrate.

The shade of the magnolias and the IP gas station was winning out over a heat already tamed by the sprinklers. So that on that stretch of road, you could sense the approaching evening, when the wealthy residents would light the mosquito coils and their grills, leaving the aroma of roast meat faintly veiled by the smoke and by the force of the wine blossoming in the decanters. As he passed by, Michele saw the beam of the television sets on the patios of other houses, small villas surrounded by hedges that at night muffled the noise that came from the nearby discotheques in Otranto, Ostuni, and Leuca. A foreshadowing of mid-August, when the city would be empty and those same residents far away.

Otherwise, I no longer feel a thing, he thought sadly, as he headed toward his father's house. After his encounter with Alberto, he'd decided to go back to Rome. The announcement at home two days earlier.

It had seemed to him that Annamaria was almost sorry. Vittorio had said: "Stay a little longer. Stay until the beginning of August. Then we can all go to the beach." In his father's gaze was a grimace that was more than a mere hope. He wanted Michele to stay. He desired it authentically, sincerely. If the young man had given him the chance, now he'd have clasped his cheeks in his old hands.

To Michele it seemed like a monstrous scene. A horror movie that, instead of ending, seemed intent on starting over again in exactly the same way, but without scenes of blood or suspense, as if the first version had never happened.

"Stay. Three weeks. What would it cost you?" Vittorio repeated.

Michele had said: "We'll see," but without conviction. He still had his brother-in-law's words in his head. He felt sorrowful, tired, he would have slept for months. A sense of solitude that was different from that through which he'd educated himself.

And then the news had arrived. The phones in the house had started ringing. There was a noise of crockery from downstairs, as if dishes and glasses were moving on their own in anticipation of a celebration. Gioia was talking at ratatat speed in her room. Michele walked past it. He listened at the door. A piercing voice, swollen with pride—a family upon whom the star of peace and prosperity had never stopped beaming. In disgust, Michele went downstairs. His father left the house. He came back half an hour later. He was carrying a bouquet of roses. Michele saw him head for the kitchen. Vittorio filled a vase with water and carried it into the living room. He put the flowers into the vase.

Then, Michele actually saw Annamaria laugh.

Not believing herself watched, the woman had moved out onto the small balcony off the living room. She'd craned her head back. She'd laughed the way silent film stars used to do when, caught in a cold light, they showed their gleaming white teeth, turning their faces to favor a gleam that could be that of eternity or of a war that had not yet broken out.

The seizure request had been turned down. They were saved. Gioia started trying on one dress after another. They were all going out to dinner together, to celebrate.

So, now, two days later, Michele was strolling through the neighborhood streets. The sorrow of having lost a sister, of having lost a mother before that, and in the end, of having lost a cat as well. It wasn't more than a human body can suffer. This was the sentence. After his encounter with Alberto, Michele felt he no longer had a grip on anything, not even the depth of his malaise. As if he could observe it only from the exterior. The cat had kept him company for four long years. So loving, so patient. A good cat. But he had brought her with him to Bari, just so he wouldn't have to go alone. He'd put her into the pet carrier. She'd gone into it, full of trust. During the train trip, she'd behaved perfectly. She'd adjusted to a place she didn't know, a house full of malevolent energies that the poor creature had struggled to ignore, because of her love for him. She'd even come up with that game, where she jumped off the top of the armoire. It had been Michele's job to protect her. And this was the result. He went past the gas station. He walked under the leaves of the plane trees, along the line of parked cars. A BMW that resembled a silver projectile. Dark marks on the bumper. Blood. Or maybe just mud, scratches.

Michele thought he could see her, the cat, frozen in the middle of the road, in her eyes the headlights of a car hurtling at sixty miles an hour. A creature used only to being petted. Evil, for someone who'd never even imagined that it existed. He thought about the rats he'd read about in the paper. Huge sewer rats that emerged out of storm drains and frightened people. It had happened in Poggiofranco, in Carrassi. The cat would have been overwhelmed. Rats with ruby-red eyes, born to violence.

But my sorrow has been amputated.

Michele walked down the cypress-lined lane. He saw the villa with its terrace emerge through the leaves. There'd been a time when he wouldn't just have imagined the cat torn to pieces by a pack of sewer rats. He would have *felt* it. He would have become her. Clara. Something inside him had shifted without his realizing it. The rotation of a room. Windows where walls ought to be, outside walls facing light instead of shade, so that the ghost could flee the unexpected.

He walked through the villa's front gate. Clearly Alberto had lied. Against the things Michele had said, he'd opposed the obtuse part of himself. The closed part, the dead part. He walked past the oleanders. The stone fountain, lined with the damp stripes of moss. He climbed up the stairs. His sister and those men. At the level of explanation, it might even be true. He pulled out the keys. He opened the front door. He went into the house. But obviously it didn't hold together. In the segment that was Clara's life (Michele had glimpsed it in its entirety in the long-ago days of his military service, when he was sunk in his delirium), there was something different from what they had tried to make him believe. He'd never know.

He crossed the living room. He said "Ciao," loudly. The house was empty. He went into the kitchen. He drank a glass of water. Then he went upstairs to his room. He stretched out on the bed without removing his shoes. He lit a cigarette. He looked at the top of the armoire. He concentrated. (Staring into the void, to make the shape of the little animal blossom inside him.) It didn't work. That's enough, he thought. Rome. Like saying Paris or Buenos Aires. Vanishing into the crowd.

He got out of bed. He went to the window and opened it. He heard the ruckus. Then in the sky he saw the airplane flying at low altitude.

Last drag. He shut the window. Now the sound of a repeated signal. Michele held his breath. He calmly observed the nightstand, then the bed. Then the armoire. Noises of settling, creaking. It happened with wooden furniture. Then a hope. His heart started beating faster. But when the noise was heard again, Michele realized that it was coming from the floor below. Someone was knocking at the door. For an instant, he transferred the hope of finding the cat in the armoire to the hope that someone might have brought her back. *Is this cat yours?* As he went downstairs, it occurred to him that it might be Vittorio, having left the house without his keys. Whoever it was knocked again. Absurd though it was, his hope was still alive. He opened the door. It wasn't his father. Something inside him began struggling. A confused, violent movement that he could no longer control.

"Hello," said Michele, shocked by what he was seeing.

The man stood there. A middle-aged man. His right leg stitched shut at the knee. Supported by a pair of crutches. His face large and stout. Moist eyes. Lips half open, like someone about to curse, or shout in your face.

"Orazio Basile," the man said, introducing himself. Nothing more.

Michele showed him in.

"An elevator?" he asked in bewilderment fifteen minutes later.

To make it clear that he wasn't kidding around, the man said that unless they held up their end of the bargain, he wouldn't hold up his. He'd tell everyone. A young woman. Naked and covered with blood, in the middle of the road. That's what he'd tell anyone who would listen.

Then Vittorio arrived. He saw his son and Orazio Basile sitting on the sofa. He went pale. Michele turned toward him. He made a tremendous effort to transform his hatred into a look of complicity.

@ClaraSalvemini:
Wise men are happy when they discover falsehoods. Idiots when they discover the truth.
10 retweets 2 favorites

@pablito82:
@ClaraSalvemini It should be the other way around.

@ClaraSalvemini:
@pablito82 Tonight anything is possible.
19 retweets 10 favorites

The medical examiner is named Gennaro Lopez and he has a terrible reputation," said Danilo Sangirardi.

Once again sitting shoulder to shoulder in the old Fiesta parked on the road to Mola, while an afternoon even sunnier than the last gleamed all around. Not far from the sea, the grass was wilting in a long reddish shadow.

Then the journalist added: "Remarkable on your part. In Italy the family is sacred. Usually people prefer to let themselves be destroyed by theirs."

Michele caught the affected coda. As if Sangirardi wanted to tell him more, but needed a greater sense of complicity.

He didn't tell him about his encounter with the Tarantine. Nothing about a naked, bloody girl on State Highway 100 the night that Clara died. He'd called him to say that he wasn't so sure anymore that she'd killed herself. Or at least not the way they said. It was likely that his father and his father's wife and his siblings had come to a mistaken conclusion. He'd asked him whether it might be possible to track down the name of the doctor who had examined the body. With every word he'd struggled to keep calm, working to restrain the fury he'd been shaking with for the past few days.

"Pretty much a total sleazeball," Sangirardi had replied.

A coke fiend. A whoremonger. Full of debts and questionable friendships. "He'd even come under a disciplinary investigation," he'd added, lighting the first delicious cigarette of the conversation. Then he'd narrowed his eyes. Even though

Michele hadn't said anything about it, Sangirardi's intuition perceived the opening. Could it be that Michele was looking for a way to act against his own family? Was that what he was asking Sangirardi to help him do? Because if that was it, the journalist let slip, there were also rumors of a wire transfer to an ARPA functionary. Maybe some money through intermediaries of some kind. A considerable sum. If Michele happened to have a way of getting into the company's offices, he might be able to find documents or receipts that could shed light on this matter as well.

"Listen," said Michele, taking a drag in turn on his Marlboro, looking the journalist hard in the face, "I understand that you might bear a grudge against my family. I can also understand that you're not especially fond of my sister," he made an effort, "even after her death. But I'm not looking to get anyone into trouble," he lied. "I just want to understand."

Sangirardi dropped his eyes, gave a fatalistic smile.

"If I wanted to get revenge on everyone who's tried to seal my lips, three lifetimes wouldn't be enough." To Michele it seemed as if he saw him sparkle. "If you want to be good at my profession, rancor is every bit as important as fear."

The blast of sunlight, unnaturally enhanced on the walls of the buildings, ricocheted among a thousand luminous circles through the windshield. Sangirardi wasn't lying. No resentment. The truth as a missing number. The truth, and that human depiction of this god that was respect for the law. That was what interested him, and he presumed that Michele was driven by the same needs. But Michele wasn't looking for the truth. Something more subtle. The black celluloid membrane inside which is imprisoned a ghost that vanishes during the developing process. He wasn't even looking for a lie, but a gesture. Something that might break the chain of meanings, so that the thirst for truth would never even spring into existence.

"Thanks for the name of the medical examiner."

"And listen, Michele . . . " Danilo Sangirardi smiled for the first time in a fragile way. Uncertain about something. Michele associated it with the veiled compliments from before, as if he were seeking the alliance that he'd started to weave, a kind of agreement that Michele considered human while for Sangirardi it clearly must have been in some way embarrassing.

"Well . . . " Sangirardi continued after overcoming the obstacle. "If you find anything interesting, I'd like to be the first to know. You understand. To write an article."

"Naturally. You gave me the contact, you get first shot. That's a promise," said Michele, hearing the ocean seethe on his right.

N ow, thought Ruggero in the privacy of his office, life might resume its normal course. Now that the seizure request had been torn to shreds in court, after his father had overwhelmed that miserable wretch with chitchat, too, sending him back to Taranto with the promise of his elevator. You could see the storm was moving away. After bursting violently two months ago, it seemed to him that he could see it inflicting itself on other, already distant lands. Once again, calm seas. All over.

Ruggero looked at the file folder. The list of patients in his appointment book. The Robert Wenner Prize certificate from the Swiss Cancer League framed on the wall. Every object gleamed in a different light than it ought to. He was almost fifty years old. He was sinking in the role of deputy director of the best-known cancer clinic in southern Italy like an insect in jelly. He thought back to the face-to-face meeting with the technical director of ARPA. Someday, he'd be appointed director. Between his consulting work and grants and fellowships, he'd earn twice as much. He pulled the lab coat off the coat rack, put it on. But the international prizes. The opening ceremonies of the conferences at the Federation of European Cancer Societies. The articles in *The Lancet* or in the *British Medical Journal*. That wouldn't happen.

For that matter, as soon as he took his position at the Cancer Institute of the Mediterranean, he'd allowed his father to talk him into handing over the documents of the Regional Medical Archives.

The magic of predestination. The pure force that erupts from certain men before they even open their mouths. He'd lost all this. He'd had it in a nascent state as a young man. He'd allowed them to destroy it. It hadn't happened to other students under Professor Helmerhorst. Ruggero observed their careers from a distance. He read the newspapers, he was interested in the statistics. Mario Capecchi, Nobel laureate in medicine, was orphaned at age four. Christiaan Barnard's father was a missionary for the Dutch Reformed Church. Pascal's father was a mathematician, not a builder and developer. Every time that Ruggero found another one, he instantly memorized the information. Descartes. Voltaire. Gandhi. Erasmus. Michelangelo. All of them orphans at a tender age. He'd wound up with a fighter more violent than any adversary he could construct with his imagination. Nine on the dot. He picked up the receiver. He dialed the extension. He told the young woman at the front desk to send in the first patient.

After five hours of examinations, he started getting organized for the next day.

He jotted down some names in his appointment book. He confirmed some appointments, tried to cancel others. He focused on the medical charts. Then he moved on to the exams. He spent two more hours reading the medical reports. Patience, concentration. At a certain point, he cocked his right eyebrow in an unnatural manner. Iron-deficiency anemia. Gastric bleeding due to altered iron absorption. He grabbed the neck of the table lamp, shifted it towards the documents. The albumin had collapsed below the warning level. The progression from the gastric mucosa to the gastric submucosa seemed undeniable. Three indicators of that kind were basically crushing proof. His father was a goner. Ruggero closed his eyes, took a deep breath, and slammed both fists down on the desk. He remained in that position for several seconds, head bowed, hands aching.

"Fuck!"

Having digested the burst of pure joy, he tried to regain the composure he'd had just minutes before.

He looked at the tray. He savored the preemptive repentance of someone with too much sugar in his bloodstream. He grabbed a chocolate profiterole with his hands. He stuffed it in his mouth.

Then Mimmo Russo, chief justice of the Bari Court of Appeals, went over to stand in front of the large picture window. The villa overlooked the water, which was being crossed by an ocean liner and lots of white sails. His wife was in Salento, baking in the sun. His children were far away. The city was emptying out. And so he—an ancient monument washed up in the summer solitude—had had to give in in the end. Call Foggia. An hour of explanations, of clarifications. Every time that he'd pushed the investigating magistrate on some aspect of the matter that made no sense, Mimmo Russo had felt—part of the give and take over the arc of the conversation—the crumbling of another fragment of his authoritative reputation. All this for a slut who was dead now, anyway.

As far as that goes, I asked for it, he thought as he dragged himself away from the enormous expanse of the picture window in the living room. He'd gotten himself into trouble at Valentino Buffante's house. He'd accepted the invitation. He hadn't underestimated the young woman's pliability. Everyone knew what these sluts were like, willing to do anything as long as they didn't have to take responsibility for the way certain evenings might turn out. He'd have sworn to her tawdriness. It was the others' degree of idiocy that he hadn't taken into account. That Costantini. The way he'd lost control. She had provoked them and he'd fallen for it. Imbecile. In these kinds of situations you need to be tough. It takes less than nothing, and from a perfectly consensual situation, well within the rules of the game, things go off the rails.

The elderly chief justice went back to the tray. Once he'd been assigned to preside over the case of a young man beaten to death outside a wine shop. It had started out with two against one. An ordinary argument. But the minute the victim had fallen to the ground, he'd made the mistake of curling into a ball with his hands on the back of his neck even before any-one had even touched him. That had unleashed the violence. The other two had started pounding him. Then a third guy joined in, someone who wasn't even involved. Then a fourth, a fifth. They'd finished him off, kicking his teeth in, for no good reason, fomented by the alcohol and a hatred that belonged to no one. A brutal energy that spread into the void, a collective fever. Perhaps a residue from a time before the first laws were chiseled into the basalt, a very distant, ferocious era, always ready to open wide beneath our feet.

He grabbed another profiterole. He stuffed it into his mouth. He continued to consider both unseemly and at the same time understandable what old Salvemini had suggested to him when he'd gone to their house for dinner. The shadow of extortion. He'd let him know that he knew. Showing it to him in the presence of his whole family. That in itself was a remarkable bit of courage. But deep down, it was still the same old show. The chief justice of the court of appeals returned to his position in front of the picture window. Still, looking out over the sea. How lovely and how stupid creation really was.

Vittorio woke up at five in the morning. He made a phone call to Turkey. Then he got dressed, had breakfast, and left the house. He got in his car. He drove off for the usual tour of construction sites. As he drove, he kept making phone calls. He talked to Turin and to Cagliari, in Sardinia. He received reports from his Spanish business partners. He was trying to catch up on all the fronts he'd neglected over the past few weeks. If he thought about what still had to be done before August, he felt ill. He was feeling reasonably well. Frail, but possessed of a new kind of serenity. The force that even old age possessed.

After making the rounds of the construction sites, a little before noon, he drove over to the administrative offices. There was still lots to be done there. And also, at lunchtime, Michele would be coming. His son was coming to visit him at work.

He took him to a restaurant a short distance from the offices. Michele ordered a pasta dish and a main course. A steak, very rare. Vittorio limited himself to a salad and a dish of grilled vegetables. His stomach was still giving him trouble. But it was a pleasure to watch his son eat. To listen to him talk, to enter his world. *A week.* At a certain point, he didn't even know how, Vittorio had managed to wheedle it out of him. "All right, Papà," said Michele, spearing what remained of the steak. He'd stay in Bari until the middle of July. Good. Very good. Maybe he'd already made up his mind a few days ago and he'd come there today to let him believe that it had been him, his old father, who had been wily enough to convince him to stay. They ordered fruit cocktail. Michele also ordered an espresso. The old man paid the check.

Before leaving the restaurant, Michele asked if it would be all right if he came up with Vittorio to the offices. He needed to make some photocopies. Also, he needed to use a computer. He needed to check his email, write a piece. In other words, work.

"As long as there's a desk no one's using, Papà. I wouldn't want to inconvenience anybody."

"Michele, what are you talking about?"

Vittorio's face darkened. He almost felt that his sorrow was twisting in his belly. He thought of how that young man must have experienced life, if after all these years he still felt the need to ask permission to make a few copies. Had he made mistakes? Like almost all fathers. And, as was the case with so many fathers who had made mistakes, time was giving him a chance to make up for it.

"Martina!" Vittorio shouted five minutes later, as he walked into the offices. "My son needs a place to work. A desk with a phone and a computer."

His tone was so solemn that it could prove embarrassing for Michele. Vittorio didn't realize that. Instead he lowered his voice, addressing the young man.

"Please. You're the boss in here. Do whatever you need to do."

At eight in the evening the employees started leaving, one after the other.

At nine-fifteen, Vittorio made the last phone call. He walked out into the hallway. The other offices were dark, the rooms empty. But Michele, motionless in his corner at the computer, was still there working. The very picture of discretion, of good will.

Vittorio went back to his office. He picked up his briefcase. He turned off the light. He went back out into the hallway, and went over to his son.

Michele stopped typing. He turned to look at him.

"I'm tired. I'm going home. Want to come with me?"

"Actually, I still haven't finished," the young man replied. "Can I stay a little longer?"

Vittorio threw his arms wide in a sign of desperation. But he was smiling.

"Cut it out with all these *can I's*," said the old man, "otherwise I'm going to have to think you're making fun of me. Do whatever you like. Should we expect you for dinner?"

"There's no need. When I'm done here, I'm going to see some friends."

"Friends from high school?"

"Something like that."

Michele smiled. He winked at something undefined that his father—convinced that he could bask in the reflection of the light that he himself had engendered—proudly associated with ex-girlfriends not otherwise specified.

Vittorio smiled in turn. "Good." He rummaged in his pockets. With an imperceptibly affected gesture, he slid the office keys across the desk. He said goodnight to his son. He left.

At a quarter to three in the morning, Michele left the administrative offices of Salvemini Construction. He was tired, his eyes were red. For five long hours he'd done nothing but open and shut drawers. He'd leafed through ledgers and accounting books, documents full of numbers and incomprehensible abbreviations. But then he'd found what he was looking for. Clutching the sheets of paper, he'd felt an obscure restorative energy spread throughout his body. A chilly green light. He'd made the photocopies.

When, many years later, Gennaro Lopez, former medical examiner of the ASL 2, the Bari health care clinic, found himself extracting from his many if tangled memories the most awful one, that is, the one that could do him the most harm, he'd choose the night on which a guy of about thirty knocked at his front door and started showering him with questions about his sister's death certificate. At the time, Lopez was deep in debt and was consuming two grams of cocaine a day. He'd managed to dodge a threatened disciplinary proceeding. He was taking Diamet, Lormetazepam, Depakote drops, he was patronizing prostitutes on a regular basis, and all this ensured that he was tormented by an elusive sense of déjà vu—the sensation that he'd read the same page of the newspaper, that he'd experienced a scene the day before and now the same synesthetic details organized themselves again before his eyes.

The problem was that the young man started blackmailing him.

And the problem was also that, at the moment he heard the doorbell ring, Gennaro Lopez was about to bend over the fourth line laid out on his nightstand, after dedicating the afternoon to a triptych (ketamine, speed, and ecstasy, to which he'd added a light acid), and he was doing it in the company of Rocco—an old partying buddy of his who had jumped off the seventh floor of the Hotel Parco dei Principi after overdosing on LSD—whose white image came back to pay him a visit every once in a while, when he found himself in this sorry state.

"Coming!"

In spite of the fact that the doorbell had already rung twice, he snorted the coke until he could feel the frozen drop. He respected the old principle that said when something unexpected happens, and you have a half-finished line, it's always best to snort the rest of it. Even if it was no one but some nosy neighbors, then at least you'd snorted it. If it was someone who'd come to beat you bloody with a pair of brass knuckles, then at least you'd snorted it.

Gennaro Lopez got up from the bed, cursing. He slipped on his sandals. He threw on a shirt. He took a few steps forward and at that point he stopped. The space between the armoire and the wall mirror was where he always got his best ideas. He turned his head slowly toward his guest.

"Go on, go see who it is."

The ghost, motionless at the foot of the bed, looked at him sternly. His figure became the long urn of light sketched by the floor lamp. *It's your house and you need to answer the door* said a voice that the medical examiner recognized as the banal extension of his own solitude.

Gennaro Lopez emerged from his bedroom. The doorbell rang for the third time. He walked down the hallway. In front of the bathroom door he shut his eyes and lengthened his stride. The bathroom, when he was in that state, was best avoided. One ran the risk of locking oneself in, curled up in the radiator recess, hands clamped to one's ears to keep from hearing the voices. Voices that wanted their money back. They threatened him, they showered him with insults. But the worst thing was that, beneath the yelling voices of his creditors, Gennaro Lopez managed to perceive something else. A warm, slow current: wails, sobs. The strangled little girl who'd been certified as a simple cardiac arrest. The criminal finished off with a blow from a bludgeon that, in his medical certificate, became a "cranial trauma caused by accidental fall."

Gennaro Lopez jerked in surprise, safely made it past the bathroom door. He finally managed to struggle down the hall. He planted his feet in front of the door, and at that point asked: "Who is it?"

In response, the doorbell rang again.

"I said: Who is it!"

"You don't know me, sir. But I need to talk to you. Please open the door. It's better for everyone."

Hadn't he heard that voice before? In any case, he was reassured by the use of the "sir." No brass knuckles. The warning had probably just been added on at the end to make up for the mistake of having sounded too courteous. And yet . . . That's where he'd heard the voice! *The sense of déjà vu.* The time-warp that still yawned open in his head. Gennaro Lopez felt as if he were reliving the same movie from the night before. As the scene progressed, he found himself sitting in the kitchen, across from the owner of the voice who giving him the third degree. A young man, clearly not armed, who never would have been able to get into his house if he hadn't been so stupid as to open the door. So Gennaro Lopez was able to reply without hesitation: "Beat it!"

The doorbell started ringing again.

"Beat it, I said!"

"Open up. Or I'll call the police."

Obviously he wasn't armed. But it was every bit as clear that, for that very reason, he wouldn't hesitate to put his threat into effect. And if the police came into his home, well, what they'd find would be more than sufficient to get him into a world of trouble.

Depressed, humiliated at the way things were working against him, Gennaro Lopez seized the door handle. He undid the security bolt with his other hand. He opened the door.

"Good evening," said the owner of the voice.

Gennaro Lopez turned pale.

In fact he found himself face to face with a young man, about thirty. Only this wasn't the one suggested by the déjà-vu. In physical terms he was—dark, emaciated, high cheekbones, his right eyelid slightly lower than the other—but the result had little to do with the sum of the parts: he emanated an obscure vibration that the medical examiner felt himself immediately engulfed by. A sensation of loss and despair, which a resulting duty to seek revenge (the extreme homage to something concerning whose reversibility we have ceased to entertain illusions) did not make less sad.

The young man slowly lifted his right hand upward, a funereal gesture that frightened the doctor even more—a force amplified by the alterations of the state of consciousness, whose power it was difficult to elude. So much so that now Gennaro Lopez was already sitting in the kitchen, across the table from the young man, just as he'd feared when he first heard his voice.

His guest tilted his head. From his features emerged a final but understanding gaze, similar to that of certain frightening Madonnas that sit enthroned at the far ends of hallways in hospitals buried in childhood memories. He clasped his hands together. Then he spoke. He asked him to tell him everything he knew about the death of his sister.

"What sister?" asked Gennaro Lopez. The tiles were suddenly crossed by a green light that immediately vanished.

"Clara Salvemini."

"And who is that supposed to be?" This time the doctor was lying. The first thing that had come to mind was the floodlight in the mortuary room. He was adjusting the intensity of the light, he was kneeling forward to examine the corpse, and now the floodlight was scalding the back of his neck. It curled the hairs on his neck, that's how powerful it was.

The young man said that it was Lopez's name that appeared on the certificate.

"How am I supposed to remember? In the past few years I must have seen hundreds of corpses." The doctor tugged at his shirt because of the sudden chill. But then, instead, he was too hot.

At that point the young man separated his hands and, with the same exasperating slowness, opened them like a goblet, as if he were effortlessly bearing up the invisible burden troubling the conscience of the man in his presence. He said that he would alert the judicial authorities. If pushed to extreme consequences, that's what he'd be willing to do. He raised his finger, with anguish, into the air, sketching in the void the numerals of a way of the cross in reverse. They would disinter the corpse. They'd compare the findings of the new examination with what they found in the document he'd drawn up. But Michele didn't want the corpse to be disinterred. The ultimate insult to his sister's dead body would be if it became the subject of an inquest, he said, with an increasingly contrite face. He was speaking from beyond a bloodstained veil, and he felt sincere sorrow for anyone who, forcing him to cross it, would be smeared with the same substance. The doctor realized that he wasn't kidding around.

"I couldn't help it," he said.

"Why."

"They forced me."

"Who forced you."

The doctor felt a chill again. If he listened carefully, it wasn't just the young man's voice. In his masculine timbre there was another one. And in the voice of the live man, the voice of the dead soul. The girl. The two voices were holding hands. This made a strange impression on him. Watching him talk, it seemed to Gennaro Lopez that his guest's tone, every so often, faded. At that point, he scraped the bottom of all his grief, which was also his strength, to extract from the depths the living figure of his sister, that is, the finest memory of her that he had, held upright by the finest memory he had of himself, so that not one but two dead people spoke through his mouth. Little brother and little sister. This was disconcerting. To see them walk together along the curve of time. Hurtled into a future they hadn't anticipated.

"Who is it that you say forced you?" asked Michele.

"I don't know," the medical examiner sniveled, overwhelmed by the suddenly resurgent wave of narcotics.

"You can't not know."

"They call me and I go." He was no longer the young man's victim but his own. "It's a matter of working out the causes of death," he said. "Sometimes I'll be called by an executive of the health care clinic. Or the director of technical operations. Usually, though, it's people I don't know. They call. I know that they're speaking on behalf of someone else, but I've never heard their voices before. At that point, in any case, I have to go examine the corpse."

In the past, Gennaro Lopez had had a clear picture of the constantly updated map that let him understand which requests he could turn down without risking grave consequences. But the number of people capable of blackmailing him had grown over the years to a frightful extent. At a certain point, the map had exploded in his head.

"I understand, but in my sister's case, exactly who would have called you?"

"A director of the health care clinic."

"The name."

"I can tell you, but it wouldn't do any good."

The young man glared at him.

The doctor met his gaze. He didn't have any problem doing that if he wasn't lying.

Michele shook his head. It seemed to the doctor that he had

just sensed the kind of maze of other names the name of the director would lead to, the links in an interminable chain that he'd have to snap one after the other to make any kind of sense of it. The young man dropped his head into his hands, probably exhausted, and that was enough to let the rising tide that was carrying the medical examiner to the height of prostration suggest the presence of another dock. Empathy. Methylene-dioxymethamphetamine. The active element in ecstasy regained some ground.

"Believe me," the doctor said at that point, driven, in spite of himself, by the fire of solidarity, "even I couldn't dig anything up starting from that guy. And what's more I can tell you something more useful about this story. The problem," he leaned cautiously toward Michele, "is that at the moment I performed the examination of your sister's corpse, there at the cemetery mortuary, well . . . I realized that I was already familiar with that body."

The young man looked at him without saying a word.

"The photos," the doctor went on, "at least a year earlier. I'd seen her photographs."

"What photographs?"

"The photographs of your sister. Those pictures were making the rounds, if you catch my drift."

He saw Michele grow sad. He felt the force of his profound displeasure that once again threatened him.

"Who was it that you say took those pictures?" the young man asked after a pause. It seemed as if the mere act of uttering those words caused him minor burns on his lips.

"A surgeon." Gennaro Lopez tried to withstand with the strength he lacked the young man's pathological unhappiness, so they wouldn't plunge, one after the other, into a deep sea with no more light or sound. "But he's not the solution to the problem either."

"And so?" Michele crossed his arms over his chest. It

wasn't clear whether he meant to intimidate the doctor or give himself a little reassurance.

The doctor heaved a sigh.

"I don't know what happened to your sister," he, said in the end. "The fractures that I found during my examination could easily have been caused by a fall. I wouldn't rule out that she actually did jump off of that parking structure. But it could have been something else, too. She could have been beaten, for instance. The external examination couldn't determine that. An autopsy would have been necessary. The one sure thing is that your sister wound up in a nasty situation. The photographs. I've never seen anything like them," he said, and he felt the sensation of when at night you drive a truck over the expansion joints on a long bridge, "but there might be a way to figure something out. A young woman. One of your sister's friends. Maybe I shouldn't call her a friend. Let's just say they moved in the same circles. I can give you her name. I can give you her phone number and address. That way you'd be free to go and talk to her."

"Let's go together," said the young man.

"What?"

"Let's go see her together. Now. Let's go see her now."

The doctor looked at him.

Michele tilted his head again. It seemed to the doctor that the young man could have remained in that position forever, so great was not his impatience but his grief; and so, when the physical body necessarily got to its feet, that would remain, the umpteenth phantom planted between the walls of his apartment.

"But it's late," said Gennaro Lopez, knowing he'd already lost.

A milky white luminosity spread out of the sky, and it was impossible to say where the moon might be. They'd gone out onto Via Corridoni, where they were surrounded by buildings that served as a protective cordon around the old city. The doctor slipped into the narrow lanes of the medieval center, Michele followed him. Behind them they could sense the vast façade of the former Dominican monastery, sliced vertically by the oversized clock tower. They passed under a tufa-stone arch. They walked past a small shrine. Their footsteps echoed through the snarl of empty streets. After more lanes and alleys, they found themselves outside the city walls, on the far side from where they'd entered. Before them lay the black waters of the Adriatic. The streetlamps along the waterfront, the lights of the hotels and the monumental apartment buildings. They were observing them as if from a hilltop watch post.

The doctor started walking up the steep street that led to the highest point of the bastions. Michele kept following him. After about fifty feet, Gennaro Lopez stopped. A squeak. They both turned to look. They were tucked away in a corner of the overlook. One of them was rearing up on its hind legs, its long snout sniffing at the air around it. The other rats were running ahead and behind. Uneasy. Venturing out of the sewers. The doctor clutched the lapels of his jacket to his throat. Now the drugs were a chilly horizontal blade, a fissure determined to suck him back down, as if the moon they couldn't find up in the sky were glowing inside him, smaller and smaller, letting him sink into the waters of an ocean at the bottom of which he'd no longer have so much as a name. Black, metallic currents. The pulverized carcasses of small animals that whirled around on themselves as they turned back into water.

"Here we are," said the medical examiner, reemerging from his journey.

A small door, varnished in white. High overhead, the green halo of a half-burnt out neon sign transformed the letters of the name of a beer into an acronym (H K E) that referred to something more intimate and less familiar. Gennaro Lopez rang the doorbell. They heard the lock snapping open. They went in, they shut the door behind them. Michele felt the sudden heat. The doctor greeted the bouncer. He went through the velvet curtain that separated the front entrance from the club proper.

They found themselves in a long, oval space. Two luminous panels immersed the room into a torrid atmosphere straight out of a tropical aquarium. At the center was a counter topped by a pyramid of bottles that seemed, thanks to the effect of the spotlights, to float in midair. At the tables, a few poorly matched couples. Men with their ties undone, young women whose fluffy hair clashed with the background music. They were drinking, smoking. The men's chubby hands were the body part that the girls paid most attention to.

As soon as the new arrivals fetched up within range of the voices, it was as if an invisible membrane were at first hindering their movement, before letting them slide through. The doctor walked toward the bar and gestured to the man making cocktails. A young man of about thirty with an anonymous face. Goatee and bandana. They chatted. The doctor turned toward Michele. They sat down at a small table. A waiter arrived with two ice-cold vodkas. The doctor drank his down in a single gulp. Michele drank, too. Then the girl arrived.

"A pleasure, Bianca," she said, extending her hand toward Michele. He started to get to his feet, but she was quicker; she leaned forward, kissed him on the cheeks. Face powder and sweat. An awkward gesture, and yet at the same time aggressive. Michele looked at her. Blonde, not even thirty, boots and a skimpy, skintight dress.

"Sit down," said the medical examiner.

The girl took a seat on the settee. She languidly ran a hand through her hair. She scrutinized them both, trying to transform a natural resentment into a channel of communication devoid of meaning. The waiter brought a caipirinha. The girl reached out and took the glass, lifted it to lips that were covered with an ugly pale-pink lipstick, neither slutty nor childish, the mark of a broad range of choice that she completely squandered, as if that, the waste itself, were her prison.

She took a sip, then moved the glass away from her mouth, careful not to set it down on the table, holding it in midair. "But are you from Bari? I've never seen you." She addressed Michele with the smile of someone whose job it is to let herself be charmed.

"Listen, Bianca," the doctor immediately put an end to any thoughts of that type of conversation, "more than anything else what he's looking for is some information about what you and Clara Salvemini got up to. You remember her, don't you? What the two of you used to do when you went out together." Then he waved his hand in the waiter's direction.

The girl widened her eyes ever so slightly, and set the glass down on the little table. She snickered. "You're looking to land me in deep shit," she said with a face that acknowledged the fact that that was where she was already. She opened her purse. She pulled out the pack of cigarettes.

"No, really," she shook her head with the fatalism of someone who is retracing the outline of bad luck in front of someone who is yet another demonstration of the same, "don't drag me into fucked-up situations."

Michele understood that the doctor held her in his grip. For some obscure reason, about which he'd never learn anything, the girl had no choice but to tell him what he wanted to know."

"No nasty situation," the medical examiner extended his hand in her direction, and the girl let him take hers, "we just want you to tell us exactly what happened to her."

"She should never have become the only attraction at the party, that's all," she said contemptuously, pulled her hand out of the doctor's.

"What party?" Michele broke in.

The waiter came to the table. The medical examiner ordered two more vodkas and a caipirinha.

"It's just a manner of speaking," the girl went on, "the parties, the orgies. She would have been better off if she'd stuck to that."

"Was she a prostitute?" asked Michele.

She made a pained grimace.

Michele looked at her.

"Oh, no, what are you talking about," and she spit out the smoke, scandalized, though it wasn't clear if she was defending the honor of Clara or the profession. "She was no whore. Not in the slightest."

"Then what?" asked Michele, relieved, confused, feeling a lump rise in his throat.

"She had . . . unusual relationships," the girl smiled slyly. "She had these men and then, every so often, she'd come hang out with us. That surgeon was the one who organized our parties." The medical examiner spun his hand clockwise, as if to suggest she skip the intermediate steps.

"She was dating some guy who owned newspapers," she went on, "but she was seeing Buffante too, that guy who got into politics. Then there was the judge. The problem is that at a certain point it turns out they started seeing each other for their own purposes. I mean Clara and those three idiots. At Buffante's house. That's where the situation got out of hand. That's what people are saying," she took another drag on her cigarette. "Fuck, everyone knows," she objected, "and you come asking me of all people."

The waiter came back with a tray.

The medical examiner drank, throwing his head back theatrically. Then he looked at Michele. He was trying to understand if he had enough.

"What do you mean, got out of hand?" the young man asked instead.

"Oh, you know," she spun her fingers in the air, focused on

stringing together a series of thoughts, "if she'd gone on spending her evenings with us, those guys wouldn't have lost control like such idiots. When there's lots of you, it eases the tension," she crushed out her cigarette, seemed irritated by Michele's failure to agree, which kept her from neatly cutting the discussion short.

"What are you talking about? I don't understand."

Another scandalized smile flashed across her face. But this time, there was a rip to be re-stitched between surprise and irritation.

"Come on . . . let's not pretend we were born yesterday," she began, crushing the stub of her cigarette, which was already thoroughly extinguished, into the ashtray. "Everyone knows that men like to hit girls."

Michele said nothing. The deeper the grief, the more time it takes before the senses are capable of perceiving it. Even the doctor remained silent.

"Anyway the incredible thing was the family," she threw in, to fill the silence. "The fact that . . . this is something else that everyone's saying," she held the topic at arm's length so that, when she picked it back up, it had less to do with her, "those three morons got themselves into a position where they could be blackmailed—"

"Listen, just one more thing," Michele interrupted her, having already understood enough, he'd known it before coming in, he just needed to understand it this way, he even understood what remained an enigma, as visible as a woman's face glimpsed through a window pounded by rain, the words that Alberto had let slip about the two engineers, details, finishing touches that he'd never be able to glimpse in their entirety, he understood enough, and yet now it wasn't the pain and grief but his sister, whether she was a ghost or whether it was just the persistence of her tracks, the living imprint that the people we've loved leave in us to go on shaping us, driving us, obsessing us with their inexhaustible voices, this then their bequest, the difference between a dead body and that which lives on, his sister was angry, he could sense that, but he needed to compare the versions.

"Yes," said the girl, rubbing her eyes.

"The times you saw her," Michele forced himself to remain focused, as if the answer depended on that, "did you talk together?"

The girl shrugged her shoulders. She took a sip from the glass. "Well," she said with weary expertise, "every now and then we'd go home together, at the end of the night. She'd give me a ride. We'd stop at a café. We'd eat breakfast before going to sleep."

"You'd eat breakfast together."

"Breakfast. That's right."

"And you'd talk."

"That's what I said. We'd have a pastry and—"

"What would you talk about?"

The girl dropped her eyes, feigned a timidity she didn't possess. "Oh, I don't know, everything, nothing."

"What did she talk about?" asked Michele. "Did she ever talk about her brother?"

"Yes, she had a brother," the girl looked him in the eye, "an oncologist, I think. He was pretty—"

"I mean *another* brother," Michele whispered, on edge, his voice clearly saying that enough was enough, they had the evidence, all they needed to do was act, "a younger brother, in Rome," he insisted, "did she ever talk about him?"

"A brother? In Rome? I wouldn't know about that. I really don't think there was another brother in Rome," the girl replied, starting to sound bored.

A few minutes later Michele got up from the settee. He turned his back on them both. He headed for the exit. It might have been three in the morning.

The sliding glass door suddenly slid open, ran violently the length of its track, and shuddered to a stop. From the pool of light in the living room a human figure emerged into the windy night. An old man, pushing sixty-five, staring wide-eyed into the darkness, his shirt hanging rudely untucked. He looked around. A shower of tiny red spots had splattered him, from his collar to the hems of his shirt cuffs. He took a few steps forward, unsteadily, like someone trying to escape a nightmare that his own body had engendered. He noticed the cloud of moths hovering in the empty air, attracted by the lights of the adjoining villa. That wasn't what he was looking for. He walked down the front steps and started walking across the lawn. The overwrought expression persisted on the long gray face. He heard footsteps behind him. A second man, taller and more powerfully built, emerged from the villa. He was staggering. He was struggling with all his might to emerge from his state of confusion. He caught up with the other man. With an effort, he placed his hands on the back of a plastic lounger.

"Well?"

"Damn it, I can't see her," whispered the other man.

The third man was inside, sitting in a chair in the down-stairs dining area. He continued to sob as he stared at his blood-spattered hands.

On the second floor of the villa next door, Signora Grazioli tossed and turned in her bed, annoyed. This was hardly the first time they'd made such a ruckus. She shut her eyes, tried to get back to sleep.

A few minutes after the crash, before the ambulances had arrived, they found the body. It was fifty feet from the road, abandoned in the dry grass. That was good luck. They'd seen her naked as a newborn, and now they were going to have to update their perspectives. They exchanged a glance. They lifted her easily, one by the shoulders, the other holding her by the feet. In silence, walking quickly, the nearly-full moon lighting their way, Engineer De Palo and Engineer Ranieri carried Clara's corpse towards the station wagon.

That night they all gather at the ex-undersecretary's villa. They're drinking, high as kites. Or else they don't drink, they don't smoke, they've never done drugs in their lives. They take it out on her. They beat her bloody. Or maybe something else happens. *They must* be drunk. *They must* be on drugs. Otherwise there's no way to explain how she could have left the villa. Naked. And it's in that state that she crosses the highway. She causes the crash. At that point they find her. Or maybe they did something else to her. What else could they have done to her. What, exactly, were they doing in there. Anyway, they find her dead. At this point he knows that. He's always known it. He acts like he doesn't. He convinces himself he doesn't. In his heart of hearts, he doesn't know it anymore. That's in his best interest. They arrange for her to be found at the foot of the parking structure. That night he must have picked up the receiver of his phone many times. He has to chase down a series of men. He blackmails the three, but never in explicit terms. An invitation to dinner, a funeral. He sends his regards. It's enough that they know there's a reason he's doing it. Forget the reason. For an instant he knows it. Then he doesn't know it anymore, as if he'd never known it in the first place. No one has any awareness now of their own worst actions. We did, once. But we don't anymore. We suffer. We blame the mechanism. Like blaming it on nature. If there's no choice, then there's no blame either. Doing something instead of not doing it. Doing it.

Michele kept thinking about it as he walked back to his father's house. After leaving the club, he'd walked the entire length of Via della Repubblica. Now he was trudging down Via Giulio Petroni. Weary, numb, he was moving through the last eddies of night wind. A concrete, voluntary action. He passed the IP gas station. He looked at the gardens of the villas, still shrouded in darkness. The silence of the sprinklers. The old 19 bus stop. He felt a tightness in his stomach. The sandwich stand wasn't even there anymore. Along the route, from the city center to the residential outskirts, he'd kept his eyes trained on the edge of the road. Under the parked cars. The sidewalks. The cat. She was dead too. The foliage of the cypresses. He saw the façade of the villa. Doing it instead of not doing it. He heard her voice.

Now he was moving through the garden. He passed the fountain. He walked up the staircase. Behind him, the chirping of the early birds. He opened the door. He took off his shoes. He went upstairs, careful not to make any noise lest the sudden awakening of any one of the members of his family ruin the perfection of the moment. A universe of mirrors that crisscross one another in turn, the lucid dream in which the murderer becomes one with his act. He went past the bathroom. Gioia's room. He kept going. From the window of his room he saw the sky as it became tinged with pink. He started undressing. It was hot, but he was shivering. He leaned over the trousers tossed onto the floor. He stood up with a cigarette between his fingers. He climbed into bed. The sheets were freshly washed. His head on the pillow. He lit the cigarette. He took a drag. Very soon, the new day. And then he was asleep. He felt a burning sensation. He reopened his eyes. He took another drag. He brushed the ashes he'd carelessly dropped off his chest. He picked up his cell phone off the nightstand. He held it in front of his eyes. He pressed on the screen. The plastic surface lit up. He went onto Twitter.

@ClaraSalvemini:
@pablito82 Tonight anything is possible.
20 retweets 15 favorites

@pablito82:
@ClaraSalvemini Even for us to meet?

@ClaraSalvemini:
@pablito82 In the meantime, try to imagine me.
65 retweets 22 favorites

@themoralizer:
@ClaraSalvemini @pablito82 Give us a few hints.

@ClaraSalvemini:
@themoralizer @pablito82 I'm wearing a short cotton dress, cut low in the front and the back, five-inch heels. Zipper up the side.
70 retweets 25 favorites

@laziale88:
@ClaraSalvemini I'm undressing you with my eyes.

This is where the exchange broke off. Michele reached an arm out into the void. He let the ash drop onto the floor. His heart was racing. The days when he hadn't had to think twice before setting fire to the house. He held his breath. Something else had appeared on the screen.

@ClaraSalvemini:
@laziale88 Apparently you were successful. Now all I'm wearing is the scent of my own body.

Michele hurled himself out of bed. He made a beeline toward his sister's room, his eyes glazed with anger. When he was in front of the door, he stopped. No one, right up until the last minute, should be ripped away from a happiness that for the rest of their lives they'd retrospectively understand as illusory. Michele took a step back. He went back up the hallway. He returned to his room. The light of day was beginning to flood everything. He went to the window. He closed the shutters. An action to accommodate the distant music of certain natural calamities. Frequency ranges that cannot be perceived by the human ear. He slipped back into bed. He shut his eyes. Catastrophes that gave not the slightest warning of their impending arrival until it was too late. He fell asleep.

The next day they all had lunch together. Ruggero would swing by later. Michele chewed slowly. He felt as if he'd been numbed. The slight disorientation of someone who's trained hard for an important match and then rests the day before. The birds were chirping in the trees. Vittorio looked at him with a hint of regret. In a few days he'd be going away. The old man watched him as he lifted forkfuls of spaghetti with lobster to his mouth, as he drank the white wine. Annamaria was surveying the scene with neutrality. Midway through lunch Gioia announced that she was going to spend the month of August traveling around Europe. She and two of her girlfriends were going to head east. Greece. Turkey. Michele asked whether they were planning to visit Cyprus. "Cyprus," Gioia smiled, "we're thinking about it." "You do know it's divided into two parts?" The dining room was flooded with light. Annamaria's voice was gently argumentative. Her idea of a return to normalcy meant giving her biological daughter a bit of a hard time, rebalancing the situation as far as he was concerned. "You'll see the sanctuary of Aphrodite," said Michele, imperturbable. Before answering, Gioia asked her father to pass her the vegetable side dish. Michele beat Vittorio to it, handed her the platter. He also served the wine. Gioia popped a carrot into her mouth. She chewed. Then she smiled. "But all we care about is the sea," she said at last. Michele smiled in his turn. The House of the Golden Cupids in Pompeii, he thought. The perfect calm of the day before.

After lunch he drank an espresso on the veranda with his father.

"So you're leaving," said Vittorio, looking at the tall grass in front of him, the maze of laurel leaves lit up by the sun.

"Sooner or later it was going to have to happen," Michele tried to joke.

Vittorio kept looking out into the garden. The wrinkles around his eyes gave him a wise expression. They heard the noise of a car. A few minutes later, Ruggero, too, appeared on the veranda.

He kissed Vittorio's cheeks. Then he hugged Michele. With energy, human warmth. He told Vittorio something about certain accounting documents to be retrieved. The old man waved his hand in a sign of assent. Ruggero went into the house. Vittorio resumed the conversation.

"We've been through some difficult times." He picked up his demitasse of espresso, by now cold, from the table. He drank. "Terrible times," he went on, "why beat around the bush? Over the past ten years, you've come home maybe three or four times in all, and never for longer than a day or two. Then you stay for two months and it's for this. I'm really sorry, I wanted to tell you that."

"Papà, don't worry." He wanted to shake him off.

But Vittorio had barely gotten started.

"Your sister," he said, enunciating every syllable, "and then all these problems that came so close to blowing us sky high. I tried to keep from telling you in terms that were too clear, I didn't want to frighten you." He looked at him with intensity. "Now, luckily, everything has been straightened out. But the damage was there before, I'm aware of it. I've thought it over, in the past few months. How could you not think it over, when all this happens." He kept looking at him; Michele felt the burden growing heavier with each passing second. "It's never been easy for me to open up," Vittorio said, "but I've come to the conclusion that, if you've been so unwilling to come back over the years, it can't have been out of malice. It was because deep down you never acknowledged this place as yours. You don't think of this as your home." His voice was trembling.

"Please, Papà . . . "

Michele felt ill at ease. His father's anxiety was sincere. But still, he understood the trick. Like hearing the truth, but proffered in such a way that it came out disfigured, so that the path leading back to the source was permanently off limits.

"If that's the way it is," the old man continued, "then it's your father's fault. That's the way it has to be. I've let myself be swept away by day-to-day problems, for years." He half shut his eyes because of the sun. "I've always kept my head down. Terrible battles, with never a chance to stop and think. I never realized what you were feeling. I failed to take into consideration your sister's state of mind. I'm doing it for the children, I thought. It's just that I was doing it in the wrong way. No breaks, no vacations. No friends. What would it all have meant, otherwise?" He's only making everything harder, Michele thought. "I was always thinking of you," Vittorio said in the end, "I'm sorry that there have been problems. I love you."

Michele leaned forward. He wouldn't have done it. But she was the one who was asking him to. He had to respect the forms of a venerable tradition. The fact that Clara paid attention even to such negligible details moved him. Michele hugged his father. He held him tight. He gave him a kiss. "And I love you, too," he said.

Once inside, he went up to his room. He looked up the number in his address book. He phoned the administrative offices of ARPA. He'd already called them once that morning. They'd asked him to call back. Once again, he asked for the technical director. The young woman at the switchboard asked him to hold. Mozart's Jupiter Symphony. Then, the switchboard operator again. The appointment had been booked.

In the afternoon, before leaving, Ruggero, too, stopped to talk with him.

Michele walked with him toward his car. The situation was strange. For two months he'd had practically no interactions with this brother who was more than ten years his elder. His patients, his career, his perennial bad temper. But now he could sense his magnetism, the tacit intention to draw him closer.

When they got to the front gate, Ruggero stopped. The convertible BMW parked a few yards away. But he didn't move.

"I know what you think about him, deep down," he said, "and I can't really blame you for it."

Michele made an effort not to reply. He was waiting. He watched the sun transform the windshield into a rectangle of light.

"You think he's a bastard," Ruggero continued, "maybe you think that he needs to be punished." He paused briefly, "I don't know who you've talked to in the past few days. Anyway, they can't have told you anything you weren't already well aware of."

Michele started. He was beginning to be afraid that Ruggero might know something. Maybe someone had called him from ARPA. He might even have been told about what happened last night. Or just guessed it, with his sixth sense. The conceit of having Michele as an accomplice was a signal of Ruggero's arrogance and at the same time of his fear.

"And yet I don't think we ought to hurt him," he continued, "we're not the ones who need to make him pay."

"I don't understand," Michele ventured.

"The punishment," said Ruggero. "We don't have to lift a finger. The punishment is on its way," he grimaced, "that's something I can guarantee you. I guarantee it as a doctor. Time is a gentleman." He left room for a pause that could swallow up the event to which he was alluding. "And at that point," he went on, "taking into account everything he's put us through, we'll get our payback. It's something we deserve. We won't have to dirty our hands."

"You mean that we'll inherit," Michele was being careful not to move a muscle of his face.

"Perhaps you can't imagine how much the company is worth," said Ruggero, "the company just has to stay intact until then."

"Of course. You're right."

"Are we sure?" asked Ruggero, focusing on the car outside of the gate.

"Agreed, I told you."

Speaking. Lying. Doing instead of not doing. It's real. Voluntary. It leads to consequences.

She tensed her muscles. As soon as the two vehicles roared past, she shot forward. She sensed death in the gust of air that had not yet dispersed over the asphalt. She crossed the street. She ventured into the lavender bushes. Behind her, other vehicles were now racing past. She started running through the dry grass. She was exhausted. Her fur was reduced to a shapeless dark gray mass. She emanated a nauseating stench. And she was hungry.

Over the past few days, the cat had wandered at loose ends through the streets of the city. Mixed up with scraps of familiar odors, she'd sensed in the air a brutality so obtuse that it left her stunned. Huge bags of garbage. The inert steel of parked cars. And voices, a racket everywhere.

As she'd made her way through the last outlying areas, the degree of familiarity had dropped along with the hope of finding her way back home. A different type of brutality made sure there was little space for anything other than sheer survival. Rather than confounding her, this kept her taut. It refined her senses. What reached her nostrils could be broken down into a myriad of new impressions. Frightening, intoxicating, each charged with nuances just waiting to be deciphered.

Despite the fact that she was safe, the cat kept running alone the curve of the field lit up by the moon. She saw on either side the mulberry trees. Then the apple trees. Black presences that radiated energy. At a certain point something shot into sight on her right side. A dark corporeal mass moving towards her. It veered off onto the left, was swallowed up by the darkness. It went back to tailing her. The part of the cat that possessed memory of her captivity interpreted it as an invitation to play. Then there was the other part. And so, without knowing why, she aimed at an apple tree that towered over the indistinct mass of weeds. She sped up. Then she suddenly whirled around so that her pursuer had the tree behind it.

Both animals came to a halt. They hunkered down, one in front of the other. No more than thirty feet between them.

The sewer rat focused on her with its beady eyes. Its front teeth were so large that it had to keep its mouth half-open. It lunged at her. Before it could sink its teeth into her, the cat leapt up, brushing past the rat's body, and when she landed back on the grass she'd unsheathed her claws. Now it was she who had the disadvantage of the apple tree at her back. She puffed herself up. The rat rose up on its haunches. But it was wounded. The cat lifted her right paw to her face and licked it. That was what definitively tilted the battlefield. The taste of blood roiled her. The part that had been underneath rose to the top, left room for nothing else. She lunged forward. The rat, in turn, lunged at her, mouth open to kill. With extreme precision, the cat's claws swiped diagonally across the rodent's eyes. The rat reeled backward onto its side. The feline was on it. She sank her teeth into the hard flesh of its neck. As she fought, she knew, she knew and she remembered at the same time. The rat squeaked desperately. In the cat's throat, something dense and deep gurgled. She'd found the artery. She was excited, electric. She felt the rat convulse one last time under the light of the moon.

T hey'd all be ruined," said the technical director, "I hope you realize that."

They were just a few yards from the sea, sitting at one of the open-air tables of a restaurant where no one had showed up yet. Ten in the morning. Behind them, half concealed by the planters full of succulents, stood the large building that housed the Regional Environmental Protection Agency. The sky over the city was clear and blue.

When Michele had started talking, the technical director wasn't certain he'd understood clearly. The request to include the area around Porto Allegro in the monitoring zone might have been a provocation. A way to tell him that the hundred fifty thousand euros was too much. They'd sent the most shameless member of the family on ahead to prod him. But why, now that the contract was signed? That part he couldn't understand.

Then, as he went on listening, he realized that the young man wasn't joking. He really was asking him not to turn a blind eye. To keep both eyes wide open. To check. To poke around. To place the mobile monitoring units on his father's land. Lead detectors, mercury detectors. Kits to evaluate radon gas percentages.

"What the hell kind of request is that?"

"I don't think there's anything left to understand."

As he was talking he felt Clara brush his skin, which ensured that his voice didn't tremble in the slightest. Synchronized swimming. Artistic gymnastics. One of those disciplines in which every cell participates in the result.

At that point the technical director had crossed his arms. He'd looked at him with pity. Black sheep. Every family had one. Resentful and thirsty for revenge. Luckily they were also completely clueless. They expected to be able to blow up bridges but knew nothing about dynamite.

"I don't know what you're talking about."

At that point, Michele pulled the photocopy of the consulting contract out of his trouser pocket. He handed it over.

The technical director felt the blow without letting it show. There it was, the dynamite. Old Salvemini must have lost his mind if he was letting this lunatic get access to the documents.

"Who can guarantee that if we include the tourist complex in the monitoring plan you won't just go ahead and circulate these documents?"

Considering the way things were turning out, he had to protect himself first of all.

"Don't include Porto Allegro in the monitoring plan and you can rest assured that the documents will circulate."

Michele ought to have given them to Sangirardi first. He'd promised him that. He'd made that commitment and he'd failed to respect it. He felt the hot wind in his face.

"All right then," said the technical director, "you've decided to create some problems for your folks. I don't know what they can have done to push you to do such a thing. But maybe you can't really imagine what the consequences might—"

"I can imagine very clearly, the consequences of my actions. I can't actually imagine anything else, if you really want to know."

"Listen, Michele," the technical director unfurled his last reserves of authority, which didn't exist, which paradoxically would have remained intact if Michele hadn't placed a Xerox of the contract under his nose, "maybe it's not clear to you what an enormous mess this new inspection will cause. This isn't going to be some monitoring operation like the others. We should have already been at this point a few years ago. The overall situation made it impossible. You want to do something. They won't let you. But you keep pushing and after a while you succeed. In the grownup world that's the way things work. We'll find concentrations of arsenic in the water five times higher than the legal limit. The dioxin levels will solve the newspaper editors' problem of what to slap on the front page for weeks. The lead will come out, and so will the copper. A bunch of animals have died. A lot of people are going to suffer. Children that haven't even been born yet are going to get sick. It's statistics," he continued, "most of it is happening on the other coast. But part of it's arrived here, too. It'll be impossible to clear out such a vast area and it will be impossible to carry out a complete reclamation." He sighed as if he needed to defuse the tension. "Your father," he said, looking at him again, "your father has absolutely nothing to do with this whole issue of toxic wastes. Last week he was cleared of all charges of having violated hydrogeological and forestry restrictions during the construction of those houses. Restrictions so complicated it would have required a whole platoon of philosophers to interpret them. A whole tangle of laws and counter-laws. And yet your father didn't break one. Respecting those regulations to the letter is impossible, but he managed to do it. The investigating magistrate had to recognize the fact. Just think. Your father respected the *ordinary* restrictions, which means that he took care not to uproot even one albino downy oak. And now," he shook his head in disbelief, "now you're asking us to go and find out whether somewhere, buried in the area of the complex, there isn't by chance something dirty. Well," he said, his voice hardening, "of course there's bound to be something there that shouldn't be. Seek and ye shall find. Too bad your father never got a penny for it. Did you ever think of that? Maybe he was forced to do it. Didn't it occur to you that he might never have had a choice? That someone, while they were building that fucking tourist village, might have ever so politely asked him to stop the work. Just for a couple of days. Enough time to come in with an earthmover and a couple of trucks, do what they had to do, and leave. Your father never made a single euro. On the contrary. He simply lost workdays. The alternative was that they would ever so politely blow up the whole construction site. Or that they'd hurt one of his loved ones."

"Unfortunately, you're not convincing me," said Michele.

He felt as if he were holding her hand, like when they were kids. She at his side. She was above him, inside of him. Everywhere.

"By doing this, you're not just creating problems for your family." The director lifted his hands, displaying his palms as if the young man were an atmospheric event, devoid of a will with which one could reason. "You're not just causing them a major financial loss. If we go there and we find something, they're well and truly fucked. I'm not just talking about the company. I'm talking about serious crimes. You're running the risk of ruining once and for all someone who did things because he had no choice about—"

"That's not true."

Michele felt he was at the peak of intensity. Then Clara vanished.

"It's not true in an ideal world," the technical director replied, "it's not true in movies and novels. It might not have been entirely true when we were born. But in the twenty-first century, that's the way things are."

Michele said nothing. The sky overhead was a slab of turquoise and Clara had abandoned him. That's how it had happened. She had released her grip on him. She had left him alone in the world. Free forever.

"Do you know what scientific discipline best explains the new century?" the man asked.

A faint sea breeze was tossing both men's hair.

"Ethology. Animal behavior," the technical director answered his own question. "Put a starving fox in front of a herd of rabbits. Run into a piazza full of doves and you'll see them fly. Find me a dove that doesn't fly."

"We aren't animals, we do strange things," said Michele.

He felt disconcerted. He was having a dizzy spell. Before him was no longer Clara, but the days that were yet to come. Empty, terrifying space, an immense blank page.

"We do what nature has decided for us. The limits are reasonably clear," the man replied.

Michele looked him in the eye. What did it all mean, if she was gone? He felt a shiver in his legs.

"We behave in ridiculous ways. We're unpredictable," he said then, and it was as if he were taking his first steps without Clara to hold his hand, proceeding in a straight line after throwing his crutches to the ground. "There was someone in the past who did for me something that they couldn't do. Acts that went against the laws of nature. Good things were done for me without any practical motive, and now I'm doing this thing. This unnatural thing. Ridiculous even for me. A miracle. Just think."

After having remained hidden for such a long time, it began to take shape. To Michele it seemed he could finally see it. The future. As magnificent and ferocious as the yawning maw of the tiger he'd read about as a boy.

The technical director dropped his hands in a sign of surrender.

"All right," he said, "I've just been wasting my breath."

EPILOGUE

T he first ones to enter were the children.

The door to the villa was thrown open—it had been two years since anyone had done that—and they started running down the hallway. They kicked up dust and flakes of dry plaster, vanished, leaving a white cloud in their wake. The little boy was seven. The girl was five. Their footsteps echoed where the living room had presumably once been. Without furniture, it wasn't easy to get one's bearings.

Then it was the father's turn. He passed from the golden autumn light through the semi-darkness of the front hall, followed by the architect. He caught a whiff of the odor into which manmade settings plunge when they're abandoned, and in which other people, caught up in a never-ending game, feel the need to establish new order.

The new owner of the house was just a little over forty. Tall, with an olive complexion. He'd married in 2004, but only recently had things started to take off financially, and even so, he couldn't really afford the villa.

He saw his children emerge from the white nebula that was the mouth of the hallway. Figures born out of the light. They were laughing. They went running past him and the architect. They went galloping upstairs. It had been the villa of the local *podestà*. A senator had sold it in the early Seventies. Then the stroke of luck. The last owners had been caught in a scandal, and the ensuing financial collapse had forced them to get rid of it quickly.

They entered a dark, airless room, with the shutters fastened tight, bolted shut for two summers in a row. The dust of dried paint whirled in a rivulet of light. The architect was delivering his sermon on the necessity of renovating the partition walls. The new owner suggested inspecting the second floor. Here the children were chasing each other around. They ran from room to room. Until the little girl found one room that was locked. She turned the handle. She pushed and pulled with all her might. Useless. The door wouldn't open. Her brother caught up with her.

The architect turned on his heels and headed off toward the stairs.

Alone now, the new owner stood for a few minutes in the partial darkness, as if that, too, was his responsibility. Weighing the symphony of deterioration before remedying it. There was something that fascinated him, but he couldn't explain it any more clearly. So he walked forward. He pushed on the door until it swung open. The light exploded into a sunburst. He saw the kitchen. He went in. He pushed past the screen, half-torn out of the French windows that gave onto the other end of the garden.

Once again the September sun warmed his face, enclosing his senses in the contentment of a circular route. Now he was on the veranda. A stack of dust-covered furniture was piled up against the picture window. Lounge chairs, serving trolleys, the canvas canopy of an old glider. One on top of another. As if they'd been heaped up in a hurry, or perhaps someone had hurled them into a corner in an ugly outburst of rage.

Trying not to knock anything over, the new owner pulled out a lounger. He dusted off the seat and the backrest as best he could with a tissue. He dragged the lounge chair to edge of the lawn. He settled onto it. He adjusted the angle and looked straight ahead. Weeds. Wild rose bushes. He heard the shouts of the children from the opposite end of the garden. Beyond the luxuriant branches of the trees, up above, two ravens chased each other through the empty air. They were plying the same cerulean surface that millions of years ago had been the domain of the flying reptiles. He ought to call his wife. The sun, softened by the eucalyptus leaves, touched his forehead. The man shut his eyes. He was so certain of his slice of good fortune that he slid into sleep and ambiguity without realizing it had happened.

AUTHOR'S NOTE

All references to events, persons, and institutions that have actually existed or now exist are strictly coincidental. Minor modifications of the topography of the places described, or of the chronology with respect to well-known historic, news, or media events have been made here and there for dramatic reasons. I would like to thank everyone who supported me in the complicated years that the writing of this novel required. My longtime friends. All the care taken by the staff at my publishing house. Those who provided me with technical consulting (in the areas of medicine, law, and construction), which I used or ignored, depending on my needs. Those who invited me to dinner, almost every week, just a short distance from home. Giovanna, who in the meantime has had a baby girl. And especially on Mondays, this book is dedicated to the medium, Chiara.

About the Author

One of Italy's most critically acclaimed con-
temporary novelists, Nicola Lagioia has been
the recipient of the Volponi, Straniero, and
Viareggio awards, in addition to the Strega.
In 2010 he was named one of Italy's best writers under forty. He has been a jury member
of the Venice Film Festival and is the program director of the Turin Book Fair. Lagioia
is a contributor to Italy's most prominent culture pages. He was born in Bari, and lives in
Rome. *Ferocity* is his English-language debut.